DANDELION ROOT

*Protects against psychic
interference*

WORMWOOD

*A drawing herb; useful for
enticing wayward spirits*

ROSEMARY

*Strengthens (or drains)
memory*

FENNEL

*Amplifies the power
of other herbs*

BELLADONNA, or
DEADLY NIGHTSHADE

A last resort

The SECOND DEATH of EDIE and VIOLET BOND

Amanda Glaze

UNION
SQUARE
&CO.

NEW YORK

UNION SQUARE & CO.

NEW YORK

Text © 2022 Amanda Glaze
Cover illustration and endpaper art © 2022 Union Square & Co., LLC

ISBN 978-1-4549-5011-0 (BN edition)
ISBN 978-1-4549-4678-6 (hardcover)
ISBN 978-1-4549-4680-9 (e-book)

Library of Congress Cataloging-in-Publication Data

Names: Glaze, Amanda, author.
Title: The second death of Edie and Violet Bond / Amanda Glaze.
Description: New York : Union Square & Co., [2022] | Audience: Ages 12-17.
  | Summary: Seventeen-year-old twins--and powerful mediums--Edie and
  Violet Bond are part of a Spiritualist show, a tight-knit group of young
  women who express unladylike talents and opinions under the guise of
  communing with spirits, but when the dark spirit responsible for their
  mother's death crosses into the land of the living, the twins race
  against time to uncover a killer who will stop at nothing to cheat
  death.
Identifiers: LCCN 2022021355 (print) | LCCN 2022021356 (ebook) |
  ISBN 9781454946786 (hardcover) | ISBN 9781454946809 (e-book)
Subjects: CYAC: Spiritualism--Fiction. | Mediums--Fiction. |
  Twins--Fiction. | Sisters--Fiction. | Death--Fiction. |
  Spirits--Fiction. | Women's rights--Fiction. | Sacramento
  (Calif.)--Fiction. | California--History--1850-1950--Fiction. | BISAC:
  YOUNG ADULT FICTION / Paranormal, Occult & Supernatural |
  YOUNG ADULT FICTION / Thrillers & Suspense / Supernatural
  LCGFT: Paranormal
  | fiction. | Historical fiction. | Novels.
Classification: LCC PZ7.1.G5882 Se 2022 (print) | LCC PZ7.1.G5882 (ebook)
  | DDC [Fic]--dc23
LC record available at https://lccn.loc.gov/2022021355
LC ebook record available at https://lccn.loc.gov/2022021356

For information about custom editions, special sales, and premium purchases,
please contact specialsales@sterlingpublishing.com.

Printed in Canada

2 4 6 8 10 9 7 5 3 1

unionsquareandco.com

Cover illustration by Marcela Bolivar
Endpaper illustrations by Maria Mann

For Blake

1

Violet was late.

Edie drew aside the thick velvet curtains of the smallest drawing room in the second-best hotel in Sacramento and peered out into the evening. The gas lamps had been lit over an hour ago, and, as far as she could tell, there was no sign of a fire or any other natural disaster brewing anywhere in the city that would prevent her sister from returning on time.

There was the last shopkeeper locking up his door for the night, donning his hat as he set out into the cool spring evening. A steady row of carriages trundled down K Street, windows open to reveal silk sleeves and feathered hats. Freshly brewed coffee from the night-lunch wagons perfumed the air, mixing with the ever-present odor of manure made even stronger thanks to the stable yards across the street.

Everyone and everything exactly where they should be. Except for her twin sister. Who was late.

Edie pulled the window shut and tugged the curtains into place with a little more force than necessary, groaning when the swish of the tasseled velvet stirred up a gust of air and blew out a candle on the table behind her. Those three paraffin candles were the only source of light in the little hotel drawing room. She'd had a devil of a time persuading the porter to extinguish the globe lights on the gaudy gas chandelier that hung from the ceiling (the second-best hotel in Sacramento had not yet been fitted for electric lighting).

But, miss. You won't be able to see!

Well, *yes*. That was entirely the point. How was anyone expected to conduct a proper séance if the client could *see* everything?

But, of course, she hadn't said that. Instead, she'd simpered and complained about a headache. When in doubt, always complain about a headache.

Now Edie pulled a box of matches from the silk pouch in her pocket. A rich aroma of dried herbs wafted out from the pouch, but she cinched the drawstring tight before the scent could pull up any memories. Then she relit the doused candle and returned the matchbox to its place.

The hotel porter would grow used to their methods soon enough. He'd have to, seeing as how this was only the first of many séances she and Violet would be conducting here while their Spiritualist tour was in town. Edie dropped to her knees and crouched under the round table, double-checking the thin piece of wire she'd looped around one of the chair legs. Next, she tested the unassuming piece of wood she'd wedged under the table, perfectly placed for a bit of levitation when the time was right.

Why anyone thought a spirit would make itself known by rattling the furniture was a mystery to her, but it's what paying customers expected, so it's what they did.

A familiar laugh trilled in the hall outside. It was followed by a male voice, pitched low. Edie stomped across the drawing room and swung open the door, her eyebrows raised.

"You're late."

A tumult of pink and black fabric soon resolved itself into two distinct figures. The first was a young man who looked to be about eighteen or nineteen, dressed in a well-tailored black suit. An unfortunate oiled handlebar mustache took up the majority of his face, making him look very much like a walrus.

Next to him was a seventeen-year-old girl wearing a pink silk dress trimmed with all the latest trifles. A monstrosity Edie still had trouble looking at without feeling a pain in her chest, since it had cost the twins the equivalent of an entire month of work. Her auburn hair was swept back into a chignon with a few fashionable curls framing her round, rosy face.

The walrus boy had the good grace to flush crimson at the sudden interruption. Edie's twin sister Violet, however, flashed a big bright smile, as if nothing in the world could ever be amiss.

"Edie!" she cried out in that musical voice of hers. "I'm dying to introduce you. Mr. John Billingsly, may I present my twin sister? Miss Edith Bond."

"Twins!" The walrus boy clapped his hands together in glee and then made a hasty bow. "By God, I thought I was seeing double. If it weren't for the hair—he made a vague gesture toward his head—"well, I'd have thought I'd gone mad."

Edie's hand went automatically to her hair before she could stop herself. It was a self-conscious gesture. One she had tried—and failed—to curb.

Violet and Edie were identical in almost every way—from the outside, at least. As newborns, they'd both possessed the same upturned noses, bright green eyes, and tufts of auburn hair. Violet's auburn had grown deeper and more complex with age, whereas Edie's had gone the opposite direction, becoming paler with each passing year until it was almost white.

Edie fixed the walrus with her coldest stare. "Yes. How incredibly clever of you to figure it out." He opened his mouth to respond, but Edie cut him off. "And while I'm sure it's a pleasure to meet you, I'm afraid we must say good night. Violet is late for an engagement."

"Edie!" Her sister slapped a hand to her chest with the same dramatic animation that had raised eyebrows at their town's yearly Christmas tableaux when their Sunday school teacher made the mistake of casting her as Mary. "Mr. Billingsly, please ignore my sister. She can be exceedingly *rude*." She directed the last word to her twin with a pointed look, but Edie ignored her.

"I may be rude, but you are late."

Edie reached out, took her sister by the elbow, and pulled her inside the drawing room.

The walrus puffed up his chest, as if he meant to protest Edie's handling of her *own* sister, but Violet only laughed and flashed him one of her show-stopping smiles. "Looks like the jig is up tonight. Come to the Metropolitan on Saturday, all right?"

Edie closed the door in the walrus's face before he could respond.

Violet spun out of Edie's grasp as soon as the door closed. "Honestly, Edie. Do you have to be so awful? John's a *theater manager*, for pity's sake. He thinks I have real talent."

Edie couldn't help it. She rolled her eyes.

"Oh, stuff it. He's very well-connected in San Francisco, I'll have you know. *And* in New York."

Edie crossed her arms. "Oh he is, is he? A man of his age and wisdom—"

"Must you think the worst of *everyone*? It so happens theater is a family business and his father—"

"I don't care if he claims to own all of Broadway, Vi! Miss Crocker will be here any minute—"

"And I am here," said Violet, peeling off her gloves. "Ready to work."

"Does that also mean you read the list I gave you?"

Violet removed her hat and hung it on a rack by the door.

"Vi. Did you read it? We have to be prepared—"

"Oh, for Pete's sake, Edie. It's a darned *cat*!"

Under normal circumstances, Edie might have laughed. As it was, she couldn't help the hint of a smile tugging at her lips. It really *was* one of their more ridiculous appointments, and they'd had their fair share of odd requests since taking up the spirit-medium profession a year ago.

5

Miss Crocker was an old maid. A very *rich* old maid; and her cat, whom she'd inexplicably named Thomas, had been her only real companion. She'd been inconsolable since his death a month ago and wanted to contact him one last time.

"Well," said Edie. "Yes, technically it's the spirit of a cat. But he was really more like a relative—"

A giggle from Violet interrupted Edie. Followed by a hiccup. Violet's eyes filled with tears as she tried to contain her laughter.

"Yes, I suppose it's all rather funny, but—"

"Funny?" croaked Violet, whose shoulders were now shaking. She reached into the pocket of her dress and pulled out the list Edie had left on the night table of their hotel room that morning. For a percentage of their fee, Mr. Huddle, the man in charge of their traveling Spiritualist tour, assisted in collecting useful information on the deceased spirit a client wanted to contact. Normally this would be particulars on the hobbies, interests, and affectations of a dearly departed relative. But in this case . . .

"Outward appearance? Black tuxedo," said Violet, reading off the list. "Favorite meal? Chicken liver, raw and chopped. And, last but not least, favorite pastimes: lying in the sun, clawing the sofa."

Violet looked up from the list, tears of laughter streaming down her face. "Edie. Come on."

The last bit of tension between them popped, and something loosened in Edie's chest. And then she was laughing, too. Great big wheezes that sent her sister into further fits of giggles. They laughed like that for a solid minute, until Violet was forced to sit down, and Edie was bent double, gripping the back of a rosewood chair.

"Can you imagine a worse fate?" asked Violet, her breathing slowly falling back under control. "For the great love of your life to be nothing more than a dirty little cat?"

Violet shook her head in horror; but for her part Edie merely shrugged and pulled out a handkerchief to wipe her eyes. She had no wish to quarrel with her twin over the nature of love, but privately she disagreed. Their mother had loved their father once; and if that's how love with a person turned out, Edie would take the cat.

There was a knock on the drawing room door, and all thoughts of mothers and fathers and love flew from Edie's mind. She straightened up and shoved the chair back into place.

"Just a moment," she called out. Then, in a low whisper to Violet, she said, "I know you think this is ridiculous, but you will do your best, won't you? Miss Crocker is likely to speak to Mary Sutton, and a good word would—"

"Yes, yes. Little fish, big fish. I quite understand, Edie. I'll behave, I promise."

As if to show she meant business, Violet settled herself into a chair and placed both hands palm-down on the table. Then, in her best, most spiritual voice, she called out, "You may enter."

The wiry old porter opened the door to admit a stout woman in a swath of black crepe. Her widow's veil fell several feet down her back. Behind her, Edie distinctly heard Violet stifle a laugh.

It *was* rather a lot, to don full mourning for the loss of a cat.

The porter gave Edie a suspicious once-over, clearly still put off about the chandelier incident, before primly closing the door.

"Miss Crocker." Edie bobbed her head and took care to keep her voice low and solemn. "I am deeply sorry for your loss. Please, take a seat. My sister Violet and I will do what we can to bring you some measure of peace."

Edie offered her arm. Miss Crocker took it and squeezed her hand eagerly. "Thank you, my dear. I know it's not common, but I do miss him dearly."

A wave of sympathy rose up in Edie, and for the length of a second she almost wished they *could* summon the poor woman's cat.

Edie settled Miss Crocker at Violet's right hand and took her place on her sister's left. "Now, before we begin," said Edie, her tone delicate, "there is the matter of—"

"Oh yes, of course." Miss Crocker's hand dove into her silk drawstring reticule and re-emerged with a bank note. Edie palmed the note quickly and slipped it into her pocket. Then she glanced over at Violet, who gave her a subtle nod of her head. They were ready to begin.

"Now," said Edie. "If we could all hold hands."

The three women interlaced their hands.

"Shall we begin with a hymn?"

Edie hated this part of the charade. But the sisters had found that beginning with a hymn tended to settle the old biddies who had any lingering doubts about the *properness* of summoning spirits.

Jesus Christ himself, Edie had often said to a wavering customer, *returned as a spirit with his resurrection. So surely our work here cannot go against God.*

They began with the first verse of "In the Sweet Bye and Bye."

There's a land that is fairer than day,
And by faith we can see it afar.

Violet's voice was sweet and pure, Edie's characteristically flat. But it was Miss Crocker who was the star of the trio. The old lady held nothing back. Her off-key mezzo-soprano thundered in the little drawing room.

For the Father waits over the way
To prepare us a dwelling place there.
In the sweet bye and bye.

Sometimes, when the religious mumbo-jumbo really got on her nerves, Edie would content herself with imagining their father's reaction if he found out *this* was how his daughters were making use of their religious education.

Not that she had any intention of his finding out.

They finished the hymn, and silence descended. After a few calculated breaths, Violet lit the dish of dried lavender at the center of the table—the smoke from the herb was a signature part of their act—and then her soft, dreamlike voice filled the room. "I feel the presence of a spirit among us."

Edie's foot found the wooden board she'd wedged underneath the table. Carefully, slowly, she put pressure on the board until the table beneath them appeared to rise off the ground.

"The spirits are here!" cried Miss Crocker.

"Hush!" admonished Edie. "My sister has fallen into a trance."

And indeed, Violet's head was thrown back and her eyes were closed. Edie pressed down with her foot on the board again, this time shaking the table until one of the candles in the center sputtered out.

"The candle has gone out," whispered Edie, awe in her voice. Miss Crocker gasped but dared not speak again.

Edie had doctored the candle, of course, trimming the wick short and digging out the wax so that, as the table shook, the molten wax put out the flame.

Violet's head jerked up and her spine snapped straight. With her body at attention and her eyes closed, she looked not unlike a puppet being controlled with a string. Edie had no desire to encourage Violet's impractical love for the stage, but the truth was, her sister was quite the talented actress.

"*Margie?*" Violet's voice croaked. Edie had been wondering what kind of voice she'd choose for the cat and was amused to see that Violet had gone for the tenor of an old man. It made sense. The cat had been *ancient* when he finally died.

"Thomas? Is that you?"

One look at the eager shine in Miss Crocker's eyes, at the nodding and bobbing of her head, and Edie knew she needn't have bothered with the theatrics after all. This woman had arrived, as so many did, ready to believe whatever they told her.

"*Dear Margie*," croaked Violet. "*I miss you so.*"

Tears flowed freely down Miss Crocker's face as she leaned across the table, and a series of questions were asked and answered.

Was he happy in the afterlife?

Yes, quite pleased. There was lots of fish.

Did he miss her at all?

He missed her terribly. But couldn't she feel that he watched over her? That he was with her always, only on a different plane?

Miss Crocker admitted that yes, she had thought she'd felt his presence, only she hadn't been sure.

"Are you really always with me, Thomas? No matter where I go?"

"*Always,*" intoned Violet. Only Edie could detect the twinkle of laughter under her words. "*Wherever there is a patch of sun, know I am there.*"

Miss Crocker sighed, and a blissful smile took over her face.

"*Only I must go now, my dear,*" said Violet. "*Know I love you always and I—*"

A cough cut Violet's final goodbye short. She cleared her throat and opened her mouth to speak again, but another cough overtook her.

This was not part of the act.

Miss Crocker turned to Edie; her eyebrows raised. "Is she quite all right?"

"Yes." Her voice was calm, but her eyes were searching Violet. "I'm sure it's just the . . . um, the tickle of the spirit. They can be quite . . . wriggly."

Violet coughed again. A deep, guttural sound.

And that's when Edie felt it. A cool breeze on the back of her neck.

On her left, Miss Crocker turned toward the window, no doubt assuming the breeze had come from a gust of night air. Edie took advantage of the woman's momentary lapse in attention to close her own eyes and reach out to feel for the Veil between life and death.

11

Except it wasn't there. Or, rather, it *was* there, but it was thinner than it ought to be. Gossamer instead of the normal thick bolt of silk.

The Veil thinned whenever a death occurred, but this was more than a single death would usually warrant. Had Violet done it on purpose? She'd lit the lavender, but the plan had never been to call a spirit through, seeing as how the spirit in question was a cat.

Edie opened her eyes and squeezed Violet's hand. Silently asking the question. *Is this you?*

Violet kept her eyes closed but answered with a small shake of her head. She hadn't done this.

A strangled sort of giggle erupted from the back of Miss Crocker's throat. She'd turned back from the window—no doubt discovering it was shut—and was now looking back and forth between the sisters with wide eyes, her lips parted in the beginning stages of shock.

Violet squeezed Edie's hand. One quick burst. *I've got this.*

A signal that Violet would discreetly handle whatever was happening with the Veil, which meant it was Edie's job to keep Miss Crocker calm.

It was for this exact reason that the twins faked most of their séances. Because while it was one thing to play at receiving messages from loved ones beyond the grave—or loved *cats*, in this case—it was quite another to truly feel the reality of death. That cold tingling at the back of your mind. The shivers up and down your spine. It was, frankly, upsetting to most people. People who thought of contacting spirits as nothing more than a parlor game to pass the time.

Edie cleared her throat, preparing to divert the old lady's attention. But then, just before she spoke, her stomach lurched and her head swam.

Something had moved in death.

But it wasn't the light touch of a curious spirit drawn to the lavender smoke. No. There was a heaviness to the movement that set her teeth on edge.

Unbidden, a memory surged into her mind. Another spirit that hadn't felt right, and a sudden, unexplainable thinning of the Veil.

Edie's heart thudded against her chest. Before she was aware of what she was doing, she lurched forward, grabbed an empty teacup saucer from the table, and slammed it down hard on top of the dish of lavender, cutting off the steady spiral of smoke.

Miss Crocker jumped, letting out a little squeal at the crash of dish on dish.

Violet's eyes flew open a second later. Wide and confused. She pinned Edie with a questioning stare. *What was that?*

But Edie only shook her head. Her heart was still pounding, her breathing shallow and tight. She closed her eyes briefly, feeling again for the Veil. It was still thin. But whatever presence she'd felt in death was gone.

Violet narrowed her eyes at Edie. Edie responded by tilting her head toward the old lady. Violet huffed but then dropped

13

back into character. She threw her head back, sucked in a great gasp of air, and cried, "I feel him depart! The spirit has left this plane!"

Miss Crocker shook her head. "Thomas, wait! Come back!"

"He has gone!" chimed in Edie.

Across the table, Violet raised her eyebrows again in question, but Edie ignored her, rising instead to help Miss Crocker out of her seat. "Come, ma'am, you've had quite an ordeal. We'll have someone fetch you tea."

"I do think," said the old woman, allowing herself to be led, "that I might take something a mite stronger. To calm my nerves, you know."

"Of course," murmured Edie. The queasiness in her stomach was gone, but her head was still dizzy. It took an effort to keep her face neutral and serene. "I'm sure that can be arranged."

Edie opened the door for her, but, before going through, the old woman paused and turned to look at her with an eager, hopeful face. "He seemed . . . happy. Didn't he, dear?"

Edie met the older woman's eyes, her heart softening at the need she saw in them. "Yes, ma'am. I think Thomas has found a great deal of peace in the afterlife."

Miss Crocker continued staring at Edie for a long, drawn-out moment. Then she gave her a watery smile and nodded her head. "Yes, my dear. I do believe you're right." She sighed and patted Edie's arm. "Well, lead the way. I'm quite shaky, and a tipple of brandy is what my old bones need."

Edie nodded back at the lady. She could feel her sister's eyes boring into the back of her head, but she didn't turn around. Violet would want to know why she'd ended the séance so abruptly, and Edie needed time to formulate an answer that would satisfy her twin. So she kept her eyes fixed on Miss Crocker, leading her through the door and into the room beyond.

2

The tall, wide-mouthed bottles filling the shelves of the Capital Pharmacy: *Druggist and Apothecary* winked at Edie as they caught the light of the late afternoon sun. The balding druggist behind the counter, however, offered her nothing but a deep, disapproving frown.

"But, miss," said the druggist, puffing up his chest to such a degree Edie genuinely feared for the middle button of his vest, "if you'd only tell me your ailment, I can recommend a mixture—"

"I don't need a mixture," said Edie. Patiently. For the *third* time. "The individual herbs themselves will be fine."

The druggist's frown deepened. Apparently, Edie was vexing to old men who couldn't understand that she knew her own mind. "What you don't seem to understand," he continued, condescension dripping from his voice, "is I am more *equipped* to fashion a pill or draught—"

"Oh, hang your pills," said Violet, walking up to stand beside Edie. Evidently, she'd exhausted her interest in the toiletry trifles displayed up front and had decided to join the fray. "Could you please, for pity's sake, give my sister whatever little herbs she asked for so we can be on our way? We've already lost enough of our day as it is."

Edie sighed, but she couldn't exactly fault the efficacy of Violet's methods. All it took was a three-second glare from her sister to send the pompous little druggist flying to the shelves to fill Edie's order.

It was the first time they were stocking up on herbs from a pharmacy. They'd managed to get by so far in their séances using nothing more than lavender. It was odd, seeing the druggist measure out a packet of mugwort from one of the many well-labeled tin containers sitting on a neatly organized shelf. Her mother's herbs had always been hanging out in the open, affixed to any available surface with bits of string or cast-off ribbons. No tiny precise handwriting distinguishing this herb from that. You had to know each one by sight and smell and touch alone.

Edie stepped away from the gleaming marble counter and turned to Violet. "Thank you."

"I still think this is a complete overreaction."

"Vi—"

"The money we're spending here would be much better put toward re-trimming my hat. Look at this feather!" Violet tilted her head so Edie could see the pure white ostrich feather that was indeed bent out of shape.

"If we get Mary Sutton's reward money," said Edie quietly so the druggist wouldn't hear, "we'll buy you a whole *new* hat."

"For nine hundred dollars, I'll expect more than *one* new hat."

Edie smiled. "*Five* new hats."

"Ten!" countered Violet so loudly her voice boomed off the walls of the shop, prompting the frowning druggist to pause in the middle of wrapping up several long sticks of rosemary with brown paper and string. But when he settled an annoyed look at Violet, she responded by simply sticking her tongue out at him.

"Vi!" whispered Edie, torn between laughter and annoyance. "Stop it!"

Violet withdrew her tongue and flashed the druggist one of her dazzling smiles. The little man harrumphed and went back to work.

Edie hooked her arm through Violet's and dragged her away from the counter. She stopped in front of an arrangement of postcards and picked one up at random to cover their retreat. She didn't want the druggist perking up his ears to try to overhear what she had to say next.

"I know you think I'm being overly cautious," said Edie, her voice low. "But we can't afford for anything to go wrong tomorrow night. Not with Mary Sutton in the audience."

Violet rolled her eyes but said nothing. Likely because she knew—as Edie did—that private séances with Mary Sutton were by invitation only. Which meant they needed to impress her on stage tomorrow night in order to secure one.

Huffing through her nose, Violet picked up a postcard of her own, but instead of looking at the idyllic landscape depicted on its front, she glared at Edie. "Nothing went wrong *last* night. I had everything under control until you went to pieces and scared that little old lady half to death."

Edie dropped her eyes and stared at the postcard in her hand. It was a color lithograph of a California orange grove, the sun drawn clear and bright. The sort often mailed to snowed-in East Coast relatives; received, no doubt, with the appropriate degree of envy.

Her sister was right, of course. She'd overreacted by cutting off the smoke so suddenly last night. They hadn't been in danger. The Veil may have thinned. Edie may have felt a movement in death. But unless she or Violet had actually *opened* the Veil, no spirit could have forced its way into life.

The honest truth was, Edie still didn't understand *why* she'd reacted like that. It had been on instinct. An unconscious response to the memory that had suddenly reared its head. A memory she normally kept buried under lock and key. One she'd never shared with her twin.

She blinked down at the postcard in her hand, surprised to find it crumpled. A crease now ran down the middle of the orange trees, marring the perfect scene. Straightening the creases as best she could, Edie tucked the card back into the rack. Then she forced her face into a neutral expression and met her sister's eyes.

"The last thing we need is a restless spirit interrupting you while Mary Sutton is in the audience tomorrow night." Edie shrugged, trying for nonchalance. "I simply want to be prepared in case I need to cross."

Violet shot her a curious, searching look. Each sister had inherited half of their mother's abilities: Violet able to channel spirits, and Edie able to cross between life and death. But unlike

Violet, Edie hadn't made use of her ability in almost a year. Not since the day their mother died.

Violet tilted her head, studying her, and Edie knew—as she often did—what her sister was going to say before she said it.

It wasn't your fault.

But she didn't want to hear those words spoken aloud. Not because she thought her twin insincere. She knew Violet believed it. But that was only because she didn't know the truth.

There was a dainty cough from the counter behind them, and they both whirled around to find the puffed-up druggist regarding them coolly. He held up half a dozen paper packets full of herbs. "That will be two dollars even, miss."

Violet groaned loudly. And inwardly, Edie was forced to agree. It was a pretty penny and would set them back significantly. She had a suspicion the little man had inflated the price, perhaps angry that Edie had rejected his fancy draughts. But she didn't want to give Violet the satisfaction of admitting that she might have gone overboard with her order. So, instead, she dug into her purse and paid the man, though it hurt her teeth to do it.

Edie tucked the herbs into her cloth bag, and then she and Violet stepped out into the bustling main street of downtown Sacramento, a steady traffic of carts, carriages, and horse-drawn omnibuses rattling past.

A chill that had nothing to do with the mild spring weather shot down Edie's back as she and Violet made their way across the city's wooden sidewalks, which—thanks to the frequent flooding of the Sacramento River—had been raised several feet above the ground.

She didn't like these sidewalks. Didn't like feeling as if she and Violet were on display as they promenaded down Third Street for everyone to see. Although she supposed it wasn't really fair to blame the sidewalks themselves. Not when she'd been feeling this same unease ever since arriving at the Sacramento train station two days ago.

Two days down. Only five more to go.

When Mr. Huddle had first announced new tour dates in Sacramento, Edie had very seriously debated skipping them, even though she knew it would jeopardize their spots in the show. After six months on tour in the East and Midwest, she'd gotten used to a certain feeling of safety. Going back to California—to a city less than a day's coach ride away from the town where the twins had grown up—felt too much like tempting fate.

But then Mr. Huddle had told her about Mary Sutton. A rich Sacramento lady offering an obscene amount of reward money to any medium capable of contacting an unnamed spirit. Reward money that not even the most prominent mediums in the West had been able to obtain. Money that—assuming the spirit this woman sought was lingering anywhere near her in the Veil—would be child's play for Edie and Violet to secure.

Seven months ago, when the last of their money had run out and the sisters were barely surviving on one meager meal a day, Edie had sworn to herself that she'd find a way to rebuild the life she'd cost them. Getting on Mr. Huddle's tour had been a start, but a lump sum like what Mary Sutton was offering could make her and Violet *truly* independent for the first time in their lives.

It was simply too good an opportunity to pass up. And besides, Edie had told herself at the time, it had been almost a year since they'd run away. Surely, going back for a single week would be safe enough.

And so far—except for the strange moment with Miss Crocker last night—things had indeed been going rather well. The tour's opening show the night before last at the Metropolitan Theater had been very well received. The twins already had several private séances lined up for the remainder of the week, and Mary Sutton herself was confirmed to attend their second show at the Metropolitan tomorrow.

Edie gave herself a little shake and mentally told her too-quickly-beating heart to slow down. There was no reason to worry. Everything was going to be fine.

She and Violet rounded the corner onto K Street and made their way toward the Union Hotel, their home for the rest of the week. Like most of the buildings downtown, it bore a faded, old-timey look. It may be 1885 in the rest of the United States; but in many parts of Sacramento, remnants of the gold-mining days that had attracted prospectors here thirty-odd years ago could still be felt. And the Union Hotel was no exception. What must have once been a shiny white facade had yellowed with age, and the wide verandas along the second floor harkened back to an architectural style popular when this land had been a part of Mexico.

But despite the obvious marks of age, the Union Hotel was an esteemed establishment—known for hosting state senators when they were in town for the legislative session—and so it was deemed acceptable by Mr. Huddle, who knew whatever money he spent on securing fashionable accommodations for his mediums would pay double when it came to attracting wealthy clientele to the séance table.

A horse-drawn omnibus rattled past them, the bright blue bus jostling along the pre-laid tracks in the center of the street, sending up a plume of dust. When it cleared, Edie spotted something in front of their hotel, mixed in amongst the line of waiting carriages and hansom cabs, that made her eyes widen in surprise.

"Is that—"

"Ruby?" cried Violet. "What on earth is she *wearing*?"

Ruby Miller, a young woman with bright blonde hair, turned at the sound of her name. Her sparkling blue eyes squinted together as she searched the crowded sidewalk, ignoring the open-mouthed stares many of the fashionable men and women streaming in and out of the hotel lobby were throwing her way. Not that Ruby wasn't used to being stared at. With her round, rosy face and petite, curvy figure, she was often remarked on as the most beautiful of the mediums on their tour. But it wasn't her beauty attracting attention today, it was her odd manner of dress.

Unlike Edie and Violet, who were both wearing long skirts and blouses buttoned up to their necks, Ruby was wearing what appeared to be a pair of bright-blue trousers that ballooned out underneath a brown plaid cutaway jacket with puffed sleeves.

Ruby spotted them in the crowd, smiled in recognition, and enthusiastically waved them over. Violet muttered something under her breath about crimes against fashion, but Edie ignored her. Her attention was focused instead on the magnificent nickel bicycle their friend was currently clutching by the handlebars. Bicycles were all the rage now; but as the sisters had spent half of the last year traveling from one city to the next, Edie'd never had a chance to try one out.

"Can you believe it?" called Ruby as the twins approached, twisting the handlebars so the metal spokes of its tires glinted in the bright afternoon sun. "I've got it for two whole days!"

Edie ran her eyes up and down the bicycle, taking in the triangular leather seat, the low sweeping center bar, and the wicker basket strapped between the handlebars. "Oh, Ruby, it's incredible."

Ruby smiled. "You're telling me! When the fella I read for this morning found out I'd never ridden a bicycle before, he lent me his sister's. She's out of town—"

"Forget about the *bicycle*," interrupted Violet. "Ruby, you look like you ran away from the circus! What are those hideous . . . *things?*"

Edie elbowed Violet's side, but Ruby only laughed. "They're called bloomers." She demonstrated by raising her right leg and pointing at the hem, which cinched at her ankle. "Aren't they marvelous? My client said I might as well wear the whole costume if I'm going to learn how to ride."

Ruby, whose pale skin did little to hide her blushes, went slightly pink at this last pronouncement. Edie tilted her head and studied her. "This fella," said Edie slowly, "seems to be awfully . . . *accommodating.*"

Ruby shrugged, but her skin went a deeper shade of pink. "I suppose that *might* be because I promised to let him take me on a picnic tomorrow before our show. He has his own bicycle, you see, and he said we could ride out to—"

"Oh, Ruby," Edie groaned. "Not *again*."

At the exact same moment, Violet said, "Oh, Ruby, is he handsome?"

Ruby's face was a deep crimson now. She was only a year older than the twins and thus far too young (in Edie's opinion, anyway), to fall in and out of love as often as she did. Especially since her love affairs *never* ended well.

Just last month, while the tour was in Rochester, she'd missed an entire weekend of shows because some worthless Lothario had winked at her and convinced her they should run off and elope at Niagara Falls. Fortunately, Ruby had come to her senses before the deed was done, but Mr. Huddle had been inches away from kicking her off the tour. The only reason he hadn't was probably due to the fact that Ruby, like Violet, was a hit on stage. She didn't have any real ability with the Veil—at least, Edie was almost positive she didn't: it wasn't something mediums generally discussed out loud—but like Violet, she was a terrific and intuitive actress.

"Well," said Edie, her voice resigned. "Just don't run off with this one, all right?"

"Oh, don't listen to her," said Violet to Ruby. "I still think the whole thing was terribly romantic."

"It was terribly *something*, all right," muttered Edie under her breath.

Violet whipped her head toward her. "What was that?"

"Oh, nothing. I was just wondering what part of a man five years Ruby's senior trying to seduce her into a lifetime of bondage is *romantic*, but maybe I'm—"

"A lifetime of *bondage*? Honestly, Edie. Not every marriage is—"

"Don't start with the *not every*—"

"Who wants to ride the bike?"

They both swiveled around to look at Ruby, who had blurted out her question loud enough to catch the attention of several passersby. Ruby wiggled the bicycle's handlebars again, making the rubber tires dance. "Come on," she coaxed. "My client told me about a path we can ride down by the river. I need *someone* there to patch me up when I fall flat on my face."

"I'll take a turn," said Edie. "Vi?"

"I'll watch," she said with a shrug. "But I don't care what *either* of you say. There's no way I'm putting on a pair of trousers and getting on that thing myself."

"Oh god, oh god, oh god!"

"You've got it, Vi. Just make sure you—"

"Don't let go, Edie! If you let go, I swear to—"

"I won't let go, Vi. I promise. Now just pedal a little faster."

"I can't! I'll fall!"

"You won't fall. I've got you. I promise."

The blue-green water of the Sacramento River flowed lazily by as Edie and Violet wobbled down the dirt path. Violet was perched on the bicycle's leather seat, her long skirts tied up in a thoroughly unfashionable and entirely scandalous ankle-showing knot, while Edie jogged alongside her, holding on to the back of the bicycle to keep her sister steady.

It was a technique she and Ruby had perfected half an hour ago when they'd helped each other learn to ride. But it wasn't until after both Edie *and* Ruby had successfully pedaled up and down the dirt path on their own that Violet had announced—to absolutely no one's surprise—that she'd changed her mind and wanted a try.

Ruby yelled out her encouragement from where she was sprawled at the start of the path, but Violet only shook her head.

"I can't," she squealed again, but low enough so only Edie could hear. "The second you let go, I'm going to fall on my face and then I'll be hideous, and I'll never become an actress and—"

Edie, winded from all this trotting, snorted through her nose.

"I'm not joking! I'll fall! I'll crash! And I know you think it's silly—"

"Vi."

"But the stage is my dream, and Mother wanted us to—"

"Vi, I'm not holding the bike."

Violet, who'd been riding on her own for the last thirty seconds, looked down at her feet and screamed. "I'm doing it! Edie, I'm riding by myself!"

Unfortunately, the shock of that realization was too much for her still-precarious balance, and she immediately toppled over.

Edie rushed forward. "Are you all—"

Her words were cut off by the thump of Violet's arms around her neck. Her sister had sprung up from the ground like a particularly spry rabbit and was now hugging her, her left cheek pressed against Edie's.

"That. Was. *Wonderful.*"

Edie's face relaxed into a smile, and she pressed her cheek more firmly against her twin's. They used to do this all the time as children: embrace cheek to cheek when they wanted to comfort each other or share some powerful emotion they couldn't name. And she could certainly feel Violet's exhilaration now.

How long had it been since they'd done this?

Violet pulled out of the hug. "I want to go again. Right now."

Edie laughed. "I need to rest first. I'm too winded to run alongside—"

"Should have thought of that before tricking me, shouldn't you? You did *promise* not to let go."

An hour later, the three young women walked back toward the hotel to prepare for their evening séance appointments, Ruby's borrowed bike, which Violet had refused to relinquish, rolling along beside them. They were only a block away from the hotel when Edie caught sight of a well-turned-out middle-aged woman standing on the corner of Front Street with a stack of what appeared to be flyers in her hands. She was wearing a yellow silk sash with the words *Votes for Women* stitched boldly across the front.

Without meaning to, Edie slowed her steps. The woman on the corner noticed. Her eyes swept over Edie, moved on to Ruby—lingering for a moment on her bloomers—and then slid over to the bicycle in Violet's hands. She gave them a brisk nod, extracted one of the flyers from her stack, and strode over to them, meeting them in the middle of the sidewalk.

"You three look like sensible young women." She held out the flyer to Edie. "I think you'd like what Miss de Force has to say."

When Edie didn't make a move to take the flyer, Ruby sighed loudly and took it herself, murmuring her thanks. The woman gave all three girls another long, assessing look, then nodded and returned to her corner, eyes back to scanning passersby.

Ruby looked down at the flyer as the three of them continued down the sidewalk. She let out a low whistle and then handed the page to Edie.

POLITICAL EQUALITY!

AN ADDRESS AT 52 SIXTH STREET

——— BY ———

LAURA DE FORCE

ON THE UNJUST TREATMENT OF

MRS. DOROTHY DRYER.

STATE ORGANIZER WOMEN'S SUFFRAGE ASSOCIATIONS,

Saturday Afternoon, March 21st

AT 3 O'CLOCK

EVERYBODY INVITED

Edie had barely finished reading the text before Violet snatched the flyer out of her hand and began to read it out loud. When she got to the name Dorothy Dryer, she paused and looked at Edie.

"Is this the woman who—"

"Who was committed to an asylum for taking medicine to prevent a pregnancy," interjected Ruby. "Yes, that's her."

Edie and Violet locked eyes, and something unspoken passed between them.

"I read all about it in the *Daily Union*," continued Ruby, shaking her head. "That good-for-nothing husband of hers just chucked her in that asylum. Never mind that the doctor told her another baby would kill her. Or that locking her up means there's no one to care for the two children she's already got."

The twins both nodded in agreement, well aware of the system that allowed male guardians—be they husbands, fathers, or brothers—to lock up women in asylums for almost no reason at all.

Ruby nodded toward the flyer. "You should go tomorrow, Edie. We have the day off until the show. And this seems like the kind of thing the *spirits* would take an interest in, don't you think?"

Ruby arched a single eyebrow, and the corners of Edie's lips twitched in response.

Unlike Violet, whose ability to channel spirits lent itself well to what the public had come to expect of a spirit medium, Edie's ability was decidedly less . . . *theatrical*. When her spirit crossed out of life and into the Veil of death, she left her body behind. And she was quite sure that even if their industrious tour manager Mr. Huddle knew of her ability, even *he* couldn't find a way to charge admission for the honor of watching Edie's skin grow cold and pale while she appeared to take a nap.

And so, Edie had found another way to earn her spot on the tour. Something that dovetailed nicely with her very unladylike interest in political affairs: trance lectures.

They were quite simple, really. Edie would walk on stage and announce to the audience that she would be channeling one of the world's great thinkers. One of the world's great *dead* thinkers, that is. Esteemed figures like Aristotle, George Washington, or Descartes. Or revered political minds like Benjamin Franklin or John Locke. One time, she'd given a particularly stirring lecture using the voice of a wise old sailor named Jed, who had a few things to get off his chest.

The truth was that it didn't matter *who* Edie channeled. As long as they were dead—and preferably male—Edie could give a lecture on almost any topic she desired, and the audience would eat it up. She liked to think the crowd was stimulated by her verbal acumen—skills she'd developed, ironically enough, from the lively theological debates she'd once engaged in with her father. It was more likely, of course, that the crowd simply enjoyed the novelty of watching a young, uneducated teenage girl use big words she shouldn't know.

Violet handed the flyer back to Edie, and she ran her eyes over the text again.

Edie had read all about Laura de Force in *The Pioneer* before her father found out about the political subscription and canceled it. Like Edie, Laura had started out as a spirit medium touring the country giving trance lectures, her thoughts and ideas attributed to the spirits she channeled. But then she'd done the unthinkable and sued Hastings College of Law in San Francisco when they refused her and another woman admittance. Sued them, and won. Now Laura de Force was a celebrated defense lawyer, and when she spoke in front of a crowd, everyone knew the words were her own.

Biting her lip, Edie folded the flyer and slipped it into her pocket. "I don't think I can go," she said. "If Mr. Huddle found out—"

"Oh, nonsense," interrupted Violet. "How will he know?"

Edie shook her head. "It's not worth the risk, Vi."

"Hang the *risk*! Besides, that man doesn't mind when you preach equality on the stage. So what if you're seen going to a speech about it?"

"He doesn't mind when *Benjamin Franklin's spirit* preaches equality from the stage," Edie corrected. "You know he's only being practical. No one would buy tickets if they thought *we* were the ones with the ideas."

Violet pursed her lips but didn't argue. This was the catch with trance lectures. Yes, they gave Edie a freedom on stage that few women enjoyed, but as soon as anyone suspected that the thoughts and opinions came from her own head, the jig would be up.

"If Mother were here," began Violet, "she'd want you to—"

"Well, she's not." Catching Violet's eye, Edie raised her eyebrows and cast a quick but meaningful look at Ruby, who was watching them both intently.

Violet pursed her lips into a tight line, turned away from Edie, and stared determinedly ahead, making it abundantly clear that while she'd received Edie's message to drop the subject, she wasn't happy about it.

Pasting a smile on her face, Edie turned to Ruby and swiftly changed the topic of conversation. A minute later, she was laughing as Ruby told them about a client who'd been so determined to catch her in an act of fraud that they'd hired a photographer to jump out from behind a silk screen in the middle of the séance, only to succeed in scaring one of the other guests so thoroughly that they'd jumped up from the table and smashed a priceless set of china.

But even as she was dutifully grinning at Ruby's story, she couldn't help but feel a plunging sense of loss as she snuck a glance at her twin. Violet's face was tight and closed off, the exact opposite of the wide, brimming smile that had transformed her face less than an hour ago. Laughing with the wind in her hair. Begging Edie to never let her go.

3

Edie slept in late the next morning, and by the time she woke up, Violet was gone. A note on the table between their beds read:

Meeting Mr. Billingsly this morning.
Will see you tonight
-V

Things had been tense between the twins last night during their séances in the drawing room downstairs. Not that their clients noticed. By now, she and Violet had become quite adept at presenting a united front even when at odds. But if Violet had taken to sneaking off in the morning before Edie was even awake . . . her sister must be more upset than she'd realized.

She shouldn't have snapped at her in front of Ruby yesterday.

Edie sank back into her pillows. The only good thing about last night was that nothing strange had happened with the Veil. There'd been no need to open it during their séances, of course. Both clients had been thoroughly researched by Mr. Huddle, the spirits they'd wanted to contact easy to discover and playact. But Edie had been on edge all the same.

She pushed the covers off and got out of bed. As she contemplated whether or not she should go downstairs for breakfast in the hotel's dining room, she realized Violet had probably breakfasted there already with John-the-walrus-Billingsly while Edie was still asleep. No doubt he'd spent the time building castles in the air while they both enjoyed their coddled eggs: castles that would crumble as soon as reality set in.

More than anything, Edie wanted to warn her sister off the walrus. The problem was, Violet had been dreaming of a life on the stage ever since, at the age of eleven, the sisters had seen a broadsheet advertising a traveling production of *Much Ado About Nothing* starring the Broadway actress Maude Adams. It didn't matter that they hadn't actually been allowed to *see* the production. Violet had proof that such a life was possible, and she'd started memorizing Shakespearean soliloquies the very next day.

Even after their father had forbidden Violet from *thinking,* let alone *speaking,* about the sinful life of an actress, their mother— quite used to disobeying her husband—had quietly encouraged it.

Edie hadn't seen the harm at the time. But now a handsome young man had arrived to take full advantage of her sister's naive hope. His real intentions were as plain as day to Edie, but pointing them out to Violet would only push her further away. All she could do was wait for it all to fall apart and hope she'd be able to pick up the pieces when it did.

who—like Edie and Violet's mother—knew the truth about death, a truth she'd imparted to her daughters the day they turned thirteen.

Death, their mother explained, was not like what their father preached from his pulpit. No heaven and hell with one death for the virtuous and one for the damned. The truth was that everyone—whether they had been good or whether they had been bad—experienced the same two kinds of death.

The first, the death of the body.

The second, the passing of the spirit.

When a person's body dies, she told the twins in that soft, dreamy voice of hers, *their spirit crosses into the Veil of death. Most spirits linger there for a time, finding comfort in the Veil's proximity to life. But eventually all spirits succumb to the same thing, a* pull *that draws them through the Veil and then . . . beyond.*

This is the second death. The final death. From which no spirit returns.

She'd gone on to explain that there were, of course, some spirits who resisted the pull. Often, that resistance could be felt by their loved ones in life, and she'd shown the twins ways to help with such things. Sometimes a spirit needed one final conversation with a person they had loved—or hated—who still walked in life. Sometimes it took a healthy dose of rosemary crossed with a hint of chamomile to help a spirit release hard memories held too tight.

Sometimes it took greater measures still.

Edie put down the knife. And then, as if in a trance, her hand moved to the white silk pouch lying on the corner of the writing desk. The one filled with herbs she kept on or near her person at all times. She loosened the drawstring and searched inside, her fingers moving past various bundles until they curled around something thick at the bottom of the little bag. Something gnarled and twisted.

A belladonna root.

Also known as deadly nightshade.

It was an herb that, when lit in death, sent any spirit within its range beyond the Veil to a final death. Including the one who had set it alight.

The first time Edie had ever laid eyes on the poisonous root had been that same afternoon a year ago. It had been her turn to take watch while her mother walked in death. It was paramount that the twins' father never find out about his wife's distinctly un-Christianlike activities, so she always made sure one of her daughters was with her when she crossed into death to seek a spirit for a client. There was still a risk of discovery, but she took it because of the modest fee she charged for her services, a fee that went directly into the small but growing savings she kept hidden behind a loose brick in her sitting room. Savings she planned to one day give to the twins.

I want you to have the choices I never had.

That afternoon, it hadn't been her father's step in the downstairs entryway that caused a line of worry to crease Edie's forehead. It had been the gnarled end of a belladonna root—instantly recognizable from her mother's illustrations—poking out of her spare pouch of herbs. A root that was so dangerous, her mother had made the twins promise to never keep it on hand.

So why did she *have it?*

Unnerved, Edie had glanced at the clock on the mantel. There was only so long a spirit could remain in death without causing harm to its physical body in life. Edie kept her crossings to about fifteen minutes. Any longer, and she'd spend the rest of the day retching up whatever food remained in her stomach. Her mother's tolerance was a bit higher; she could withstand a half hour in the Veil without any significant effects.

Except, by Edie's count, her mother's spirit had been in the Veil much longer than her usual half hour that afternoon. That fact, combined with the ominous presence of the belladonna, sent Edie scurrying across the room until she was kneeling in front of her mother's still, impassive face.

Her white-blonde hair—the color leached by three decades of crossing into the Veil—was coiled in its usual bun on top of her head. Her lids were closed, hiding the bottle-green eyes she'd passed down to the twins. Her skin was pale and cold to the touch, her breathing so infrequent it was undetectable to the untrained eye.

But all that was to be expected after spending more than a few minutes in the Veil. From the outside, everything appeared fine—so perfectly normal that Edie knew she should ignore the niggling sense that something was wrong.

But she didn't.

Instead, she set aside the belladonna root, lit a bundle of lavender, and opened the Veil.

As soon as her spirit crossed into death, Edie was surprised to catch the interwoven scents of fennel, wormwood, and hellebore.

It was a rarely used herb combination capable of binding a spirit to a caster's will and forcing them beyond the Veil to a final death. A drastic measure her mother only took when a spirit's haunting of a loved one in life reached the point of extreme distress.

After ensuring that the Veil was closed behind her, Edie sprang up from her seated position and rushed toward the scent. The ever-changing Veil had taken on the aspect of a forest that day, and she had to weave through a grove of trees before she found her mother's glowing spirit seated cross-legged in a grassy clearing, her back to Edie. Mist was a constant in death, and it billowed around her mother, giving her spirit's outline a soft, hazy glow.

The sight was so familiar that, for a moment, Edie allowed herself to relax, accepted the fact that she'd overreacted, and even mentally prepared for the lecture she'd no doubt receive when her mother discovered she'd entered death alone without permission.

But then she looked up, saw the spirit standing at the edge of the clearing, and all of her relief fled.

The smoke from her mother's herbs wrapped around the spirit in crisscrossing binds of deep gold, like a shimmering spider's web. But it was clear, even from Edie's vantage point several feet away, that the herbs weren't having their usual effect. The combined smoke should have immediately sent the spirit beyond.

But it hadn't.

And there was something else: the light from the spirit was bright enough to indicate that it was one of the recently dead, but instead of a constant, steady glow, the spirit's light appeared to be . . . flickering. In and out. Like a candle's flame.

Edie had never seen a spirit flicker like that before.

She took another step forward; and as she did, her mother's head swiveled around, her eyes widening in alarm.

"Edie?"

Behind her, the web of herbsmoke started to fade. Edie flinched. Her approach had distracted her mother, causing her to break her connection with the smoke, weakening her bind on the spirit.

Edie reached for her own herb pouch. She could fix this.

But before she could open it, her mother jumped up from her seated position and closed the distance between them. "You need to go back, Edie. Now."

"But I—"

"Now, Edie! I don't have time to explain."

Edie hesitated, her eyes bouncing between her mother and the spirit at the edge of the clearing. The net of gold smoke was nearly gone now, and the spirit—unsteady pulses of light emanating from its form—would soon break free.

She didn't understand what was happening or *why* her mother was trying to send this strange, spasming spirit beyond the Veil. She only knew she'd risked overstaying her time in death to do it, so it had to be important.

"But I can help. I can—"

Edie's words were cut off by a sudden shift in death. A change in pressure that made her head spin and her stomach lurch.

The Veil had thinned.

Except that wasn't possible. Because neither she nor her mother had lit lavender or any of the other crossing herbs. A quick glance told her no new spirit had appeared, which meant the Veil hadn't thinned because of a recent death.

"What was—"

Her mother's hands seized her shoulders and turned her around. "You need to run, Edie. Get out of range."

Edie twisted her neck around. "But why—"

"Get to that tree." Her voice was tight and urgent. "The twisted oak past the clearing." She gave Edie a strong push. "Get to the tree, open the Veil, and cross."

The shove sent Edie stumbling forward, but she quickly regained her balance and turned back around. The spirit was completely free of the binding herbs now, and Edie could finally see its features unobscured. It was the spirit of a man. Tall and thin. Middle-aged with hollowed-out cheeks and dark, almost black, hooded eyes.

And he was moving toward them. Fast.

Her mother strode across the clearing to meet the spirit. She shot a quick glance over her shoulder, and when she saw that Edie hadn't yet moved, her face twisted in what could only be fear. "Go. *Now.*"

It was a tone that brooked no argument. Before Edie knew it, she was stumbling back and running full-tilt for the twisted oak. Seconds later, she was fumbling with a lavender bundle from her pouch, her fingers shaking violently as she lit the tip and reopened the Veil.

It was in that moment—just before she crossed out of death—that she caught it. A scent on the mist. Fresh and green. Like unripe tomatoes blooming on a vine.

Get out of range.

Too late, the true meaning of her mother's words dawned on Edie. A scream of denial tore from her throat as she spun around. Surely she was wrong. Surely her mother wouldn't—

But she had.

Edie watched in horror as her mother raised one arm high above her head, a belladonna root—nearly identical to the one Edie had found next to her body in life—clutched in her glowing hand, black smoke billowing from its twisted end.

The mist rippled with motion as the spirit moved past her mother, toward Edie. But it didn't matter. Not with the black smoke curling up from the belladonna. Smoke that would seize onto every spirit within range, forcing them forever beyond the Veil.

The smoke didn't care that her mother was still alive. That she had a body breathing in life. Two daughters who *needed* her. Belladonna was indiscriminate. And Edie knew, even as she fell numbly back into life, that when it took that flickering spirit, it would take her mother, too.

Now, back in her hotel room, Edie squeezed the gnarled root she'd kept since that day. She forced her fingers to release it, uncurling each digit one by one. Slowly she slid her hand out of the silk pouch, cinched it closed, and picked up her mother's knife one more time, a new determination thrumming in her veins.

She'd never told Violet the truth of what happened that day in the Veil.

Her sister had burst into the sitting room while Edie and her mother were both still in death. She'd been the one to see their father kneeling before his wife and daughter, shouting their names and shaking their cold, seemingly breathless bodies.

Violet had seen him recoil in shock as Edie's skin suddenly bloomed with life. As her eyes snapped open and she'd thrown herself over their mother's body, reaching out in vain for any remaining connection to her spirit. Begging her, through gut-wrenching sobs, to find a way back to life.

Unnatural daughters.

You will *be saved.*

Later, Edie had let Violet think she'd never found their mother in the Veil. That she'd come back empty-handed only to feel their mother's spirit pass beyond. She justified the lie by telling herself she didn't want to condemn her sister to the same agonizing state of unknowing. Of not understanding *what* had happened and *why*.

The twins had run away that night. After locking them in their room, their father had left to make immediate arrangements for their *treatment*. But Edie and Violet had tied their sheets together, climbed out the window, and taken first a mail coach, and then a ferry, to San Francisco.

Although Violet had managed to retrieve the small sum of money their mother had hidden away for them, it wasn't enough to last them more than a few months. Taking up the spirit-medium profession had made sense, given their natural gifts. But Edie had had other motivations as well.

While Violet had been sleeping fitfully on the mail coach the morning of their escape, Edie had found something tucked in between the bank notes and legal tender wrapped in one of their mother's old handkerchiefs.

A hand-written list of three names.

Two of the names, Edie had eventually tracked down thanks to her newly developed contacts in the local medium trade. She'd been able to confirm her suspicions that these women were the contacts her mother corresponded with to set up her appointments, but unfortunately neither of them knew anything about her mother's final client.

The last name on the list she tracked to a set of rooms off Market Street where an irate landlady told Edie that yes, a Miss Nell Doyle had let these rooms the past three years. But that was before she'd absconded in the middle of the night without paying up her room and board.

So, by the time she and Violet left on Mr. Huddle's Spiritualist tour six months later, Edie was no closer to discovering the identity of her mother's last client—or the reason she'd procured the deadly nightshade—than she'd been the day she died.

Blinking, Edie glanced back down at the knife in her hand. This time, when she gripped it, her hand didn't shake. She sliced off the edges of the wormwood stems, put the knife aside, and picked up a small piece of unbleached string. With it, she tied the end of the herbs with a tight, secure knot.

Next, she unspooled a second, longer string, folded it in half, and began the careful process of wrapping up the herbs into a bundle, crisscrossing the longer string into an X shape with each firm knot.

Once she was finished, she slipped the bundle into her white silk pouch.

Then she picked up a packet of dried hellebore stems and began the process all over again, her hands remaining steady as she worked until the morning had passed and her pouch was full.

Edie was brought along with it, pressed up against tightly packed bodies until she had a clear view of the woman in front.

Laura de Force was exactly how Edie had imagined she'd be: stately and elegant. Her dress simple but flattering; the only adornment a yellow rose—the color of women's suffrage—pinned to her chest. Her light brown hair was tied back into a practical knot, but there were several loose strands around her face, giving the impression that nothing about this woman was content to remain contained.

Laura de Force raised her gloved hands and the applause died down.

"For too long," she called out, her voice clear and assured, "there has been a system of repression and oppression practiced toward women. Too often, the little girl who dares to voice an opinion in opposition to, say, her brother's view on some subject, is met with the exasperating and insulting reminder of her inferiority, expressed as '*Well, you are a girl. What do you know about it?*'"

The crowd buzzed in angry acknowledgment. And though Edie booed along with them, a small corner of her mind couldn't help but remember a different kind of man: the father she'd known as a young child. A man who, once he'd sensed her interest, encouraged her to read the newspaper along with him in the mornings. His bright-blue eyes dancing with pride when she used what she'd read to bolster an argument. A father who'd brought her with him to an empty church when he practiced his sermons, patiently explaining the art of oratory.

The man he'd been before everything changed.

You aren't a child anymore, Edith. I've indulged this unnatural interest long enough.

"Both law and gospel," continued Laura de Force, "have joined against woman to render her position in life unnatural and subservient. In law, she has always been a ward. First of her father—and second and always of her husband. But I stand before you today, and I tell you that woman is no longer content to remain a subject!"

Another cheer rose up. This time Edie joined in, yelling until she felt hoarse.

Laura held up her hands for silence, waiting for the crowd to settle down before she continued. "Mrs. Dorothy Dryer," she said solemnly, "wife and mother of two, is but the latest of too many women to suffer at the hands of the unjust laws of this country. Laws which are *made* by men. *Interpreted* by men. And *administered* by men. This government, which runs on taxes *paid for by women*, compels women to obey laws to which they have not given their consent! And then, those same laws imprison them and commit them, without a trial by a jury of their female peers!"

Another roar from the crowd, this one with some bite to it. Rage shimmering around its edges.

"I have here a list," called out Laura, holding up a sheaf of paper with official-looking writing printed along its front, "of acceptable reasons for a man to commit his wife, daughter, or ward to an asylum for the insane. And believe me when I tell you, the burden of proof does not fall to *him*!

"You know, of course," she continued, "that taking medicine to prevent a pregnancy—even when that normally happy occasion will cause great harm to the mother—is on this list. But so too is the practice of *reading of novels!* The crime of providing *bad company,* and even the offense of *experiencing political excitement!*"

Another angry murmur from the crowd, like the steady, ominous buzzing of bees.

"You show me a single man," cried out Laura, "who has been sent to such a place as this"—she held out a hand and indicated the black metal gates behind her—"for *expressing political excitement.* For if this is indeed a crime of the mind, then believe you me, I have a long list of men whose minds must be as feeble as they come!"

The crowd around Edie broke out into an appreciative tension-breaking laugh. But Edie did not laugh. She didn't even smile. Instead, her eyes focused on the black metal gates behind Laura de Force, taking them in properly for the first time, her eyes widening at the large gothic monstrosity beyond the gates, complete with dark stone walls and a multitude of towers and turrets.

And there. A sign along the top that read: SACRAMENTO ASYLUM FOR THE INSANE.

Edie's entire body froze.

She should not have come here.

But before she could turn and flee, there was a scuffle near the edge of the crowd. A group of men were forcing their way toward the front. Her eyes caught an ominous flash of white around the neck of a man in the front of the group. A clerical collar, peeking out from underneath a black suit.

Edie tried to back away, but the crowd was too tightly packed for it not to cause a scene and draw attention. Her heart hammered in her chest. A voice rose into her mind.

Unnatural daughters!

Her body shivered, just as it had that day a year ago when her father had slammed the door to her and Violet's bedroom, turning over the lock with a key.

You will be saved.

The man with the clerical collar spoke.

"Turn your eyes away from this sinful daughter of Eve!"

But no. The voice was all wrong. High and nasal, where her father's was deep with the barest hint of an old lisp.

The minister shouted again. "Return to your homes!"

It wasn't him.

"Return to your womanly duties. Forget not the words of St. Paul, who proclaimed in the fourteenth chapter of Corinthians, verse thirty-four: *Let your women keep silence in the churches: for it is not permitted unto them to speak.*"

Edie had heard that verse quoted before. But by a different man.

Laura de Force turned to look at the protesting minister, her gaze steady and unshaken. But Edie didn't share her confidence. She had eyes only for the police officers moving in toward the crowd.

She must have missed their presence before. She'd been too entranced by Laura de Force's words. Too in awe of a woman who could speak with such authority in her own voice. So mesmerized,

Edie hadn't even realized she'd delivered herself to the gates of the exact asylum that would have been her fate and Violet's, had they not escaped that night a year ago.

A hysterical kind of laugh bubbled up to her lips. She might as well have donned a straitjacket and tied a bow around her neck.

She needed to get away from those black gates. *Now.*

Edie whipped around and began pushing through the crowd.

Behind her, Laura de Force spoke again. "For too long," she said, her words bouncing off Edie's back, "the stronghold of the church has been the ignorance and degradation of women!"

Other women began noticing the encroaching police officers as well. Edie caught more than one worried glance. She quickened her pace.

Up near the front, the minister was speaking again. But Edie only caught every other word, *blasphemy* seeming to be a favorite.

And then, just as she was nearing the sidewalk, a ruckus broke out in the middle of the crowd. Seconds later, a police whistle blew. It was all the officers were waiting for. They moved in toward the crowd of women, determination on their faces.

Edie glanced over her shoulder and saw one of them, a beady-eyed officer with greasy hair poking out from underneath his round helmet, making his way toward her.

Panic seized her chest and for a moment she was unable to breathe. It was unlikely she'd be arrested, but this officer could detain her as a witness. Discover her name. Her *real* name.

She picked up her skirts, turned, and ran toward the sidewalk. But her path was blocked by something tall and solid. Edie rammed into it with such force that she lost her balance and would have tumbled to the ground if a hand hadn't reached out and gripped her elbow, pulling her upright. She was aware of something white fluttering to the ground.

"Miss, are you all right?"

Edie looked up into the concerned face of a young man. A rather good-looking one, she couldn't help but notice despite the threat at her back. He was hardly older than she was—seventeen or eighteen if she had to guess—dressed in a respectable, if somewhat worn, linen sack suit. He had pale skin and a mop of dark, untidy curls peeking out from beneath his hat. And he was staring at her with concerned brown eyes. Kind eyes.

One of his hands was still holding her elbow. The other had reached down to swoop up the white thing that had fluttered to the ground, tucking it into the breast pocket of his suit.

Another police whistle blew. And all at once, Edie had an idea.

She gripped the young man's hand and quickly adjusted her arm so it was looped through his. Then she stood up on her toes and said, in a low, urgent tone, "Screw up your face and say something mean."

The young man furrowed his brow. "Excuse me?"

"A little better than that!" Edie adjusted her grip on his arm. "Try looking down at me and sort of shaking your head. Like you're very disappointed—there, that's good."

It wasn't *actually* good. Although the young man was indeed shaking his head, he looked much more confused than he did angry. But it would have to do.

Edie jerked his arm, pulling him toward the sidewalk. "Now, you have to make it look as if you're dragging me away."

"Miss," interrupted the young man. He had the barest hint of a Southern drawl. "I really don't—"

But he stopped talking when Edie suddenly halted. She turned and looked him straight in the eye. And for just a moment, she let her bravado drop away.

Her guard was up again in seconds, but whatever the young man saw in her face for those few brief moments must have been enough to persuade him to play along, because, the next thing Edie knew, there was a hand on the small of her back, guiding her firmly—but gently—away from the crowd.

Edie played at resisting. And under the guise of some general wiggling, she threw a look over her shoulder. The police officer who'd been heading her way had turned his attention to a different unaccompanied young woman.

Edie turned back around and allowed the young man with brown eyes to lead her down the street. She was close enough to detect a faint woodsy scent on his skin. It was mixed with something sharp Edie couldn't quite identify, but she focused on it anyway in order to ground her panicking mind.

It wasn't until they turned the corner that Edie allowed herself a breath of relief. She quickly disentangled herself from the young man, her mind still somewhat numb with dread, and set off toward the opposite side of the street.

He'd let go of her easily, but when she began to cross the street he called out. "Wait!"

Edie tensed.

"Is that . . ." He paused, as if unsure what to say. "Is that it?"

She turned and raised her eyebrows. "I'm not going to thank you for playing the role of male guardian," she said, her tone both cautious and haughty. "So if that's what you're waiting for—"

"No," he said, cutting her off with a shake of his head. "I only mean . . . it's just. Are you all right?"

For one traitorous moment, Edie considered the question.

Was she all right?

Her heart was still hammering from being so near the gates of that asylum. The asylum she would be locked inside of if their father found them. And she had just been feet away from a police officer. A police officer who might very well have her name and Violet's—their real names, anyway—listed as local underage runaways.

Edie met the young man's eyes with a defiant stare. "Of course I'm all right," she said, drawing herself up to her full height. "Why wouldn't I be?"

And then she turned on her heel and set off down the street. Her bones were shaking and there was a sheen of panic-induced sweat on her brow, but there was something else thrumming through her as well. A new kind of focused clarity.

Inspiration had finally struck, and she had a trance lecture to prepare.

the topics of her trance lectures with one, or both, before going up on stage.

Leaning over the notebook, Ada and Lillian read the open page at the same time. A minute later, Lillian straightened up and whistled. "Not pulling your punches tonight, are you?"

Ada swept her eyes once more over Edie's list of arguments before picking up the notebook and handing it back to her. "The inequality in marriage laws is biting off a lot, Edie. Even for you. May I ask what put this particular bee in your bonnet?"

Edie shrugged, trying for nonchalance. "Seems like an important topic."

Lillian shot her an assessing look, and Edie tried not to flail underneath it.

While Lillian wasn't *actually* able to heal a person by placing her hands on them and invoking the spirit world, she did have an uncanny knack for diagnosing people. Always the first to know if someone had had trouble sleeping the night before. Always there with a cup of tea when you were feeling low. It would be no surprise at all if she'd sensed that Edie's interest in this topic was not purely academic.

When Lillian continued to stare at her expectantly, Edie turned away and made her way back to the easy chair.

She didn't want to talk about the real reason behind her sudden burning need to attack a common law that voided a woman's personhood after marriage. A law that prevented a woman like her mother from leaving with her daughters after the quiet, curious man she'd fallen in love with at nineteen had been so thoroughly transformed by the views of his church's elders.

"If you must know," said Edie, eager to change the topic, "I attended a speech by Laura de Force this afternoon that gave me the idea. Not," she added in a hurried tone, "that Mr. Huddle needs to know about it."

"*Hm.*" Lillian crossed her arms and leaned back in her chair. "I'm not sure how I feel about that woman."

Startled, Edie's eyes flew to Lillian. "I'd have thought you of all people would support her. A woman who is using her considerable influence to protest the unjust confinement of a perfectly sane, innocent woman to an asylum?"

"But that's just it," cut in Ada. "Someone like Laura de Force is happy to publicly throw her support behind a woman like Dorothy Dryer. A respectable, as you say *innocent*, woman. But I don't hear her—or anyone high up in the state suffrage association, for that matter—raising a ruckus about all the women going missing from Belden Place."

A pall fell over the women at Ada's words.

Quietly, Lillian said to Edie, "Ada received another letter this morning."

Edie looked over at Ada. "The same as the others?"

Slowly, Ada nodded. "Polly Edwards. I don't think you ever met her."

Edie shook her head. When she and Violet had first arrived in San Francisco after running away from home, they'd met some of the women who lived in a particularly seedy alley called Belden

Place. Women who offered their services as spirit mediums, but who were also compelled by circumstance to offer other, less respectable services as well.

Edie and Violet hadn't been in the city long enough to know many of them before leaving on Mr. Huddle's tour, but Ada and Lillian were well connected in that world. And so they'd received word when, five months ago, one of the women they knew from Belden Place was picked up by the police under the selectively enforced vagrancy laws. This kind of arrest in itself wasn't uncommon, but the fact that the woman hadn't been seen or heard from since, was. Equally alarming was that all requests made for information about her whereabouts had been met with bureaucratic silence.

And then another medium had gone missing in the exact same manner.

And then another.

"How many is that now?" Edie asked. "Five?"

Ada shook her head. "Polly makes six."

"And no one has any idea—"

"It's like they disappeared into thin air," said Lillian. "And no one gives a damn about it. Ada and I aren't the only ones who've written to the local suffrage chapter. Hell, we've written to *anyone* who might have any influence at all to get some answers. But evidently the powers that be don't want to be associated with a half-dozen missing women of *ill-repute*."

Lillian's words sent a shiver up Edie's spine. How close had she and Violet come to being forced to live that life?

Reaching across the table, Ada took Lillian's hand and squeezed it. Lillian sighed, brought Ada's hand to her lips, and brushed a kiss across her knuckles.

At that same moment, the door to the Green Room opened. Lillian and Ada immediately broke apart as Emma Foster's pale, heart-shaped face peeked around the frame.

Emma, a gifted musician who, like Ada, was obliged to give the spirits credit for her original compositions, was only a year older than the twins, but she somehow seemed younger. Perhaps because of her tendency to ramble nervously whenever she didn't have a musical instrument in hand.

"Oh, *there* you are, Edie," said Emma, her wide blue eyes relaxing in evident relief. "Mr. Huddle's looking for you. Could you go and meet him in the lobby? He said to tell you to be quick about it, but I didn't think to look for you in here. Which is silly because you're always here. But I'm afraid he might be a little put out that it took me so long. So, if you wouldn't mind—"

"I'll go at once," said Edie, cutting the poor girl off before she talked herself into a nervous fit. "Thanks for letting me know, Emma."

As Emma nodded and retreated out of the room, Edie sighed and bent to slip her shoes back on. In addition to giving trance lectures, Edie acted as a sort of helper to Mr. Huddle from time to time. A necessity since it was Violet—with her winning stage presence and uncanny séance ability—who had gotten them a spot on this tour. Edie's trance lectures were acceptable but by no means a favorite act. And so Edie found additional ways to earn her keep.

Shoes fastened, she tucked her pen away and scanned the notebook page on which she'd sketched out the basic points of her lecture. There was quite a bit left to fill in, but Edie was rather good at doing that while on stage—letting the words flow naturally, rather than planning them out too much in advance. Just like her father used to do with his sermons.

Tearing off the page with the writing, Edie folded it and tucked it into the hidden inner pocket of her dress right next to her silk herb pouch. After a quick goodbye to Ada and Lillian, she set off toward the lobby.

❦ ❧

A middle-aged man with an impressive set of whiskers and a round, ruddy face strode across the carpeted lobby of the Metropolitan Theater.

"Edie! Just the girl I was hoping to see!"

"Mr. Huddle," said Edie, extending her hand. He brushed his lips over her gloved knuckles, the lingering scent of tobacco smoke wafting off his jacket and tickling Edie's nose. "How are the numbers looking for tonight, sir? I trust our special guest will still be in attendance?"

Mr. Huddle chuckled and bestowed Edie with a conspiratorial wink. "Oh yes, indeed. And your Mary Sutton isn't the only one, my dear. I have an extra little job for you tonight, if you're up for it."

"Of course, Mr. Huddle. As long as I'm free to watch Violet's séance."

"Oh yes, you'll be free as a bird to attend your—oh, but I believe this is our young man now! What excellent timing!"

The lobby doors opened with a light swoosh and a cold gust of air washed over the back of Edie's neck. She turned around to greet the newcomer, caught sight of a mess of untidy black curls, and then immediately turned back around.

"Mr. Huddle!" The slight Southern drawl was unmistakable. "It's a pleasure to meet you, sir. Sorry to have kept you waiting. Blasted tire went flat, if you believe it."

"Not at all, young man," said Mr. Huddle amiably as he strolled over to greet him. "Now, is it my age or are you lot getting younger by the year?"

"I'll be eighteen next month, sir. And I assure you, my editor is confident I'm more than up—"

"Oh, I'm sure you are. Young, sharp minds. That's what we need, I always say! And I'll tell *you*, this couldn't be better timing. For here is the young lady I wanted you to meet!"

Edie was still standing with her back to the lobby doors, which was unconscionably rude. She would have to turn around soon. There was no way out of it, although her stubborn mind still dashed around looking for possibilities.

She couldn't exactly flee the lobby. Mr. Huddle would simply find her again backstage and question her strange behavior. And hiding was out of the question anyway, since she'd already been seen. Well, the back half of her. No, there was no way out. She would have to face this head-on.

Edie turned around.

The young man's brown eyes narrowed in confusion Then they widened with understanding and recognition. He was dressed in the same casual way he'd been earlier that afternoon at Laura de Force's speech. A somewhat wrinkled linen sack suit, the sleeves rolled up, revealing ink-stained fingers. He'd removed his hat, allowing a few errant curls to fall onto his forehead. A notebook poked out from the breast pocket of his coat.

Edie walked forward to greet him, a mild smile plastered to her face.

"Ah, here we are," beamed Mr. Huddle. "Miss Edith Bond, may I present Mr. Lawrence Everett? Mr. Everett's a reporter who's going to do a little article about us."

Heat crawled up Edie's neck at the frank interest she felt in Mr. Lawrence Everett's gaze, but she forced herself to meet his eyes with as much ice as she could muster. "It's a pleasure to meet you, Mr. Everett."

She emphasized the word *meet,* and she could tell, by the way his lips quirked, that he understood her silent demand.

"Please," he said, offering her a small bow, his eyes never leaving her face. "Call me Laws."

Edie blinked at the familiarity. Then she braced, preparing for him to mention their meeting earlier that day. But an entire second passed by. And then one second more. And Laws Everett did nothing but smile.

Mr. Huddle clapped his hands together. "Well, this is excellent! Edie, you're to show young Laws about. He's from the *Sacramento Sting*, you know. Excellent paper."

Edie's brows shot up. It *wasn't* an excellent paper, actually. She'd read enough of the *Sting* since arriving in Sacramento to know the pages included more sketches than words and that the editors seemed more interested in lampooning a subject than in providing credible reporting.

But there was no point in explaining that to Mr. Huddle. He was a dog with a bone when it came to any possible opportunity to increase their flagging ticket sales.

"I'd like you to arrange for some interviews with the ladies," Mr. Huddle continued. "Won't that be grand?"

"Yes," said Laws, his eyes dancing. "I'm so looking forward to learning more about your . . . uh, your little show here."

Edie stood up straighter. "Our little *show*?"

"Oh, come, Edie," admonished Mr. Huddle. "No need to bristle. Laws here is going to get us some excellent publicity. Isn't that right, my boy?"

The older man strode forward and flung an arm around Laws. "And I'll tell *you*, Edie here is the best one to show you about. Her twin sister is one of our finest mediums. Just wait until you see her tonight. You'll be moved to tears. See if you won't!"

Laws's eyebrows raised a hair, and he directed another piercing gaze at Edie. "Twins? Well, that must be . . . *convenient*."

Mr. Huddle laughed off the comment. "Excellent, excellent. Now I'll pop off to let the gals know you'll be coming through. And I'll get together those testimonials I promised to send you home with, young man. Edie, a quick word?"

Edie shot Laws an annoyed look and then followed Mr. Huddle to the other side of the lobby.

"Now, my dear," said Mr. Huddle in a low, disapproving tone. "I'm quite sure you know what I'm about to say?"

He gave her a knowing look, and Edie caught a not-often-seen flash of steel underneath Mr. Huddle's normally genial face. For one wild moment, she thought he'd found out about her attendance at Laura de Force's speech after all. Is that why the reporter was here? Had he somehow discovered her identity and ratted her out?

"Yes," said Mr. Huddle, no doubt correctly reading the panic on Edie's face. "It was a little far, wasn't it? I must say, Edie, we got more than a few . . . *complaints* afterward. Farming and fruiting pays for this city, you know."

It took Edie a full two seconds to understand what Mr. Huddle was saying.

"My trance lecture on Wednesday," said Edie slowly. "On the inequality faced by farm wives who do as much work as the men but share none of the profits. Women who not only help with the crops but must also—"

"Yes, yes," cut in Mr. Huddle, throwing a nervous glance back at the reporter. "Can't very well have the, er . . . *spirits* calling out a bigwig's livelihood and still expect a good write-up, now, can we?"

That caught Edie up short. She too shot a look at the reporter. "Are you saying that because the owner of that man's paper is also in the farming business—"

"I'm merely suggesting," said Mr. Huddle in a tone that told her this wasn't a *suggestion* at all, "you find a spirit for tonight's performance who has somewhat less . . . *political* views."

"Less political," Edie repeated.

"Exactly," said Mr. Huddle, clearly happy that Edie was catching on. "What about Joan of Arc? Always such a hit. A nice talk on the virtues of female sacrifice would be just the ticket. Can't go wrong there, can we?"

"But, Mr. Huddle—"

"That's a good girl. Now, I'll pop right back with those testimonials." Then, nodding in the direction of Mr. Lawrence Everett, he said, "And you'll keep your eye on that one, won't you, dear?"

Without waiting for her response, Mr. Huddle scurried off. Edie opened her mouth to call after him and then promptly closed it, clenching her teeth hard against the temptation. Mr. Huddle wasn't a cruel or unreasonable man, but he could be surprisingly ruthless when it came to ticket sales. And right now, their livelihood depended on his goodwill. Edie sighed through her teeth. Another reason why they needed Mary Sutton's substantial reward money. So no man—not even the seemingly affable Mr. Huddle—would have the ability to control her life.

"So."

Edie jumped at the voice behind her. That lout of a reporter had followed her across the lobby without her noticing, which was annoying, because Edie was normally very aware of her surroundings.

She turned to face him. And then immediately wished she hadn't. There was something knowing and mischievous in those brown eyes of his. Something that set the hair along her arms on edge.

Forget her fear of Lawrence Everett telling Mr. Huddle about her presence at a political speech. This boy had seen her run from a policeman. He was a reporter. With resources. He could find things out about her—and Violet—that Edie didn't want found.

He opened his mouth to speak, but Edie shook her head and turned around toward the backstage door. She needed a moment. A moment to *think*.

"If you'll excuse me," she said, starting to walk away, "there are a few items I must attend to before—"

"Oh no, you don't." Laws jumped in front of her, blocking her path. "I know where to find you now. There's no point in running again."

Edie pulled up short. "Are you threatening me?"

He slapped a hand to his chest in mock agony. "*Threatening* you? How could you think such a thing, Miss Bond? It's Edie, though, isn't it? May I call you Edie?"

"Edie is what my friends call me."

"Edith then, since although we may not be friends, surely you can't deny we're acquainted."

Edie narrowed her eyes but said nothing.

"Look," he said, holding up his hands, palms out, in the universal gesture for *I mean no harm*. "I'll level with you, *Miss Bond*. I need a story. One good enough to convince my editor that he didn't make a mistake bumping me up to reporter. And I think *you're* the one to help me get it."

Edie cocked her head to the side. "I've already agreed to give you a tour. What else could you want—"

"What I want," said Laws, taking a step toward her, eyebrows raised knowingly, "is the *real* story. And I think you know exactly what I mean."

Edie crossed her arms. She knew a skeptic when she saw one, and she wasn't about to let some ambitious junior reporter destroy the livelihood of every woman on this tour just because he was looking for a story to print in a third-rate paper that would become fish wrappings the next day.

"There's money in it for you, too," said Laws, mistaking her silence for consideration, "if that's what you're worried about."

He took out the pad of paper from under his arm and flipped the pages, revealing a crisp banknote tucked inside the folds. Then he opened the pad to a blank page and took out a pen from his coat pocket. "Why don't we start with the kind of setup you have here. You lot love your stagecraft, don't you?"

Edie schooled her face into a polite smile. "It would be my pleasure." Laws's eyes lit up. "Which would you like to see first? The trick wires on the stage, or the vat where we mix up the ectoplasm?"

The smile dropped from his face. "I suggest you take my offer more seriously."

"And why on earth would I do that?"

"Well." His eyes flicked over her shoulder to where Mr. Huddle had last been. Then he took a step closer to Edie and lowered his voice. "It seems to me you're pretty keen on keeping the truth of your whereabouts this afternoon mum. And I've got no problem with that, Miss Bond. As long as you're amenable to helping me out a bit."

"Why, Mr. Everett." It was Edie's turn to slap a hand to her chest. "Whatever could you mean? I was in my room at the Union Hotel all afternoon."

"Surely you don't mean to deny that—"

"Oh, but I do."

This time, it was Edie who took a step toward him. Their noses now inches apart. This close, she could smell the same woodsy scent she'd detected earlier this afternoon, only now she was able to identify it. Sandalwood. And something else. The sharp, oily smell of ink.

Edie had learned a few things since taking up the medium profession. Namely, she'd learned to read people. And she had an instinct about this boy. A feeling he had no intention of giving her up to Mr. Huddle. Maybe it was the kind eyes. Or maybe it was the way he'd asked if she was all right back on the street corner this afternoon, as if he'd genuinely wanted to help. Whatever it was, she'd decided to call his bluff.

Lawrence Everett opened his mouth to speak, but only managed to sputter. "I . . . uh, well."

Edie hid her exhale of relief under a smile.

"I think we understand each other, Mr. Everett." She took a step back and allowed herself a discreet breath of non-woodsy air. "I'll inform Mr. Huddle that you will, regrettably, be unable to write a story after all. I'm sure he'll understand that another reporter needs to be assigned. Perhaps someone with a little more"—she paused, slowly dragging her eyes over his face—"experience."

She turned toward the backstage door. But just before she'd opened it, a voice called out.

"Oh, Miss Bond?"

Edie took her time turning around, her eyebrows raised. They dropped only slightly when she caught sight of the silver bicycle now propped up under Laws's arm. She'd been vaguely aware of it leaning against the lobby doors but was only now getting a proper look at it. It was a little different from the one Ruby had borrowed. The center bar jutted straight out from the handlebars toward the seat, instead of sloping down in a graceful curve, but it was still just as tempting. Looking at it, Edie could almost feel the wind whipping in her hair, could taste the freedom she'd felt yesterday when pedaling full-speed on Ruby's borrowed bike.

Some of that yearning must have shown on her face, because Laws tilted his head to the side and smiled in a knowing way. "Do you ride, Miss Bond?"

Edie tore her eyes away from the bicycle, crossed her arms, and frowned.

"Because if you did," he continued, his eyes blazing into hers, "I think you should know that I have a strict policy of letting my friends borrow this bicycle whenever they like."

Edie narrowed her eyes. "We're not friends."

Laws shrugged. "That, Miss Bond, is entirely up to you." They stared at each other for another moment. Long enough for her to notice the flecks of gold in his brown eyes.

Then he wiggled the handlebars of the bicycle, breaking the tension as the front wheel jerked to the left. "Could you show me a place to store this? I'd hate for it to get nicked while you're giving me that tour."

6

"And here," said Edie, leading Laws off the stage and through the wings, "is the backstage hall where the mediums prepare before the show. We have about half an hour until curtain, so I believe we'll have time for a quick hello with a few of the ladies."

Laws flipped through his notebook, his eyes roving over the very few notes he'd taken during their tour of the theater. "Well, Miss Bond, I must say I think you've done a remarkable job on this tour."

Edie tried to mask her surprise. She'd been priding herself on doing a remarkably *bad* job. "Have I?"

"Oh yes. So far you've managed to steer me away from examining the stage for any hidden rigging by summoning a man who, I am pretty sure, was not actually there to manage the lights."

That was true. Edie had summoned an usher who was not yet dressed in his livery and told Laws it wasn't safe to remain on the stage while the man cleaned the glass in the lamps.

"Then," continued Laws, "you spoke in a frankly upsettingly loud voice as we were passing a grouping of what I assume are members of your little troupe who were pumping those nice old ladies for information on their recently deceased husbands."

Drat. So he *had* been able to hear that.

"And while I'm sure I can expect the same level of . . . assistance in these interviews, I do wonder if I might be able to conduct them *alone*?"

"Oh, Mr. Everett. As much as I would love to indulge such a request, I'm afraid it simply wouldn't be proper. You'll be meeting these women in their dressing rooms, you see, and, well . . ."

Edie trailed off and enacted a delicate shrug as if to say *What can we do?*

Laws sighed in a resigned sort of way. "Very well, then. Please do lead on."

Hiding a satisfied smile, she turned down the backstage hallway, Laws falling into step beside her. "And at what point," he asked, "will I have the opportunity to interview *you*, Miss Bond?"

A muscle in Edie's jaw jumped, but she kept her voice light as she said, "I rather thought you were doing that now."

They approached the door separating the backstage hall from the dressing-room corridor. Laws jumped forward to grasp the handle, holding it open as Edie brushed past him. "If that's the case, Miss Bond," said Laws as he fell back into step beside her, "then I wonder if I could ask about your trance lecture the other night. Such a unique and timely topic. The inequality in earnings for farm wives."

Edie shot him a glance. "You were, um—you were in the audience on Wednesday?"

"Of course," he said, eyes dancing. "You didn't think I'd show up to interview a bunch of . . . spirit mediums"—he injected as much skepticism as possible into the words *spirit* and *mediums*—"without first doing my research, did you? Although"—he lowered his voice and tilted his head closer to Edie's—"I must admit, I didn't recognize you this afternoon when we—"

"As to my lecture," said Edie, cutting him off. The less said about their encounter at Laura de Force's speech, the better. "I'm afraid I'll have to disappoint you. I am unable to comment on the content after I leave my trance."

"Oh? And why is that?"

"Because they are not my words. They are the words of the spirit I channel, and I do not recall them after they are spoken."

"Ah," said Laws, his eyes searching her face. "Well, that *is* a shame. I thought the point was rather well-argued. And it's a topic I'm sure our readers would be curious to learn more about."

Edie shot him an assessing look. It was a good attempt on his part. Appeal to her vanity. Her desire to be seen as *smart*. To claim her own words and ideas. But she had no intention of rising to the bait. Because if she so much as *uttered* an opinion of her own on this topic, she knew the article in the newspaper the following day—*if* you could even call the *Sting* a newspaper—would not be a heartfelt treatise on the way society failed the women working their fingers to the bone on farms without any share in the profits, but rather a salacious tidbit about a medium admitting herself to be a fraud. Along with what would likely be an unflattering cartoon of Edie's face.

Fortunately, there was no need to answer his question because they had arrived at their first destination. A quick knock from Edie and the dressing-room door flew open, revealing a petite, birdlike woman in her late thirties. Like Edie, she was dressed in a pearl-white gown, although she'd added quite a few more ruffs and feathers to hers.

"Oh, Edith dear," she said in a high, almost childlike voice, "I thought I heard your voice." Without waiting for an introduction, she turned to Laws and grabbed his arm. "And *you* must be the young reporter Mr. Huddle told me about. My, aren't you a handsome one? And eager to hear all the details, I'm sure."

Laws, who was at least a foot taller than the woman now clutching his arm, looked down at her with what could only be described as utter bewilderment. "Er, yes. Details are always . . . appreciated."

He shot Edie a questioning glance; and although she was enjoying his confusion, she supposed she really ought to make the proper introductions. "Miss Cora Bradley, may I present Mr. Lawrence Everett of the *Sacramento Sting*. Mr. Everett, Miss Bradley is one of our most celebrated spirit mediums. As I'm sure you're aware, she was quite famously summoned to the White House on a number of occasions and was instrumental in helping President Lincoln end the war."

Laws's eyebrows shot up. "Is that so?"

The corner of Edie's mouth twitched, but she managed to keep a mostly straight face as she said, "Indeed. We, as a country, owe her a great debt of gratitude."

79

Cora, apparently unable to wait even a second longer for the spotlight to shine on her, began pulling Laws into her dressing room, not unlike a spider reeling in its prey.

"You know," said Cora, "it was dear Mary Todd who first summoned me. Her husband, dear Abe—may the spirits keep him—was quite distressed, you see, and Mary thought I might be able to help. I was only thirteen at the time! Yes, yes. I can see you're surprised. But, you understand, the spirits called me early into their service."

Edie followed the pair into the dressing room, not bothering to hide the satisfied smirk on her lips. On any normal day, she would have jumped through fire if it meant escaping another recitation of Cora's glory days, but she was petty enough to enjoy watching Lawrence Everett suffer the ordeal. He thought she was keeping him from the real bones of their show? Well, let him have Cora Bradley unfiltered. See if *that* didn't change his tune.

Cora began by telling Laws the story of her older brother, who had died fighting for the Union in the War Between the States. It was his spirit who had first contacted her when she was only a little girl. And, although Cora was a complete and total fraud now, Edie was rather sure young Cora *had* spoken to her brother's spirit as a child. It was a common enough backstory for women working as spirit mediums today.

The ability to open and close the Veil of death *at will* was rare. And those who could were careful about showcasing it. Even the recent popularity of Spiritualism couldn't erase the secrecy and fear born of being burned and hunted as witches for hundreds of years.

But while a consistent ability was rare, the occasional interaction with death was not. Most so-called mediums had discovered their "gift" after they lost someone dear to them. A child or lover was the most common. A spirit who would linger near them, making their presence felt in life—even murmuring in their ear— before moving beyond the Veil to a final death.

But just because someone like Cora had once communicated with a loved one in death, that didn't mean she could call down someone else's dear Aunt Mildred at will. And so Cora—like most spirit mediums—faked her trances, whether they were conducted for President Lincoln at the White House or for an audience of two hundred on stage.

Edie let Cora prattle on until Laws's eyes had fully glazed over. And then, just for fun, she let her go on for a few minutes more. When she finally stood up to announce it was time to move on to the next interview, the look Laws gave her was almost grateful.

She'd intended to introduce him to Ruby next, but when she checked her friend's dressing room she found it empty. Not wanting Laws to pick up on anything, she quickly closed the door. Mr. Huddle would see red if Ruby missed *another* show because of a handsome young man. Even one with a bicycle.

Fortunately, Laws said nothing as she moved past Ruby's door and knocked on Ada Loring's. Laws spent a thoroughly enjoyable (to Edie, at least) quarter of an hour trying to trick Ada into taking credit for the poems she'd recited on stage their opening night. But, like Edie, she insisted she was *but a vessel for the spirits.*

"But you must spend a lot of time traveling," said Laws, a note of desperation in his voice. "Do you pass the time reading any . . . influential works?"

A beatific smile broke out on Ada's face. "Well, as a matter of fact, I do. There's a special book I keep close at hand. Would you like to see it?"

Laws nodded eagerly and leaned forward in his chair. Ada swiveled around and reached across the small vanity until her fingers closed around a thick book bound in simple black leather. She stared at it lovingly for a moment before passing it over to the reporter.

Laws opened it to the first page, and his face fell. "Oh. It's, um . . . well, it's the Bible."

A laugh burst out of Edie's mouth. Laws shot her an annoyed look.

Ada caught Edie's eye and gave her the quickest of winks before saying, "Yes indeed. The word of God keeps me company at all times."

Flora McCarthy was next.

Unlike mediums such as Violet, Cora, and Ruby who claimed to channel a variety of spirits, Flora—a twenty-one-year-old girl of proud Irish descent with bright orange hair and freckles to match—only claimed to be in contact with *one*. A single spirit who was immune to fire, since that was how he had supposedly died. And when Flora was possessed by that spirit, she too could not burn.

It was an impressive bit of stagecraft.

She would bring a lit kerosene oil lamp on stage with her and invite a member of the audience to test the lamp's bell-shaped glass shade. After they confirmed it to be exceedingly hot, Flora would pick up the burning-hot glass with her bare hands. The audience always gasped at that part, gasps that only increased in frequency and volume as she continued holding the hot glass for several long seconds, her face neutral and serene. She would then return the glass cover to the lamp and invite another audience member on stage to confirm that not even a single burn marred her delicate hands.

Flora ushered Edie and Laws into her dressing room, but Edie had barely gotten through the introductions before Laws made a beeline for Flora's cosmetics and creams.

"Mind if I take a sniff?"

Flora raised her carefully shaped eyebrows—the same bright orange as her hair—and shot Edie a surreptitious look.

Edie was equally surprised. She hadn't expected Laws to know about the special liquid Flora smothered on her hands before a performance: a mix of camphor, aqua vitae, quicksilver, and liquid styrax—a preparation that, once dried, protected the skin from fire and burns for a short period of time.

"Sniff away," cooed Flora, her voice amused. "I had no idea this article included a section on our beauty regimes, but I'm happy to oblige. That one," Flora added, as Laws picked up a small green jar and examined its contents, "is particularly good for spots. I'd encourage you to try it on your nose, but I'm afraid it's rather too late for that."

Since Flora made the special mixture in her hotel room before arriving at the theater, there was nothing for Laws to find, a fact he soon came to realize himself. After a few compulsory questions to Flora about her act and her background, Edie led the reporter to his last victim of the evening.

Lillian was back in the Green Room, her various mixtures spread out and neatly labeled on the table before her. Earlier, with Ada and Edie, she'd been wearing her everyday clothes, but she'd since changed into her elaborate costume. Like the rest of the mediums, she was dressed all in white. But instead of a flowing dress, she wore a kind of belted robe that made her look like an angel who'd escaped from a heavenly choir. Even the drape of the robe along her back gave the suggestion of wings.

When Edie and Laws entered, Lillian was busy scribbling in a notebook that Edie knew kept an account of each of her patients.

"Lillian," Edie began. "May I introduce you to—"

"Lawrence Everett," said Laws, cutting her off and striding past her into the room. "From the *Sacramento Sting*. I saw your act on stage Wednesday night."

Lillian looked up from her notebook, her black hair piled high on her head, a polite, welcoming smile on her face. "Of course. Mr. Huddle told me all about your article, Mr. Everett. It's a pleasure to meet you."

Laws's only response was a kind of humming sound at the back of his throat. He then proceeded to sit down on the small settee across from Lillian's chair without being invited.

Lillian shot a quick, questioning glance to where Edie stood hovering just inside the doorway. Edie nodded to indicate that she would stay for the interview, but then she shifted her attention back to Laws.

There was a sharpness to his features now that she hadn't noticed before. A crack in the affable demeanor he'd kept up during Edie's abysmal tour and throughout the other interviews. Prior to this moment, it had almost felt to Edie as if she and Lawrence Everett had been playing some kind of game. He was a skeptic, yes. But a skeptic who seemed to find all of this rather . . . amusing.

But he wasn't amused now. That hint of laughter was gone from his eyes, replaced by a hawklike intensity that raised the hair on the back of her neck. Was this the real reporter underneath the act?

Laws leaned forward in his seat, his eyes never leaving Lillian's face. "I understand that you fashion yourself a spiritual healer, Miss Fiore. Is that correct?"

Lillian's normally kind eyes narrowed. "I don't *fashion* myself a healer, Mr. Everett. I *am* one."

The smile that crossed Laws's face didn't meet his eyes. "And as a healer, Miss Fiore, you dispense medical advice to your . . . *patients*. Some of whom are very ill. And yet—unless I am mistaken—I do not believe you have received any sanctioned medical training. Is that also true?"

Lillian's eyes flashed.

"Mr. Everett," said Edie, stepping forward. "I assure you that Miss Fiore practices the utmost care when—"

"I would prefer," interrupted Laws in a calm but cold voice, "to hear it from the *doctor* herself."

Lillian stiffened in her chair. *"Doctor?"*

Edie almost groaned aloud. Laws had done it now. "Perhaps we should continue this interview at another time. The show is close to—"

But Lillian stopped her with a wave of her hand, her eyes remaining on Laws. "I am not a *doctor*, Mr. Everett. And I would thank you to refrain from using that term to describe me."

Laws gripped his pen and began to write. "So you admit it? That you have no medical training? Do you tell your *patients* as much?"

Lillian's eyes narrowed. "There is nothing to admit *to*. I have never, nor *will* I ever, claim to be a part of that heinous and dangerous institution."

Laws stopped scribbling and looked up at Lillian. If Edie hadn't been so anxious at the turn this conversation had taken, she might have been amused at the confused frustration on his face.

"I'm afraid I don't understand, Miss Fiore. You, who have admitted to having no actual medical knowledge, who waves her hands over a patient in order to cure him of his ills? *You* claim that anyone within the medical profession is dangerous?"

Lillian said nothing for several moments. Then she crossed her arms over her chest and leaned back in her chair. "Do you know where I was this morning, Mr. Everett?"

His only response was to raise his eyebrows.

"I was checking in on a patient who, prior to *my* care, had been bedridden for months after following his *doctor's orders*. This *doctor* prescribed a tincture of opium and snuff to cure his ails. His wife came to me, quite distraught. It took some doing, but eventually we persuaded the man to take a medicine of a simpler nature. He was up and about this morning for the first time in months."

Laws shrugged. "That's but one lucky incident—"

"Are you familiar with calomel?"

His brow furrowed. "I believe so. It's a powder, isn't it?"

"Yes," said Lillian, her voice heavy with disdain. "The *miracle drug*. If the doctors are to be believed, calomel is a cure for everything from syphilis, cholera, and gout to tuberculosis, influenza, and even cancer of the blood."

"Well," said Laws, his pen hovering uncertainly in his hands, "I'm not sure if a credible doctor would claim—"

"Oh, but they do. It is the most oft-prescribed medicine in our great country, Mr. Everett. Do you know what calomel consists of?"

Laws pursed his lips together. "I'm afraid I've never looked into the matter."

"No," snapped Lillian. "Of course you haven't. Calomel is a formula of mercury and chloride. Can you imagine what the effects would be on a body if this drug were overused?"

Laws stared mutinously at her but provided no answer.

Lillian held up a finger. "Gangrene of the skin, for one." She released a second finger. "Loss of teeth, for another." A third finger.

"Deterioration of the gums. I could go on." She uncrossed her arms and leaned forward in her chair. "The mercury in that powder is not a miracle cure, Mr. Everett. It is *poison*. Plain and simple. So, in answer to your earlier question? No, I am not a doctor. I do not cut people up to satisfy my own egotistical curiosity. I do not see human life as an experiment. I am a *healer*. I commune with the spirits to assess the ills of the body, and I then prescribe natural, simple remedies to heal them."

"While that's all well and good in theory, Miss Fiore, your disdain for the medical profession is—"

"Justified."

Edie stepped forward. This interview had gone on long enough. Somehow Mr. Lawrence Everett had managed to get under Lillian's skin—*not* an easy feat for the normally unflappable healer. Edie had underestimated him.

"Thank you so much for your time, Lillian. But I'm sure you need to get ready for—"

"No," said Lillian, her eyes still on Laws. "This young man is curious about my *disdain* for the medical profession, Edie. I believe he has a right to know my story. He's even welcome to print it, although we both know he won't."

At that, Laws raised a brow.

"Lillian," said Edie. "I don't think—"

"I was married at the age of sixteen," said Lillian, her back now ramrod straight, her eyes still fixed on Laws. "My only job in this marriage was to produce children for my husband. A job at which I did not succeed."

Edie took a step back. She knew this story, but hated hearing it all the same.

"I suffered three miscarriages within a year before finally giving birth to a stillborn babe. It was after this birth that the doctors began to come. I was too deep in my grief to recognize then what was happening. It wasn't until they loaded me into the back of a carriage that I understood. My grief was all my husband needed, you see, to commit me to an asylum for the insane."

Edie heard Laws's sharp intake of breath and saw his eyes grow wide. It was the first time she'd seen anything but hostility on his face since the interview with Lillian had begun.

Lillian caught the gesture. "You're familiar with the conditions of these asylums?"

His jaw visibly clenched. "I'm aware they can be quite . . . horrible."

Lillian nodded absentmindedly. "Horrible. Yes. That's as good a word as any." Her eyes stayed steady, but her voice took on a faraway tone as she continued. "The building was kept freezing at all times and the clothes we were forced into were threadbare. Useless against the constant chill. Most of the women were blue with cold. Some lost their fingers and toes."

A chill traveled up Edie's spine. The black gates of the Sacramento Asylum towering in her mind.

"And then there were the ice baths. A favorite treatment. I'll never forget the time a pair of nurses came to me unannounced and bound my hands and feet before throwing me into a tub of dirty water and ice. I had had the gall to complain to a doctor, you see, about the rancid meat and the coppery taste in the food. Women were getting sick from it. He dismissed my claims, of course. Calling them the imaginings of a diseased mind.

"The nurses beat me for telling. But apparently that hadn't been enough. So they threw me in that tub and held my head under the ice-cold water until I nearly drowned. They brought me up for a breath, only to submerge me again, over and over again until I gave up all sense and hope. Until I begged God to let me die."

Edie could see the image in her mind. Had seen it in her dreams many times since Lillian had first told her and Violet of her ordeal. Sometimes it was Lillian in the tub. Sometimes the person she saw in her dreams, ice water clogging her veins, was Violet.

Lillian went on to describe the morphine and chloral that the women were drugged with in such great quantities that even the sane ones lost their minds. She recounted the women's organization that had worked to free her, persuading the doctors to release Lillian into their care. How once she'd been freed from the asylum, the struggle to rid herself of the dependence on the drugs had been immense. How she had been sick for months. And that was only the physical pain.

Edie's stomach churned, and she was forced to lean against the dressing-room wall to combat the trembling in her knees.

Her father's face flashed into her mind. Twisted in shock and then righteous fury as he dragged her and Violet out of the sitting room, their mother's body lying cold and empty behind them.

You will be saved.

As if from a distance, Edie heard Lillian speak again. She tried to focus on her words. Tried to let them ground her in this place and time.

"So you understand, Mr. Everett"—Lillian's voice was sad but firm—"why I am unable to hold the medical profession in high regard."

There was a moment of silence after Lillian spoke. Edie slumped a little lower against the wall as she focused on getting her breathing back under control.

Laws stood up. "Thank you, Miss Fiore, for sharing your story with me. What you describe goes against all tenets of human decency. If you would be so kind as to write out the names of the particular institutions and persons involved, I'd like, with your permission, to reach out about corroborating the events you describe."

Lillian's eyes widened in surprise. Edie knew she'd told reporters this story before, after she'd first been released. They'd all deemed it not worth looking into further.

"You have my permission, Mr. Everett. I shall see that you get the particulars you need."

Laws nodded. Then he turned quite suddenly toward Edie. But she was so preoccupied with keeping her legs steady underneath her that she failed to gather herself in time. She felt, rather than saw, his eyes make a quick but thorough examination of her slumped form, the heat from his gaze causing her skin to flare with a prickly kind of awareness, starting at her feet and traveling up the length of her body, until his eyes settled on her face.

In that moment, when her green eyes met his brown, Edie knew she'd made a mistake. That whatever reaction she'd had to Lillian's story had intrigued him. Because the way Laws Everett was looking at her now? With his brow furrowed and his head tilted ever so slightly to the left? It was the way someone looked at a puzzle they desperately wanted to solve.

Edie pushed herself away from the wall and—thank goodness—managed to stand up on steady feet. "If you'd be so kind as to follow me, Mr. Everett, I'll find an usher who can show you to your seat."

7

By the time Violet bounded into their dressing room, *after* the show had already begun, Edie was surprised that she still had any hair left on her head, considering she'd spent the last twenty minutes all but pulling it out.

"Violet, where have you—"

"I know, Edie. I know."

"It's ten after!"

Violet threw off her hat and began unbuttoning a walking dress. It was a new one Edie had never seen before. Lilac, with a deep purple trim. "I'm well aware of the time, thank you."

"Well excuse me for assuming you'd lost the ability to read a clock! Silly me. Thinking that with *Mary Sutton* in the audience tonight, you might actually want to arrive at some reasonable—"

"I have forty minutes before I'm set to go on," said Violet, as she pulled the suspicious lilac garment over her head. "I don't know why you're—"

"Twenty minutes. Ruby's not here, so Flora opened. Lillian's on now, which means you have *twenty* minutes. Something you would know if you'd arrived along with the rest of—"

"What happened to Ruby?"

Edie rolled her eyes. "What do you *think*?"

Violet shook her head and laughed. "Oh, Ruby."

"I don't see what's so funny. Mr. Huddle's furious. Cora blabbed and told him about the client she went on that bicycle ride with, and after the Niagara Falls incident, it doesn't exactly take a genius to put two and two together. Honestly, one no-good scoundrel *winks* in her direction and she forgets about everything that *actually* matters."

Without meaning to, Edie's eyes flicked down to the lilac dress now pooled at Violet's feet. She'd bet her last nickel— and that was saying something, considering the current state of their funds—that another no-good scoundrel had given her sister that dress. A scoundrel who bore a remarkable resemblance to a walrus.

Violet followed her twin's gaze. "Just what," she asked, her tone deceptively light, "are you trying to imply, Edie?"

Edie tore her gaze away from the lilac dress. "The only thing I'm *implying* is that you are late. To the most important evening of our lives. I'd think that's enough to be getting on with, don't you?"

Violet pressed her lips together but said nothing. She took a white silk dress off a peg in the wall and pulled it over her head. Then she walked over to Edie and, without a word, presented her back. Edie stopped her pacing and did up the little pearl buttons. When she was finished, she patted Violet once on her shoulder.

Violet walked over to the vanity, plopped down on a chair in front of the mirror, picked up a bottle of face cream, and began applying the lotion to her face in light, delicate dabs.

"There's another thing," said Edie, watching her sister's reflection in the mirror. "Mr. Huddle has arranged for a reporter from the *Sacramento Sting* to do a piece about the tour. He's already interviewed some of the mediums."

Violet's eyes widened in the mirror.

Edie squinted back at her. "I know what you're thinking. And the answer is no."

Violet recorked the face cream and opened a jar of face powder. "The answer to *what* is no, Edie?"

Edie crossed her arms. "I've met this reporter, Vi. He's too observant by half. And that's on top of the fact that the *Sting* is only looking to make us the subject of their latest joke. This isn't an opportunity to charm him into writing something about your future career on a Broadway stage."

Violet swept her white rabbit's-foot brush into the jar of powder and began applying a light layer to her face. "So you're telling me that if Mr. Huddle asks me to speak to this reporter, I'm to . . . refuse?"

Edie shifted uncomfortably. "Of course not. That would look suspicious."

"Well then, color me confused."

"Oh come off it, Vi. Just . . . if you *have* to speak to him, try to make it quick. And be sure to stick to the story, all right?"

Violet's eyes narrowed. "Oh, is *that* what I should do?" She dropped the rabbit's-foot brush onto the counter and slammed the lid back on the face powder with a loud *clang*. "Thank goodness you reminded me. Because I was *going* to tell him the whole sorry tale of two sixteen-year-olds who fled their father's house via a rope of tied-together bedsheets while their mother's body grew cold in her sitting room. But now that you've reminded me *not* to say that, I suppose I won't. Whatever would I do without you to keep my head on straight!"

"Vi," Edie hissed, "will you *please* keep your voice down?"

Violet stood up from the chair and wheeled around to face her. "I swear, Edie, if you tell me what to do one more time—"

"Well maybe if you acted like a responsible person once in a while, I wouldn't feel the need to remind you of even the most basic—"

A knock at the door cut Edie off mid-sentence. Both she and Violet were breathing hard, chests heaving and their colors high. Edie forced a deep breath, then met her sister's eyes, silently asking a question.

Violet gave a terse nod.

Edie turned toward the door. "Come in!"

The door opened, and Emma's heart-shaped face popped in. "Oh, hello, Violet. Edie, Mr. Huddle asked me to tell you Cora just went on."

Edie nodded. "Thanks, Emma. I'll be there directly."

Emma's gaze flicked between Edie and Violet for a brief second. Then she nodded, retreated out of the room, and shut the door.

After Emma left, the twins stood in tense silence. Edie knew she should apologize for losing her temper. She wasn't happy Violet was late, but that wasn't exactly unusual, and she had—after all—made it in time. On some level, Edie knew she was really just upset with herself for letting her guard down, however briefly, with Lawrence Everett. And she was still on edge after what had happened at Laura de Force's speech. Finding herself standing in front of the Sacramento Asylum. Mistaking the minister in the crowd for her father. It had all set her on edge. And now she was taking it out on her sister.

She wanted to tell Violet all that. Unburden herself the way they used to. Receive absolution in the form of Violet folding her into her arms so they could promise each other that everything would be all right.

But instead, all she said was, "I should go backstage."

After a moment, Violet nodded.

Edie turned to leave. But when her hand reached the door handle, she paused. Without turning around, she said, "Be careful tonight, Vi."

When Violet said nothing in return, Edie opened the dressing-room door and set off down the hall.

Edie waited in the wings as the applause for Cora died down. Like Ruby's, her séances relied solely on whatever information

Mr. Huddle's audience plants managed to glean, but she always managed to pull something off that was rather good. It wasn't uncommon for her to receive the biggest applause of the night. That is, until Violet went on.

Cora glided off the stage, her face beaming. Mr. Huddle introduced Edie and gave her a significant nod as they passed each other in the wings. A reminder of their conversation earlier, about the content of her speech. But he didn't have anything to worry about. She'd already resigned herself to *channeling* Joan of Arc.

A smattering of tepid applause greeted Edie as she stepped out into the soft glow of the gas jets, the familiar aroma of cigarette smoke mixed with the heat of two hundred bodies and a dozen warring perfumes floating up to greet her.

As she took her position at center stage, she allowed her eyes to drift over the crowd, even though she could only make out the first few rows of red velvet chairs. Her gaze swept again across the audience and then, just as she was preparing to throw back her head to *allow* the spirit of Joan of Arc to take over her body, voice, and mind, she caught a movement in the front row of the crowd.

It was Laws Everett. Flipping over a page in his notebook.

He must have noticed Edie's eyes on him, because at that moment he raised his eyebrows with an amused, expectant look, almost as if he were saying *I'm here and ready to be impressed*.

It was a challenge she should definitely ignore. This wasn't a crowd eager for political discussion. This was an audience here to be entertained.

Edie tilted her head farther back and prepared again to take on the guise of Joan of Arc. And then Laura de Force's face flashed into her mind, just as it had appeared earlier that afternoon as her words rang over the gathering crowd. Words that didn't ask for change, but *demanded* it.

Someone cleared their throat in the crowd. Skirts rustled against cushioned seats. Edie had been on stage for almost a minute now. It was past time to begin her speech.

So why were her lips refusing to move?

She took another deep breath, and this time she closed her eyes. Then she opened them again.

She couldn't do it. It was as simple as that. She couldn't stand on this stage—today of all days—and preach to the crowd about the beauty of martyrdom. As if that was all a woman was good for.

Her eyes cut again to Laws in the audience. He was the only face in the front row who didn't appear to be bored. Instead, he looked positively riveted. His eyes fixed on her with an intensity that made her shiver.

Earlier, he'd tried to goad her into admitting that her lecture on farm wives was inspired by her own ideas. That was something she couldn't admit to without losing her spot on this tour. But there *was* something else she could do.

This time, when Edie threw her head back, she sucked in a great, noisy gasp of air. She jerked her body and straightened her spine. Then she lowered her head and looked out into the crowd. When she spoke, it was with the kind of calm, quiet authority she was only allowed to use when in the guise of a man.

"My name is Benjamin Franklin."

The rustling in the audience stopped, and Edie felt a jolt of energy as two hundred pairs of eyes focused their attention on her.

"I have been to the other side, and I return tonight to speak to you of a grave injustice in this land. I journey back from the land of spirits tonight with the sole purpose of opening your eyes to the inequality dealt to women in the marriage laws of this great country of ours."

A different kind of rustle rippled through the crowd: hundreds of patrons shifting uncomfortably in their seats.

But Edie stole a glance at only one of them. A curly-headed audience member seated in the front row. A young man who leaned forward in his seat, poised his pen over a piece of notebook paper, and kicked his lips into a smile.

"I will tell you," continued Edie with that same unfiltered confidence, "about the horrors faced by good, God-fearing women whose babes are unjustly ripped from their arms, whose hard-won earnings are taken by their husbands only to be lost in gambling dens. I will tell you how, across this country, the common law not only allows this, but *enables* it.

"Tonight, I will tell you the truth. As only a spirit can."

8

Violet was a vision on stage.

Edie, who had spent the remainder of the show hiding from Mr. Huddle in Lillian's dressing room, watched from the wings, one eye on her twin and the other looking out for the grey-haired tour manager who would certainly have some choice words about her lecture topic when they finally came face to face.

She still wasn't exactly sure what had come over her during her act. Letting Laws Everett provoke her with nothing more than a look? Directly defying Mr. Huddle? Putting everything the twins had worked for at risk because of some self-righteous whim? That was Violet's sort of move, not hers. And even though Edie didn't *think* Mr. Huddle would kick them off the tour for this, she'd have to do some world-class groveling to make it right. With him as their conduit to Mary Sutton—or, more accurately, to Mary Sutton's reward money should they secure a private séance after tonight— inviting his displeasure couldn't have come at a worse time.

Violet was never going to let her live this down.

At least her twin was doing well tonight. *Better* than well. Violet was on her second faked séance of the evening and the audience was already eating out of her hand. By the time she got to the third séance—in which she would actually open the Veil of death—there wouldn't be a skeptic left in the house, rich Mary Sutton (hopefully) included.

At the moment, Violet was playing her favorite role of all, that of a long-lost lover. In this particular case, the lover in question had died young, before she and the elderly gentleman on stage could be married. He had been heartbroken and remained a bachelor his entire life. But now, in his twilight years, he wished finally to marry.

This information, Edie knew from the backstage gossip, had been relatively easy for Mr. Huddle's audience plants to discern because the gentleman on stage had brought his intended bride with him to the theater tonight. The town gossips in the crowd had spoken of little else.

"*My dear*," said Violet, her voice quivering and soft. Her eyes closed, chin tilted up. "*Do you imagine I have not longed for this? That I have not watched you from beyond, hoping you might finally find love on the earthly plane?*"

The old gentleman shook his head and brought a handkerchief to his eyes. His shoulders shook as silent sobs overtook his frail form.

"*Go*," said Violet with so much force that the spiral of white lavender smoke swirled at her release of breath. "*Find what love you can in this life.*"

The old man on the stage was weeping openly now, all care of decorum evaporating along with the wisps of smoke.

"Know there is room in my heart for you both."

Violet let her last words linger in the air for the length of a heartbeat. Then she sucked in a great, gasping breath, snapped open her eyes, and said, in her normal musical voice, "The spirit is gone!"

The audience let out a collective satisfied sigh, and the old man reached across the round table, took both of Violet's hands in his own, and shook them heartily, his gratitude evident in his teary eyes and glowing face.

After that, there was the usual hubbub and bustling about as a red-coated usher escorted the man back to his seat. Excitement bubbled in the crowd as they whispered amongst themselves, wondering who would be called to the stage next. Edie took advantage of this transition moment to peer farther out behind the curtain, hoping to catch a glimpse of Mary Sutton in the crowd.

The gas jets focused on the stage made it hard to see most of the audience, but there, in the center of the third row, Edie caught the distinct figure of little old Miss Crocker. Arranging a séance for the sweet lady's cat may have been a bit ridiculous, but when Edie saw whose ear Miss Crocker was excitedly whispering into, she decided it had most definitely been worth the fuss.

Seated next to Miss Crocker was Mary Sutton herself. Edie recognized her instantly from Mr. Huddle's description. She was in her mid-forties. Her clothing was rich and of the latest style.

Her pale skin was lightly powdered, and her light brown hair was arranged in fashionable curls gathered atop her head.

She looked every inch the typical society lady, and yet Edie knew there was nothing typical about Mary Sutton. Or rather, *Doctor* Mary Sutton. The first female doctor ever to be appointed as staff at the Sacramento County Hospital, an appointment that had resulted in a quarter of the male doctors quitting on her first day, if Mr. Huddle's detailed client-research was to be trusted. And it usually could be.

Not for the first time, Edie wondered *who* a woman like that would be so desperate to contact. Because while Mr. Huddle's scouts had provided a detailed report about the woman's impressive strides in the medical profession, they'd turned up nothing when it came to former husbands, lovers, or partners. Her aging parents were still alive and well. And she had no siblings, deceased or otherwise.

Edie glanced back at Violet on stage, who was busy preparing a new dish of lavender to light, and then looked back at the woman in the crowd. Unlike little old Miss Crocker next to her, Mary Sutton's eyes were not shining with anticipation and wonder. In fact, she seemed rather . . . unimpressed.

But Edie wasn't worried. They may not have hooked the doctor yet, but this next bit was sure to do the trick.

On stage, Violet lit the herbs and closed her eyes. The crowd fell silent.

From the outside, there was nothing about Violet's spirit calling now that looked any different from her earlier, pretend attempts. Only Edie could know that, this time, Violet was scanning through the nearby spirits lingering in the Veil, choosing the one she would invite to cross.

After a few silent moments, Violet opened her eyes and spoke. "Margaret? Is there a Margaret Brown here tonight?"

The crowd rustled as members of the audience craned their necks, trying to spot the lucky woman before the surprise left her face. And since it was the last visitation of the evening, more than a few patrons—those not blessed with the name Margaret Brown—allowed their disappointment to show.

Mere seconds later, a figure rose in the middle of the audience and quickly made her way down the aisle. A red-coated usher waited at the foot of the steps and assisted her onto the raised stage.

The woman was dressed all in black. An inky lace veil fell over her eyes, affixed to a hat that was several seasons out of date. Even from where she stood in the wings, Edie could see the sallow skin not covered by the veil. Pale and sickly, as if it had been some time since she'd seen the sun.

The usher deposited her safely into the chair across the table from Violet and then melted back into the wings.

Violet spoke again. "Margaret Brown. There is someone here tonight who would speak with you."

The woman made no reply to this. She merely pushed her black veil out of her face and stared at Violet with a fragile, desperate hope. It was an expression the twins had seen many times before.

Violet nodded, acknowledging the woman's silent plea. Then she closed her eyes once again and tilted back her head.

Edie felt the moment the Veil opened. A small, delicate tear just wide enough for a single spirit to slip through.

"*Mama.*"

It was Violet's mouth moving, but the words were not her own.

A particular kind of hush fell over the crowd. The kind of hush that explained why Violet saved the real spirit visitation for last. Because there was something different about the way she spoke now. Something otherworldly and strange shimmering around her edges, a tingling in the air impossible to fake.

As in her previous two séances, Violet kept her eyes firmly shut. The difference was that while, earlier in the evening, that bit had been for show, this time Violet's normally piercing green eyes were replaced by those of the spirit. If she opened them now, Margaret Brown would see her own child staring back.

The silence in the theater deepened. Anyone with even the slightest sensitivity to death would be feeling it now. The dark tug at the back of their mind. A long-suppressed animal instinct recognizing what the conscious mind refused to see. It was a dangerous thing to do in front of a crowd, to reveal so clearly one of life's great mysteries. People claimed to desire answers, but deep down they didn't really want to know. Deep down they preferred the fairy tale of a God in heaven and an everlasting life.

Edie herself had preferred it once, as a child. She'd loved nothing more than sitting at her father's knee, listening with rapt attention to the stories he told her about a God who loved them all. About the place in heaven he held for her.

"My Edith," he would say when it was just the two of them, as it often was in those early days. Before everything had changed. "God loves you and will always keep you safe."

Edie used to repeat those words to herself at night before she went to sleep. That is, until the night of her and Violet's thirteenth birthday. Until their mother had shown them the truth about death. Later, she'd be angry she had ever believed her father in the first place. Furious that she'd been naive enough to listen to a man who chose an outdated book over his own daughters. But that night four years ago, she'd felt only loss.

That was why the twins always made sure to leave a trail of crumbs behind. A trail that could lead a person back to the safety of that story, if that's what they preferred. *This* moment may feel real to them, but later on they might say *I heard that Mr. R spilled all the details of his engagement to a chatterbox probing the crowd. Surely that girl is a fake, and it's all a scam.*

The key was to leave enough doubt in their minds to wonder later if any of it was real, while also allowing them to glimpse— even if only for a moment—a piece of the truth.

"*Mama, it's William. Are you there?*"

"Yes," gasped Margaret Brown, her body lurching toward Violet as if she wanted to grab the young woman in her arms and clasp her to her breast. "I'm here, my sweet boy." A sob escaped the woman's throat. "I'm here, my darling."

More tears emerged as the conversation continued. Personal details were conveyed to convince Margaret Brown—who didn't need much convincing at all—that her son was here with her tonight. She even nodded in appreciation at Violet's suggestion, still in the spirit's voice, but quite clearly (to Edie, at least) from Violet's mind, that Margaret Brown put off her mourning clothes, insisting that a year was long enough to grieve.

Edie managed a quick glance at Mary Sutton in the crowd—just long enough to note that the woman no longer seemed *un*impressed—when a strangled cry drew her attention back to the stage.

It had come from Violet, who was now doubled over in her chair, her body shaking in a series of spasms. From across the table, Margaret Brown stared at her in silent horror, and every single member of the audience went eerily still.

Edie took a step toward the stage—audience be damned—but stopped when Violet raised her arm high above her head.

"The spirit," she said, her voice strained and hoarse, "is restless."

Silence was replaced by anticipation as an excited murmur rippled through the crowd. Edie watched as Violet slowly straightened up in her chair, the muscles in her neck straining with the effort to keep the spasms under control.

Edie immediately blinked her own eyes shut and reached out to feel for the spirit of the young boy currently housed within her twin's mind.

But he wasn't there.

A different spirit had taken his place.

Her eyes flew open. At that exact same moment, Violet turned around in her chair. She pointed her face directly at Edie and opened her eyes. Only for a second. Just long enough for Edie to see that their edges were pooling with black.

Before she could react, Violet had closed her eyes again and turned back to Margaret Brown. "He wants to hear the lullaby," she croaked. "The one you used to sing."

It took less than a second for Edie to understand the message her twin had wanted to impart. Violet was buying her time. Time to go into the Veil, find out what was going on, and salvage this before the crowd caught on.

Edie didn't allow herself to stop and think about what she was doing. Didn't stop to remember the last time she'd gone into death. Instead, she whirled around and threw herself into a deserted corner backstage where the glow from the gas lights didn't reach.

On the stage, Margaret Brown was murmuring a sweet, singsongy lullaby, tears edging her tremulous voice.

Edie fell into a cross-legged seat on the dusty backstage floor and pulled her silk herb pouch out of the pocket in her skirt. She extracted one of the bundles of lavender she'd made that morning and took out a match, preparing to light it. As soon as she did, the smoke from the lavender would assist her in opening the Veil just enough to allow her spirit to cross from life into death.

Her heart thudded in her chest. Sweat trickled down the back of her neck. She did one final check of her surroundings, ensuring that her body would be as hidden as possible while her spirit walked the Veil. To any passerby, it would appear as if Edie had merely closed her eyes while sitting upright and still. But if they came too close, they'd find her body cold and seemingly without breath. *That* would be harder to explain.

A hacking cough from the stage. Violet breaking into Margaret Brown's song.

There wasn't any time to waste. Edie lit the match and set the tip of the lavender alight. The sulfuric tang of fire filled her nose, and an opaque puff of smoke rose into the air. Then she took a deep breath, closed her eyes, and crossed into death.

9

The first thing Edie saw when she opened her eyes in death was a thin wall of mist. Delicate white wisps that danced and shimmered in the air before her.

Two blinks later, and she was also taking in the sight of a beautiful sunrise. Streaks of pink and orange and yellow filling the sky, casting a soft hazy glow over a long stretch of sand that sloped into a brilliant blue sea.

Edie had been surprised, the first time she crossed into the Veil at the age of thirteen—her mother's hand held firmly in hers—at how lifelike death appeared. But her mother had squeezed her small hand and said, "Oh, darling. Death *is* life."

Tonight the Veil appeared as a picturesque oceanfront. Sand at her feet. The steady whoosh of a tide. But that first time with her mother, death had taken the form of a meadow with rolling hills. Edie had been delighted by the soft grass under her feet. The slope of hills against a cloudless sky. Even the cold fingers of mist licking at her spirit had not dampened her awe.

She felt no such awe today.

Whatever comfort this place had once been for her—whatever bond it had forged between her and her mother—was gone.

After closing the Veil, Edie pushed herself up from her seated position in the sand, slipped the lavender bundle back into her pouch, and sniffed the misty air.

She caught the scent at once. The lingering aroma of lavender that Violet had lit on stage; stronger in death than it had been in life. She followed the scent at a run, and it was only moments later that she came face to face with the spirit of a young boy. Edie recognized the feel of him at once. This was the boy Violet had called into life to speak to Margaret Brown.

A quick assessment told her his spirit was bright with a clear, steady light. Not as bright as it would be if he'd died very recently, but bright enough to indicate that he had plenty of time left before he would feel the pull of a final death.

Like Edie, he wore the clothes he had last worn in life. In Edie's case, it was the blue plaid skirt and shirtwaist she'd changed into after her trance lecture on stage. In the young boy's case, it was a nightshirt that went just past his knees.

The boy looked up as Edie approached, his eyes wide with shock. No doubt he was confused as to why his time with his mother had been cut so abruptly short. Edie drew closer to the boy with the intention of saying something to calm him, but then he shifted to the right, revealing the opening Violet had made in the Veil.

Edie froze at the sight.

Her sister knew how to pierce the Veil. How to make the slightest nick of an opening, like the precise prick of a needle in cloth. But the tear before her now was the opposite of precise. It was ragged, uneven, and far too large, evidence that whatever spirit had forced its way into Violet's mind was strong.

Strong and reckless.

Her fingers flew to the silk herb pouch in the pocket of her skirt. She needed to act fast. Pull this spirit out of life—and out of her sister's mind—before Violet lost the strength to resist. From her pouch she pulled out a dried bundle of wormwood and a small box of matches. Pausing just long enough to focus her mind, Edie struck a match and lit the herb on fire.

Unlike in life, the smoke of herbs had color in death. The color of wormwood was a delicate light green, its smoke curling up in spirals, cutting through the lingering mist. A thick, rich aroma accompanied the smoke, reminding Edie of roast turkey with a sprig of mint, although her mother had always claimed it made her think of stew. Whatever the particulars, it was a savory scent that smelled indescribably of home, too lifelike for spirits to resist.

Edie waited until enough smoke had risen from the herb bundle in her hand. Then she widened her stance, raised her arms, and directed the rising pillar of wormwood smoke toward the gaping tear in the Veil.

She felt a small tug of victory when the smoke followed her commands, pouring through the opening into life. She'd only practiced this particular maneuver a handful of times, and even then only with her mother by her side.

She felt the moment the spirit responded to the smoke. It was quick. Which meant Violet must be keeping up a decent fight for control of her own mind. Once she was sure the smoke had a solid hold, Edie raised her arms again and pulled both smoke and spirit back through the Veil.

Her eyes searched the swirling column of wormwood smoke as it poured back into death. She was looking for the spirit that should be trapped inside, but couldn't find even a hint of brightness. Not so much as a single speck of light.

Had the wormwood failed? Had *she* failed?

But no. There was *something* there. Something twisting within the smoke. Something dark, pulsing with an uneven rhythm that—

Edie stumbled back.

That wasn't a spirit.

She watched in terror as a pulsing black mass rose to its full height within the wormwood smoke.

Then she turned on her heel and ran.

It wasn't a spirit that had tried to force its way into Violet's mind.

It was a shadow.

A shadow left behind in death is a dangerous thing.

The words of a bedtime story their mother had told them as children. A tale meant to frighten and keep them alert. Nothing they were ever supposed to actually see with their own eyes.

The sand sank around her feet as she ran, slowing her down. Edie cursed aloud. She needed to cross back into life before the shadow reached her. But she had to put enough distance between them first. She couldn't risk it following her through.

Glancing back, she saw a blurred, humanlike shape break free of the wormwood's hold, the light-green herbsmoke fading harmlessly into the mist. It lurched toward her, a jerky movement without any grace but with plenty of speed.

Edie picked up her pace; but even as she did, she could feel the shadow gaining behind her.

Another glance over her shoulder revealed that a ropelike tendril had detached from the shadow's murky form. It slithered toward her with even greater speed.

A strangely calm part of her brain informed Edie that she was never going to get far enough away. That her only chance of ever again returning to life was to light the last of her lavender now, and cross.

But doing so brought with it a terrible risk. This shadow had gotten very close to possessing her sister's mind. Only the strength of Violet's resistance—born from years of their mother's training—and Edie's interference in death had prevented it. If she opened the Veil now, if the shadow followed her through to the packed Metropolitan Theater, it could have its choice of bodies to possess, bodies who would have no idea how to resist.

Her mother's face flashed in her mind. Exactly as she'd seen it that day in the Veil a year ago. Her usually soft dreamy eyes had been wide with fear, but her mouth had been set in a grim, determined line, a smoking belladonna root held high in her hand.

Edie stopped running and turned to face the shadow. She wasn't going to outrun it. But maybe there was another way.

And then—a flicker of light at the corner of her eye.

A second spirit had approached, this one full of light. A young boy in a nightshirt that fell just past his knees.

Edie blinked in shock. She had forgotten about the child.

But before she could call out a warning and tell him to run, the boy's spirit darted forward with surprising speed. He placed himself between Edie and the shadow's approaching form, a small speck of light facing off against a wall of night.

The scream that erupted from Edie's lips was somewhere between a warning and a sob. Because she knew—even as she formed the words—that it was already too late.

The shadow's tentacle-like strands wrapped around the boy's neck only a split second after he appeared. A gurgled scream burst out of his mouth as the shadow lifted him into the misty air. Edie had one last glimpse of his terrified face, eyes wide with surprise and fear, before the shadow broke the poor boy's spirit in two.

The rest happened fast, but the speed made it no less horrible to watch. Bending over the boy's broken spirit, the shadow lowered the blurred mass that served as its head and proceeded to drink in the light still shining off the boy.

In less than a second, he was drained completely. What little remained of his spirit fell apart like dust, floating away to join the Veil's ever-present mist.

Belatedly, Edie remembered his name. Remembered what his mother had called him from the stage.

William.

William Brown.

Soon, that name would be all his mother could recall of the beloved child she had lost. Even now, the light of his memory would be dimming in her mind. Memories of a boy who had died too young. Who had been brave even in death. Whose soul would now never find a final peace beyond.

Sorrow engulfed her even as the shadow, its feeding done, shifted and turned to face her.

The mist rippled in response to its movement, bringing with it a scent that tickled her nose. A sharp aroma, wafting off the shadow in pulsing waves.

Fresh and green. Like tomatoes on the vine.

The scent of belladonna.

Edie!

Her mother's voice. Frantic and worried. Just as it had been that day in the Veil.

Edie!

She had ordered Edie to stop. Stop and turn around. But Edie hadn't listened. She had wanted to help.

Edie!

Another scent filled the air around her. Mingling with the mist. Cutting through the bitter-green belladonna. Lavender . . . and something else. Something that reminded her of life.

Edie looked up as the shadow made its final lunge toward her. One of its ropelike tendrils inches from her face.

How long would Violet remember her? Would it be days, or only hours, until she became an unreachable ghost in her sister's mind?

Edie closed her eyes. Heard her mother's voice call her one last time.

Then she fell into black.

10

Violet's laughter tore through the air. As sharp and clear as a bell.

"A scary one. Tell a scary one, *please*!"

Edie sat up in bed to protest. Scary stories before bed gave her nightmares. But before she could speak, Violet shoved a pillow into her face and pushed her back against the sheets.

"Violet, please don't suffocate your sister."

Their mother was using her *stern* voice, but she couldn't quite hide her amusement.

Violet huffed, but lifted the pillow. Edie blinked up at her sister's flushed face and rosy cheeks, her green eyes wide and pleading as she leaned down and whispered, "Please Edie? The scary ones are so much more *fun*."

The other side of the bed dipped as their mother perched next to Edie. She was clad in her usual cream-colored dressing gown, her white-blonde hair hanging in a braid down one side of her neck.

"Edie, darling. It's perfectly all right if you'd rather—"

"No," said Edie, turning toward her mother with grim determination. "I want a scary one, too, please."

Behind her, Violet squealed in delight and wrapped her arms around Edie, giving her waist a grateful squeeze. Edie smiled and settled more deeply into her sister's arms. If bad dreams came, Violet would hold her through them.

Eyes crinkling, her mother reached out and tucked a lock of hair behind Edie's ear. Ever since Edie had started crossing into the Veil a year ago, her hair color had started to fade. And although she'd never said it aloud, Edie suspected her mother knew that a tiny part of her mourned the loss of her once–deep-auburn mane.

After getting up to turn off all the lamps but one, their mother returned to the bed, tucked them more securely under the covers, and began to speak in the soft, lilting voice of story.

"In life there are many things little girls would be wise to fear. But in death there is only one."

Edie shivered at the ominous turn in her mother's voice, and Violet wrapped her arms more tightly around her.

"A shadow," their mother crooned, "is the dark side of our soul. The scared, cruel, sometimes vicious part of us. When your shadow is contained within the whole of you, when it's tempered by your light, there is nothing to fear. But a shadow left behind in death is a dangerous thing."

Violet's breath hitched, and it was Edie's turn to give her a reassuring squeeze.

"No spirit," continued their mother, her usually green eyes dark in the low lamplight, "who has escaped into life can leave their shadow behind forever. They are tethered together, for now and always.

"But if a spirit resists the pull of its shadow, if it refuses to return to death, they condemn their shadow to an endless, mindless hunger. Desperate to reunite with the one who abandoned it, a shadow will consume any unfortunate spirit who crosses its path. It will drain whatever light that spirit still holds, taking even the memories that keep them alive in the minds of those they loved in life.

"So when you walk the mists of death, my dears, when you dare to open the Veil, be always wary of the shadows. And should you ever come across one, you must promise me. You must promise to—"

Edie stiffened as Violet's arms disappeared from around her waist. She jolted up in bed as cold mist filled the room, thick as sea fog. A thin spiral of black smoke curled into the air, cutting through the white mist. With it came a fresh green scent.

Like unripe tomatoes on a vine.

A scream lodged itself in Edie's throat. She was no longer cuddled between the sheets of her childhood bed, but standing in the Veil of death. And there, in the distance, a glowing hand shot through the air, a burning belladonna root gripped between forefinger and thumb.

"Run!"

Her mother's voice, tearing through the mists of the Veil.

And then both smoke and mist were gone. Only the belladonna root remained, but now it lay half-hidden in a silk herb pouch on the floor of her mother's sitting room, just as it had that fateful day a year ago. Flames from a fire in the grate danced across its twisted form, giving the shriveled herb an ominous glow.

And there was something else. There, by the fireplace. A white flash of parchment. The corner of a piece of paper her mother had put in the grate to burn.

Edie remembered her doing it. Remembered watching her feed a single sheet of paper to the flames. She'd been curious about it at the time. Tried to sneak a peek while her mother's back was turned. But it had burned before she could make out the words.

Or had it?

Suddenly, she was kneeling by the fire, the heat from the flames searing her face. Leaning forward, she could just make out what appeared to be the final lines of a letter, written in a delicate feminine hand.

grief seems genuine. And yet I find myself compelled to advise caution, my dear.

Ever yours,

N.D.

"N.D."

Those initials set bells of recognition ringing in her head.

Where had she seen them before?

Reaching out, she made to snatch up the slip of paper from the hearth; but before her fingers could reach it, the fire flared up, consuming the letter entirely.

And then it was Edie being devoured by the flames. Blistering heat crawling up her arms. Smoke choking her nose and mouth. A heavy weight pressing down on her chest.

She couldn't breathe.

She couldn't—

⸙

Edie woke with a gasp.

Air filled her lungs as she took in frantic, halting gulps. Her heart was thudding against her chest, and she was covered in sweat.

Someone had removed her clothes, except for her linen shift, which now clung to her cold, clammy skin. A white coverlet lay on top of her, along with a thick flannel blanket. She threw off the heavy weight, realizing as she did so that she was in a bed. And not the childhood bed of her dream, but her bed in the room she shared with Violet at the Union Hotel.

Before she could wonder how *that* had happened, a wave of nausea rose up. She barely managed to tip herself over the side of the bed and grab the white clay bowl placed there, before the contents of her stomach emptied themselves in a stream of bile.

She closed her eyes against the pain in her head; but as soon as she did, an image of the shadow rose in her mind. Little William Brown's terrified eyes. His mother's tearful, hopeful face as she gazed at Violet on the stage.

Her head spun, and she retched into the bowl again.

Finally, once she was sure there was nothing left in her stomach that could possibly come up, she carefully lowered the bowl to the floor and forced herself to sit up and take stock.

She was alone in the room. Violet's bed stood empty and unmade on her left. To her right, a faint grey light filtered in through the lace curtains of the room's west-facing window.

Faint, grey *morning* light.

Her heart skipped a beat. How long had she been asleep?

Nausea was a common side effect when interacting with the Veil, but passing out for hours on end most certainly was not. Then again, Edie had never encountered a shadow before. She'd also never been pulled back into life by someone else. Which she now realized is what must have happened. The voice calling her hadn't belonged to her mother after all, but to her twin.

Which meant Violet had opened the Veil.

But she hadn't known about the shadow.

Any sense of calm Edie had regained upon waking up in a safe bed vanished in a sudden, urgent haste to find her sister.

She needed to see Violet's eyes.

Ignoring the protesting aches of her body, Edie forced her legs to swing over the side of her bed, planted them on the scratchy wool rug, and stood up.

And then she sat back down again. Or, rather, she *fell* back down again because her legs were too wobbly to support her weight.

This was a problem.

At that moment, the door to their hotel room flew open and Violet waltzed into the room. She was wearing a thick, lacy dressing gown belted at the waist, and her auburn hair was piled on top of her head with a few loose strands curling around her face. Violet's flushed pink cheeks, coupled with the distinct scent of rose oil she added to her bathwater, told Edie her sister was returning from the bathing room at the end of the hall.

Edie redoubled her efforts to stand. This time she managed it.

"Edie! You're awake!"

She barely had time to brace herself before Violet's arms wrapped around her and she lost her balance again, falling onto the bed.

"What are you doing up?" cried Violet as she pushed Edie back toward the pillows. "Lillian said you're to rest all morning!"

But Edie was too busy reaching her hands up to either side of Violet's face to answer. Too busy holding her steady as she peered into her eyes.

Green eyes.

Clear, without a trace of black.

Relief filled Edie as she slumped against the pillows. Violet made a tutting sound in the back of her throat and picked up a small amber bottle from the nightstand. "Here," she said, holding it out to Edie. "You should take a little more of this."

Curious, Edie sniffed the bottle. "What is it?"

"Lillian left it for you. She tipped most of it down your throat last night and said it would help—but, oh, never mind that. Edie, I don't think you're all right. You're very pale."

Edie reached out to take the bottle and took another sniff of its contents. She detected distinct traces of licorice, fennel, and dandelion root. "Lillian left this?"

"Yes," said Violet. "And she'll be livid if I tell her you aren't staying in bed."

Edie ignored the edict and re-capped the bottle without taking a drink, her mind turning to her spiritual healer friend and to the way she'd approached the sisters backstage after their first show with the tour. A show in which Violet—eager to make a good impression—had opened the Veil not once, but twice during her act. There had been a . . . protective air about Lillian ever since then, when it came to Edie and Violet. Something she'd chalked up to Lillian's self-proclaimed role as tour mother, despite being only twenty.

But Edie couldn't help but wonder if there was perhaps another reason Lillian had taken a special interest in them. If she could possibly have sensed their abilities. If perhaps, like Edie's trance lectures, Lillian's spiritual healer persona was a cover-up act.

Edie had just encountered—for the first time in her life—a shadow in the Veil: the dark part of a spirit left behind when they crossed out of death and into life. A shadow in the Veil meant there was a spirit walking in life, housed in the body of someone who may or may not have known they were possessed.

Could Lillian be the person who'd opened the Veil? Had she let a spirit escape?

Edie needed to find out.

This time she had no trouble pushing herself off the bed, although Violet sighed pointedly when she teetered over to the vanity table and poured a pitcher of water into the basin that stood at the ready.

"What happened after I crossed?" Edie asked, dipping a washcloth into the bowl. "I remember being in the Veil and then—"

"*I* should be asking *you* that, E! I nearly fainted when I saw you backstage. I kept waiting for you to come back, and when you didn't, I . . ."

Violet trailed off, and Edie knew they were both remembering a different time, a year ago, when their mother had spent too long in death. Only *she* hadn't come back.

"To be entirely honest, I panicked. I lit lavender and rosemary—"

"Rosemary?" Edie paused in the middle of wringing out the cloth. So that was the second herb she'd detected. The one that made her think of life. Rosemary was a memory herb.

"It was an impulse. I'm not quite sure why I added it. I think I was afraid you'd gotten lost, and it just felt right in the—"

"That was smart, Vi. Really smart."

Violet shook her head. "I'm only glad it worked. You know I've never called someone living through before, and I wasn't even sure how big to make the tear. But I was still spooked by that spirit.

It had such a dark presence, Edie. And so I made an opening as small as I could, and I closed it the *second* I felt you come back. When you fluttered your eyes, I almost broke down and wept right there. But then that reporter found us—although *how*, I've no idea—and suddenly Mr. Huddle was there, muttering something about Joan of Arc, and—"

"The *who*?"

"Mr. Huddle and the reporter who—"

"Lawrence Everett? From the *Sacramento Sting*? He was backstage?"

Violet nodded. "He helped John—er, Mr. Billingsly, I mean—get you into the carriage and up to bed. But who *cares* about all that? Are you going to tell me what happened? Why in the world didn't you cross back on your own?"

Under the guise of washing her face, Edie wiped the wet cloth over her forehead and eyes, avoiding her sister's impatient gaze.

She should tell her about the shadow.

She should also tell her that in all likelihood someone nearby—someone in this city—had been possessed by an escaped spirit.

But then again . . .

Edie glanced at her sister. Coming to a split-second decision, she removed the wet cloth from her face and ran it down her neck, over her chest, and under her arms before dropping the cloth back into the basin. Her clammy skin screamed out for a proper bath, but she didn't have even a moment to waste.

"When I crossed," said Edie, removing her sweaty linen shift and pulling a new one out of the chest of drawers, "I found a spirit that was fading. It's feeling the pull but refusing to pass beyond until it's given a message to someone in life."

Pulling a petticoat out of the drawer, Edie shot a surreptitious glance in her sister's direction. Violet's brow was furrowed, and her teeth were digging into her bottom lip. Her thinking face.

Guilt welled in Edie's gut at the lie, but she forced it back down. It's not that she didn't trust her sister. She did, implicitly. It was only that Violet was the sort of person who never let fear stop her. If Edie told her about the shadow, Violet might open the Veil and try to confront it herself. Better to tell a small lie now, to protect her impulsive twin, than to tempt her with the truth. Once she'd gained a little more control over the situation, Edie would tell her everything.

"A spirit that was fading," said Violet thoughtfully. "Do you think that's what I felt then? Because I don't think I've ever . . ." Violet shuddered and trailed off.

Edie turned back to the dresser so Violet couldn't see her face. She'd chosen to say the spirit was fading and resisting its final death, as a way to explain the darkness Violet would have doubtless felt. Neither she nor her sister had ever encountered a shadow before, and she was hoping Violet would accept this explanation. Acting as a channel between the living and the dead was also exactly what their mother had taught them to do—albeit usually for a fee.

"I think that must be it," said Edie. "I felt it too. In the Veil."

There was a beat of silence as Edie selected a faded pinstriped blouse from the dresser. Her heart wanted to hammer against her chest, but she forced her breathing to remain steady and slow.

After another moment, Violet spoke.

"Did the spirit give you a name of the person in life?"

Edie hid the relief on her face by slipping her arms into the blouse and bowing her head to do up the buttons. "Only a first name. And the name of a church."

Spirits weren't known for the specificity of their conversations. Without significant help, they were more likely to recall images—the color of a loved one's eyes, for instance—than they were legal names or a current address.

"I was going to stop by and speak to the pastor this morning," Edie continued. "See if I can track down an address."

Violet nodded thoughtfully. This was the type of errand they'd both known their mother to undertake on occasion. Before her sister could question her further, Edie changed the subject. "I don't suppose Mr. Huddle happened to send word as to whether—"

"As to whether rich Mary Sutton and her nine-hundred-dollar reward have agreed to a private séance?"

Edie glanced sharply at her sister, who was now lounging against the pillows on Edie's bed with a cat-got-the-cream smile on her face.

"He did," said Violet with a teasing lift of her brows. "And don't think I've forgotten about all the hats that money is going to buy me."

A smile lit Edie's face, and then she was running to the bed, launching herself at Violet and pulling her into a hug. "Oh, you did it, Vi! You *hooked* her! I knew you would!"

Violet laughed and returned the hug. "She wants us at her house tomorrow night. The details are in Mr. Huddle's note over there."

"Oh, Vi." Edie squeezed her sister one more time and then straightened up. Her cheeks were damp with tears, but she didn't care. "This is going to make everything all right again. You'll see. No more bowing and scraping to Mr. Huddle's every whim. We'll be *independent*. We could run an inn like those sisters we met in Pittsburgh. Do you remember them? And I know you said farms are dirty, but there's something to consider there. We could hire people to help with the—"

"Edie." Violet's lips pursed, and there was a frown between her brows. "I'm not sure if we should—"

"Oh, I know, I know." Edie pushed herself off the bed and returned to the wash basin so she could wipe the happy tears from her eyes. "You're right, of course. It's too early to celebrate."

And it *was* too early. Mary Sutton wanted to do a séance tomorrow night, which only gave Edie today and tomorrow to find the escaped spirit and reunite it with its shadow. Otherwise they risked having to cut the séance short if the shadow appeared again, forfeiting the reward money.

"Edie, that's not . . ."

But instead of finishing her thought, Violet trailed off and chewed her lip, watching silently as Edie finished getting dressed. It wasn't until Edie was bending over to tie up her boots that she spoke again. "I'd offer to go with you to the church, but I've promised to meet Mr. Billingsly this morning. There's an important theater director he wants me to meet about an audition."

"That's all right," said Edie, grateful to the walrus man for once. "I'll be fine on my own."

"I was also supposed to tell you that Mr. Huddle wants everyone at the theater at three o'clock today. I've no idea why, but Lillian suspects it's one of his new schemes."

Edie groaned as she finished lacing up her boots. "I'd better really hurry then." Straightening up, she grabbed a few hairpins from the top of the dresser and hastily gathered her hair into a bun at the top of her head. "If I'm late, could you tell Mr. Huddle that I had an appointment and I—"

"Yes, of course I will. Only before you leave, Edie, I have to tell you that I'm worried about Ruby."

This brought Edie up short. "Ruby? Why?"

"I don't think she came back this morning. I knocked on her door on my way to the bath, but there was no answer."

Edie raised her eyebrows. "Couldn't she still be asleep? Or maybe she's gone out again?"

"Maybe, but I find it odd that she would—"

"Vi, is it possible this could wait? Ruby's always running off somewhere or other, and I really don't have much time if I'm to be at the theater at three."

Violet's frown deepened, but then she shook her head and stood up from the bed. "Of course. And Edie, you'll tell me if you need help with that spirit, won't you?"

Nodding, Edie turned toward the door and tried to ignore the fresh guilt that tugged at her. She'd already kept the truth about their mother's death from her sister, and now she was adding another lie on top of the first.

But it was only for a little while. Just until she knew a bit more.

Before she could change her mind, Edie called out a final good-bye to Violet, threw open the door, and tore off down the hall.

11

Edie rang the bell of a pale blue house on the corner of a mixed residential and business area off J Street. Then she stood back on the porch to wait for Lillian Fiore to answer.

As a spiritual healer, Lillian needed somewhere more discreet than a hotel to see her private clients, and so Mr. Huddle arranged for the renting of small homes or private offices. She was likely with one of her private patients now and would be irritated at the interruption, but Edie couldn't afford to wait.

When there had been no answer after another minute, she rang the bell again.

And then she rang it for a third time.

Finally she heard the sound of quick footsteps inside the house. The front door swung open, revealing Lillian's very annoyed face.

"Edie?" The annoyance quickly transformed to concern. "What are you doing here? You're supposed to be in bed!"

"I'm feeling much better," said Edie, hoping that the walk from the hotel had returned some color to her cheeks. "And I'm here because I need your help."

Lillian glanced over her shoulder into the little house. "All right. You'd better come in. I'm with a patient, but you can wait in the—"

"No need." Edie took a deep breath. There was no use stalling, and she didn't want Lillian's patient accidentally overhearing what she'd come to say. Reaching into the pocket of her skirt, she pulled out the little glass bottle Lillian had left with Violet. "Violet said you gave this to me last night."

Lillian shot the bottle a perfunctory glance. "That's right. You were faint, and I—"

"Licorice, fennel, and dandelion. Those herbs combine to protect the mind against psychic interference."

Lillian's gaze sharpened, her expression turning instantly wary.

Heart pounding, Edie took a step closer to where her friend stood on the porch.

"You know about us, don't you?" She kept her voice quiet. Barely above a whisper. And yet it still felt too loud. "You know what Violet and I can do."

Lillian's eyes went wide, and her face drained of color. For several long seconds, she did nothing but stare at Edie, as if she'd suddenly sprouted several additional heads. Then she gave herself a little shake and crossed her arms over her chest.

"Yes," she said. "I know."

"For how long?"

Lillian shifted on her feet. "Since that first show in Chicago. When Violet opened the Veil."

"So you're also able to—"

"No." Lillian shook her head. "My mother . . . she was like your sister. I'm only able to sense it. Feel when it's open. Impressions, sometimes, of what's happening in death." Eyeing Edie thoughtfully, she continued. "I've never met anyone who can cross before."

That wasn't surprising. Edie's mother had told the twins that while the ability to open the Veil was rare, the ability to cross was rarer still.

"How do you know I can?"

"I didn't. Not for sure, anyway. Until last night."

Edie nodded. If Lillian had felt her crossing, she was very sensitive to the Veil indeed. Distantly she wondered if that same sensitivity was what made her friend such a naturally gifted healer.

But sensitivity to the Veil wasn't enough to bring a spirit through into life. She had hoped Lillian was the medium responsible for the escaped spirit and its shadow. Evidently she was not.

But that didn't mean she couldn't help Edie find out who was. Lillian had been traveling the Spiritualist circuit for a lot longer than the twins. And unless Edie's instincts were much mistaken, her friend was part of the same whisper web of women her mother had belonged to.

"I'm sorry to come here like this, Lillian. To bring all this up now. But . . . something's happened, and I—"

"Something? What kind of—"

"I don't have time to explain it all now. But it's absolutely vital that I find and speak to anyone you know of—anyone on the tour or anyone here in town—who's capable of opening the Veil. I need names, Lillian."

Lillian was silent for a long moment. Then, regret in her eyes, she shook her head. "I'm sorry, Edie. But I can't help you."

"You *can't?* Or you won't?"

"It's . . . that's not the way it works."

"Lillian, I wouldn't ask if it weren't important."

"I know, Edie. But . . . you have to understand, these are women who are only trying to make a living. Women who live in fear of being found out by the wrong people. Women whose ancestors were *burned at the stake.*"

Lillian swept her gaze up and down the street. Then she stepped closer to Edie and lowered her voice even further still. "Those mediums who have been disappearing? Some of those women have *real* ability, Edie. I'm not saying it has anything to do with why they turned up missing. Lord knows there are enough perils in the world for women as it is. But I have a responsibility. Just like I would to you and Violet if anyone ever came asking—"

"If someone that you *knew* and *trusted* sought you out and told you Violet and I were in danger? That our lives were at stake? Well, in that case, Lillian, I hope you'd give our names at once."

Lillian's eyes narrowed. "What do you mean *in danger?* Edie, exactly what is it that's going on here?"

Edie ignored the question, reaching out and squeezing Lillian's hand instead. "Please, Lillian. You can trust me. I promise no one else will know."

Lillian looked like she was about to say something, but at that same moment a high-pitched nasally voice sounded from inside the house.

"Miss Fiore? Is everything quite all right?"

Lillian sighed. "That'll be Mrs. Wilson. I can't keep her waiting much longer." She hesitated for a moment, as if torn. Then she said, "Wait here a moment."

Lillian dashed into the house and emerged a few moments later holding a small white card with black lettering printed on the front. "I don't think anyone else on the tour can do . . . what you're asking. But, here."

She held the card out to Edie, who took it and read it at once.

MADAME PALMER
CLAIRVOYANT & FORTUNE TELLER BY CARDS AND PALMISTRY
LADIES 50¢, GENTS $1
625 F STREET, SUITE A. BETWEEN SEVENTH AND EIGHTH

Edie looked back up at Lillian. "Madame Palmer? Who is she?"

"A friend. I first met her in San Francisco, but she's recently set up shop here. She's . . . well, Nell is an extremely private person, but her ability is genuine. If you tell her I sent you—"

"What did you say her name was?"

Lillian started at the sharpness of Edie's tone. "Nell Doyle. I haven't had a chance to visit her yet, but I assume this new *Madame Palmer* moniker is meant to sound more mysterious. It can be difficult to attract clients in a new town."

Edie nodded along with Lillian's words, but she was only half-hearing them.

Nell Doyle was the last name on her mother's list. The medium who had skipped town without paying up her rent.

And there was something else. An image from the strange dream she'd had before bolting awake this morning. The last lines of a letter, flickering in firelight. A letter that contained a warning. Signed by someone with the initials *N.D.*

Hope flared to life inside Edie, and her fingers curled around the business card, crushing it to her palm.

"If you can wait until this evening," continued Lillian, "I'll be free to go with—"

Edie shook her head. Already she was turning to leave, her feet itching to be off. After a year of searching, after she'd all but given up on ever learning more about the identity of her mother's last client . . .

"That's all right, Lillian. It's better if I go alone."

Lillian looked like she wanted to object, but then Mrs. Wilson called her name again from inside the house. "I'd better go. Whatever this is, Edie, promise me you'll be careful."

❦

Edie held up the card in the bright afternoon light and checked the address again.

The broad red-brick building before her was just north of downtown, a half-dozen blocks from the river, and it featured several hand-painted signs hanging along the awnings advertising a variety of shops and offices housed within.

Yes, this was definitely the correct address.

Unfortunately, it was also the location of about half a dozen uniformed police officers who had set up a crude perimeter around the entrance to the building, holding back a crowd of curious pedestrians.

She closed her eyes and took a deep breath. This was the second time since arriving in this city that she'd been within a few feet of police officers—a habit she and Violet generally avoided, seeing as how they were underage runaways in the eyes of the law. At least at Laura de Force's speech she'd been able to walk *away* from the police when she'd spotted them.

This time, she needed to go toward them.

Opening her eyes, Edie set her jaw, picked up her skirt, and strode forward. A tall barrel-chested policeman stepped in front of her. "Sorry, miss. Can't let you by just now."

She offered him a tight smile. "It's all right, officer. I have an appointment."

He looked down his nose at her. "Not today, you don't."

"It will only take a minute."

She tried to breeze past him, but he blocked her path again, this time sliding one hand to rest on the pommel of his shiny black nightstick. "Now, miss. I'm asking you nicely to hold it right there."

"But, officer," said Edie in her weakest, most helpless voice, "it's really a matter of the utmost importance. Isn't there any way I could slip on by?"

The officer stared down at her, unmoved. Edie cursed inwardly. If Violet were here, they'd already be in the building by now. Still, she had to try.

Edie fluttered her eyelashes. Then she rolled her eyes upward, put a hand to the back of her forehead, and swayed. She was just preparing to swoon into the officer's arms when a familiar voice called out her name.

"Miss Bond?"

She whipped her head around. But, as her body was already listing to the side in preparation for her fake-faint, the sudden movement of her head had the effect of throwing her off balance. The sidewalk loomed before her. Her aim was off now. Instead of falling onto the officer as she'd planned, she was going to land awkwardly on the hard ground.

Edie closed her eyes, preparing for impact. But instead of dirt and gravel, she suddenly found herself leaning against something soft and warm.

She opened her eyes.

Laws Everett was staring down at her, a grin on his face.

"What," he asked, his voice low enough so only she could hear, "are you up to now?"

Edie closed her eyes again and groaned.

"Oy! Everett!" It was the officer's voice. "The girl all right?"

"I don't know," Laws called back. He lowered his voice again and spoke to Edie. "*Are* you all right?"

Edie blinked her eyes open. She was in it now. Might as well see the thing through. "I need to get inside that building," she said in a whisper. Then, although it killed her pride to do it, she added "please."

Laws stared down at her for a moment, his expression intensely curious. Then he lifted his head and called out to the officer: "She's just a little faint, sir. All right if I take her inside to sit down?"

The officer grunted. But then he sighed and said, "Fine. But make it quick. Detective Barney's arriving any minute, and you know how he is."

Laws nodded and tipped Edie back onto her feet. He kept one hand on the small of her back as he swept her past the circle of uniforms and into the red-brick building.

The interior of the building was a well-lit lobby. To the left of the entrance was a long corridor with several office doors spaced out along the hall. Light streamed in from two front-facing windows, and there were unlit gas sconces mounted along the walls.

As soon as the door closed behind them, Laws removed his hand from her back, crossed his arms across his chest, and raised an eyebrow. "It's nice to see you up on your feet again, Miss Bond."

Her cheeks flushed hot.

"Yes," she stammered, suddenly remembering that Violet had said *he* was the one who had gotten her into the carriage last night. "I suppose I should thank you. For last night, and . . . well . . ."

"Not at all. It was my pleasure to be of help."

Edie nodded. "Yes. All right. Well."

She stared at him for a long moment. Then she turned on her heel and set off down the hall.

Footsteps thudded behind her. "Now, wait a minute. Just where do you think you're going?"

Edie kept walking, checking the letters above the office doors. "I told you I needed to get inside this building. I meant it."

Laws grabbed her elbow, pulling her up short. "Officer McNally let you in here because you're with me. I can't very well have you poking around a crime scene."

Edie blinked. "Crime scene? What are you talking about?"

"Didn't you see the uniforms stationed outside this building? What did you think they were here for? The scenery?"

Edie shook her head. "I didn't . . . Look. I'm not here to *poke* around a crime scene, all right? There's someone I need to see. Once I've done that, I'll be on my way."

Laws tilted his head. "Who do you need to see?"

Edie avoided his eyes. The last thing she needed was a reporter for the *Sting* catching wind of this particular errand. He'd probably assume she was here to get dirt on the locals from a fellow medium. A practice that was actually quite common. "It's personal," said Edie. "A woman's affair." That should shut him up. "Now. If you could please release my arm."

Laws stared at her, his now-familiar brand of curiosity burning on his face. "All right," he said. But instead of releasing her arm, he tucked it into his own, as if they were lovers about to embark on an afternoon stroll. "Let's go."

"It really is a very personal matter," Edie began, but Laws shook his head, cutting her off.

"Sorry. But it took me months to get in good with those coppers outside. And a reporter can't risk losing that inside track. It's my reputation on the line, Miss Bond. You go with me, or you don't go at all."

Edie hesitated. She could wait. Come back tomorrow. But she had only a day and a half until the Mary Sutton séance. The shadow needed to be gone by then.

Her mother's handwritten list flashed into her mind.

"I have a condition."

Laws raised an eyebrow but said nothing. Waiting.

"Everything you see? None of it's going in your paper. I want your word on that."

Laws smiled. "Miss Bond. I wouldn't have it any other way."

Edie narrowed her eyes but quickly realized that was as much reassurance as she was going to get. She sighed and set off down the hall, trying to ignore the press of Laws's arm in hers.

Halfway down the hallway, she paused in front of a door marked SUITE A. Except the door wasn't shut. It was already standing open. Edie made a move to step inside, but Laws pulled her back.

"Wait," he said. "You can't go in there."

Edie pulled her arm away. "We already went over this. I simply need to—"

"No!" Laws grabbed her waist and pulled her back into the hall. "I mean, of all the rooms in this building, you can't go in *there*." All humor was gone from his eyes. "*That's* the scene of the crime."

12

Edie stared at Laws, unblinking.

Then she pulled out the business card and double-checked the suite number. Her eyes slid back to the open door. There, in hand-painted lettering, were the words: MADAME PALMER, CLAIRVOYANT AND SPIRIT MEDIUM.

Laws pulled her farther into the hall. "I can't say I'm surprised," he muttered darkly. "I'll bet Francie Palmer was the first stop of every traveling medium coming into this town. Or *used* to be, anyway."

Edie stopped walking, forcing Laws to pull up short. "What do you mean *used* to be?"

Laws met her gaze evenly. "I'm sorry. But Frances Palmer is dead."

Edie stared at Laws uncomprehendingly for several long moments.

Frances Palmer is dead.

But that wasn't possible. Because that would mean Nell Doyle was dead. And Edie had only just found her.

"Miss Bond, are you—"

"I need to see her."

"You . . . what now?"

"Ne—I mean, Frances Palmer. I need to see her body."

Edie made to push past Laws into the suite, but he quickly moved to block her. "She's not in there anymore, Miss Bond. The report came over the wire three hours ago. The coroner already took the body, declared the death an accidental overdose."

"An overdose? Of what?"

Laws shrugged. "Couldn't say. But it's been known to happen. These gals take some stuff to fake a trance—make it look authentic. Maybe give it to their clients as well. That's why the detective is on his way. The death seems pretty open-and-shut, but he wants to know if she's got more of that stuff stashed away."

Edie had heard of people experimenting with sedatives in order to access the *other side*, as it was often called. In a way, it wasn't that different from the herbs she and Violet used. But Lillian had said Nell Doyle's ability was genuine, and Edie believed her. She'd have no reason to experiment with dangerous drugs.

Closing her eyes, she forced her mind to quiet so she could reach out for the Veil. Normally, when a spirit crossed over into death, it left an imprint of sorts. Very faint. A slight thinning of the Veil that lasted for about a day. But Edie didn't feel anything here.

"The police think she died *here*? In this office?"

"They don't *think* it. The report we got said this is where they found the body. Or, rather, where her client found it. Apparently

146

the old biddy was quite put out because Frances Palmer hadn't shown up for their regular appointment yesterday evening. So the lady came around this morning to give old Francie a piece of her mind. Didn't exactly work out like she'd planned."

Edie dug her fingers into her palms. Nothing Laws was saying made any sense. This was *not* the place where Nell Doyle, or Frances Palmer, or whatever her name was, had died.

She was sure of it.

So why were the police saying it was? Had someone moved her?

A shiver went up the back of her neck. Something here was very, very wrong.

Peering past Laws, who was still hovering in the doorway to block her advance, Edie swept her eyes across the interior of the office, which had been set up to look like a cozy parlor. Two armchairs were facing each other, with a table in the middle set for tea. A rectangular velvet pouch that Edie was sure held a deck of tarot cards lay in the table's center.

And there, hanging on a rack of hooks just inside the doorway: a small metal key.

Edie glanced up at Laws. Two things had become quite clear to her in the last minute. The first was that she needed to find out more about this woman and about the manner of her death. The second was that she couldn't do it now. Not with Laws breathing down her neck and a pack of police officers outside.

It took tremendous effort, but somehow Edie managed to tamp down her fiercely beating heart so that she sounded almost nonchalant when she said, "I don't suppose I could just take a *quick* peek inside?"

And then, without waiting for his reply, Edie pushed past him and stepped into the office suite. Laws reacted quickly. He lunged forward and made to grab ahold of her elbow again. Edie faked a gasp as his hand neared her, only just managing to whirl out of his grasp. Her shoulder banged painfully against the inside wall of the office, her hand colliding with the wall rack just long enough to slip the little key off its hook.

"Honestly, Mr. Everett," said Edie, her hand balling into a fist around the key, "you needn't haul me out of here like a sack of grain. If my presence is not desired, I shall see myself out."

With that, she turned on her heel and set off down the hall.

She'd only just rounded the corner when the front door of the building creaked open and a deep voice boomed in the hall.

"It's just this way, Detective."

Edie's steps slowed and her heart gave an ominous thud. She could hear Laws behind her around the corner, muttering angrily as he set the office back to rights. She slipped the key into one of the pockets she'd sewn into her skirt and forced her face into a neutral mask of polite disinterest as the police officer Laws had spoken to outside made his way down the hall.

Next to him was a second man. The detective, she surmised. He was also wearing a police uniform with two silver bars stepped onto his sleeve. A pair of heavy iron handcuffs hung from his belt, clinking against each other as he walked. He was clean-shaven with thin lips and beetle-black eyes. Eyes that narrowed as he approached Edie.

The detective turned to the younger officer. "McNally. What is *she*—"

Edie cut him off. "Thank you again, Officer, for allowing me to sit down. It's all that fresh air, you know. It quite goes to a girl's head."

The detective's eyes snapped back toward her, narrowing further. The younger police officer—McNally—cast a nervous glance at the detective. Edie had the distinct feeling that if it came down to it, this young officer would deny having offered her entry rather than admit insubordination.

Her eyes darted to the handcuffs at the detective's waist. Only for a second. But when she looked back up the slight tightening of his mouth told her he'd noticed.

Edie forced a smile. "Good day, Officers."

She stepped to the left, meaning to pass them by; but at a look from the detective, the young Officer McNally moved into Edie's path, forcing her to halt her steps.

"Now, miss," began the young officer. "Why don't you—"

"Oh, there you are, darling." Edie jumped in surprise at the sound of Laws's voice behind her. *How had she not heard him coming?* "Are you quite recovered?"

"I, uh—"

Before Edie could utter any actual words, Laws reached out and tucked her arm in his, turning to the young officer who'd blocked her path. "Thanks again, McNally. My poor girl went quite faint back there. You're a good man."

"Oh," said McNally. "I, uh—"

"And if it isn't Detective Barney," said Laws, turning to the detective. "Any chance you'd like to give me a quote about this Bill Higgins business? Word is, he's not the only one of your officers on the take. Care to comment?"

Edie didn't think it was possible for Detective Barney's eyes to narrow further, but somehow he managed it.

"Everett," he said in a cool voice. "I don't believe the press are allowed back here. Were you perhaps hoping this stunt would provide you with an invitation to a cell at the station?"

Edie tensed, but Laws only laughed. "No need for that, Detective. We both know I wouldn't be there for long, even if such an invitation were issued. So how about I save us both the trouble and take my leave?"

With a tip of his hat, Laws gave Edie a less-than-gentle tug and set off down the hall, not pausing to wait for permission. Edie hurried along beside him, matching his stride with her own.

Two heartbeats later, they burst through the building's double doors and out into the bright California sun. They didn't slow their pace as they exited the building, and Edie kept hold of Laws's arm until they were well past the circle of uniformed police, her earlier bravery with the officers having all but disappeared.

"Miss Bond," said Laws, as he kept pace beside her. "Are you all right?"

Edie nodded and kept her gaze straight ahead. "Perfectly."

"Well, I'm glad to hear it. And if that is the case, might I ask that you, er—loosen your grip just a bit? It's only I do sometimes like to use this arm."

"Oh." Edie halted mid-step and released Laws's arm in the same movement. "I'm so sorry. I—uh. I didn't realize I was . . ."

"It's quite all right. You appear to have had a bit of a shock."

"Oh. Yes. I really wish you wouldn't do that."

"You wish I wouldn't what? Intercede when it comes to officers of the law?"

"No. I wish you wouldn't sneak up on me like that. You walk very quietly and it's . . . unsettling."

Laws barked out a surprised laugh. "Well, I do apologize." And then, after a thoughtful pause, he added, "Although you really ought to take up your complaint with the sheep."

It was such an odd thing to say that Edie's head snapped up of its own volition, all her awkwardness forgotten. "The *what*?"

"The sheep." A half-smile inched onto his face. "Not much fun to be had as an only child growing up on a farm. So I got pretty good at sneaking up on the sheep."

"But . . . why would you *want* to sneak up on sheep?"

"To scare them, of course." He tilted his head to the side, studying her. "Haven't you ever seen a sheep jump up when it's scared?"

"I can't say I've had the pleasure. Do they do something interesting?"

"Well, I'm not sure it's interesting as much as it's just plain funny. Their eyes get all big and they do this little wiggle—"

For a second, it seemed as if Laws was going to demonstrate what this sheep-wiggle looked like, and in that moment Edie could see exactly what he had been like as a little boy. Full of laughter and joy and curiosity. And something else, too. Something sad and lonely. A boy all alone on a farm, trying to make playmates out of sheep.

But he seemed to remember where he was before any wiggling could emerge. "Now that we've satisfied your curiosity about the sheep, Miss Bond, how about you return the favor and tell me why you were visiting old Francie Palmer?"

Instantly Edie's walls went back up. "Thank you for your assistance, Mr. Everett. It is much appreciated. However, I must now be on my way. I wish you a good day."

After taking a second to get her bearings, she turned south and began to walk at a brisk pace. With any luck, she'd make it to the Metropolitan Theater in time for Mr. Huddle's summons and then, by the time that was done, the police would have vacated the building.

A set of steps to her right made her pull up short. Laws was walking along beside her. "Mr. Everett, I believe I said I no longer required your escort."

Laws, who had stopped walking when she did, smiled back at her innocently. "I would never presume you did."

"Then why, may I ask, are you following me?"

"I'm not. Although it does appear we're going in the same direction. Would you prefer it if I walked a few steps behind you?"

"I—well. No, I suppose that would be rather strange."

Laws nodded in assent. "I agree."

"Well," said Edie, hesitating. "All right."

And then, because she couldn't think of anything else to do or say, she began walking again. Laws did, too. They continued that way for an entire block, without speaking, the sounds of rattling carts and carriages filling in the silence between them.

When they reached the end of one of the raised sidewalks, Laws offered his arm to Edie so he could assist her as she descended the ramp to street level. He kept her arm in his as they crossed the street and then ascended the next ramp onto the subsequent sidewalk block. Only once they were atop the wooden platform did he release her.

"So," said Laws conversationally, "were you and Francie old friends?"

Edie stiffened. She was about to offer a quelling reply when it occurred to her that while neither she nor Lillian knew much about Nell Doyle's life as Frances Palmer, Lawrence Everett might.

"Perhaps. Did *you* know the lady at all?"

Laws snorted. "I wouldn't go so far as to call her a lady. Although she was good at divesting people of their coin, I'll give her that."

So she'd been a popular medium. That explained how she'd been able to afford to rent her own place of business. Had she become popular by opening the Veil frequently? Is that how the spirit had escaped?

"Bit high-and-mighty to some people's minds, old Frances. Heard some of the coppers say that's why they might be adding mediomania to the cause of death."

"Adding *what*?"

"Mediomania. A misalignment of the . . . er, internal female organs that's said to cause mediumistic hysteria, delusions of grandeur, and—"

"I know what it *is*," cut in Edie, whirling to face him. "What I find appalling is that you would take such utter drivel as fact."

Laws stopped walking. "Who said I did?"

"You just—"

"What I *said* is that's what the police think. There's a local man, a Dr. Henry Lyon, who happens to be very outspoken on the matter of mediomania and the need for treatment."

Treatment.

A memory of her father's face flashed into her mind. A key turning in the bedroom lock.

You will be saved.

"He's got everyone in a lather about it," continued Laws. "I've been trying to secure an interview with him, as a matter of fact, but so far he's—"

"An interview? You're going to *print* what that vile man has to say?"

Laws's eyes flashed. "I'm a reporter, Miss Bond. Interviewing subjects and reporting on those facts is my job."

Edie's eyes narrowed, but her blistering retort died on her tongue, because at that same moment her eye caught on something just behind Laws that made the hair on the back of her neck stand up.

Something large, black, and looming.

She'd been so focused on their argument that she hadn't realized her feet were treading the same path as the day before when she'd gone to hear Laura de Force speak. In front of Sacramento's Asylum for the Insane.

And now, here it was again. The black iron gates rising high into the sky. Ominous, even on a sunny spring day.

"Miss Bond?"

It was only when Laws spoke that Edie realized she was staring, open-mouthed, at the building beyond the black gates. Even from her distant vantage point on the street, she could see the outlines of bars on the uppermost windows. Put there so that not even the most desperate of the patients would have the recourse to jump.

And there was something else, too, something she couldn't quite name. A pressure in the back of her head. A warning in her stomach. A wrongness. Not unlike what she'd felt in poor Madame Palmer's office.

She shook her head.

Nerves.

Fear.

She couldn't let them master her. Not here. Not in front of present company. Edie tore her eyes away from the building and began walking again, her pace somewhat quicker than before. She braced herself for a question from Laws about her sudden interest in a building meant for criminally insane people. Inwardly, she prepared an answer that had something to do with poor Dorothy Dryer, the woman who had been sent there for attempting to prevent a pregnancy that might have killed her. But when Laws did ask a question, it wasn't the one she'd expected.

"You and your sister," he said, "seem rather young to be traveling alone. Did one of your parents not want to accompany you?"

Edie looked at him in surprise. She was prepared for this question. She always was. But she thought it strange that he would ask it now. Still, she schooled her face into a neutral expression and said, "Our parents are deceased."

"I see. I'm sorry for your loss."

"Thank you."

"Another relative, then? An aunt? Or a cousin?"

Edie kept her eyes straight ahead. "Violet and I are alone in the world. And perfectly capable of taking care of ourselves."

"Of course. I didn't mean to imply otherwise."

"Is there a reason for this line of inquiry? It's not that I mind, of course. It's only that Mr. Huddle indicated the focus of your article would be on the tour itself."

"Oh yes," said Laws. "It is. I was only hoping for a little color, you know. To get a sense of the . . . whole person, as it were."

"Well, I'm afraid there's not much to tell when it comes to us. Violet and I lost our parents about a year ago. That's when we decided to put our skills to use. And it brings us great joy to do so."

"Does it?"

Edie looked at Laws sharply. "Of course it does."

"It's only"—Laws paused, as if not quite sure how to put his next words—"I couldn't help but overhear your conversation with Mr. Huddle in the lobby the other day. About the political nature of your speeches."

Edie's face burst into flames. He'd heard that?

"Eavesdropping is a terrible habit."

The side of his mouth quirked up. "Actually, I would say that eavesdropping, in my line of work, is rather a plus—"

"Well, you didn't understand what you heard. It might have seemed as if Mr. Huddle was suggesting that I . . . well, that I had some control over the contents of my trance lectures. But it's very well known that a medium has a choice as to what kind of spirit she summons. And he was merely asking me to—"

"To choose a spirit with less-radical political views. Yes. That's what I gathered."

Edie stared at him, confused. "I don't understand. If you aren't questioning the validity of my trances, then what are you—"

"Oh. I don't believe your trances are real for a second, Miss Bond. But you are correct that the little conversation I overheard gives me nothing I can use to discredit you. I bring up the subject merely because it seems that *someone* ought to tell you your skills are being wasted."

"My—my *what*?"

"Your skills at oratory. Your ability to make a cohesive and convincing argument. Your brain, Miss Bond. It is being wasted on a crowd of gormless sycophants who would rather believe a spirit is speaking through you than believe a young woman is capable of making a sound point."

Edie stopped walking and stared at him in disbelief. How many times had she had this exact same thought? How many times had she lamented this precise irony? So, why was she so angry all of a sudden? Why did she want to scream at this young man?

Laws took a step toward her. "You don't need to live a lie, Miss Bond. You're an intelligent young woman. You could do great, important things."

Right. That was why she was angry.

Edie started walking again. Laws hurried to catch up. "If I've offended you, I—"

"Offended me?" Edie whirled around to face him. "You haven't offended me, Mr. Everett. You have merely put your naiveté on display."

"My *naiveté*?"

"You're right," said Edie. "*Naiveté* is the wrong word. It is your ignorance that is showing."

"I beg your pardon—"

"You deign to inform me I am wasting my skills? You suggest I go out and do *great, important things*. Fine. Let us say I take that excellent advice. What exactly do you suggest I do? Shall I become a newspaper reporter, like you?"

"Well, there are worse—"

"Tell me, how many women work at your newspaper?"

Laws blinked and said nothing.

158

"You needn't name them all," said Edie. "Perhaps just one. One name."

Again, Laws said nothing.

"You can't name one. Because there aren't any."

Laws met her eyes. "There are women who work as typesetters—"

"As typesetters? So working as typesetter would serve as a better avenue for my *brain*, as you so bluntly put it?"

"Well, no—"

"I thought not. Perhaps instead you might suggest I run for some kind of political office. Make use of my *oratorical skills*. After all, a handful of women have tried it. Remind me, Mr. Everett, did any of them *win* the office?"

"Well—"

"Of course they didn't. They didn't stand a chance. How could they, when women aren't even allowed the vote!" Edie took a step closer to Laws. "This is not a country built for women, Mr. Everett. But I don't expect you to understand that any more than I expect you to understand anything about me, my life, or the choices I've had to make in it."

"Edie, I—"

"Perhaps I can leave you with some unsolicited advice of my own, Mr. Everett. The next time you feel the desire to tell someone you've just met what to do with their life? *Resist it*."

With that, Edie turned on her heel and left. This time, Laws didn't follow.

13

Edie burst into the lobby of the Metropolitan Theater, her cheeks pink and her breath coming up short. She'd practically run the last five blocks, partly because she wanted to put as much space between herself and Lawrence Everett as possible, and partly because she honestly couldn't believe she'd purposefully antagonized a reporter.

What was *wrong* with her?

She pressed her back against the lobby wall—thankful the room was empty—and tried to catch her breath.

All was not lost.

She had set out to speak to Nell Doyle, and death would not stop her from completing that task. It only complicated things a bit.

Reaching into the pocket of her skirt, she fingered the key she'd swiped from right under Laws Everett's nose. She'd return to the office on F Street this evening, after the police were gone, and conduct a thorough search of the woman's office. She wasn't sure what, exactly, she hoped to find. But instinct told her there was more to this woman's death—and life—than met the eye.

One more deep, steadying breath and then Edie was pushing herself off the wall and making her way to the backstage hallway. She threw open the double doors and froze.

"*Violet?*"

Her sister skidded to a halt in the hallway, her shoeless, stocking-clad feet sliding on the polished wood floor. "Edie! You're here!"

"Where are your *clothes*?"

Violet, who was stripped down to her petticoat, corset, and chemise, laughed as she padded over and looped her arm through Edie's. "Oh, just wait until you see, Edie. I think he's truly lost his mind this time. But I won't deny it's a heap of fun!"

Before Edie could ask any more questions, Violet dragged her down the hallway, paused outside the Green Room, and opened the door with a flourish.

Edie blinked against the riot of color that assaulted her eyes. Every single surface of the usually quiet, peaceful room had been covered in swaths of bright fabrics, many of them stamped with loud, garish prints. Mediums from their tour, all in various stages of undress, filled the room. Some of them were chatting loudly as they lounged on the fabric-covered furniture; others were standing with their arms outstretched while a bustling team of seamstresses took their measurements or checked fabric samples against their skin.

"Apparently," said Violet from beside Edie, "white is out, and color is in."

Edie shook her head in amazement. "I thought we were all supposed to look like ethereal angels."

"It seems angels aren't selling enough tickets at the moment. Flora said Mr. H got the idea from a review of P.T. Barnum's newest tour. It's a hit, of course, and all the women wear bright colors and bold patterns. Hence our new costumes."

"But *we* aren't a circus!"

Violet raised an eyebrow. "Aren't we?"

Edie's sputtered reply was drowned out by a commotion in the center of the room where someone had dragged a mirror from one of the dressing rooms and placed a pedestal in front of it. Cora Bradley, who'd so successfully flummoxed Laws Everett last night with her claims to White House fame, had now turned her considerable talents upon the woman who appeared to be the head seamstress.

"I'm so sorry to make a scene, my dear," sang out Cora in a voice clearly meant to be heard by everyone present. "But I'm afraid this color simply won't do. The spirits do not prefer me in purple. They have made those feelings *quite* clear."

Violet's hand flew to her mouth to cover a snicker, and Edie turned her head to the side to hide a smile of her own. But when she caught sight of Lillian across the room, deep in conversation with their spiritual musician Emma, her smile faded. Telling Violet she'd return in a moment, she made a beeline for Lillian.

"I'm so sorry to interrupt," said Edie as she approached the two women. "But Lillian, I was wondering if I could steal you for a moment?"

Lillian's gaze shot to her, quietly assessing. "Of course." Turning to Emma, she said kindly, "And Emma dear, do hold that thought. I find your deconstruction of Schubert to be endlessly fascinating."

Blushing, Emma mumbled an affirmative under her breath, and then Lillian was following Edie out into the hall.

"Edie," she started as soon as they were alone. "What's happened? You look as if—"

"I need you to tell me everything you know about Nell Doyle."

Lillian's eyes widened. "But I've already—"

"She's dead, Lillian."

"*Dead?*"

"The police were there when I arrived this morning, investigating. They say she died in her office salon, but she didn't."

Lillian's face drained of color. She didn't ask how Edie knew the police were wrong about the location of Nell's death. She didn't need to.

"There's something wrong here, Lillian. I'm sure of it. And so I need you to tell me everything you know about her. Did she have any family? Close friends? Where did she live in town?"

Lillian's brow creased, and she shook her head. "Edie, I want to help, it's only . . . I don't think I knew her very well."

"You don't *think*?"

"I didn't," said Lillian, more forcefully. "I haven't thought of Nell Doyle in months, and that's only because I happened to have found her letter while I was sorting through—"

"Why did she leave San Francisco? There must have been a reason."

"All the letter said was that she'd had to leave rather suddenly. She gave me her new direction. Her new name. Told me to call if our tour came to town."

A need to leave town *suddenly*. The adoption of a new name.

Had Nell Doyle been running from someone? The same someone *N.D.* had warned her mother about in that letter?

And yet I find myself compelled to advise caution, my dear.

It wasn't enough information. She needed to know more.

"That *can't* be all you remember about her, Lillian. You must—"

A screech from inside the room cut off Edie's words.

"*He wouldn't dare!*"

Both Edie and Lillian whipped around at the sound of Violet's outraged voice. When they rushed back into the room, it was to find Cora, half-swathed in fabric of a particularly unflattering shade of canary yellow, facing off against Violet, whose hands were on her still only partially clothed hips, elbows stuck in the air, murder on every line of her face.

"Well, I don't see why not," simpered Cora. A quick dart of her eyes made it clear she was both aware of and excited by their audience. "She's crossed him one too many times, if you ask me. That's the problem with you young girls. No *respect* for the calling. Why, I remember when the spirits first—"

"Oh, shut it," cut in Flora, her orange hair clashing brilliantly with a bright pink gown that one of the seamstresses was in the process of pinning. "You're just jealous because, after Violet, Ruby beats you in applause half the time."

"Ruby?" asked Lillian as she and Edie joined the group. "Has she come back?"

"No," said Violet, shooting an accusatory look in Cora's direction. "But apparently Mr. Huddle has already declared her off the tour."

"I don't know why you're glaring daggers at *me*," said Cora. "*I'm* not the one who ran off with another—"

"We don't know that she ran off with anyone," bit back Violet. "For all we know, she's disappeared just like those girls at Belden Place. And here you are, *crowing* about it."

"Well," huffed Cora, her color rising, "Ruby certainly does fit the model, doesn't she? That girl will toss up her skirts for just about—"

Edie almost didn't catch Violet's arm in time. And it was only thanks to Lillian, who had quickly stepped between Violet and Cora, that Edie got a firm enough grasp on Violet's elbow to pull her away.

"Let go of me!" hissed Violet, struggling in Edie's grip. "I need both of my hands if I'm going to *wring* that hack's little—"

"Okay," cut in Edie, loudly. "That's enough. Excuse us, everyone. Please."

There was a general murmur of disappointment from the mediums and seamstresses who'd paused to watch the scene, but everyone dispersed quickly enough, allowing Edie to drag Violet over to the far side of the room. Out of the corner of her eye, she was grateful to see Lillian, assisted by the fortuitous arrival of Ada, guiding a still-spluttering Cora into the hallway.

Spinning her sister to face her, Edie put a hand on each of her shoulders. "What on earth were you thinking? If Mr. Huddle hears about this—"

"I know, Edie. I know." Sighing, Violet ran a hand over her face. "The truth is, I *wasn't* thinking. Cora just made me so mad, and I . . ."

She sighed again. Then she raised her eyes to Edie's. "I don't think she ran off. Ruby wouldn't do that. She wouldn't let me worry like this."

Edie pressed her lips together, afraid to say anything that might rekindle her sister's temper. But Violet wasn't having it.

"What is it? Why aren't you saying anything?"

Releasing Violet's shoulders, Edie took a step back. "I don't know what you want me to say."

Violet's eyes narrowed. "Well, it might not kill you to try the truth for once."

Edie started, her gaze cutting to Violet. Had she imagined the double meaning behind her sister's words? Were they still talking about Ruby?

"You could, for example, just come out and *admit* you and Cora are two peas in a pod. Both of you convinced Ruby would run off with some man without so much as leaving a note!"

Edie crossed her arms. "While I don't exactly care for the image of me and Cora as a pair of matching vegetables—"

"This isn't a *joke*, Edie!"

"I'm not saying it is! It's only that . . ."

166

Edie hesitated, unsure of how to say the next part.

"It's only that *what?*" prompted Violet.

Edie sighed. "It's only . . . did Ruby tell you last time? Before she ran off to Niagara Falls?"

"No," said Violet. "But we all knew where she was—"

"Only because Flora saw her and that man as they were leaving with their bags. She didn't actually *tell* anyone. But she *did* tell us only two days ago about her client. Her very *handsome* client."

"I don't see what that has to do with anything," mumbled Violet, but Edie saw the flash of uncertainty in her eyes, and she hastened to push her advantage.

"They had plans for a picnic yesterday morning. It hasn't even been two days. If they decided to go on a jaunt for the weekend, they couldn't be back by now even if they *wanted* to. And as for Mr. Huddle kicking her off the tour, you know half of what he says is bluster."

Violet opened her mouth to say something, but Edie spoke over her. "I'm not saying we shouldn't worry. I'm only saying . . . maybe we don't need to panic just yet."

Violet glanced up from under her lashes. "Do you really think so?"

Edie nodded. "I do. You know I love Ruby. But this is exactly the kind of thing—"

"Miss Bond?"

Both sisters turned toward the head seamstress who had called their name.

"Which one?" asked Violet.

"Together please," she replied, waving them over to where the mirror and pedestal were placed. "Your *ensembles* are to correspond."

Before following, Edie shot her sister a quick glance, her eyebrows raised. *Are you okay?*

After a short pause, Violet took in a breath and nodded. Together, the sisters made their way to the center of the room where the head seamstress, who distractedly introduced herself as Miss Laurent, was busy directing a harried-looking assistant who was balancing two bolts of fabric in her arms.

The first was an emerald green patterned with dark blue stripes. The second was an exact reverse of the first: deep cobalt shot through with green.

Taking the emerald first, Miss Laurent unfurled a long swath and held it up to Violet. The warm jewel tone brought out the richness in her auburn hair, the fabric such a perfect match for her coloring that Violet's skin seemed to glow.

Humming in satisfaction, Miss Laurent handed the green fabric back to her assistant and picked up the blue. But when she repeated the process with Edie—holding a sample of the cloth up against her pale, blonde hair—there was no satisfying hum. Instead, her elegant features creased into a frown.

Edie shifted uncomfortably. Although she and Violet were technically identical, their coloring—thanks to Edie's blonde, almost white, hair—did not match. The gorgeous rich colors that complemented Violet made Edie look sickly and pale. She didn't know why Mr. Huddle had gotten it into his head that their costumes should match in some way, but surely this woman should be warned that her task was impossible.

Edie opened her mouth to tell her as much but stopped when she felt Violet's hand slide into hers. Startled, she looked over at her sister. Violet gave her hand a light squeeze; then she tilted her head and pressed her cheek against Edie's.

At the touch of Violet's skin against hers, Edie's entire body relaxed. She pressed her cheek more firmly against her sister's and allowed her eyes to flutter shut as Miss Laurent withdrew the blue fabric and began rattling off instructions to a second, equally harried-looking assistant who'd rushed over to help.

As her eyes closed, a memory unlocked in Edie's mind. She and Violet at eight years old, engaging in one of their rare but beastly fights. Over an emerald ribbon.

It had started when their father, in a rare show of indulgence, had instructed each of his daughters to choose a ribbon from a shop downtown. The twins had been truly identical then, and Edie had selected a length of deep green satin that brought out the red in her auburn hair. Violet had chosen a light pink ribbon, but had quickly realized it didn't suit their coloring nearly as well as the green.

She'd asked to borrow Edie's ribbon; but for the first time in her life, Edie hadn't wanted to share with her twin. Holding the green ribbon against her hair—letting the smooth satin brush through her fingers—brought her a deep sense of satisfaction, and she'd wanted to keep that feeling all for herself.

But Violet—unused to this lack of sharing—had snatched the green ribbon out of Edie's hands and fled the house. Edie gave chase, screaming at her to give it back. Her fingers were inches away from grabbing the fluttering end of the fabric when Violet, clearly aware the game was up, tossed the green ribbon into the steadily flowing creek behind their house.

"If we can't both have it," her angry voice called out over the rush of water, "then neither of us will!"

The green satin bobbed on the surface of the cold, clear water for one long second, before the current carried it away.

Edie had refused to talk to Violet for the rest of the day. It was the longest fight they'd ever had, and it lasted until their mother climbed into the bed where Edie had been sulking and took her crying daughter into her arms.

"I'll never forgive her," Edie had sobbed into her mother's warm shoulder. "She did it on purpose. She's selfish and vain and I only wanted one thing and she couldn't even let me have it. I . . . I *hate* her."

"Oh, darling." Her mother's voice was soft and clear, her hands rubbing circles against Edie's back. "I know you feel that way now."

"I'll always feel that way," persisted Edie, determined to hold on to her anger. "And nothing you say will change my mind!"

Gently, her mother lifted Edie off her shoulder and held her at arm's length so she could look her in the eye. "Edie, darling. Do you know, there are so many things I want to give you. So many things in this world that sometimes I don't know if I'll ever manage them all."

Glumly, Edie nodded her head.

"But there is one gift, darling, that I did give to you. Something that makes up for all the rest. Do you know what it is?"

Edie pressed her lips together. She guessed her mother's line of thought but didn't want to answer.

A small smile tugged at her mother's lips, but she kept her voice serious as she said, "I gave you a sister who will always forgive you, Edie. Who will always understand. One day you'll come to realize just how precious that is. How much stronger it makes you."

At Edie's look of outraged disdain, her mother gave in to her smile and pulled her daughter back against her chest, holding her and rocking her until Edie's tears were spent and she drifted off into a fitful sleep.

It was sometime later that Edie heard the door to the bedroom open again, followed by the soft padding of stockinged feet. She knew it was Violet, but she didn't turn around as her sister climbed into bed next to her. Instead, she curled her body into an even tighter ball so that only the skin of her right cheek was showing.

It was this bit of cheek that Violet found, pressing her face against her sister's.

It was the first time they'd ever done that.

As soon as their cheeks touched, Edie felt a rush of emotions from Violet. Confusion that Edie had wanted to keep something from her. Guilt over stealing the ribbon. Remorse for having thrown it away. Fear that Edie would never forgive her. Terror that her sister was lost to her forever.

It was the terror that shook Edie out of her own wallowing self-pity. She'd pressed her cheek more firmly against her twin's; and when she felt Violet's sigh of relief, she'd known her sister understood.

All was forgiven. Always.

Edie's last thought before she and Violet drifted off to sleep—warm in each other's arms—was that their mother had been right.

A loud *clap* split the air, tearing Edie away from the memory and forcing her back into the present moment.

At least a dozen bolts of fabric now lay deposited at her and Violet's feet, but apparently the search had not been in vain. Miss Laurent, whose hands had been the source of the clap, was beaming at them from a foot away as one of her assistants held up a swatch of soft, sage-green fabric to the space where Edie and Violet's faces touched.

A sudden coldness on her right cheek made Edie flinch. Violet had straightened so they were no longer touching, the warmth from her skin quickly fading away. Looking over at her sister, Edie found Violet staring at her. There was a searching look on her face. Her head tilted to the side, almost as if she were waiting for something.

As if she expected Edie had something to say.

But then Miss Laurent moved toward them, her hands sweeping up the fabric from her assistant. "*Yours*," she said, directing her chin at Edie, "will be trimmed with pale pink. And *yours*," she said to Violet, "with emerald. Yes?"

Violet smiled her signature smile and stepped forward, reaching out to touch the sage-green cloth. She then proceeded to *ooh* and *ahh* as Miss Laurent detailed her plans for the design of their gowns.

Edie stayed where she was, silently submitting to an assistant who rushed up to take her measurements. She watched Miss Laurent and her sister chattering happily away with a strange emptiness in her belly. As if she'd missed a step when walking down a flight of stairs.

14

This time, when Edie walked up to the red-brick building at 625 F Street, there were no policemen to greet her. In fact, the entire building housing Nell Doyle's place of work was quiet and still, all the shops and offices closed for the evening.

She let herself into the building and paused in the small foyer, gripping the key she'd placed in her pocket earlier that afternoon. The sun was still hovering low in the sky, but very few of its rays penetrated the dim hallway, making it easy for her to stick to the shadows as she made her way down the corridor to Suite A. Earlier, when she'd come here with Laws, that door had been standing open. But now it was closed, the red cursive writing on the glass catching the fading light.

Madame Palmer, Clairvoyant and Spirit Medium.

She pulled the key out of her pocket and held her breath. She hadn't had time to test it when she'd swiped it this afternoon, and if this key was for a different lock . . .

But it fit perfectly in the keyhole. And when the lock turned over, Edie let out a sigh of relief. Maybe luck would be on her side after all. She slipped inside, relocked the door, and returned the stolen key to its place on the rack.

It was dark in the room, with only a single window high up on the wall. She spotted a kerosene lamp on a spindly-legged tea table, and, after removing the glass chimney, she picked up the box of matches sitting next to the lamp and lit the wick. Then she replaced the chimney and turned the lamp down low until it emitted a soft buttery light.

After offering up a silent apology, Edie then proceeded to do a thorough search of the woman's things, starting with the small writing desk in the corner. The room already had a ransacked feel, proving that while the police were most definitely incorrect about the manner of the medium's death, they were quite serious about finding out what they could about the woman herself.

She found a few calling cards, likely from potential clients, but no appointment book. No personal letters at all, and certainly nothing addressed *to* or signed *from* a Miss Nell Doyle. And nothing with Edie's mother's name either. Not that she'd dared to hope for that.

There was an innocuous-seeming list of items to buy at the grocer that the police had deigned to leave behind in a wastepaper bin. Edie held it up to the kerosene lamp, mentally comparing it to the writing she'd seen on the letter in her dream. Her memory of it was hazy, but Edie thought the handwriting *might* be similar.

But that didn't tell her anything she hadn't already suspected.

Frustrated, she returned the list to the wastebasket where she'd found it and swept her eyes across the room. And that's when she saw it, peeking out from between the cushions of an armchair.

A scrap of white.

She leapt across the room and pulled at the white fabric, her heart swelling when the full item came into view.

A pouch of herbs.

Dropping to her knees, Edie poured the contents onto the rug, sorting through neatly labeled packets of lavender, wormwood, hellebore, feverfew, bay leaves, and—

Edie snatched her hand back as if she'd been burned.

There. Sitting on the cozy woven rug was a twisted belladonna root, its tip black and burned.

I find myself compelled to advise caution, my dear.

Nell Doyle had warned her mother. And apparently she'd taken precautions of her own.

It couldn't be a coincidence that there was a shadow in the Veil that reeked of belladonna, as if someone had tried—and failed—to force it beyond.

Edie cast a glance at the locked office door.

She'd been planning to wait for this: cross into the Veil when she was safely back at the hotel and call the woman's spirit there. But the urgency heating her veins was at a boiling point now, and she couldn't wait another minute.

Gingerly, Edie returned the belladonna to the discarded pouch along with the rest of the herbs. Then she settled into a cross-legged position and pulled out her own bundle of lavender, trying to ignore the way her hands were shaking.

She would be prepared for the shadow this time. She would keep her lavender at the ready and cross back at the first sign of its approach.

And what if you don't? What if the shadow breaks you apart, and Violet never finds out why you didn't come back?

Edie shook the thought aside, took out her box of matches, and lit the tip of her dried lavender bundle. A steady spiral of white smoke rose into the air. Closing her eyes, she felt for the edge of the Veil, let out a deep breath, and slipped into death.

❧ ❧

This time, the Veil of death appeared as a forest with thick curtains of mist rising up off the ground and blanketing a grove of tall, twisted trees. It wasn't the same forest Edie had seen when she'd crossed into death after her mother a year ago, but it was similar enough for her to feel a sharp pain of longing at the center of her chest.

But this wasn't a time for mourning or grief or regret. She'd crossed into the Veil with a purpose. And time was short.

She closed the Veil behind her but kept the lavender bundle in her hand, ready for a quick escape into life should the shadow arrive. At the same time, she extracted a bundle of dried rosemary from her pouch. Nell Doyle had been dead for only a short time, so it was likely that her memories of life would still be fresh; but Edie had prepared the memory herb anyway, just in case.

Clutching the rosemary bundle in one hand and the lavender in the other, Edie opened her mouth and whispered a name.

"Nell Doyle."

The name echoed around her, both amplified and distorted by the ever-present mist. Every nearby spirit would have heard her call. Quite possibly the shadow as well. She could only hope Nell was the closer of the two.

A minute passed by.

And then another.

Edie was preparing to call the woman again when she caught sight of a soft light beyond a distant ring of trees.

A spirit was approaching.

She squinted her eyes, trying to discern what she could through the thick white fog.

It appeared to be a woman. Long, curly hair framing a round face. Edie had expected Nell Doyle to be fully dressed, since she'd supposedly died at her place of work. But the spirit approaching her now was wearing what seemed to be a thin nightdress or shift. Had the woman died in her sleep, after all? Had her body later been moved and dressed again?

Edie took a few steps toward the spirit, careful not to scare it away. As she did, the mist cleared before her, and the spirit's face was revealed.

Edie halted mid-step.

This wasn't Nell Doyle's spirit. This was—

"*Ruby?*"

The spirit paused a couple of feet away from Edie, looking up from the ground. And as she did, Edie's heart turned to stone. There was no mistaking the identity of the spirit before her. There were Ruby's bouncy blonde curls. There was her round curious face. There were her wide bright eyes.

But Ruby couldn't be *here*. Ruby had run off with her latest young man. She couldn't be . . .

Edie shook her head against the word, but her mind forced it through anyway.

Dead.

Ruby.

Dead.

Edie rushed toward the spirit of her friend, weaving through the trees. "Ruby! Ruby, what happened—"

But before Edie could reach her, the spirit held out her hands, shook her head, and . . . flickered. In and out. Like a sputtering candle flame.

Edie froze, her hand flying to her mouth. She'd seen a spirit flicker like that exactly one time before. Minutes before her mother had died.

Ruby opened her mouth and spoke.

"Beyond . . ."

Her voice was weak and soft. Almost too low to make out.

". . . the black . . ."

Her spirit flickered in and out again as she spoke. It seemed as if every word was costing her a tremendous effort.

". . . gates."

The flickering increased in intensity, like a flame caught in the wind. Ruby's face became a blur as she fell to her knees, the mist swallowing her up and surrounding her like a shroud. Edie rushed forward, and this time she didn't stop until she was kneeling in front of her friend's spirit. A spirit whose light was far too weak for one so recently dead.

"Ruby." Edie's voice broke on the word, but she forced herself to continue. "I don't understand. What gates? What's beyond them? What *happened* to you, and why are you—"

Ruby shook her head. Then she raised her chin and looked into Edie's eyes. This close, Edie could see that her normally happy, carefree face was twisted in pain. Pain and something else. Something urgent. Had Ruby died a violent death? She wouldn't be the first spirit to ask for vengeance.

"Edie." Ruby's voice was weak. Broken and rasping. As if she'd screamed for so long, her voice had given out. "The darkness . . . the eyes . . ."

For one long second, Ruby's trembling stopped. Her light held still and steady enough for Edie to make out the terror on her face.

And then she spoke again. A single word.

"Hurry."

Her spirit flickered again. Just once. And then . . . she was gone. Disappeared into the mist as if she'd never been there at all.

Edie stared at the place where Ruby's spirit had been. Icy-cold tendrils of mist licking her face, her arms, the back of her neck. She didn't understand what had just happened. Where had Ruby's spirit *gone*?

She hadn't been pulled beyond the Veil. Edie had seen spirits succumb to their final death. Witnessed their last halting walk past a thick wall of mist. None of those spirits had disappeared like Ruby had. Blinking out like a doused flame.

It couldn't be a coincidence. Ruby's light sputtering in and out, exactly like the spirit her mother had faced in the Veil a year ago.

Now, Edie! I don't have time to explain.

Frustration surged at the memory of her mother's words. Explain *what*? What had her mother known that Edie hadn't? Had something happened to the spirit of that man her mother had tried to bind? Had he been . . . damaged in some way? Had the same thing happened to Ruby? And what had Ruby been trying to tell her?

She might have stayed liked that all night—kneeling on the cold forest floor, turning Ruby's strange words over in her mind, careless of the toll it would take on her physical body to stay so long in death—had it not been for the scent that reached her.

Fresh and green. Like unripe tomatoes on a vine.

Her head snapped up. Eyes searching the Veil. It took her less than a second to see it. At the edge of the forest beyond a line of trees. A dark, nebulous form.

She scrambled to her feet, shoving the rosemary back into her pouch at the same time she extracted her box of matches.

The shadow lurched forward, moving toward her with unnatural speed. But it wasn't fast enough. Edie struck a match and set her lavender bundle aflame, using the light purple smoke to open the Veil. Closing her eyes, she hurled herself back to her body in life, closing the Veil behind her the instant after she crossed.

When she opened her eyes again, she was still sitting cross-legged on the floor of Nell Doyle's office-salon.

Only now she wasn't alone.

Laws Everett was kneeling before her.

15

Edie flew to her feet. Fast. Too fast, considering the dizzying aftereffects of the Veil. She swayed to the side. Laws reached out a hand to steady her, but Edie spun away before he could touch her.

Ruby.

Ruby was dead.

Violet had sensed something was wrong, but Edie had dismissed her concerns. They hadn't even *looked* for her. And now Ruby was—

"I must admit, Miss Bond, that I now understand why you keep *this* part of your act off the stage."

Edie blinked at the young man before her. It was dark in the room, with only the soft glow of the chimney lamp to stand against the shadows. But she could still make out the mocking challenge in his face. Could hear the lazy confidence behind his words.

Because he thought this was all a joke.

He thought *she* was a joke.

Ruby is dead.

"Why are you here?"

For a second, Laws seemed taken aback by her abrupt tone. But he quickly gathered himself again. "I could ask you the same—"

"No," snapped Edie.

Ruby was dead. But she'd asked something of Edie. She'd asked her to *hurry*.

"You followed me here for some reason," Edie continued, her tone icy and brisk. "You will tell me what it is, and then you will leave me be. I've done nothing wrong, and see no reason for you to *stalk* my every—"

"You broke into a crime scene, Miss Bond."

"I didn't break in."

"No," agreed Laws. "First you stole the key."

It took considerable effort to keep her face blank. So *that's* how he knew she'd return here. She'd been so sure he hadn't noticed her slipping the key into her pocket earlier this afternoon, but she really should have known better. His hawk eyes missed nothing.

But none of that mattered now. Ruby was dead, and she'd asked her to hurry.

Hurry to *where*, she had no idea. But she wasn't going to figure it out with Laws Everett's too-observant eyes fixed on her. She needed to get rid of him. She needed time alone to *think* while Ruby's plea was still fresh in her mind. Oh, how she wished she'd never met him. Wished she'd never sought out his help that day at the—

Edie gasped.

The black gates.

"Black gates," said Laws, his voice confused. "Black gates of what?"

Only then did Edie realize she'd voiced her thoughts aloud. Cursing her carelessness, she turned on her heel and yanked open the office door, pausing only for a moment when she belatedly remembered that she'd locked the door behind her.

"As a key was not readily available," Laws said from behind her, "I'm afraid I was forced to pick the lock."

But Edie was past caring about locks and keys. Without another word, she strode through the open doorway and barreled out into the hall, her mind whirring with the implications of her realization.

Could the black gates Ruby had spoken of be the heavy iron gates Laura de Force had spoken in front of? The asylum gates Edie had inadvertently returned to only this afternoon, that had sent a shiver up the back of her neck?

And there was something else Ruby had said.

The darkness. The eyes.

Edie had crossed into death hoping Nell Doyle's spirit would be able to tell her the identity of the person possessed by the escaped spirit. But Edie had found Ruby's flickering spirit instead. And she'd spoken about the darkness in someone's eyes.

The eyes were always the tell in a possession. It was the reason Violet closed hers when she channeled a spirit, so no one would notice the change. If Ruby had noticed something strange about a person's eyes, did that mean she'd come face to face with whoever the spirit had possessed? Was that who had killed her? Could the manner of her death be the cause of the strange flickering?

Hurry.

Footfalls sounded behind her, and Edie was annoyed—but not surprised—when Laws fell into step beside her.

"So, did you honestly expect that little trick to work?"

Edie's head snapped toward him. "Excuse me?"

"That business back there with you sitting on the floor and ignoring me when I called your name half a dozen times. Did you actually expect me to fall for that?"

They'd reached the lobby now; but before Edie could open the door, Laws stepped forward and held it open for her. She lowered her head, purposefully avoiding his eyes, and barged past him into the late afternoon light.

In her shock of grief over Ruby, Edie had barely considered the fact that Laws had just witnessed her crossing back from the Veil. It had been dark in the room. Had he noticed the lifeless state of her body? Had he seen the change when her spirit returned?

She shot a sideways glance at him. The low-hanging sun hit his face at a slant, casting his cheeks in sharp relief. Sensing her gaze, he looked down at her, his eyes bright with curiosity.

But those eyes were always curious. Always bright. How could she tell if this was curiosity of a different kind?

Maybe the best course of action was to change the subject and pretend nothing out of the ordinary had happened at all.

"I'd appreciate it," said Edie, "if you could keep tonight's incident between the two of us."

Laws's mouth quirked. "Do you mean the part where you stole a dead woman's key under the nose of the police, when you illegally entered her place of work, or when you proceeded to fake a séance for an audience of none?"

She turned her head away and set her eyes straight ahead. So much for changing the subject.

"How about this," said Laws, his voice amused but pointed. "You admit what you were *really* doing in Frances Palmer's salon tonight, *and* why you came to see her earlier today. Then I just might be persuaded to keep this breaking-and-entering business under my hat."

When Edie said nothing, Laws spoke again. "Come now, Miss Bond. You seem like a good sort. Think of how it will feel to get the truth off your chest. I can even promise anonymity if you confess."

Edie stopped walking and turned to face him. She didn't have time for this.

"It seems as though you want me to admit something, Mr. Everett. Would you care to enlighten me as to the charge?"

Laws, who had stopped walking when Edie did, met her gaze with a thoughtful, assessing stare. Then he lifted his eyes and did a quick sweep of the busy street around them, bustling with late afternoon traffic.

With a tilt of his head, Laws motioned her toward a small alleyway between two buildings. Reluctantly, Edie followed.

The alley was narrow, which meant there was less than a foot between them when Laws fixed her with an expectant look and said quietly, "There is only one reason for a traveling medium to visit someone like Frances Palmer. You sought to buy information from her about her clients in the city. And then, when you found out about her accidental death, you decided to wait for the police to leave and return to look through the poor dead woman's files. Tell me, could you hear me coming in the hall? Is that why you decided to fake the trance? Because I must admit, that's the one part I don't fully understand."

As Laws spoke, Edie realized there was no reason to worry about what he had or hadn't seen. He wasn't the first to glimpse the truth of death, only to chalk it up to an act. And he was only dogging her steps now because he believed she'd been caught red-handed in the act of cheating.

Fraud was, of course, a punishable offense. More than one enterprising medium had been fined or sentenced to time in jail for it. But Laws had no real evidence. And Mr. Huddle was rather adept at handling these types of accusations.

Not that Laws needed to know that. He needed to think he'd won. That he'd gotten what he'd come for so he would leave her alone.

If Violet were here, she'd already have handled this foxhound of a boy. But she wasn't. And so Edie did her best to force a blush, and then she dipped her chin and lowered her eyes in what she hoped looked like shame. "Excuse me, Mr. Everett. But I—"

She turned away from him and let out a little sob. It started out fake, but then Ruby's face flashed back into her mind. Bright with laughter, like it had been the day they rode her borrowed bicycle down the river path.

Ruby's spirit, weak and flickering.

The bitter taste of guilt flooded her mouth. A gaping hole opened in her chest as sorrow, frustration, and regret warred within her.

And then it was her mother's face taking over her vision. Scared but determined. Black smoke blotting out her form. Smoke that then morphed into something tall and looming. The metal gates of the Sacramento Asylum for the Insane.

Adrenaline shot through her veins. Fear gripped her heart. By the time Edie turned back to face Laws Everett, the tears shining on her cheeks were real.

"Miss Bond, I—"

But Edie shook her head, cutting him off. "You've found me out, Mr. Everett. When you print your account of tonight in your paper, my sister and I will be discredited and ruined. We will be kicked off the tour. Our livelihood gone. If you seek to involve the law, then we will be . . ." Edie choked on another sob. "But I hardly expect you care about that."

His eyes traced the tears on her face, and for a second Edie thought he might be softening toward her. But then his jaw hardened and his eyes narrowed. "And what about the people you deceive, Miss Bond? Do you care about *them*? What about the grieving mothers whose money you take so they can *talk* to a son who is dead and buried? How do you defend your lies then?"

She knew she should leave it there. Let him have the last word. But her emotions were too raw, and the judgment in his eyes incensed her. She'd never felt the need to justify what she and Violet and *Ruby* had done in order to survive. But she did now.

"How do we defend *our* lies?" Edie took a step forward, her own eyes narrowing in return. "How do *you* defend *yours*?"

His brown eyes flashed. "I believe you've become confused, Miss Bond. *You* are the one who profits off lies and cheats. Whereas I—"

"Whereas *you*," interrupted Edie, "would print the lies of that vicious quack, Dr. Lyon. Do you know the supposed *cure* for mediomania, Mr. Everett?"

When he didn't answer right away, Edie barreled on. "It's a so-called 'rest cure' in which the *afflicted* woman is subjected to the will of a male doctor. The *healing* comes when she can no longer assert a will of her own!"

A muscle in Laws's jaw ticked. "You seem to be laboring under some misapprehension that simply because I *report* an expert's view on a subject, that I—"

"Oh yes," cried Edie. "You're only *doing your job*. Well, I've read the third-rate rag you call a newspaper, Mr. Everett. A paper whose only intent is to tear people down. Whose owner has no qualms about taking money to advertise *miracle cures* for every conceivable ailment without a single word of caution. A paper that oh so conveniently makes light of the rampant corruption in the state legislature because the man who decides what you print belongs to the same elite club. So what if those same men are all bought and paid for by those who profit off the backs of *children* working in their mills and the unpaid labor of *women* all over this country?"

Edie's chest was heaving now, and her breath was coming up short. There was a loud shout from the street followed by the high-pitched whinny of a horse. A reminder that despite the relative privacy of this alleyway, she and Lawrence Everett were not alone. And yet she couldn't look away from his brown eyes, no longer bright and curious, but blazing with something she couldn't name.

"You should be careful, Miss Bond." He took another step toward her, his voice low and soft. "Because it almost sounds as if you're questioning my integrity."

He was close enough now that Edie had to lift her chin to meet his eyes.

"'Integrity'? Is *that* what you call standing aside while the rich and powerful commit their sins? Choosing instead to attack *us* for claiming the small corner of the world to which we are allowed? Women like Lillian Fiore who, after experiencing the worst humanity has to offer, has dedicated her life to providing some small comfort to those who have been failed, or outright harmed, by the medical profession. Ada Loring, whose only crime is to delight audiences with her brilliant mind. Flora McCarthy, who puts wonder in their eyes. My sister and—"

She swallowed down the sob that rose in her throat.

"My sister and . . . Ruby Miller. Who give grieving mothers, fathers, daughters, and sons a last chance to say goodbye. You have eyes that cut to the truth of things, Mr. Everett. And yet *these* are the criminals you seek to punish?"

A single tear raced down her cheek. Followed by a second and a third. She didn't bother to wipe them away.

Laws's eyes flitted over her face. His hand twitched at his side, and Edie had the strangest feeling that he wanted to reach out to her. For one breathless second, she wanted him to. Wanted his hand buried in her hair as he pulled her to his chest. Wanted to feel the rumble of his voice as he told her everything would be all right.

Except that it would be a lie. Because everything *wouldn't* be all right. Not if she didn't get rid of this boy right now.

Edie blinked and took a step back. Laws cleared his throat and shoved his hand into his pocket.

"I will take my leave of you now, Mr. Everett. I believe you'll understand why I say with full sincerity that I hope to never see you again."

And then, without so much as a backward glance, Edie turned on her heel and set off into the fading light. She forced her beating heart to slow and focused on getting her breathing under control. There was one more stop she had to make before confronting the heavy black gates and the asylum that lay beyond.

16

Edie pushed her way through the doors of the Union Hotel, her feet heavy as she made her way up the stairs to her and Violet's room on the third floor.

Violet had known that something about Ruby's sudden disappearance was wrong, but Edie had dismissed her concerns. Violet was going to be devastated. She was going to be angry. And when Edie came clean about the shadow in the Veil—she couldn't very well hide that any longer—Violet was going to . . .

Well, Edie had no idea how her sister would react. She only knew she deserved whatever came.

And what about Nell Doyle? What about the names on Mother's list? Are you going to tell her about that?

Are you going to tell her everything?

Edie bit her lip as she reached the top of the staircase and turned the corner. If she was going to sneak into the Sacramento Asylum tonight on the last orders of Ruby's spirit, she was going to need her sister's help.

Edie inserted the key and opened the hotel room, her mind still a whirl of indecision. She could start slow. Gauge Violet's reaction, and then decide if—

"EDIE!"

She barely had time to look up before she was enveloped in a fierce hug, Violet's rose-oil scent wrapping around her like the warmest of shawls.

"Oh, Edie! I'm so glad you're here!"

Violet eased her hold and pulled back, revealing a face that was positively glowing. The joy in her face was staggering, and for a second Edie lost her own breath. She couldn't remember the last time she'd seen Violet so . . . happy. It was infectious. Before Edie knew it, the worry, fear, and confusion that had been roiling in her gut since seeing Ruby's spirit fell away, and she was returning her sister's smile.

"Well, what's all this?"

Violet laughed her trilling laugh and leaned forward again, placing her cheek against Edie's just like they'd done during the fitting. And as always, the position allowed Edie to immediately feel what her twin was experiencing. A steady wave of pure, unfiltered joy.

"I'm happy for you," whispered Edie into her sister's ear. And it was true. Even though she had no idea what she was happy *for*. "But I'm also dying of suspense."

Violet laughed again, squeezed her hand, and sighed a happy little sigh. "The audition, Edie." Her voice was full of wonder as she spoke. As if she couldn't believe her own words. "I got it.

The director cabled John, inviting me to read with the rest of the cast tomorrow morning in San Francisco. John hired a coach for tonight. He's waiting downstairs, and I know it will be a slog, but I'm too excited to sleep a wink anyway. And I'm so glad you're here, so I could tell you—"

She pulled back from their embrace, her smile falling as she took in Edie's face. "Edie? What is it? What's wrong?"

But Edie wasn't looking at Violet. She was taking in the state of their hotel room. Between the two of them, the twins owned a rather limited wardrobe, and it seemed every single article of it—from dresses and skirts to scarves and shoes—had been liberated from its respective peg, drawer, or box and laid out on the bed, draped across the back of a chair, or set precariously atop the dresser.

But it was the sight of Violet's powder-blue valise, sitting peacefully amidst the chaos, that held Edie's attention. Her traveling case. Packed and ready to go.

Somewhere in the room, under the many piles of clothes and hats, was Edie's matching case. Identical but for the dents and scuffs in different places. For the first time in the history of their lives, Violet's bag was packed, and Edie's was not.

Edie tore her eyes away from the traveling case and looked back at her twin.

Violet was going to leave her.

The realization made her feel oddly light. As if her limbs had ceased to exist. The practical part of her brain reminded Edie that this was only an audition. One single night away. But her bones—

what she could still feel of them at least—knew it was more than that. Violet had wanted this her whole life. Edie had discounted it as an impractical distraction that would never come to pass.

She had been wrong.

"What about the Mary Sutton séance?" asked Edie, wincing as she heard the desperation in her own voice. "It's tomorrow night."

"I know, and John promised we'd be back in time. The audition is in the morning, and then we'll take a steamer back first thing. Only . . ." Violet paused. Her eyes swept Edie's face, and then, in a careful voice, she asked, "Are we going ahead with the appointment? Did you find what you . . . needed?"

Edie stiffened. "What I needed?"

"For that spirit. It could cause a problem, couldn't it? If it interrupted tomorrow night?"

Edie shot her twin a searching look. Violet blinked back at her. But there was something beneath her politely curious expression that warned Edie to proceed with caution.

"No," said Edie, turning slightly to take off her hat and gloves. "I haven't yet. But I will. I won't let us miss this chance."

Violet opened her mouth as if to speak, but then she shook her head and pressed her lips together.

Once again, a persistent voice in Edie's head urged her to tell her sister everything, come what may.

She placed her hat atop the dresser as another thought occurred to her. Telling Violet everything would stop her from leaving. No audition, no matter how important, would outweigh

Ruby's last plea from death. Violet may hate Edie once she learned the truth, but she would stay.

Edie turned back to Violet, the words on the edge of her lips. But then she froze, arrested by the lines of worry that had formed on her sister's face, marring her earlier joy.

A year ago, Edie had promised herself that she would build a new life for them. A better life than the one she'd cost them. And here Violet was, with a real shot at the life of her dreams.

All she needed was for Edie to step aside and let her take it.

Setting her jaw, Edie walked over to Violet's bed and picked up the packed powder-blue valise. Infusing her voice with as much cheer as she could muster, she said, "You shouldn't worry about all that now, anyway." Walking over to Violet, she held the bag out to her. "You should be focusing on your audition."

Violet reached out for the bag, but then paused before taking the weight of it, her hand resting next to Edie's on the leather handle. "Is that it? Is that all you're going to say?"

Edie hesitated. "I . . . well. I know I'm not supposed to wish you good luck, but I hope you know that I . . . hope it goes well."

A flash of disappointment crossed Violet's face. She took the handle of the traveling case and turned toward the door. But then, before opening it, she paused. Without turning around, she said, "I can't wait forever, you know."

Edie's chest went tight. "I don't . . . can't wait for what?"

Violet didn't move from her position at the door, only turned her head so she could meet Edie's eyes. "I can't wait forever for you to tell me what made you like this. Why my sister—the most opinionated, determined person I know—has spent the past year living like a rabbit afraid of her own shadow."

Edie's face went hot, her stomach churning at the unfairness of her sister's words. "If anyone is going to be giving lectures, Vi, I'd think that I—"

"Oh no," said Violet, turning fully to face her now. "I think I can recite this one from memory. You're worried I'm not being realistic. That I'm not making practical choices. Do you know what I always want to say to that?"

Edie met her sister's eyes but said nothing.

"That at least *I'm* not living every moment in fear. At least every thought going through *my* head isn't about what could go *wrong*."

"No," said Edie quietly. "You made that my job instead."

The laugh Violet let out this time was not full of joy. It was dark and cold, and Edie's heart twisted in pain when she heard it. "You've become so good at lying, Edie. I wonder if you even know when you're lying to yourself."

"What's *that* supposed to mean?"

Violet shook her head, her eyes steely. "I never understood how you could think I was that stupid, E. How you could *actually* think I had no idea."

Edie froze, her blood turning to ice.

"I don't know what happened to you and Mother that day in the Veil. But I know something did. That look on your face now? Like you're being haunted? You wore the same one right after she died. It came back two days ago. Are you going to tell me why?"

Violet's question hung in the air between them. Silent. Waiting. And every second Edie didn't respond, every moment of silence between them, gave it even more weight. Until it became a thing so solid, Edie could have reached out and touched it.

And still Violet waited. Waited for Edie to say something. Confess, maybe. Or lie again.

But Edie couldn't speak. Couldn't *move*. Base survival was taking over every other instinct, as if she were caught in a predator's gaze and being still as a stone was the only way to stay alive.

Finally, Violet sighed. She adjusted her hold on the powder-blue case, turned the silver knob of the hotel room's door, and slipped out into the hall. Her footsteps padded along the carpet in the hallway, growing fainter with each step. They paused for a second at what might have been the top of the stairs. But, instead of turning back, they continued on down the stairway. Until finally there was nothing more to hear.

Until Edie knew her sister was well and truly gone.

17

After Violet left, Edie stared at the back of the door for what might have been hours or what might have been minutes.

The tingling lightness in her limbs intensified until she felt as if her body could float away. But even as her mind fought to retreat from the pain of watching her sister leave, a distant but persistent voice told Edie she had to *move*.

Haltingly, she obeyed. Drifting in a kind of daze, she sifted through the clothes Violet had strewn on the floor until she found the black skirt and blouse she'd worn in the months following their mother's death. The same voice prompted Edie to open the drawer of the writing desk and slip the leather sheath containing her mother's bone-handled knife into the pocket of her skirt.

Less than fifteen minutes later, Edie was in the hotel lobby— although she had no recollection of how she'd gotten there— pushing through the doors and out into the setting sun.

As she headed west on K Street, she was dimly aware of passing the stables housing the mules that pulled the omnibuses—her feet avoiding the extra piles of manure out of pure instinct—and walking past the train station she and Violet had arrived at less than a week ago, where a young boy had been selling armloads of bright yellow California poppies for twenty cents a bunch.

But even as her feet padded along the wooden-planked sidewalks and her arms wrapped around her body in response to the early-evening chill, Edie had the distinct feeling of being separate. As if she had left her body and was watching these actions from afar.

And then a voice sounded behind her shoulder, followed by a whistle and a chorus of laughter.

Male laughter.

"Well, that one isn't half bad! Are you, girlie?"

And just like that, Edie came crashing back into her body.

The pain she'd been avoiding—the hole in her stomach that had formed at Violet's parting words—took the wind out of her for a second. But even that was quickly pushed aside as Edie whirled around to see a group of sailors, clearly out for a night of drinking, stumble out of one of the many gambling dens lining the waterfront. One of the sailors—a greasy-looking young man with black, beady eyes—was close enough for Edie to smell the stench of fish and sweat wafting off his body. As her eyes fell on him, his thin lips twisted into a smile.

Edie shoved her hand into her pocket, clutching the leather sheath of her mother's knife, and then she ducked her head and ran.

On her left, the lazy current of the Sacramento River flowed by, washed pink in the setting sun. But on her right, more saloons and gambling dens lined the street, their windows aglow with muddy yellow light, and the rooms filled with bellowing men accompanied by women in low-necked gowns.

What had she been thinking, walking along the waterfront this close to night? She should have hired a hack, no matter the cost.

But the answer, of course, was that she hadn't been thinking.

Slowing, Edie risked a glance over her shoulder. A cold tingling on the back of her neck warned her that she was being followed, but one quick peek revealed that the sailor who'd called out to her was still leaning against the gambling den's wall, a spider waiting for the arrival of its next prey.

She allowed herself a single sigh of relief. Then, sidestepping a drunk passed out on the street, she picked up her pace again to a brisk walk. She'd gotten lucky. But she couldn't afford to slip up again. She needed her head on straight for what lay ahead.

Five minutes later, Edie reached the suspended steel railroad bridge. She continued to have the uneasy feeling that she was being followed, but she spotted no one behind her each time she turned around. Soon she was making her way up G Street, the boisterous hoots and hollers from the waterfront fading away. And then . . . she felt it.

A familiar pressure in her head. A warning in the pit of her stomach.

Half a block more and she saw it. Looming before her. High stone walls behind black metal gates. A sign along the top that read: SACRAMENTO ASYLUM FOR THE INSANE.

Earlier that afternoon, she'd assumed that her physical reaction to this place was nothing more than nerves. Fear of what her life would be like if her father found her and forced her beyond those gates for a lifetime.

But now she understood what she'd missed before. That pressure at the back of her head? The twisting in her stomach? It was a response to a thinning of the Veil.

Ruby's words rose in her mind.

Beyond the black gates.

Hurry.

Edie took a couple of steps forward. The bars of the gate were too close together for her to squeeze through, and the stone wall surrounding the property had to be at least ten feet high. She wouldn't be able to climb it on her own.

And on her own is exactly what she was.

I can't wait forever, you know.

With an effort, Edie forced Violet's words from her mind. Ruby's spirit had given her a task, and Edie had let enough people down for one day.

Her eyes scanned the asylum walls again. There were a couple of large oak trees sprouting up around the walls. Night would be falling soon. Maybe she could wait for the cover of darkness and then climb up one of the trees? And then to get down, she'd . . . jump? No, she'd be sure to break an ankle, and then where would she be? She'd need to find some rope. She could tie the rope to a tree branch, and then—

"We should really stop meeting like this."

Startled, Edie jumped into the air and, at the same time, she tried to turn around toward the voice that spoke. The result was a kind of midair spin that threw her off balance.

A hand reached out to steady her.

"That," said the grinning face of Laws Everett, "is exactly what the sheep used to do."

18

Edie wrenched her arm out of Laws's grasp.

He let her go and took a step back, giving her space. Before she could demand to know what he was doing sneaking up on her in the middle of the sidewalk, Laws held up a hand and spoke.

"Before you ask. This time I *did* follow you."

Edie's eyes narrowed, but Laws kept speaking.

"I told my editor I wanted to pursue the story your friend Lillian told me about. The one about the asylum."

Edie's mouth snapped shut. That had *not* been what she'd expected him to say.

"He said no. So I said I'd do it on my own, and then I quit."

"You quit your job at the *Sting*?"

Laws nodded. "I came to find you at your hotel because, well, you were right. I became a reporter because I wanted to help people find out the truth of things. And I think I . . . well, the honest truth is I was biased toward you. You and your friends. I had my reasons, but I should never have—"

"What were they?"

Laws tilted his head in question.

"Your reasons for your bias?"

"Well, Miss Bond. It's a long—"

"Call me Edie."

Mortified, Edie had to stop herself from slapping a hand over her mouth.

Why had she said that?

"Edie it is," said Laws, a smile tugging at the corner of his lips. "But only if you call me Laws."

Unable to form actual words, Edie only nodded.

"Well, *Edie*." Laws shifted on his feet. "If you really want to know—"

"I do."

This time his smile broke through. But it disappeared as quickly as it had come. "Okay, then." Shoving his hands in his pockets, Laws stared at a fixed point on the sidewalk. "As you may recall, I grew up on a farm. With sheep." He shot her a quick teasing glance before dropping his eyes again. "My father owned it, but he died when I was twelve."

"I'm so sorry."

"Thank you. It was a hard time. Harder on my mom, though. She didn't . . . take his death well. So when a traveling medium came to town claiming she could speak to the dead, she was the first to book an appointment. Gave every last penny we had—including money she'd gotten from taking out a mortgage on the farm—to that woman. When she ran out of money to pay the medium, she took her own life. Left me a note saying not to worry. That she'd contact me from the other side." His eyes flicked up to Edie's face, and though it was only a second before he dropped his gaze again, Edie saw the raw pain there. "Obviously still waiting for that bit to happen."

Edie stared at Laws's bowed head. Speechless.

Her mind reeled back to the question he'd asked her in the alleyway.

And what about the people you deceive, Miss Bond? What about the grieving mothers whose money you take?

She'd been so confident in her reply to him. So dismissive of his concerns.

"Laws. I'm sorry. I don't . . . I don't know what to say."

He looked up at her then, this time maintaining eye contact. "You don't have to say anything. It's not your fault."

"But I—"

"I mean it," said Laws, cutting her off. "You asked, and I told you. It's as simple as that." Drawing his hands out of his pockets, he crossed them in front of his chest. "I think, instead, we should talk about exactly *how* you were planning to go about trespassing on private government property."

Edie's eyes widened. "I have no idea what you're talking about."

"Sure you don't. Which is why it's only for the sake of conversation that I mention the last time I tried to gain entrance to this building in my—admittedly misguided—attempts to gain an interview from the reclusive Dr. Lyon, I noticed watchmen strolling the perimeter. Watchmen who will spot you in a second, even if you *did* manage to scale those gates."

Edie's stomach fell. She hadn't thought of that.

"Unless you have a different plan?"

Of course she didn't have a different plan.

"I'm sorry to douse your spirits."

"Again," said Edie, "I have no idea what you're talking about. I am out for a stroll."

"Right. Love a good stroll myself. Especially while wearing all black attire that is not at all suspicious. Of course, if that *is* the case, then I suppose you also wouldn't be interested in hearing about the man I may or may not have on the inside of that asylum?"

Edie's gaze shot toward him.

"Ah. I *thought* that might interest you."

"Why?"

Laws raised an eyebrow. "Why is he on the inside? Well, some of us work *honest* jobs for a living. Not something I'd expect you to know much about—"

"No. Why are you telling me this? Why would you want to help me, *um* . . ."

"Why would I want to help you break into a state-run insane asylum?"

Edie winced at the bluntness of his words, but she didn't deny them.

Laws's eyes twinkled. "Well, I could tell you that it's part of the story I'm now committed to writing. That I want to see the inside of that place when they haven't had time to prepare for a press visit. But that wouldn't really be the truth. And I'm not sure our budding friendship can take the weight of any more lies, are you?"

Edie said nothing. He took a step toward her. "I'll level with you, Edie. As a reporter, I pride myself on having a certain . . . nose for the truth, if you will. An instinct that I've learned to trust. And that instinct tells me you're mixed up in something big. Something you shouldn't be facing alone."

Alone.

But Edie had never been alone. She'd always had Violet.

Laws shoved his hands into his pockets. "Look, you've given me no earthly reason to trust you. Hell, you've been lying through your teeth since the moment we met. And yet, for some reason I do. Trust you, that is." His eyes lost their humorous expression and he regarded her with a serious, thoughtful gaze. "So, to answer your question? I simply want to help. Which leads me to a question of my own."

Edie met his eyes. "Oh? And what is that?"

Laws raised an eyebrow. "Are you ready to trust me back?"

⊂℟℈⊃

A half hour later, Edie was leaning against the rough bark of an oak tree, attempting to eat her half of a cheese sandwich that Laws had obtained from the horse-drawn night lunch wagon across the street.

"Might as well eat while we wait," he'd said while breaking the sandwich in two.

When Edie had asked—for at least the twelfth time—*what* exactly they were waiting for, Laws had merely winked and said she'd see soon enough.

Prior to securing the sandwiches, Laws had found a boy willing to take a note to his "man on the inside." But then, after Edie had refused to answer *his* questions about *who* or *what* she was looking for inside the asylum, he had in turn refused to answer *her* questions about what would happen next. They'd been at a stalemate ever since.

Edie shifted against the tree trunk. The bark was rough and sharp against her back, and it was nearly impossible to find a position in which a small rock or root wasn't jutting into her thigh. Laws, who had long since gobbled up his half of the sandwich, was sprawled on his back atop the leaf-strewn ground. One arm was flung over his eyes, and he looked for all the world like he was in the middle of a nice, pleasant nap.

Not that Edie could see more than his basic shape and outline. The sun had set half an hour ago and darkness had fallen. Not wanting to arouse any suspicions by lingering a block away from the asylum after dark, Edie and Laws had retreated into the bit of foliage just outside the glow of the recently lit streetlamps.

Edie swallowed a bite of cheese sandwich. It tasted—through no fault of the cook—like sawdust in her mouth. "Exactly how much longer are we supposed to wait?"

"Any minute now."

"You said that twenty minutes ago."

Laws shrugged, his shoulders rustling the leaves. "This criminal business takes time. And proper planning."

"I am *not* a criminal."

"Oh no?" More rustling as the shape that was Laws propped himself up onto his elbows. There was just enough light from the rising moon and the glow of distant streetlamps to illuminate the teasing glint in his eye. "Silly me. I thought breaking and entering was still considered a crime in this country. Unless, of course, you'd care to enlighten me as to what exactly you—"

"No."

A laugh rumbled in his throat. "Thought not."

The leaves rustled again as Laws stood up from the ground. After shaking out the coat he'd been lounging on, he stuck his arms through the sleeves and peered out past the trees toward the street. Then he turned back to Edie and held out a hand.

Edie stared at it, making no move to take it.

"I hope you're not having second thoughts now, because I do believe our man has arrived."

Ignoring his outstretched hand, Edie sprang up from the ground and made her way toward the street.

The traffic on Sixth Street had kept up a steady pace for the last hour or so, hansom cabs, hacks, and fine black carriages regularly rattling past. But it wasn't a fancy black carriage that pulled up along the sidewalk now. It was a small four-wheeled cart, a single horse at its head. The wooden cart had been painted a dusty shade of blue, and stenciled along the side were the words:

WAH LEE

WASHING & IRONING

Laws approached the cart and lifted a hand in greeting. Edie grabbed his elbow and yanked him back. "I thought you said you had a man on the inside!"

"Well, what do you think this is?"

"I think it's a laundry cart."

"Exactly," said Laws with a wink. "A laundry cart that's going *inside*."

Before Edie could explain that this was not *at all* what she thought he'd meant by having a way in, the driver of the cart leaned forward, poking his head out from the front of the cart.

"Lawrence Everett," called the driver. "You better believe I'll be sending you the bill for this rush job."

The driver was a young man of East Asian descent who seemed to be around Laws's age. A plain black homburg hat was pushed back on his head, revealing that, despite his dry tone, his eyes danced with a mischievous glint. Laws gently disentangled himself from Edie's grip and walked toward the driver.

"Oh, come on, Tom. You know I'm good for it."

"All I know," said the driver—Tom, apparently—"is that after this, we're square."

"Square?" Laws shoved his hands into his pockets and let out a short whistle. "Let's not get ahead of ourselves now—"

"If that's how you're playing this"—Tom picked up the reins of the horse and nudged the tawny animal forward—"then I believe I have other places to be."

The cart rolled forward a foot before Laws yelled out, "All right, all right! Have it your way. You do this for me and we're square. All right?"

The cart stopped. Tom's head poked out again, a full grin on his face now. "In that case, you two had better hop in before someone sees."

Laws nodded once and then headed to the back of the cart. When he noticed that Edie wasn't following him, he stopped and turned around. "Well? Aren't you coming?"

Edie stuck her hands on her hips. "*This* is your plan? To hide in the back of a laundry cart?"

Laws smiled. "It's okay. You can admit you're impressed."

"Impressed?" Her voice came out like a squeak. "Someone is bound to search the cart! It's near half past eight! Surely deliveries are done for the day. This is all going to look highly suspicious."

The gnawing feeling of doubt in her stomach was quickly turning to despair. *This* was what happened when she let other people take charge. It was never going to work. She needed to cut her losses now and come up with a new plan.

"Oh, don't worry about that," said Laws, his expression the opposite of concerned. "Tom here will take care of that part. Won't you, Tom?"

From the front of the cart, Tom raised a hand in acknowledgment but didn't turn around.

"See? He's got it." Laws took a couple of steps toward her. Lowering his voice, he said, "This is going to work, okay? You've just got to trust me a little bit."

Her jaw tightened. Easy for him to say. He was a reporter. If he got caught by the wrong people in there, he'd probably get nothing more than a slap on the wrist. Hell, he'd probably get a front-page article out of the experience. But if Edie got caught...

Her eyes slipped toward the black metal gates, just visible down the street. The tingling pull in her stomach hadn't gone away. And Ruby's words were still fresh in her mind.

Hurry.

Could she really turn around now?

Laws stretched out his hand again, palm up. "Whaddya say, Edie? You want to hop in the back of this laundry cart with me and sneak into a state-run asylum?"

A smile inched onto her face. She was mad to do this. But she reached out her hand and plopped it into his.

Laws's own smile lit up his entire face. He pulled her toward the cart and unlatched the back door. Edie sneezed as an aroma of bright, clean soap tickled her nose. Laws helped her inside the little wooden cart and then scrambled in behind her. They covered themselves in a few dozen squares of neatly folded white sheets. Once they were as covered as possible—which was not very covered at all: anything more than a cursory look would surely get them caught—Laws banged his fist twice on the side of the cart.

And then they were off, the little wooden cart rattling along the dirt road toward the black metal gates.

ℂ ℠

Laws and Edie did their best to carve out their own space within the wagon. They were both lying on their backs, sheets piled on top of their bodies from head to toe. But while the laundry cart was no doubt big enough to do its normal job, with two nearly full-grown bodies inside, it was . . . cramped.

She could feel every point of contact between Laws's body and her own: his right shoulder jammed up against her left; the edge of his hip rolling into hers whenever the cart rumbled over a rough patch in the road; his pinkie finger pressed against the back of her hand.

Her entire body was far too warm. And her heart was thudding too loud and too fast against her chest. Maybe it was because of the boy pressed up next to her. Or maybe it was because, after spending a year trying to stay one step ahead of her father's plan for her, she was now willingly walking—or, rather, rolling—toward that very fate.

Maybe this was a terrible idea. Maybe she should throw these sheets off right now and demand that Laws stop everything. Tell his friend Tom to turn this cart around. She didn't have to do this. It was too late to save Ruby. She could let the Veil sort itself out. Forget Mary Sutton's money. Ignore the haunting similarity between Ruby's flickering spirit and the spirit her mother had faced.

But before she could decide whether she wanted to stop this mission or not, the swaying stopped and the cart lurched to a halt.

Gravel crunched as heavy footsteps approached the left side of the cart. What sounded like a ring of metal keys jangled against someone's leg. The footsteps stopped and a deep, gruff voice spoke. "Evening, Tom. Bit late for deliveries, isn't it?"

Beneath the sheets, Edie held her breath. But Tom didn't miss a beat. "Hi there, Samuel. And boy, are you telling me. I was about to head home when they sent me out with this load. I guess Nurse Harris ordered a rush."

"A rush? That's not like her."

The tang of the laundry soap tickled Edie's nose again, and she risked bringing a hand to her face so she could pinch her nose shut with her forefinger and thumb.

"All I know's what they tell me," said Tom. "But if you don't want it now, I can come back tomorrow."

"No, no."

Edie thought she detected a hint of fear in the gruff man's voice.

"If Nurse Harris wanted 'em tonight, better not get in the way of that. She'll have her reasons."

"She always does," Tom agreed.

A low, appreciative laugh rumbled in the man's chest, and then he said, "All right, then. Hold tight, and I'll open the gate."

But then, just as the footsteps started up again, Edie lost her battle with the laundry soap and sneezed.

Laws's body went rigid beside her.

"What was that?" said the gruff voice.

"What was what?" Tom seemed to be trying for that same lazy tone, but he wasn't quite succeeding.

"Thought I heard somethin'." Footsteps crunched toward the back of the cart. Edie's heart pounded in her chest. Sweat broke out on her brow.

She would have to run.

They weren't inside the walls yet. She could wait until the man opened the back door of the cart, spring out, and then sprint for all she was worth. But what if he got hold of her before she could get away?

Laws shifted next to her. She felt him turn his head to the side. Then his lips were pressed up against her ear. "I'll jump out first and distract him." His voice was barely a whisper. "Then you run."

Edie shook her head. She didn't need his help. She didn't *want* his help. What if he failed to distract the guard? Then, by waiting to run, she was giving up the element of surprise.

Laws grabbed her hand and squeezed it. "Look, Edie. I know, all right?" His voice was so low she could barely hear him. "Just trust me."

What did he mean, "he knew"? He knew *what*? She wanted to press him, but the footsteps were getting closer.

And then Tom's voice rang out. "Don't tell me this place has got to you too, Samuel. Always took you for one of the hardier types."

The footsteps stopped. "And just what's that s'posed to mean?"

"Well, isn't that how it starts? Hearing imaginary voices and all that? Word is, that's the first thing happened to Charlie before he, well . . ."

Tom trailed off.

"You heard about that, eh?" Samuel's gruff voice was somber. "That was a bad business with Charlie. He was a pal of mine."

"Sorry to hear that," said Tom.

There was a moment of silence. And then Samuel spoke again. "S'pose we might as well get you on your way. Reckon one of us ought to enjoy their evening."

The footsteps reversed course, heading away from the cart. There was the sound of a key turning in a lock. And then the groan of metal scraping against gravel. But Edie didn't allow herself to take a full breath until the little wooden cart lurched forward, its metal wheels rattling along the gravel drive and through the black metal gates.

19

The next time the cart lurched to a halt, Laws squeezed Edie's hand and released it. It was only then that she realized how tightly she'd been holding onto him.

"That's our cue," he said, voice low.

It took some maneuvering to extract themselves from the sheets without completely destroying the neatly folded squares. In the end, it was Laws who wriggled out first, followed by Edie, her feet landing on the packed dirt with a soft thud.

Her eyes immediately took in the bleak, multistoried gothic building that loomed before her. Its dark stone facade swallowed up the light from the rising moon, but the muddy yellow light of the gas lamps installed at the front door provided enough illumination for Edie to see the iron bars along the windows. A shiver crept up her back at the sight. This building truly was one giant cage.

Laws left her side and trotted up to the front of the cart. He and Tom exchanged a few brief whispered words and then, to Edie's dismay, Tom clicked his tongue at the horse and his cart jerked forward, rattling on toward the back of the building.

"Wait!" Edie rushed up to Laws. "He can't just leave us here. He has to get us inside!"

Laws turned toward her, his face washed blue in the light from the rising moon, and shook his head. "Tom got us past the gate, but there'll be someone to meet him for the delivery. We don't want any part of that. Not to worry, though." Laws set off toward the building, Edie at his heels. "I myself didn't actually make it *in* the building last time, but Tom said the halls in the east wing should be empty this time of night, apart from a couple nurse patrols on the hour."

They were careful to keep to the shadows as they skirted around the building, avoiding the pools of gaslight that lit the stone front steps. The closer they got, the more intense the twisting in Edie's stomach grew.

They were halfway around the building when Laws tapped her shoulder. She paused and followed the point of his finger. "There," whispered Laws. "Does that window look open to you?"

It was a ground-floor window, one of the few without bars. Edie approached it and found that it was slightly ajar. Unfortunately, the opening was also about three feet above her head.

"I'll lift you up," whispered Laws. "You check to make sure it's empty, and if it is, I'll climb in after."

She'd rather have found a way through the window on her own, but the truth was she needed a boost. "Fine," she whispered back through clenched teeth. "But don't get any ideas."

Laws coughed, as if he were stifling a laugh. But he only said, "You have my word."

Edie tiptoed up to the window and then stood still as Laws wrapped his hands around her waist. "On three," he whispered low in her ear. "One. Two. *Three!*"

On the third count, Laws bent his knees and lifted Edie into the air with a small grunt. His fingers dug painfully into the sides of her waist, but Edie ignored this, focusing instead on grabbing the lower ledge of the windowsill.

Her fingers hooked around the thick wooden edge of the frame, and she hauled herself up. When she was midway through the window, she paused—trying not to think of the undignified way her skirts were billowing around her calves—and did her best to take in the room. It appeared small, dark, and uninhabited, which was good enough for her. She kicked her feet for momentum and then launched herself the rest of the way through. The drop wasn't far, only about five feet. And she managed to catch herself with her hands before landing in a heap on a cold, tiled floor.

She'd only just managed to right herself when Laws's face popped up in the window. He soon landed in a heap of his own— it was some consolation that his maneuvers weren't any more graceful than hers had been—before jumping back up to his feet.

The only illumination in the little room was a shaft of moonlight streaming in through the window, but it was enough to see that they'd ended up in some kind of storage room. There was a broom in the corner, a shelf of what appeared to be folded yellowing towels, and several amber glass jugs lined up along the floor.

"Well," said Laws, his voice a low whisper. "That's my end done. It does appear that we've successfully made it inside."

Edie nodded once to show she'd heard him; but, instead of answering, she closed her eyes so she could focus on the peculiar sensation of the thinning Veil. She was close enough now to whatever the source was to feel a little tug. Forward and to the right.

When she opened her eyes again, Laws was staring at her. There was only the moonlight to see by, but it was enough for Edie to discern that he was studying her with more intensity than his usual brand of curiosity allowed. She tensed, readying herself for the inevitable interrogation; but, much to her surprise, Laws merely bowed his head and murmured, "After you."

Edie nodded again, reached forward, and placed her hand on the doorknob of the little storage room. And it was there—in the seconds between reaching for the door and easing it open—that Edie realized she was glad Laws Everett was here with her.

She had no idea what she'd find here tonight. Was Ruby's body somewhere in this asylum? Would she find the person possessed by the shadow's escaped spirit? And what about the living humans who ran this place? If Edie and Laws were caught, and if Edie was later identified, chances were good she'd never see the other side of those black gates again.

And even though she couldn't tell Laws any of this—had no intention of ever doing so—she couldn't deny there was something bolstering about his presence. Something about the never-ceasing challenge in his eyes that made her feel just a little bit more . . . brave.

The hinges on the storage-room door only whined a little as Edie carefully pushed it open. Beyond the door was a long, narrow hall. There were no lamps lit, and the glow of moonlight did little to illuminate the space. Edie pulled a packet of matches from her pocket and struck one, allowing its flickering flame to illuminate the hall for the seconds it took for the fire to travel the length of the little stick.

In that time, she saw that the hallway was lined with wooden doors. All closed. All fitted with metal locks. And although the hallway itself was quiet, she could just make out a few faint sounds coming from the other side of the doors. Confirmation that the inhabitants of the asylum had been locked away for the night.

Her heart clenched at the sight of those locks, but Edie forced herself to focus on the twisting of her stomach instead, a sensation that felt stronger when she turned to the right. So right she went, Laws following a few steps behind.

When the first match flared out, Edie lit a second one. And that's when she caught sight of another, shorter hallway a couple of feet to her left. She tiptoed toward it and peered around the corner. The second hallway terminated in a dead end, and it had a single door on its right side.

Edie's stomach lurched.

A second later, the match flared out. She lit a third one and held it up.

The door at the end of this second hallway was different from the others. For one, it was metal instead of wood. For another, there was a sign bolted to it, the writing on which she couldn't make out from this distance.

But Edie didn't need to see the writing to know—to *feel*— that whatever she was looking for was on the other side.

The third match sputtered out. She pulled out a fourth one and was preparing to light it when suddenly she was seized from behind. A hand clapped over her mouth.

She tensed, but then a familiar voice hissed in her ear. "*Shhhh. Someone's coming.*"

Edie nodded quickly to show she'd understood. Laws took his hand away from her mouth and reached down to grab her hand instead, pulling her back to the storage room. Together, they slipped into the little room, closing the door softly behind them.

Not fifteen seconds later, the sound of footsteps—two pairs, it seemed to Edie's ears—clicked down the hallway toward them. Each step was accompanied by the metal clang of what sounded like a ring of keys.

The footsteps stopped several feet to the left of Edie and Laws's storage room. There was the sound of a key turning in the lock, and then the hinges of a door squeaking open.

"I thought," whispered Edie, "that Tom said the nurses did their checks on the hour."

Even in the dimly lit room, Edie could see a muscle in Laws's jaw jump. "Apparently," he whispered back, "he was wrong."

Less than a minute later, the door thudded shut again. The lock turned and clanked shut. The footsteps continued on and then stopped at what must have been the next door. Again, the lock was turned. Again, the hinges creaked. The door was open for about thirty seconds before it was slammed shut and locked once again.

The footsteps progressed to the room directly next to their storage room. In one synchronous movement, Edie and Laws turned to meet each other's eyes. Laws tilted his head toward a section of the wall that would be hidden when the door swung inward. It wasn't the most secure of hiding places, but it was the best option they had. Edie nodded back at him, and together they tiptoed over and pressed their backs against the wall.

The clicking footsteps approached their storage closet, and both Edie and Laws held their breath. But the footsteps didn't stop. They continued past them, stopping instead a few feet to their right. Another door was unlocked and then slammed shut again.

They both released their breath at the same time. Laws caught her eye and smiled in relief. Edie couldn't help but smile back.

But they didn't dare move from their hiding spot behind the door just yet. Instead, they waited for several minutes until the footsteps faded away down the hall.

Then, after another minute of silence, Laws spoke. His voice was low. "Tom may have been wrong about the timing, but if they're doing their rounds, then now's the time to make our break."

Edie nodded. "There's a door across the hall that I need to get inside."

Laws paused. She could feel the question on his lips. His desire to know where they were going and why. But once again, he surprised her with a simple nod. "All right, then. Let's go."

This time, it was Laws who eased open the door, holding it for her. Edie lit another match, and the two of them scrambled as quickly and quietly as they could down the hall until they came to the large metal door. In the second before the match sputtered out, Edie caught the words printed on the small sign bolted to its front.

EXPERIMENTAL WING. AUTHORIZED ACCESS ONLY.

The next match revealed two metal deadbolts affixed to the door a few inches below the sign.

Laws sucked in a breath. A quick glance told Edie that he'd come to the same conclusion she had. This door was locked from the outside. It wasn't meant to keep people from getting *in*, it was meant to keep people from getting *out*.

It took her two deep breaths before she worked up the courage to slide the deadbolts and pull open the door. On the other side, a narrow flight of stairs led down to a pit of darkness. As her eyes adjusted, she could see there were a few gaslight sconces spaced out along the wall to her right, flickering with a wan yellow light.

She looked back once at Laws, whose face was barely visible in the dark corridor, and then she started down the steps. There was no banister, only a faded brick wall sweating faintly with moisture and reeking of mildew.

As she descended the stairs, the twisting in her stomach grew. By the time she was halfway down, it had transformed into the familiar seasick-like nausea Edie associated with a thinning Veil.

They were getting close.

When she finally reached the bottom of the stairs, her head was swimming with dizziness, and beads of sweat had sprouted on her brow; but she paused at the base of the stairs only long enough for Laws to catch up before she started walking again, this time down another long corridor with more gas lamps flickering on the wall.

It ended at a second door, this one locked from the outside as well. Edie slid the deadbolt and swung open the door. Then she doubled over in pain.

"Edie!"

Laws was by her side in an instant. "Edie, what's wrong? Are you hurt?"

But Edie could only shake her head. The nausea and dizziness had spiked as soon as she'd opened that door. It hit her hard. Harder than ever before. Not even her first experience with death—when she'd been young and unprepared—had affected her this way.

There was something wrong with the Veil in this place. Something . . . unstable about it. It was much thinner than it should be after a recent death. Thinner than it should be after several *hundred* recent deaths.

She shook her head again, trying to clear it. The only way to understand was to keep going. She needed to pull herself together and get through this door.

Edie forced herself upright and took in small sips of air through her nose, letting them out through her mouth. Just like her mother had shown her that first time she'd interacted with the Veil.

"Edie," said Laws, his hand reaching out to hold her elbow, "you don't seem all right. And I think that . . . maybe we should go back. There's something wrong with the air in this place. It's making my head spin."

Edie glanced over at him. So Laws was feeling the effects of the thinning Veil, too. At any other time, she might have enjoyed this. A skeptic getting his first real taste of the spirit world.

But this wasn't any other time.

Instead of answering, Edie forced her body to straighten up the rest of the way and wiped the sweat off her forehead with the back of her sleeve. Then she set her jaw and took a step toward the weak yellow light of the room beyond.

Laws's hand on her elbow tightened, gently but firmly pulling her up short.

"Edie." His voice was whisper-light. "Are you sure you want to do this? It's not too late to go back."

She turned to look at him. And even in the low light, she detected something far too knowing in the young reporter's gaze.

Look, Edie. I know, all right?

She didn't know what he'd meant back in the laundry cart, and at this moment she didn't want to know.

Gently, she extracted her arm from his. He didn't protest. She took in a deep breath and inched toward the corner, flattening her back against the wall. When she was as close as she could be without being seen, she twisted her body so she could peer around the corner.

It was a dark, dank square of basement lined with white metal beds. The kind you might see in a hospital, if the beds in hospitals also had cages around them. Because that's what they were, Edie realized. Metal cages that had been constructed in a square around the beds, ready to trap their occupants inside.

Whoever was being kept down here hadn't even been afforded the space of a cell.

Edie's eyes swept over the space. It looked like only one of the beds was currently occupied; it held a slim figure clad in a dirty white smock. The figure moaned softly. An expression of pain so hopeless and mournful, it was clear they expected no one within earshot to care.

Edie rounded the corner and inched toward the bed. It held a woman with bright blonde hair pinned up in what looked to have once been a rather intricate and stylish coiffure, but that was now matted and tangled. Edie glanced again around the room, and—satisfied that it was empty, besides the inhabitant in the bed—moved again toward the blonde woman.

As soon as she saw the woman's sleeping face, Edie froze.

Laws bumped into her from behind, startling Edie out of her stupor. She launched herself toward the bed and fell to her knees, fingers clutching at the metal wires of the cage.

Her voice was a mix of pain, disbelief, and awe as she choked out a single word.

"Ruby?"

20

There was another whimpering moan from the bed.

And then Ruby stirred in her sleep, her eyelids fluttering but remaining closed.

Ruby.

Ruby, whose spirit she had seen in the Veil.

Ruby, who wasn't dead at all, but was here.

Alive.

Ruby, who had told her to hurry.

"Ruby! Oh, God, Ruby. I'm here!" Edie shook the metal cage. "*Please.* Ruby, you've got to wake up!"

But Ruby only fluttered her eyes again.

Laws knelt beside her. "Do you know this girl?"

Edie nodded, while at the same time taking in every inch of the cage. Where was the lock? There must be some kind of opening they used to get people in and out of these horrible things.

"Who is she?"

Edie stood up and began walking along the cage, her fingers exploring it for any unseen edges. "Ruby Miller," she murmured to Laws. "She's part of our tour. You were supposed to interview her the other night, but—"

"But she didn't show," Laws finished for her, understanding dawning in his voice. "By God. Was she here the whole time?"

Edie shook her head. "I don't know. I don't understand what's . . . just look for a keyhole, will you? Some kind of door or hatch. We need to get her out of here."

Laws stood up and began examining the cage himself. "Edie, what's going on? How did you know about this basement? And why would a medium from your tour end up in this . . . this cage?"

Edie shook her head but didn't answer. She didn't understand what was going on herself. She had been sure Ruby was dead. How else would her spirit have been able to contact Edie in death? She'd been in the wings for many of Ruby's séances, and she'd never once felt even the slightest shift in the Veil. It wasn't possible that Ruby shared Edie's ability to cross in and out of death at will.

Unless she'd been hiding her ability.

And yet even if that were true, it didn't explain what Ruby was doing in this basement or why the Veil was so thin here. Whatever Edie was sensing—whatever was causing this twisting in her stomach—it couldn't be Ruby's doing alone.

Just as she was beginning to despair, Edie's fingers caught on an uneven edge of Ruby's cage. She crouched down and found a small round padlock that blended in almost perfectly with the cage. And now that she knew where to look, she could see the outline of a small square door.

231

"Here's the lock," whispered Edie. "We need to find—"

At that moment, heavy footsteps sounded from the far side of the basement, opposite of the direction the two of them had come from.

Edie and Laws locked eyes. And then her hand was in his again, and they were scurrying to the far edge of the room.

"Over here."

Laws pulled her toward a free-standing wardrobe, wrenched open the door, pushed Edie inside, and then scrambled in after her. The wardrobe was empty, apart from a single wool coat on a hanger in the middle of a horizontal wooden bar. Laws pulled the double doors shut, plunging the tiny space into darkness. The only remaining light came from a tiny crack where the two closet doors met.

Less than a minute later, a high-pitched nasal voice filled the room. "Thank you again for coming, minister."

"The pleasure is mine, doctor. I was intrigued by your note."

Edie's mouth fell open in an audible gasp. Laws clamped a hand over her mouth.

"Yes," replied that first nasal voice—a doctor, apparently. "A very promising result, I must say. I'll be eager to hear your thoughts."

Two pairs of footsteps continued across the basement. One set was quick and erratic, the other heavy and sure.

"This patient, she is one of yours?"

It was the second voice speaking again. A voice that sent chills down Edie's spine. A voice that shouldn't—*couldn't*—be here now.

"Funny thing," replied the nasally voiced doctor. "But she's from one of those traveling acts—charlatans all of them, I've always thought. I'll admit my expectations were not high. But we received reliable information from a . . . *client* of hers, and I must say I'm quite glad we took the chance."

The logical part of Edie's mind told her this was not happening. That what she was hearing could not possibly be true. That the thin Veil in this basement had scrambled her brain. Caused her to imagine what was not really there.

But even as her conscious mind clung to denial, her body shivered with the truth.

She knew that second voice. Deep and serious. With the barest hint of an old lisp.

Her eyes swiveled around the tight, enclosed space of the little wardrobe. It had seemed like such a clever hiding space only a moment before. But now it felt so pathetically insufficient. A single sheet of cheap wood was all that stood between her and the man who held her freedom in his hands.

And it was becoming harder and harder to breathe. Did the wardrobe hold enough air? What would happen if she passed out and crashed onto its floor? He would certainly find her then. Here, of all places.

A little hysterical bubble of laughter worked its way up her throat at that uniquely horrible thought, and Edie was suddenly very glad that Laws's arm was still wrapped around her, his hand covering her mouth. It was both entirely inappropriate and completely necessary, because she could no longer trust herself to not make a sound.

The footsteps in the basement slowed to a stop.

"Here we are," said the doctor. "As I said, still a way to go. But after the unfortunate, er . . . well, that is to say, I'm rather pleased with her body's response to the first dose. Very promising, as you can see here."

There was a pause in the conversation as some papers rustled. And then the second voice spoke again. "This is the correct body temperature? You are sure?"

"Oh yes, quite."

"And yet the pulse of her heart—"

"Stayed strong, yes."

A slight pause. "I see."

"Yes," said the doctor, a smug note in his voice. "I thought you might."

"This is indeed promising. I'm grateful you sent for me so quickly. We shall give her another dosage tonight."

"Tonight?"

"Yes. Now. As soon as can be arranged. Is that a problem?"

"No, no, of course not. It's only—well, another dosage so soon. The thallium can be, well . . . fatal if taken in excess. We wouldn't want another incident wherein we—"

"The incident you speak of has been taken care of. I have assurances from the chief of police himself. Remember, doctor, it is our duty to cleanse the soul. Cleanse the soul, and the body will follow."

There was another pause. A pause in which Edie didn't need eyes in order to know exactly what kind of expression had crossed the second man's face. A furrowing of the brow. A downward turn to the lips. A minor tilt to the head that radiated discontent.

She and Violet both knew that look, and the tone of voice that accompanied it, like they knew the backs of their own hands. It was one of their father's favorites.

"This woman here is a child of God," continued her father. "It is our duty to return her to that righteous path. I do not shirk my duties, doctor."

And yet as terrifying as it was to hear her father's voice *here* of all places, it was the words he spoke that truly turned her blood cold. How had he become this? How could the man who'd once sat her on his knee and spoken in awed, reverent tones about the mysteries of God's plan be speaking with such heartless apathy about a woman's death?

The question that had haunted Edie for years, even before that fateful night a year ago, rose up again in her now: What had happened to the father she'd once loved?

"Well, no. Of course, when you put it that way," said the doctor. "I only meant to say that with a subject this promising, we wouldn't want to—"

"She is in God's hands now. How long until the second dose will show results?"

"Ah. Well. If you insist on . . . yes, all right. She should be ready for observation within the hour. The subject has been sedated, and I'll first need to—"

"Very well. Send for me when you're ready. In the meantime, I will retire to pray for the girl. Her mind may be broken but, God willing, we will save her soul."

"Yes, minister. Of course. Thank you again for coming."

One pair of heavy footsteps receded out of the room and down the corridor. As soon as those faded away, the doctor made a noise in the back of his throat that sounded a lot like a sigh. He mumbled something indistinct and then his light, quick footsteps began puttering around the basement. A minute later, there was a squeak of metal.

Edie leaned forward, toward the crack in the wardrobe doors. Laws's arm—which was still around her shoulders so that his hand could cup her face—tightened against her, but Edie shook her head and then carefully extracted herself from his grip. She pressed her left eye up against the crack between the doors and was just able to see a sliver of Ruby's bed.

It was difficult to make out much from her angle, but it looked like the doctor had opened Ruby's cage and was holding her limp arm out while simultaneously inserting something below her elbow.

Metal clanked again as the door to Ruby's caged-in bed was shut and relocked. The doctor stood and walked over to a long wooden shelf to the left of Ruby's bed. There was some more rustling and the clink of glass striking glass.

Then the doctor turned around. Edie drew back from the crack in the wardrobe, holding her breath as his quick footsteps crossed the room, retreated out into the corridor, and then faded away.

As soon as she was sure he was gone, Edie turned to Laws. "We need to get her out."

21

Edie paced around the basement room. Then she turned back to Laws, who was kneeling in front of Ruby's caged-in bed. "Hurry!" she hissed for the third time in thirty seconds. "He could be back at any moment."

Laws ignored her. Just as he'd ignored her the last two times she'd urged him to hurry up with the lock after they'd failed to find the key the doctor had used. She still had her doubts that he could get the thing open. He'd broken the first hairpin right away—but, thankfully, Edie had plenty to spare.

The only good news was that whatever the doctor had given Ruby seemed to have woken her up a little. She was now moving around on her bed. Still groggy, but slowly coming around. Edie could only hope she'd be able to walk. Her own body was still nauseated from the too-thin Veil, along with the vibrating terror that had taken up residence in her bones since hearing her father's voice.

The lock on Ruby's cage clicked.

Laws let out a soft whoosh of air, and Edie rushed back to the bed. He unhooked the padlock from the cage and opened the square door. Edie reached inside and caught hold of Ruby's arms, carefully guiding her friend out. Ruby's eyes remained closed, her movements sluggish and clumsy, but she didn't fight against Edie's hold.

Laws started down the corridor. "I'll check to make sure the stairway is clear."

Edie nodded and adjusted her grip on Ruby so her friend was half sitting on the edge of the bed and half leaning against her. As they waited, Edie's gaze shifted to a wooden shelf along the left side of the basement room. Her father and the doctor had spoken about some kind of dosage. The mere fact that her *father* was having these kinds of discussions was so incomprehensible that she had to shove the question of *why* from her mind and focus instead on *what*.

What were they doing down here?

Carefully, she detached herself from Ruby so that her friend was leaning against the side of her open cage. Then she hurried over to the wooden table and studied the various glass bottles lined up on the shelf.

She recognized a few of the names.

Laudanum. The medical version of opium. That was likely what had been keeping Ruby under. Calomel. The cure-all Lillian often railed against. Something called Erythroxylum coca that Edie had never heard of. And then a small bottle marked thallium. That was the medicine the doctor had mentioned. The one he had just given Ruby a second dosage of.

Footsteps ran back into the room, followed closely by Laws's whispered voice. "It's me," he said, his breath fast. "Stairway's clear. We should go. *Now.*"

Edie nodded, swept up the bottle of thallium, and dropped it in the pocket of her skirt next to the silk herb pouch. Laws had already gotten one arm under Ruby, and Edie hurried to take the other side. Together, they made their way down the corridor. The stairs, however, were too narrow for three people at once, so Laws took the bulk of Ruby's weight, and even then, he had to sidestep the whole way up.

When they finally made it to the top, they paused on the other side of the door, listening for any footsteps. After a minute, Edie nodded at Laws, and he eased the door open.

The hallway was empty. Edie closed the door behind them and refastened the twin deadbolts. Then she looped her arm around the other side of Ruby's waist, and she and Laws all but dragged her across the hallway into the same small storage closet they'd broken into. It was an ordeal to get the groggy girl through the open window, but somehow, with Edie pushing her from behind and Laws ready to catch her below, they managed to get Ruby out of the building and onto the grounds.

The three of them hurried through the dark toward the black metal gates. It was only then that Edie's steps slowed.

"How are we going to get—"

"I have a plan," said Laws, cutting her off.

"What kind of plan?" Edie hissed.

Laws turned to look at her over Ruby's head and grinned. "Trust me."

❧ ❧

Five minutes later, Edie and a barely conscious Ruby were tucked behind a pair of large oak trees as Laws strode toward the gate, his pen and notebook held prominently in his hand.

"I say," called Laws to the middle-aged white man who was clearly in charge of opening and closing the gate. "What would a fellow like you say to an interview with the *Sacramento Sting* about the working conditions here?"

The man's eyes went wide at Laws's approach. He stood up from the simple pine chair that had been set unceremoniously next to the gate, revealing a large, round belly and a rolled cigarette in his hand. The man looked around frantically, as if expecting another couple of reporters to emerge from the surrounding trees. "How'd you get in here?"

Edie recognized the man's voice. This was the same guard Tom had spoken to when she and Laws had been hiding in the back of the laundry cart.

"*How* I got in is unimportant," said Laws. "The point is that I did. On your watch, it seems. So, how about that interview?"

Edie squinted her eyes and saw the portly man turn his head toward the main building. If he called for help, they'd be lost.

"The name's Samuel, isn't it?" said Laws.

That got the man's attention. He turned back to Laws, his mouth hanging slightly open.

"Now here's the deal, Samuel," Laws continued. "My editor is meeting me on the other side of that gate in . . ."—he paused and made a show of checking his watch—"five minutes' time. And since it was about a half hour ago that I crossed onto these grounds, I'm guessing that if he does publish anything about my little . . . foray, the records will show *you* being on duty at the time of my arrival. Is that right?"

"Now, see here," the man stammered. "I don't know how you got in, but I've got a family to feed, and I can't go about—"

"Ah, I see what you're saying, Samuel. Of course, when you put it that way, the impossibility of you consenting to an interview becomes quite clear. Far be it from me to endanger the livelihood of a family man."

Laws crossed his arms and tilted his head to the side, as if thinking. "Okay, Samuel. Here's what we'll do. I'll explain to my editor that you were unable to consent to an interview, but that you were helpful in providing general background information for this asylum. The date of founding and other innocuous tidbits like that."

The man watched Laws's face intently, mouthing the word *innocuous* to himself as Laws spoke.

"I think," Laws continued, "that will persuade my editor to keep any information leading to you out of the article. He'll be livid at *me*, of course, but it's the least I can do for a family man. How does that sound?"

"Well," said the man, his forehead crinkling deeply. "I think that, uh—"

"Excellent. Then we are agreed. Now. If you'd be so kind as to open the gate, I'll be on my way and will trouble you no more."

The man paused, and although it was hard to see in the lantern light, Edie thought she detected a narrowing of his eyes. "If you got yourself in," he said, voice wary, "I can't see as why you need my help gettin' out."

Laws paused for the briefest of moments. And in that same second, Edie's stomach lurched and her head spun. Next to her, Ruby began shaking uncontrollably. And although she didn't understand why, or how, Edie knew immediately what was happening.

Ruby had opened the Veil.

But only for the briefest of moments. Already, she could feel it closing again.

And then another lurch as the Veil opened . . . and closed.

Opened and closed.

Edie's stomach twisted, and it was all she could do not to fall to her knees. The dizziness in her head was unbearable.

How was this possible? Neither she nor Ruby had lit any herbs.

We shall give her another dosage tonight.

Her father's voice, speaking to the doctor in the basement. Edie thought of the glass vial of thallium she'd slipped into the pocket of her skirt. Was this what the drug did? Was it compelling Ruby to open the Veil?

Next to her, Ruby's body gave a violent jerk, and then she went stiff as a board. Edie bent down to adjust her grip on Ruby's waist and, as she did, her friend's eyelids fluttered open.

Edie froze at the sight.

Ruby was looking back at her—not with her usual hazel eyes, but with eyes of deep black.

But then Ruby blinked, and the glow from the gas lights along the asylum walls caught on a flash of dark hazel green wrapped around the black of her iris.

The drug. It must have dilated her pupils.

"Ruby," whispered Edie urgently. "Just hold on. Hold on for a little bit longer."

Her friend's eyes rolled up and her eyelids fluttered closed again. Distantly, Edie heard Laws speaking again with the man at the gate. Something about Laws's editor. How easy it would be to find the man's full name.

Ruby swayed. If they didn't get her out of here soon, she would collapse.

And then . . . the sound of footsteps heavy on the ground. The groan of metal scraping against gravel. Edie strengthened her hold around Ruby's waist, reached into her pocket to quickly squeeze the leather sheath of her mother's knife for luck, and then darted forward.

She didn't care if the man at the gate was looking her way. She didn't pause to check her surroundings. Ruby seemed ready to pass out at any moment, and since Edie was in no shape to carry her, she'd be forced to choose between leaving her friend behind or staying on the wrong side of those black gates.

She managed to keep them to the shadows at first but was forced to veer into the lamplight when they crossed the threshold of the open gate.

There was a shout from behind them. Followed by a loud *thump*.

A man's voice yelled something Edie couldn't make out, but she didn't turn around.

And then her feet were falling on the hard wooden planks of the raised sidewalks. They were past the gate. Outside the walls of the asylum.

But even as her feet slapped against the wood, she heard the sound of pursuit. Deep voices raised in alarm. She quickened their pace as much as she could; but, beside her, Ruby's legs were failing.

They weren't going to make it.

Ruby would be caught again, only this time she wouldn't be alone. This time Edie would be taken with her. And when her father realized who else had been caught? What would happen then?

A voice sounded from the street on her right.

"Edie! Quick!"

It was Laws. And he was sitting in a plain wooden cart, sporting a bloody lip, and holding the reins of a terrified-looking donkey. Edie stumbled up to the cart, carrying the other girl along. "What," she gasped. "How—"

Laws shook his head. "No time. Here, hand her to me."

Edie tried to haul Ruby up toward the cart, but at that moment the last of Ruby's consciousness gave way, and she fainted outright. It was all Edie could do to catch her before she fell. Laws swore and leapt down from the driver's seat. He took Ruby in his arms and, with a grunt, lifted her up and placed her as gently as he could into the back of the cart.

He turned to help Edie in, but she was already scrambling in after Ruby. "Go!" she screamed at Laws. "Now!"

Laws flew back into the front seat and leaned forward to stroke the neck of the indignant-looking donkey who was braying with an anxious, wheezing sound. Affecting an air of calm Edie did not at all share, Laws muttered soothing words to the donkey, continuing to stroke its neck until—to Edie's immense relief—the animal trotted forward. And while this donkey would never win a blue ribbon for speed, she could have kissed the hairy thing anyway because it was at least faster than the two men who burst out of the gates of the asylum on foot.

They were getting away. For now, at least. And once again, it appeared she had Laws Everett to thank.

22

The donkey cart cleared the asylum and turned right on Fourth Street. Laws urged the poor beast to trot along as fast as its short legs could move. But would it be fast enough? And where could they go?

Laws seemed to be thinking the same thing. "I don't think we can go to the police," he shouted over the rattling of the cart, his eyes glancing back briefly at Edie before turning again to the road. She nodded her head in agreement, and then, realizing Laws couldn't see her, shouted her agreement back.

She'd heard what her father said in that basement about the chief of police. And although he hadn't been specific, Edie was sure he and the doctor had been talking about Nell Doyle's death. She still couldn't make sense of the fact that her father—her *father*—had been the one to say it, but the meaning was still clear as day. The asylum they'd broken Ruby out of was state-run. What was happening in that basement had to be sanctioned. And whatever they'd done to Ruby, they'd done to Nell Doyle first. It had killed her, and the police had covered up the true cause of death.

No. They couldn't go to the police. Or authorities of any kind.

In the cart next to her, Ruby let out a soft, whimpering moan. Edie grabbed a wool blanket that was stuffed in the corner of the cart—it smelled strongly of onions—and wrapped Ruby up in it. She could still feel her friend trying to open the Veil. Could still feel it thinning. Although, by now, Edie had managed to temper her own reaction to it so she was no longer nauseated beyond control.

Leaning forward, she called out again to Laws: "Turn right up there. We need to take her to Lillian Fiore's house. It's on J and Sixth."

"*Lillian Fiore?*" Laws turned again to look at Edie. Even in the faint glow of streetlamps, the incredulity in his bright eyes was clear. "Edie, whatever is going on with that girl, she needs a *real* doctor. Not someone who's going to call on imaginary spirits to help!"

"We're taking her to Lillian," Edie yelled back. "You can drive us there in this ridiculous cart, or I can drag her there on foot. Your choice."

"For chrissakes, Edie—"

"You said you trusted me, Laws Everett? Well, I trust Lillian. And I'm telling you to take us there. Right now!"

❧ ❧

Lillian opened the door in a floral dressing gown that had been hastily thrown over her nightclothes, the kerosene lamp in her right hand revealing a pair of eyes that were still heavily lidded with sleep. But as soon as she caught sight of Ruby's limp body suspended between Edie and Laws, those sleepy eyes snapped to life.

She didn't waste time asking what had happened or why they'd come to her. She simply opened the front door as wide as it would go and said, "Bring her in. Quick."

Lillian lit the way with her lamp as Edie and Laws followed, all but dragging poor Ruby—who was still wrapped in the onion-smelling blanket—between them.

A door at the end of the hallway opened, and a new person hurried toward them. It was Ada, also clad in a dressing gown, a lit candle in her hand.

"Lillian, what has—*Edie*? Is that—"

Ruby chose that moment to wake up.

Edie's stomach lurched as the Veil opened again. A scream tore from Ruby's lips and she started thrashing violently against Laws and Edie's hold. Edie wrapped her arms around her, trying to soothe her. But Ruby resisted, her hands pushing against Edie's waist, hips, and shoulders in her desperate bid to get free.

Swearing under his breath, Laws bent down and swept his arms under Ruby's knees, hefting her flailing body up with a grunt of effort and cradling her in his arms.

Lillian rushed forward and threw open the door to a small sitting room. "In here," she said tightly to Laws, gesturing to an upholstered daybed in the center of the room. "Lay her down there."

Laws obliged. And to everyone's shock, the second Ruby's back touched the daybed, her thrashing stopped and she lay still once more.

After whispering a few hurried instructions to Ada, who nodded and quickly set off down the hall, Lillian lit two wall sconces, filling the room with a soft, hazy light.

"Now," said Lillian, rolling up the sleeves of her dressing gown, her eyes on Ruby. "Tell me what happened."

Edie reached into her pocket and pulled out the little glass vial she'd swiped from the shelf in the basement. "Here. This is what they gave her."

Lillian took the bottle and held it up to the light. "Thallium?" Her eyes cut to Edie. "This has been administered to Ruby? You're positive?"

Edie nodded. "Do you know what it is?"

Lillian's mouth formed a grim line. "It's a kind of poison. A potentially deadly one. Where was she? Who did this to her?"

"We found her in the basement of the Sacramento Asylum for the Insane," said Laws.

Lillian's face drained of color. She nodded once in acknowledgment of this information—her own memories of being drugged in an asylum written clearly on her face—and then she carefully lowered herself to perch on the edge of the daybed, picking up Ruby's wrist to check her pulse. She closed her eyes for a few long seconds. When she opened them again, her gaze found Edie's.

"The Veil. Can you feel how it's—"

"Lillian." Edie jerked her head toward Laws and risked a subtle shake of her head.

But Lillian ignored her. "It's not open, but it's not closed either. I can't quite—"

"Mr. Everett," said Edie, turning to Laws. "Perhaps you would be more comfortable waiting outside while Miss Fiore examines—"

"We don't have time for that," cut in Lillian. "You're the one who brought him here, Edie. Right or wrong, there's no time to correct it now."

"Lillian!" Edie turned back to the healer. "Will you *please*—"

"Mr. Everett," interrupted Lillian. "Do we have your word that you will not speak—or write—about whatever you see or experience here tonight? Remember, if you will, that a young woman's life hangs in the balance."

A brief moment of silence followed Lillian's question, during which Edie didn't dare turn around to look at Laws but, instead, quite literally held her breath.

"Yes," said Laws, his voice quiet and steady. "You have my word."

"Good." Lillian turned back to Edie. "The Veil," she repeated. "It's—"

"Unstable." A tingle at the back of her neck told Edie that Laws was watching her, but she forced the thought aside. Lillian was right. Ruby was all that mattered now. "It's Ruby. She's been trying to open it, but it closes again at once."

"But Ruby's never shown any ability—"

"I know, but . . . I saw her earlier tonight, Lillian. In the Veil. I thought she was dead, but then . . ." Edie hesitated, searching for the words. "Is it possible thallium could do that? Could it give someone the ability to cross?"

Lillian's eyes widened. She leaned over Ruby and lifted her eyelids, peering at the pupils underneath. "If it can," she said after a few tense moments, "it's not working as it should. It's almost as if she's—"

"Trapped," finished Edie, realization dawning as she thought again of the strange way Ruby's spirit had flickered in the Veil. So similar to the spirit her mother had died trying to force beyond.

Lillian nodded, looking back up at her. "She's not like you or Violet. She wouldn't know how to come back. Edie, do you have your herbs?"

Edie met Lillian's eyes and nodded.

She was going back into the Veil.

23

Edie didn't so much as glance at Laws as she took a cross-legged seat on the rug next to the daybed where Ruby lay. If he recognized her position from earlier this afternoon when he'd snuck up on her in Nell Doyle's office, he said nothing about it aloud.

In fact, Lillian was the only one who'd said anything at all in the last several minutes. "You may have to compel her," she repeated for the third time while tucking an extra blanket around Ruby's shivering form, "if she resists."

Edie nodded but said nothing as she pulled a fresh bundle of lavender out from her pouch.

Lillian finished tucking Ruby in and then turned to Edie. "Should I send for Violet? If anything happens, she may be able—"

"No. She's . . . unavailable."

Lillian tilted her head in question. But when Edie volunteered no more information, she nodded once. "All right. I'll do what I can for her body in life. But Edie . . . you need to hurry."

Edie made no response to that, concentrating instead on taking a box of matches out of her silk pouch. She could still feel the heat of Laws's gaze on her, but she once again pushed that thought away, forcing herself to focus instead on Ruby. Ruby, whom she'd thought was gone. Ruby, whom she could still save.

For a brief moment earlier, she'd considered telling Lillian about the shadow in the Veil, but then she'd quickly decided against it. She couldn't risk her friend deciding it was too dangerous for Edie to cross.

Lighting a match, Edie held it to the lavender bundle until it caught flame. Then she closed her eyes and crossed again into death.

A misty field of pale yellow wheat greeted Edie when she opened her eyes in the Veil. The stalks huddled together in thick batches nearly as high as her head.

She swore under her breath even as she closed the Veil and replaced the lavender stick in her pouch. It would be difficult to find Ruby's spirit in a field as thick as this, and she'd hoped to avoid calling out her friend's name—or making any kind of noise—in order to avoid attracting the shadow.

Edie squared her shoulders and set off through the tall stalks of wheat. She'd have to search for Ruby's spirit by eye. With any luck, she wouldn't be too far from her body in life.

She moved in slowly expanding circles, searching inch by inch. A couple of times, she thought she saw a shining person-like shape through the stalks; but by the time she'd reach the place, she would discover it was only the mist playing tricks, gathering together and billowing up in a cloud of fog that appeared humanlike until Edie jumped forward, her fingers closing together on nothing but freezing-cold air.

It was hard to keep track of time in death, but Edie estimated it had been a quarter of an hour since she'd crossed from life, and still there was no sign of Ruby's spirit.

What if the poison had won out? That doctor in the asylum had said it could be fatal. Edie was convinced that the drug had killed Nell Doyle. What if—

Edie yelped as she tripped over a bit of uneven ground, falling forward and crushing stems of wheat with her knees. Cold mist closed in around her, thick and white, but before she could push herself up to continue her search, she caught sight of something bright on the ground next to her.

A light that flickered in and out.

"Ruby?"

Edie clamped her hand to her mouth, immediately regretting the volume of her voice. Shaking her head at her stupidity, she fell to her hands and knees and crawled forward toward the flickering light. Toward what she hoped was her friend's spirit.

She reached her seconds later, and was both relieved to have found her and dismayed at her state.

As before, Ruby's spirit was flickering wildly. And now that Edie knew what to look for, she could see that Lillian's assessment had been correct. Ruby's spirit had not fully crossed into death. But neither was she still in life.

She was somehow trapped in between.

And the flickering wasn't the worst of it. The light from Ruby's spirit was far too low. A sign that her spirit was succumbing to the pull of a final death. Edie needed to open the Veil properly and get Ruby back to life before that pull won out.

Raising herself to her knees beside Ruby, Edie leaned in close and whispered her friend's name.

"Ruby, it's Edie."

Ruby didn't react. Her eyes remained closed, her spirit spasming with each flicker of light, giving no sign she'd heard Edie at all.

"Ruby," Edie tried again. "We need to cross back into life. I need you to open your eyes and do exactly as I tell you."

Ruby's only response was to let out a soft moan.

You may have to compel her.

Lillian had warned her, but the thought of binding her friend's spirit to her own will felt profoundly wrong. That was something only done to restless, troublesome spirits. To those who'd overstayed their time in the Veil.

Edie rummaged in her silk herb pouch until she found a bundle of rosemary, the memory herb Violet had used to help Edie remember her ties in life. She struck a match and set the herb on fire. Moments later, a light blue smoke rose up in spirals. Edie directed the smoke toward Ruby until she was surrounded in a sheen of shimmering blue.

A few seconds later, Ruby opened her eyes.

"Edie?"

Her voice was weak.

"Ruby! Oh, Ruby, I'm so happy to—but we don't have time for that now. Listen. We have to go back. I need you to—"

But Edie stopped talking as a look of horror crossed Ruby's face. Her friend's eyes had gone wide, and she was frantically shaking her head back and forth. So fast that, between the flickering and the rapid movement of her head, her spirit form appeared as a blur.

"No," said Ruby, muttering under her breath. "I won't go back to it. Don't make me go back."

"Not to the asylum," said Edie, leaning closer to her friend. But Ruby gasped in terror at Edie's movement, continuing to violently shake her head.

Ruby tried to push herself up off the ground, but she wasn't strong enough to stand.

"Please," she moaned again. Her voice was ragged and weak. "I can't." Reaching out with flickering hands, she grabbed a stalk of wheat and half-crawled, half-pulled herself away from Edie. "Too strong. I can't—"

Her words broke off in a sob.

Edie's heart sank. Ruby had remembered, all right. And she was terrified of the memories the rosemary smoke had brought back.

Edie knew what she had to do next, although she hated herself as she extracted the bundle of hellebore from her silk pouch. But if Ruby wouldn't allow Edie to help her cross back into life, then Edie would have to force her by taking away her free will and binding her spirit to Edie's instead.

Ruby continued to moan the word *no* over and over again, dragging herself farther and farther away as Edie lit the hellebore, its distinct coffeelike scent filling the misty air.

Apologizing silently in her mind, Edie drew on every ounce of her focus and sent the hellebore smoke hurtling toward her friend. Shimmering pale pink ribbons wrapped around Ruby's spirit in a web of crisscrossing binds. Within moments, her spirit collapsed and her struggling ceased.

Keeping her eyes firmly fixed on her now-immobile friend, Edie extracted the lavender from her silk pouch and lit the herb alight. She was acutely aware that one errant thought, one moment of distraction, could sever her link with the binding herbs. Or, worse, send Ruby's spirit to a place Edie did not intend.

So she didn't so much as blink as the soft purple lavender smoke filled the mist with its calming scent, allowing Edie to carve out an opening in the Veil wide enough for Ruby's spirit to pass through.

"I'm so sorry," said Edie again, this time aloud. Closing her eyes, she took hold of her friend's spirit and gave her an unceremonious *shove* toward life.

Ruby could only obey.

24

Edie blinked open her eyes to a field of flowers. Delicate yellow daisies dancing in the glistening sun. And underneath her, something soft and plush that didn't feel at all like a field of wheat. Or the rug next to Ruby's daybed.

"You're awake."

Her eyes flew open the rest of the way. This time, they met a pair of worried brown irises. "You've been out for almost half an hour," said the voice connected to the eyes. "Miss Fiore, Miss Loring, and I were beginning to worry."

Edie's mind struggled to make sense of what this person was saying. It was harder than it should have been. There was something wrong with her head. It seemed to be spinning in circles. She closed her eyes again, and a single image flashed against her eyelids.

Ruby. Her flickering spirit succumbing to Edie's will, forcing her back into life. The bind draining Edie's strength.

Her eyes snapped open again, and this time she took in the reality of her surroundings. She was not in a field of flowers. She was in what she now recognized as the main sitting room in Lillian's rented house. The flickering gaslight sconces along the walls cast shadows on the yellow wallpaper, making it appear as though the illustrated flowers danced.

Edie herself was lying on a settee. Laws was sitting in a chair to her left, his brown eyes catching the light from a candle on a side table nearby. As soon as he saw her looking at him, he leaned forward in his chair. "Edie. What—"

"Oh, good, you're awake." Lillian bustled into the sitting room, a chipped, flower-patterned teacup balanced in her hands. Laws stood up, retreating to the fireplace, and Lillian immediately took over his chair.

Edie pushed herself up to a sitting position. "Ruby. Is she—"

"Resting comfortably," said Lillian. "Ada's watching over her. Now, drink this."

Lillian held the steaming teacup up to her lips, but Edie shook her head. "I need to speak to Ruby as soon as possible. It's important."

Lillian sighed and tipped the teacup back, forcing Edie to choose between opening her mouth to drink or allowing the hot liquid to dribble down her chin. In the end, it was a combination of both.

Fortunately, after Edie had spluttered and gulped down half the cup of ginger-lemon tea, Lillian seemed to decide that was enough because she set the cup down and said, "You won't be speaking to Ruby at all tonight. You may have brought her spirit back, but her body is still suffering the effects of that horrible drug. I gave her something to help her sleep. She'll be out the rest of the night."

"But . . . isn't there anything you can do to wake her up?"

"Not," said Lillian, with a stern look, "without compromising her already-precarious health."

Edie's face went hot at the judgment in Lillian's eyes. "Of course, you're right. I'm sorry. It's only—"

Edie paused and shot a look at Laws. He stood in profile to her, appearing to inspect a few knickknacks on the mantel. But Edie didn't assume for one minute that he wasn't straining to hear every word she and Lillian said.

She lowered her voice to a whisper. "The thallium. Lillian, I think it does allow someone to cross. Except—"

"Except without your control."

Edie nodded. "But why force it on someone? Ruby was too unstable to contact or influence a spirit. What would be the purpose?"

Lillian shook her head. "I don't know, Edie. I've been thinking about it, and all I can say for sure is that it's dangerous. And I could be wrong, but I have a theory that it only had this effect on Ruby because she had some inherent ability with the Veil. One I doubt she was even aware of. I don't want to even *think* about what effects that same drug might have on you or Violet."

An image of the flickering spirit her mother had faced rose into her mind. Had that spirit been a victim, too? An experiment like Ruby? Had her mother sought the spirit out on purpose? And why had it been so vital that she force it beyond the Veil?

Some of Edie's frustration must have shown on her face, because Lillian reached out and patted her knee. "Whatever the

260

answer is, we aren't going to find it tonight. You're done in. You need to go back to the hotel and get some rest. Mr. Everett has agreed to make sure you get there in one piece."

Edie's eyes went reflexively to Laws. He was looking directly at them now, no longer pretending not to eavesdrop.

She looked back at Lillian. "I'm not sure that's the best idea."

"It's the *only* idea. We're out of beds with Ruby here, and in your state I don't trust you to get home alone." Lillian looked Edie up and down. "Do you feel steady enough to walk?"

"Lillian," said Edie again, her voice pleading. "I really can't—"

"If you are still too weak to walk," said Laws from the fireplace, the tone of his voice making it clear that he'd heard every single one of her whispered words, "I would be more than happy to employ the services of a carriage."

Begrudgingly, Edie looked over at Laws and met his eyes from across the room. The look he gave her made it absolutely clear that the moment they were alone, he was going to ask every single question he'd been holding back since they rolled past those asylum gates.

You brought him here. Right or wrong, there's no time to correct it now.

Lillian's words. And from the expression on Laws's face now, she supposed she was about to find out the exact price of that trust.

Edie set her jaw and pushed herself up off the settee, pleased to find her head much steadier after the concoction Lillian had forced down her throat. "There will be no need for a carriage. I'm perfectly capable of walking on my own."

Laws nodded. Then he crossed the room and stood by the entrance to the hallway that led to the front door. The reporter in him was clearly ready to get the interrogation underway, but Edie ignored him for the moment, turning to Lillian instead. "You'll let me know the moment she wakes?"

Lillian nodded. "I promise. Now go and get some rest."

Edie hesitated. It felt wrong to leave Ruby here. Ruby, who may be the only person alive who had the answers Edie sought. But, on the other hand, she also knew Lillian was right. It had been a very long, very tiring day. A glance at the clock on the mantel told her it was half past midnight now. If she was going to have a chance of figuring any of this out, she was going to need some sleep.

And Ruby would be safe here with Lillian and Ada. She could also be sure of that.

Edie nodded and thanked Lillian again for her help. Then she swept past Laws and threw open the front door.

◈ ◈

The air was cool as Laws and Edie stepped out into the night. He paid a boy to return the donkey cart to the shopkeeper he'd hastily borrowed it from, and then he and Edie turned toward her hotel without a word.

She'd been expecting the barrage of questions to begin right away and was therefore surprised when they walked the first two blocks in silence, only the occasional rattling of a late-night carriage or hack filling the quiet between them.

She was so distracted by this unusual reticence on Laws's part that when they cut across K Street at the intersection of Third, she wasn't paying attention to the terrain, and the hem of her skirt caught on one of the omnibus tracks, nearly landing her flat on her face. Edie yelped and Laws instinctively reached out and grabbed her arm just in time, steadying her.

She untangled her skirt and regained her footing; but when they started walking again, Laws didn't let go of her arm. And somehow she found herself not pulling away. This close, she could easily smell the faint scent of sandalwood clinging to his skin.

Silence continued to stretch between them; each second driving Edie more and more mad. All she'd wanted since meeting this boy a couple of days ago was for him to stop asking questions and leave her alone. And now here she was, desperate to know what was going on inside his head.

She was about to give up and start the dreaded conversation herself when Laws suddenly stopped walking. His hold on her elbow pulled her up short, and she twisted around to face him.

"Why did you let me believe you were a fraud?"

Surprised, Edie blinked up at him. "What did you just say?"

He took a step toward her. "If you're truly able to cross into the spirit world, why did you let me—no, why did you *encourage* me—to think you were a fraud?"

Edie stared back at him. She wasn't exactly sure how she'd expected this conversation to go, but Laws quickly and easily accepting the reality of death—and her ability to cross into it— was *not* one of them.

She raised her eyebrows. "What makes you so sure I'm not a fraud now?"

"No. You can't do that with me now, Edie. Not after what I saw happen back there with you and your friend Ruby."

"Maybe it was a trick. You said it yourself. Us mediums are full of them."

His grip tightened on her elbow, letting her know exactly how he felt about having his words thrown back at him. "And what," he asked, his voice lowering, "about what happened in the asylum? Are you going to try and deny that, too? You forget that I was there with you in that wardrobe. That I *felt* your reaction when that minister—"

"Don't!"

"—spoke. And while I'll be the first to admit there's a lot going on here I don't understand, I know more than you—"

"You don't *know* anything, Lawrence Everett." Heart pounding, Edie tried to take a step back, but Laws pulled her closer instead.

"I know," he said, his gaze fixed on hers, "that Bond isn't your real name. I know you and your sister are not, in fact, alone in the world. I know your mother is dead, but that your father is very much alive. A circuit preacher based in Marysville. A well-respected family man who is desperate to find his runaway daughters alive."

Stunned, Edie could do nothing but stare at him.

His eyes swept over her face, assessing her, before continuing. "I know you told me that I knew nothing about you and nothing about your life. I know I wanted to change that, and so I asked my editor about you and your tour. He was in San Francisco for a couple of years before this, and I thought your name might ring a bell. It didn't. But then I told him a little more about your sister and your trances on stage. I happened to mention the difference in the color of your hair."

His eyes drifted up past Edie's face, landing on the white-blonde hair piled atop her head. Her face heated under his perusal.

"And that's when my editor told me about some gossip he'd heard while covering a mayoral election up north in Wheatland a year ago. A story about a well-liked circuit preacher who'd lost both his wife and his twin daughters in the same night. The wife had died, and the daughters had run off. It was the description of the twins that stuck with him, though."

With his free hand, Laws reached up and pulled loose a strand of Edie's hair. Holding it between his forefinger and thumb, he turned it over, examining it in the moonlight. "The twins were described as identical. Except for the hair. One auburn. The other pale blonde."

Carefully, almost reverently, he tucked the loose strand behind her ear. His fingers, warm and rough with calluses, hovered at the place where her pulse thrummed against her throat.

"I'm fairly positive I know *who* that minister in the basement was tonight, and that I know now why you and your sister ran. I also know I meant what I said outside those asylum gates. About your needing help."

His fingers trailed along her throat, pausing when he reached the corner of her jaw. Edie fought the urge to lean into his hand. She needed to get away from this boy who'd seen too much. *Knew* too much.

"I know," he said, his lip twitching, "that you want nothing more than to run right now. I know running is what you do when you're scared. And I know you are terrified right now."

Edie jerked at his words. She made to pull her elbow out of his grasp, but Laws reached down and took her hand instead, pressing it flat against his chest, his hand covering hers.

His hold was loose. She could have easily broken away.

She should break away.

But then he was speaking again, his voice low and soft, his eyes boring into hers.

"I know you were incredibly brave tonight. I know I haven't been able to stop thinking about you since you first barreled into me on that sidewalk. I know that as soon as I saw you again in the Metropolitan lobby, a part of me realized I'd never want to let you out of my sight again."

Closing the last of the distance between them, he tilted his head toward hers. "But there's still one thing I *don't* know, Edith Bond."

His breath skipped across the delicate skin at her throat as he spoke. Edie's fingers curled into a fist, the fabric of his shirt twisting in her hands. She could feel the beat of his heart against her palm. Fast and racing. His pulse matching her own.

"I still don't know," he whispered, his lips so close she could almost taste them, "if you're ready to trust me back."

For a long moment, Edie found it impossible to breathe. All she could do was stare into Laws Everett's eyes. Eyes that stared back with an intensity that set her blood on fire. And then she was lifting her chin. Going up on her toes. Pressing her lips to his.

She knew she shouldn't. Knew that this wasn't just a kiss, but a promise. A promise to trust this boy with the truth about her and Violet's past. The truth about their lives.

You've become so good at lying, Edie.

Violet's words.

She didn't want to lie anymore.

As soon as her lips touched his, Laws responded in kind. A soft growl rumbled in the back of his throat, and then Edie wasn't thinking about anything except the feel of his hand tightening against her waist. His fingers spreading across the small of her back, pulling her close. His other hand tracing the edge of her jaw before settling at the base of her neck, tilting her head so he could deepen the kiss.

And then her hands were moving, too. Traveling up his arms, his neck, and tangling in the curls of his hair.

When she accidentally knocked his hat off his head, they both pulled back in surprise.

Laws laughed softly. Edie laughed, too, and started to apologize, but Laws only shook his head, pulled her close, and kissed her again.

And even as she kissed him back, reveling in the feel of his lips moving against hers, a small voice inside her insisted that she shouldn't be allowed to feel this way. Warm and safe in this boy's arms. Not with her father's chilling words still ringing in her head. Not with the image of Ruby's tortured face haunting her mind.

But even as she acknowledged that truth, she recognized another one as well.

She wanted this.

This boy.

This moment.

His ink-stained fingers soft and steady as they cradled the back of her neck. The sighs deep in his throat. The answering sighs in hers.

This feeling of being known. Seen. Of not running away, but running *toward*.

And so she threaded her fingers more deeply into his hair, pressed her lips more firmly to his, and let herself have it.

25

The next morning, Edie woke to bright sunlight streaming in through the hotel's lace-curtained windows.

It had been well past two in the morning by the time she'd finally returned last night. She and Laws had spent at least an hour on a park bench around the block from her hotel, Edie telling him, in between kisses that made her melt, everything he needed to know about why she and Violet had run. About their real abilities. Her mother's list of names. Frances Palmer's true identity.

About their father's threat.

Laws had been confident that he could uncover a money trail that would reveal who was supporting—or at the very least turning a blind eye—to whatever experiments were going on in the basement of the state-run asylum.

"I can find the connections," he'd said again, holding her in his arms a few feet away from the hotel lobby doors. "But Ruby's disappearance won't go unnoticed. You should keep your head down for the next couple days. Nothing to draw unwanted attention."

Her face warmed at the memory of what had come after those words. A final good-night kiss that had started off quick and light but had rapidly transformed into something else. Something that had left them both panting for breath.

Smiling, Edie sighed and stretched her arms above her head. The clock on the bedside table told her she'd slept in late—it was already ten o'clock—but that still gave her hours until Violet was due back from the city for their séance with Mary Sutton that evening.

A séance they might have to cancel. Her stomach twisted in disappointment at the thought. And then it twisted in something else.

Hunger. She was *starving*.

Rising, she quickly got dressed and headed down to the hotel dining room, where she wolfed down toast, two hard-boiled eggs, and a cup of coffee. After checking to make sure Lillian hadn't sent her a message, she finally managed to make it down the hallway for the bath her body had been craving. She kept it short, but it was no less wonderful for that.

Back in the room, she brushed out her long wet locks, spread them over her shoulders to dry, and retrieved her bundles of herbs. Once Edie finally told Violet everything about the shadow, their father's inexplicable presence in the asylum, and Ruby's narrow escape, she may very well want to cancel their appointment with Mary Sutton. And she'd probably be right to do so. It seemed wholly inconsequential in light of yesterday's revelations. But at the same time, she and Laws had both agreed that it would be prudent for Edie not to make any noticeable alterations to her schedule. And there was the still-undeniable fact that opportunities like this—money that meant *real* independence—didn't come around often for girls like them.

So she'd decided to prepare the herbs anyway. Just in case.

Picking up the blue skirt she'd worn yesterday, she reached into the pocket for her mother's bone-handled knife.

But it wasn't there.

Quickly, she dug her fingers into the other pocket, but the knife wasn't in there either.

Holding up the skirt, she gave it a vigorous shake, but nothing fell from its folds. Dropping to her knees, she began a thorough search of the floor, rifling through the various articles of clothing Violet had left strewn about in her haste to pack last night.

After several minutes of frantic searching, Edie was forced to accept that her mother's knife wasn't anywhere in the room.

Had she lost it last night?

She remembered running her fingers over the leather sheath for luck just before she'd made a dash for the asylum gates with Ruby at her side. Could she have lost it afterward in the jostling donkey cart? Or was it possible that Lillian might have it? It could have slipped out of her pocket when—

Edie froze in the act of picking up a lace chemise, the cream-colored garment fluttering to the floor as a vivid memory from last night flashed in her mind.

Ruby's sudden return to consciousness. The way she'd crashed into Edie halfway down the hallway of Lillian's house. Her hands gripping Edie's waist to keep herself from falling. Those same hands dropping against Edie's right hip. It had only been for a moment, but—

A terrible possibility rose into her mind. She didn't want it to be true. It *couldn't* be true, and yet. . . .

I won't go back to it. Don't make me go back.

Black eyes staring up at her in the moonlight.

In less than a second, Edie went from eerily still to a blur of motion. She threw off her dressing gown and shoved herself into the first available clothes she could find. Her hair was still damp and loose about her shoulders, but she didn't have time to care.

The beat of her heart kicked up to a fevered pace and stayed that way as she raced down the hotel stairs and burst through the double doors into the late-morning light. A clatter of hooves announced the arrival of a hansom cab. Without sparing a thought for the expense, Edie yanked open the door, yelled Lillian's address to the driver, and threw herself inside.

The horse set off at a trot, and the cab lurched forward. A distance that had taken Edie and Laws twenty minutes to walk last night took only ten minutes in the hansom. But as Edie paid the driver and sprinted up the steps to Lillian's porch, a blood-curdling scream sounded from inside the house, telling her she was already too late.

Gripping the handle, Edie tried to push open the front door, but it was locked.

"Lillian!"

Edie banged against the door with her fist.

"Lillian, let me—"

"Nooooooooooooooo!"

That was Ada's voice. Barely recognizable through the hacking sobs.

"Give it to me, Ruby."

Lillian. Her tone was calmer than Ada's, but it was clear from the palpable tension in her voice that she was scared.

No, it was clear she was terrified.

Edie turned sideways and threw her shoulder against the door. It didn't budge.

"Please, Ruby," said Lillian again, her voice raised loud enough to be heard over Ada's sobs. "Give me the knife. Ada—no. Let her have her space. Ruby and I are talking now."

"That isn't Ruby," cried Ada. "Lil, please. She doesn't—"

But Ada's warning was drowned out by a low, guttural sound. A scream of pure, unfiltered agony.

"Ruby, no! Ada, we have to stop her. Ruby—"

"*Stay away!*"

The voice that growled those words both was Ruby's voice and was not Ruby's voice. It was as if her usual laughing cadence had been tainted.

Influenced.

Possessed.

Pulling back her fist, Edie banged it again against the door. She grabbed the door handle with both hands and shook it so hard, the wood frame rattled.

She screamed Ruby's name.

I won't go back to it. Don't make me go back.

When Ruby's spirit had said those words in the Veil, Edie had been so sure she was talking about the asylum, that she hadn't wanted to go back to that basement of horrors.

But that wasn't what she'd meant at all.

Too strong.

I can't.

A sob racked Edie's throat. She called Ruby's name again. The knuckles of both her hands were red and bleeding from pounding against the wooden door, but she didn't notice or care.

The truth of what had happened was so clear to her now. Ruby's black eyes hadn't been a side effect of the drug. They had been a sign of the shadow possessing her, just as it had tried to possess Violet on stage.

The thallium had forced Ruby to open the Veil, and the shadow, mindless in its hunger to reunite with the spirit that left it behind, had forced its way through that opening and into Ruby's body in life.

But Ruby had fought, refusing to relinquish control. The flash of hazel Edie had seen in her eye was evidence of that. When it became too much, Ruby had escaped into death. To the one place the shadow would not follow.

Don't make me go back.

Too strong.

I can't.

But Edie had cut off her escape. She'd weakened her by suppressing her will. Then she'd forced her back into the battleground that was her body in life.

Ruby hadn't stood a chance.

Without warning, the front door to Lillian's house flew open, and Edie stumbled forward. Strong hands gripped her shoulders, keeping her from falling, and Edie looked up into Ada's tear-stained face. There was a thin scarlet slash across her left cheek.

"Ruby," Edie choked out, her voice hoarse. "Is she—"

Ada shook her head. Not letting go of her grip on Edie's shoulders, Ada led her around the corner to the sitting room.

Lillian was there. Sitting in the middle of a braided blood-stained rug. Ruby's curly blonde hair fell in a curtain across Lillian's lap, her head lolling back at a strange angle.

Edie's knees gave out.

Ada tried to hold her upright, but Edie pushed out of her hold, fell the rest of the way to the floor, and crawled on hands and knees to where Lillian sat sobbing over Ruby's slack, unmoving form.

She didn't need confirmation to know that Ruby was dead. She could feel it. But she reached out anyway and pushed aside the sheet of curly blonde hair.

Bright red blood poured from a jagged cut across Ruby's throat. It pooled in Lillian's skirt and ran down Ruby's neck, chest, and arms in tiny gruesome rivers.

Numbly, Edie dropped her gaze to Ruby's limp hand. There, in the center of her palm, lay Edie's mother's bone-handled knife, its metal blade drowning in Ruby's blood.

Her eyes didn't leave the knife when, after several long moments, Lillian spoke in a hoarse, halting voice.

"The sedative wore off this morning. We tried to . . . restrain her. But we didn't know about the knife. She went after Ada first. Then me. And then she . . . oh God."

Lillian dissolved into sobs again. A hand landed on Edie's shoulder, squeezing it gently.

"Just before she . . ." Ada shuddered, looking away from Ruby's crumpled body. "It was the only time she was herself. She saved us."

A dazed remoteness settled over Edie as she forced her gaze away from the bloodied knife and back to her friend's empty body.

It was sometimes possible to bring a spirit back to life if you acted swiftly enough. But Edie could feel, even from here in life, that, like her mother, that would not be possible with Ruby. Whatever she had done—or whatever the shadow had done to *her* once Ruby had forced them both back into death—had severed the link between her body and her spirit permanently.

Ruby was gone.

And it was Edie's fault.

Again.

She was only dimly aware of what happened next. At some point, she found herself sitting on a bed—Lillian and Ada's, perhaps—with a mug of tea growing cold between her palms.

Sometime later, a tug on her hair told her that someone was brushing the tangles out of her now-dry locks and braiding the strands into a rope down her back.

Her bloodstained clothes were removed from her body. And then a voice—Lillian's, she realized—was speaking in a low, soothing tone. Telling her that she and Ada were taking care of everything. That Edie was in shock. That she needed to rest now.

The last thing Edie remembered was her head resting against a pillow as her eyes, heavy with unshed tears, finally gave up and fell shut.

26

Edie woke to voices outside the bedroom door.

The sunlight, which had been streaming in through the lace curtains earlier, had faded to dusk. A lit oil lamp on the bedside table cast the room in a soft yellow glow.

"You can't stop me, Lillian. I need to see my sister right—"

"But she's only just—"

"I don't care."

The door to the bedroom flew open, revealing Violet's frantic face. She was still wearing her traveling clothes, and there were loose curls frizzing about her face, thanks, no doubt, to her trip up the river.

"Edie. What—"

"Ruby's dead."

Somehow, Edie had managed to push herself up into a sitting position on the bed. She was only wearing her linen shift, and the chill from the early-evening air bit into her bare arms, but she didn't draw the covers around herself. Whatever numbness her earlier shock had provided was gone now, replaced with a burning ball of grief and shame lodged deep in her chest. She welcomed the cold.

Behind Violet, Lillian slowly closed the door, giving them privacy.

Violet threw off her cloak and hat, but didn't advance farther into the room, hovering just inside the doorway. Her gaze was a mix of wariness and concern as she took in her twin.

"Lillian said Ruby was possessed. But I don't understand how that—"

"It was a shadow," said Edie, her voice low and hollow. "The same shadow that tried to force its way into your mind the other night."

Violet's forehead creased. "But that was a fading spirit. You said—"

"I lied."

She tried to keep Violet's gaze. Tried to force herself to face what she'd done. But when her sister's eyes went wide and she silently shook her head in confusion, Edie looked down at her hands in shame.

"No," said Violet. "You wouldn't do that. You wouldn't keep something like that from—"

"I did." Edie's words came out forcefully. Tonelessly. It was the only way she could manage them. The only way she could keep the twisting ball of fire in her chest from erupting and consuming her whole. She need only hold it at bay a little longer. Just long enough to tell Violet what she needed—no, what she *deserved*—to hear.

"And that's not all I lied to you about," Edie continued. "Last night, I didn't tell you that I'd seen Ruby's spirit in the Veil. I thought she was gone then. But I didn't tell you, even though you'd been right to worry. You *knew*, and I didn't listen—"

"Edie, even if we had—"

"No," cried Edie. She wouldn't allow Violet to comfort her. Not when there was still so much she didn't know. "It's my fault, Vi. They had her. In the basement of that horrible asylum. And *he* was there. Father was there, and they were forcing her to—"

"Father?"

Edie's eyes flashed up at the tremor in her sister's voice. Violet was no longer standing but had sunk into an overstuffed reading chair to the left of the door. She was staring back at Edie with wide, confused eyes. "I don't understand. Why would—"

"No," cut in Edie bitterly. "You don't understand. And that's *my* fault. Just like it's my fault Ruby died. Just like it's my fault—"

White-hot pain tore through her chest. Inside, a dam was breaking. There was fire in the back of her throat. A blinding sting behind her eyes. And then the tears she hadn't yet shed for Ruby came crashing through her in angry, blistering waves—the force of them so strong, she struggled to breathe.

"Just like it's my fault," said Edie, forcing her words out between the gasping sobs, "that Mother never came back."

"Edie . . ."

"You were right last night." Tears continued to streak down her cheeks, but Edie managed to find just enough air to get the next, vital words out. "I did lie to you about what happened in the Veil that day. I told myself I was protecting you. Protecting *us*. That if I could just find out what *really* happened. Who she'd met with. Why she had the belladonna—"

"*Belladonna?* Why—"

"But that was just another lie. I was never going to tell you, Vi. I *couldn't*. I—"

"You can tell me anything, E. I promise, no matter what it is."

"I *can't*. Even now—"

A fresh sob cut off her words. It clawed its way up her throat and stayed there, blocking her voice. Cutting off her air. Black dots blurred her vision.

Black like Ruby's eyes.

Black like the smoke curling up from her mother's hand.

Despair tore through her at the realization that she was going to fail at this, too. Violet deserved the truth now. Had *always* deserved it. But Edie was too broken, too much of a coward, to give it.

And then it was as if a weight had been lifted off her body. The grip on her chest eased, and her lungs filled with air. Something warm and soft pressed against her tear-soaked face.

Violet's cheek, leaning against her own.

It took several long minutes of being held; several deep inhales of her sister's familiar rose-oil scent mixed with the musk of travel for Edie's breathing to fall back under control. And when it did, it was Violet who spoke. Her voice a whisper against Edie's skin.

"I think it's time now, E. Time for you to tell me everything."

Closing her eyes, Edie pressed her cheek more firmly against her sister's. Then she took a deep, trembling breath and, in a halting voice, she began.

CR SD

The sun had fully set by the time Edie finished speaking. Her throat was raw, her eyes were rimmed red, and her head was pounding. But at least she could say, for once, that she'd left absolutely nothing out.

Violet had been as shocked and confused as Edie was about their mother's procurement of the belladonna. She'd asked Edie a multitude of questions about the list of names she'd found, despairing—as Edie had—that none of them could shed light on the identity of their mother's final client or the strange spirit she'd encountered in the Veil.

"And what about that letter from your dream?" Violet had asked. "N.D. *has* to be Nell Doyle. This poor Madame Palmer woman. But why didn't she come when you called her in the Veil?"

Edie had shaken her head. It was something she still didn't fully understand. Although after what had happened with Ruby, she did have a horrible guess.

"Lillian thinks thallium enhances any inherent ability with the Veil, and according to her, Nell Doyle had plenty. Much more than Ruby. If they did to her what they did to Ruby, she would have been forced to open the Veil. The shadow would have sensed it. Crossed. Possessed her. But before anything could happen—"

"The poison killed her."

Edie nodded. "Thallium is fatal if taken in excess. That's what that doctor said."

"And after her body died, after her spirit crossed . . ."

Violet trailed off.

An image of a little boy flashed into Edie's mind. William Brown, in a nightshirt that fell just past his knees. The shadow breaking him apart. Absorbing his spirit.

It was, in all likelihood, the same fate Nell Doyle had met. Once her ability to open the Veil was gone, the shadow would have had no more use for her.

When Edie told Violet about hearing their father's voice in the asylum basement, her sister hadn't said much at all. Only wrapped her arms more firmly around Edie, holding her tight.

And that was how they lay now. Wrapped in each other's arms, the blankets from Lillian and Ada's bed heaped over them, their breathing evenly matched.

After a few more moments of this, Violet sat up in the bed and looked down at Edie.

"Come on."

Edie blinked up at her.

"You need to eat something. Or at least drink a glass of water."

But Edie didn't want to move. She wanted to stay this way forever, wrapped in the safe cocoon of her sister's arms. Delay indefinitely the realities that awaited them outside this room.

Violet was, however, nothing if not stubborn, and she soon had Edie out of bed, wrapped in one of Lillian's dressing gowns, and sitting at a small round table in the middle of a modest kitchen. She set the kettle to boil and slid a plate in front of Edie. It contained two pieces of bread, heavily buttered just the way she liked it.

"Eat," said Violet, her voice vibrating with a rarely used tone of command.

It had been hours since Edie's hurried breakfast in the hotel restaurant, but she still wasn't the slightest bit hungry. She forced herself to take a bite anyway.

Violet busied herself with making the tea while Edie continued to chew mechanically. There was no sign of Lillian or Ada. Had they taken Ruby's body away?

Two steaming mugs landed on the table with a soft thud. Violet followed soon after, sliding into a chair across from Edie. Lifting one of the mugs to her lips, Violet prepared to take a sip, paused, and then set the mug back down.

"I have to tell you something."

Edie paused mid-chew, lifting her eyebrows.

"It's not the right time for it. But I don't want to keep it from you either. It's something that could . . . change things."

Chewing her lip, Violet stared down into her untouched mug of tea. Whatever this was, she was nervous about saying it. Worried about how Edie would react.

Edie swallowed the lump of bread a little too quickly, coughed, and then managed to say, "Tell me, Vi. Whatever it is."

Nodding, Violet continued staring down into her tea. Then, in a voice so soft Edie almost couldn't make out the words, she said, "I got it."

Edie's brow wrinkled. "Got what?"

Violet's eyes lifted. They were wide, but not with fear or sorrow. No, these eyes were bursting with barely contained excitement.

"I got the part in the play. Rehearsals start next week for a three-month run in San Francisco. There are plans for a tour after that. Maybe even all the way to New York."

Edie's mouth fell open, but no words came out.

"It means leaving the medium tour," Violet continued, her words coming out in a nervous rush. "I wouldn't be going with you all to Oregon. It means—"

She was cut off by the sound of Edie's chair legs scraping against the wooden floor. In less than a second, Edie had rounded the table, pulled Violet up, and wrapped her arms around her. "I'm so proud of you," she whispered fervently into Violet's ear. She thought she'd used up the last of her tears, but there were fresh ones streaming down her face now. "You did it, Vi. I am so, so proud."

Violet let out a surprised, hesitant laugh. "But you're crying, E. Do you really—"

"Happy tears." Edie released Violet and held her at arm's length so she could see her properly. "I'm happy for you. So incredibly happy."

"You don't mind that—"

"No."

"And you won't—"

"Of course I'll miss you. But this is your shot, Vi. You have to take it. I *want* you to take it."

Violet searched her face for another few moments. Edie let her. She had nothing to hide from her sister. Not anymore.

And apparently it was enough. Because a split second later, Violet's face broke out in an ear-splitting smile. A squeal erupted from her throat, and then her arms were wrapped around Edie's neck.

"Oh, Edie," she sighed against her cheek. "Do you think it's possible to be both deliriously happy and also terrified and heartbroken all at the same time?"

Edie settled Violet's head more securely between her neck and shoulder as her mind touched on the still-raw grief of Ruby's death. On the tremor of absolute terror the memory of her father's voice sent thrumming through her veins. All this wrapped up in an overwhelming pride she felt for her sister, and the unbridled relief of being truly connected to her once more.

"I think it must be possible," Edie whispered back. "Because that's exactly how I feel right now."

For several long moments, the sisters stood there in silence. Holding each other.

Then Violet straightened up and stepped back from the embrace. Tilting her head, she fixed Edie with a determined stare. "I think we should keep our appointment with Mary Sutton tonight."

Edie blinked once. Twice. And then she shook her head. "We can't. Not with—"

"No, listen. That appointment, that reward money . . . Edie, that's *your* dream. True independence. If you get that money, you could have that dirty farm you talked about."

"I don't think I really want a—"

"Your inn, then. Or anything else you want. The point is that you would have *choices*. That's all Mother ever wanted for us." Stepping forward, Violet reached out and took both of Edie's hands, squeezing them. "I found my choice, Edie. And I made it. I want you to find yours."

Despite everything, a flare of desire rose up in Edie at her sister's words. "But what about the shadow? It's still in the Veil. It might be stronger than ever, after Ruby—"

"We'll be fast," cut in Violet. "First sign of it, and we'll close the Veil. It might mean not getting the money in the end, but at least we'll have tried."

Edie opened her mouth to protest that it was still too dangerous, but once again Violet headed her off. "Plus, we know it's there now. If you have to cross, you'll keep lavender at the ready. And you know the shadow won't be able to possess me the way it did Ruby."

Edie couldn't deny it. Unlike poor Ruby, Violet knew how to control—or at the very least *resist*—spirits that entered her body. If the worst happened, she could hold on long enough for Edie to close the Veil. And it was also true that Edie *had* escaped quickly into life the last time she'd encountered the shadow in death.

"I don't know, Vi. It seems—"

"Risky? Dangerous? Ill-advised and exciting?"

Edie let out a little laugh. "Yes. All of those things."

"Then let's do it, Edie. Let's go get what you want. Let's get what you deserve. Together. Okay?"

Edie looked into her sister's bright, determined eyes.

Together.

For the first time in a year, she and Violet truly were together, with no more lies and secrets between them. She'd forgotten how strong that made her feel. How utterly invincible.

She didn't need to say the words. Violet read the decision on her face. With a squeal of excitement, she lunged forward, planted a kiss on Edie's cheek, and then rushed off toward the hallway.

"You'll have to wear the spare outfit I packed in my valise," she yelled back over her shoulder. "Thank goodness I couldn't decide which one to bring. And then I need you at the dressing table, Edie. We have less than an hour before we should leave, and I'll need at least half of that to deal with the *travesty* that is your hair."

27

The scent of magnolia blossoms and ripening oranges filled the air as Edie and Violet made their way up the tree-lined walkway to Mary Sutton's stately Queen Anne–style house.

Before leaving, they'd found a note from Lillian in the sitting room explaining that she and Ada had gone to see a local client of hers whose *discretion* she trusted.

Discretion for Ruby's burial, Edie's thoughts had filled in, her heart sick as Violet read the note aloud.

When they reached the wide porch of the Sutton home, Violet shot Edie a bracing look and squeezed her hand. But before she could reach out and knock, the door swung open and a tall, ginger-mustached butler, dressed in a suit finer than anything Edie had ever seen their father wear, filled the door frame.

"The Miss Bonds, I presume?"

Without waiting for an answer, the butler ushered them inside.

"Dr. Sutton will see you now. If you'll follow me?"

He led them down a richly decorated hallway and into a room that was unlike any lady's sitting room Edie had ever seen.

A mix of distinctly feminine articles—rich, luxurious carpets; silk, floral-patterned upholstery; and elegantly carved end tables—sat side by side with towering piles of thick medical tomes, half-unrolled anatomy depictions, and even a fully articulated skeleton propped up on a stand by the window.

It was the kind of room Edie had never dreamed of having but now wanted desperately for herself. Although, in her fantasy, she'd swap out the medical titles for ones on law and philosophy. But the principle of the room would remain the same. Trappings of knowledge that were currently reserved for men, strewn unapologetically in a woman's domain.

And there, sitting at a small round table in the center of the room was the woman Edie and Violet had risked so much to meet.

Mary Sutton was much as Edie remembered from her spying session behind the curtain at the Metropolitan Theater. Her dark hair was fashionably but simply arranged, and her pale skin was powdered just so. She was immaculately dressed in a stylish mauve suit with a matching purple jewel sparkling against her throat. Only the slight smudge underneath her eyes hinted that she might spend her evenings reading in low light.

As the sisters entered, Mary stood up from her chair, the eyes above those dark circles—so light blue they appeared almost grey—crinkling with a genuine smile as she approached them.

"Welcome, welcome."

Her voice was rich, resonant, and brimming with inner confidence. She reached out her hands to Violet first, pulling her close and kissing her twice, once on each cheek. Then Mary turned to

Edie and repeated the gesture. "I cannot tell you how wonderful it is to *finally* meet you both. Although," she added, grey eyes twinkling, "I suppose I am at the advantage, having already seen you both on stage."

"The pleasure is ours, ma'am," murmured Edie. Next to her, Violet smiled and murmured something equally indistinct.

"Now," said Mary, gesturing back toward the table set up in the middle of the sitting room, "you must let me know if we've arranged everything to your satisfaction."

They followed her back to the table, where three unlit candles had been set up in a circle atop a white lace tablecloth. "Your Mr. Huddle assured me you needed only a few candles," said Mary as she took her seat at the table. "But I am rather used to the mediums I meet needing quite a few more supplies."

"Mr. Huddle is correct, ma'am," said Violet, taking the seat Mary offered her. Edie followed suit, sitting in the chair to Violet's right and Mary's left. "It's best to dim the lights before we begin— to better welcome the spirits—but a little candlelight won't scare them off." Violet took her own silk pouch out of her pocket and extracted a small brass dish. "We've brought everything else we need with us."

She placed the dish at the center of the table and proceeded to empty the last of her dried lavender petals into the dish.

Mary watched the process with rapt fascination. "Oh, how wonderful." She reached out a single gloved finger and nudged the herbs inside the dish. "I saw you burn something similar on stage the other night, dear. Do tell me, what is its purpose?"

"The herbs," said Violet smoothly, quite used to this question, "assist us in contacting the spirit world."

"How fascinating." Mary gave the herbs another gentle poke with her finger, and then raised her eyes again to look at Violet. "How lucky, my dear. That you possess such an extraordinary gift."

"Yes," said Violet. "I thank our great Lord every day that he saw me fit to bear it."

The lady murmured a polite agreement and retracted her hand from the herbs.

"Well," said Edie, with a quick look at Violet to confirm that she was ready. "If you'd like, ma'am, I believe we're ready to begin. All that's left to do is turn down the lights."

"Lovely." Mary rang a small silver bell at her elbow. "I am so eager to begin."

A moment later, the ginger-mustached butler reappeared, this time carrying a tray with a single glass cup balanced in the middle. He deposited the tray in front of Mary, who thanked him and then asked him to lower the lamps. As the butler set about turning down the gas wall sconces, Mary sipped from the cup he'd brought.

"I'm afraid you must think me rude," she said, indicating the cup. "But I can assure you that you would not want to partake in this particular draft. It's rather bitter stuff. A new medicine mixture I'm experimenting with that must be taken at very particular times."

"Oh, not at all," said Edie in a polite tone. And then, because her curiosity got the better of her, she went on to ask, "Do you often experiment with new medicines on yourself?"

"Oh yes." A gleam of excitement lit in Mary's eye. "Some of my ideas are rather . . . new, I suppose you could say. And as one of the few women in my field, finding study participants is not always easy. And besides, I could hardly ask a patient to take anything I myself haven't tried, could I?"

Edie returned her smile.

The butler put out the last of the lights and withdrew. The only illumination now came from the pair of flickering candles Violet had lit in the center of the table. Edie glanced at her sister, who nodded her head.

"My sister will soon enter into a trance," said Edie, pitching her voice low. "She will then attempt to call forth the spirit of the one you seek. Is there a name that she might call to those on the other side?"

"A name will not be necessary. The spirit I seek is by my side. If your sister's gift is true, they will come to me without being called."

Edie dipped her head. She'd expected this response. Mr. Huddle had told the twins that every other medium had tried—and failed—to secure a name for the spirit Mary Sutton sought. It simply meant that Edie would indeed need to cross into the Veil and hope the spirit in question was as close by as she claimed.

And that she would find it before the shadow appeared.

Next to her, Violet spoke. Her voice solemn and soft. "We are ready to begin."

Violet held out her hands, palms up, and the three women interlaced hands. Edie had borrowed a thick pair of gloves from

Lillian's wardrobe in the hopes that they, along with the barely there candlelight, would keep Mary Sutton from noticing the change in her body when she crossed into the Veil.

"Shall we begin with a hymn? 'In the Sweet Bye and Bye,' perhaps."

Edie closed her eyes and took a deep breath to begin the first verse but was quickly cut off by Mary.

"I believe we can dispense with the hymn portion of the evening." The edge to her voice was unmistakable, and Edie felt another jolt of kinship with this woman.

"Very well," said Edie, taking the adjustment in stride. She glanced sidelong at Violet, but her twin didn't need the reminder. She'd already let go of Mary's and Edie's hands so she could light the lavender in the brass dish. Within seconds, a steady stream of light grey smoke was spiraling into the air, and Violet had retaken Edie's and Mary's hands.

"Now, if we could all close our eyes," murmured Edie. "And turn our energies inward."

Edie waited until she was sure Mary had obeyed this request. Then she closed her own eyes and tuned her senses toward her sister, waiting for Violet to open the Veil. As soon as she did, Mary's hand jerked in hers. An unconscious response to the strange sensation that accompanied the opening, and a sign that she was more sensitive to death than most. Not uncommon among healers, nurses, and doctors who had visited their fair share of deathbeds.

Edie squeezed Violet's hand to indicate she was ready. Then she took a deep breath and crossed into death.

A gust of wind blasted her in the face.

Edie blinked open her eyes but was immediately forced to close them against the force of the gale. Mist swirled around her in angry, frantic swarms, and she had to cup both her hands over her eyes in order to open them a tiny slit. But even then she could see very little. The mist was too heavy and thick to see more than a couple of feet ahead.

Her first thought was that she'd never be able to find the spirit Mary Sutton sought in this.

Her second was that she'd never known death to take on the aspect of a storm.

And then, as if in answer to both those thoughts, something bright appeared on her right. A spirit moving toward her like a bobbing lantern in a sea of fog.

She stayed very still as the spirit approached her. With the Veil as uncharacteristically turbulent as this, she didn't want to accidentally scare it off. She would let the spirit come to her, and then she'd find out if it was the one with which Mary wanted to talk.

As the spirit drew closer, she was able to make out what appeared to be the form of a woman, her hair pulled back in a simple, elegant knot.

There was something familiar about the way she walked. The way she tilted her head and looked at Edie as she approached. But it wasn't until the spirit was a few arm's lengths away that she realized why.

"So," said the spirit of Mary Sutton, her bright features coming fully into view. "This is death."

28

Edie stumbled back as Mary's spirit drew closer, allowing her to see what had previously been obscured by the thick mist.

Mary's spirit was flickering in and out.

She'd been dosed with thallium.

But how? When? And why would someone—

"The cup."

Edie whispered the words, but Mary heard them. She smiled and stopped walking. "You're as much to thank for my presence here as the thallium, Edith. Until now, I've only managed to catch glimpses of this place."

Mary tilted her head up, taking in the storming clouds of mist. At the same time, Edie thrust her hand into her silk pouch and pulled out a box of matches.

"Although, I must admit, your mother implied there would be a bit more beauty than this."

Edie froze, an unlit matchstick in her hand.

"Tragic, how she died."

Edie's grip on the matchstick tightened. "How did you know my mother?"

Mary's eyes ran up and down Edie's spirit form in a hungry kind of way. "If only I'd known Lena had daughters, it would have saved us so much time."

At the reference to daughters—plural—Edie's insides unfroze. She had to get back to life. Back to Violet.

She struck a matchstick and then cursed when a gust of wind blew out the flame. Mary watched her pull out a second match with the same clinical interest she'd shown at the séance table only moments ago, making no move to stop her. Edie didn't pause to wonder why. This time the flame held, and as soon as the lavender smoke thinned the Veil, she closed her eyes and crossed.

The first thing she heard in life was a scream.

Violet's scream.

Her eyes flew open at the same moment that someone clasped a pair of cold metal manacles around her wrists.

Everything came into focus quickly after that. The lamps in the sitting room had been relit, the steady hiss of gas filling the air. The ginger-mustached butler was back and was standing in the center of the room, talking to a man in a police uniform with two silver bars stepped onto his sleeve. She recognized him at once as the thin-lipped detective who'd been investigating Nell Doyle's death.

Next to Edie, Mary's eyes blinked open. Without sparing Edie a single glance, Mary stood up from the table and made her way to the butler and the detective.

A second, younger officer was in the process of clasping a pair of manacles on Violet's wrists. This had been the source of her sister's scream.

"You'll be quiet," said the young officer as he closed the second handcuff around Violet's wrist. "And you'll do what you're told."

"And why," screeched Violet, "would I do that?"

Violet tried to stand up from her chair, but the young officer pushed her back down.

Across the room, the detective—Detective Barney, Edie distantly recalled—bowed his head to Mary and spoke in a solicitous tone. "My apologies that you have to see this, ma'am. But I'm afraid these two fit the description we told your man here about."

The detective nodded to the ginger-haired butler, who returned the gesture with a civility teetering on boredom. As if a trio of officers arresting two young women in the middle of his employer's sitting room was not out of the ordinary at all.

"What *description*?" cried Violet. "We were engaged for a private séance, and as far as I know, that isn't against the law. Will someone please tell me what the *hell* is going on?"

Mary reared back, as if Violet had slapped her in the face. "Oh, dear," she said, shaking her head with a great degree of dramatic effect. "The girl is quite deranged. You say it was *murder?*"

The police officer behind Edie chose that moment to yank her up from her chair. Cold metal bit into the sensitive flesh at her wrists, causing her to yelp in pain.

"It's looking like a kidnapping gone wrong, ma'am," continued Detective Barney. "We received a tipoff about some out-of-town folk who abducted an invalid from the local asylum for their own devil-worshipping purposes. It seems their . . . *ritual* went wrong and the girl wound up dead."

"Kidnapped?" cried Edie.

At the same time that Violet screeched, *"Devil*-worshipping?"

The police officer who was detaining Edie yanked at the metal cuffs around her wrist, causing another sharp burst of pain. "You'll both be quiet," he hissed. "Unless you want to confess to murdering the girl right here and now. Save us all some time."

"Expect they'll hang," said the younger officer who was now hauling Violet toward the hallway. "Nasty, the way they cut out that poor girl's throat."

Violet twisted around, her frantic eyes seeking out Edie's.

They'd seen Ruby's body.

Coming fast on the heels of that realization was another. *Had they arrested Lillian and Ada, too?*

"I must apologize again, ma'am," the detective was saying to Mary, "for barging into your home like this. The manager of their so-called *tour* was quite reticent to give out your address, but it was urgent that we find these criminals before they managed to slink away."

"Oh, I quite understand, Detective. And I applaud your commitment to justice. Truly."

There was a theatrical quality to Mary's voice now when she spoke. She didn't sound at all like the warm, intellectually curious woman who'd welcomed them into her home.

"But if I may," she continued. "I've had the opportunity to observe these young women. I myself am a medical doctor, and it is my firm belief that they are both suffering from an acute case of mediomania, and cannot—"

"No!" cried Edie.

"—reasonably be held accountable for their actions. It is therefore my professional recommendation that they both be delivered to the local asylum, where I will have the opportunity to oversee their treatment myself."

Edie surged forward, ignoring the dig of metal against her wrists as the officer held her back. "Don't you *dare*! Don't you—"

"If you'd like," said Mary, speaking over Edie, "I could subdue them for the journey. As you can see, the disease can make them quite . . . rabid."

Mary looked at her then. Her eyebrows raised in challenge.

And all at once, Edie understood how this woman had known their mother. Why she knew about her death.

Mary Sutton had been her final client.

This séance. The reward money. It had all been some kind of trap. For reasons Edie still didn't understand, Mary Sutton wanted to find mediums with the same abilities as their mother. And Edie had played right into her hands.

A scream from Violet pulled her back into the present moment. Her sister was being hauled out of the room.

"Edie!"

"Vi!" she called back. "Violet, I'm—"

Mary Sutton stepped forward, blocking Violet's retreating form from view. Her gaze raked Edie up and down, a fanatical light gleaming in her grey eyes. "I'm so glad to have found you, Edith. You and I are going to do great things."

Edie's eyes shot to where the detective stood behind Mary. Surely he'd heard that strange comment. Surely he'd insist that *before* Edie and Violet could be turned over into her hands, their case must be heard by a judge?

But that's not what Detective Barney said. Instead, he inclined his head toward Mary in a respectful bow. "I'll take my leave now, ma'am. A pleasure, as always."

With a grunt, the officer holding Edie's manacled hands pushed her forward. She stumbled over her feet, and he let her fall to her knees. When he yanked her up again, she felt a sharp pain in her left shoulder.

A pleasure, as always.

Mary had done this before. With other women. Other *mediums.*

Ruby.

Nell Doyle.

The mediums from Belden Place? Women who'd been picked up for indecency by another police department and then never heard from again.

"You're a lucky girl," sneered the officer behind her. "To have a nice, respectable lady take an interest in saving a pretty little neck like yours."

Lucky.

The word echoed through Edie's mind as she was thrown down the front steps of Mary Sutton's house.

Lucky.

Violet was already in the back of the police wagon when Edie was roughly shoved in. Her sister's hands—like Edie's—were shackled.

Lucky.

The two wooden doors to the wagon were left open, affording passersby a full-on view of the two young women huddled inside. Two young women whose lives were supposed to truly begin today.

When the officers returned, each carrying a cup of what Edie knew to be the sedative Mary Sutton had promised, Violet fought tooth and nail against it, half the liquid spilling down the side of her cheek.

But Edie, knowing that all was already lost, simply tilted back her head and opened her mouth. The liquid was sour as it trickled down her throat, but she forced herself to swallow every single drop. And when the darkness came up to claim her, she embraced it without a fight.

29

When Edie woke, she was in a cage.

She was also dressed in a white smock stained yellow from too many washings, the herb-pouch she always kept in her pocket was gone, and she was lying on top of a reed-thin mattress. But she didn't need to sit up and get a proper look around to know where she was. She was lying on a caged-in bed in the basement of the Sacramento Asylum.

Another thought burst through the fog of leftover sedatives. *Violet.*

Violet would be here, too.

Edie jolted upright so fast, the top of her head collided with the ceiling of the metal cage around her bed, the clang echoing in the cavernous basement. Wincing in pain, she turned to her right and discovered a figure lying on the bed next to hers, so close that the metal links of their individual cages were almost touching.

It was dark in the basement. The few gaslights along the wall were turned down low, producing a dim, muddy light. But a single kerosene lamp on a nearby table allowed Edie to make out Violet's shape through the metal caging. She was curled up on her side, her back to Edie, dressed in an almost identical smock.

Edie got on her knees and leaned toward the second bed.

"Violet!"

She didn't dare raise her voice above a whisper. Violet rolled over, her face catching the light, her eyes red and puffy from crying.

Whatever defiance she'd shown earlier in the police wagon was gone. She looked resigned now. Lost. It made Edie sick to see it.

You and I are going to do great things.

Mary Sutton's final words came back to Edie. Clearer now than they had been earlier, when the shock of the woman's betrayal had still been fresh.

You and I.

No mention of Violet. No mention of Edie's sister who could not cross into death.

And all of a sudden, Edie knew what she needed to do.

Reaching into her hair, she dug out one of the multitude of hairpins Violet had used to create her coiffure in preparation for the séance. Moving quickly, she straightened the pin and curved one end of it with a twist of her fingers, just as she'd seen Laws do last night.

The round holes in the cage were only about two inches wide, but Edie managed to poke two fingers through, the hairpin extended between her pointer finger and thumb.

If she could just get the end of the pin into the lock . . .

"Vi," she said, as she attempted to twist her fingers into an impossible angle. "I'm going to try to pick these locks. If I can, you need to run. There's a hallway to our left, but it ends in a door that's locked from the outside. So you should take the exit on the right instead. I'm not sure where it leads, but I think it's your best—"

"What do you mean *I* should take it? If you get those locks open, we'll go *together*."

Edie shook her head. "She only wants me, Vi. I don't understand why, but I know that if you leave before she . . . I think you can get away. You just have to—"

"You want me to *leave you here*? That's your plan?"

The hairpin slipped from her grasp, landing with a soft *ping* on the basement floor. Edie banged her free hand against the cage. "*Yes!* My God, Violet, yes. Don't you see? We wouldn't even *be* here if not for me! Mary Sutton was in the Veil when I crossed."

"But how—"

"Her spirit was flickering. In and out." Edie tore another pin from her hair, straightened it, and twisted its end. "I think it was thallium that she took before the séance. But she needed *us* to open the Veil for her. And she knew about Mother, Vi. I think . . . I think Mary Sutton was her last client. I think she's been looking for me—or someone like me. The reward money was a trap all along. And I walked us right into it."

"Edie, I—"

But Violet's words were cut off by the sound of a door creaking open. Then the thump and squeak of wheels rolling along the concrete floor. Several pairs of heavy footsteps approached, growing louder and louder until a dark shape took form just outside the pool of lamplight.

A man stepped into the light.

He was dressed in a black suit with a white clerical collar around his neck. When his eyes landed on the twins locked inside their cages, his dark eyes narrowed. Edie scrambled back to the far end of her caged-in bed. Next to her, Violet let out an involuntary whimper.

A second figure stepped into the pool of lamplight, a bright purple jewel glittering at her throat.

"Now, girls," said Mary Sutton. "Is that any way to greet your father?"

Edie stared at the man before her.

Her father.

The same man who'd once promised that his God would always keep her safe. Who'd taught her how to speak in front of a crowd, even if he'd never intended her to use the skill. She tried to reconcile that man with the one staring at his daughters now, with nothing but icy contempt.

There was another whimper from Violet's neighboring cage. Followed by a different sound. Soft and hissing.

Edie tore her gaze away from their father and looked at her twin. Violet's eyes were wide, her face pale. And she was whispering something. The same word over and over again.

Eyes.

The eyes.

Edie's head whipped back, taking in their father properly for the first time. She'd heard his voice last night, but she hadn't seen his face—a face that had grown haggard in the past year, his cheeks sunken and hollow. The severe black suit and white collar couldn't hide how loose his skin hung on his bones. Even in the low lamplight, she could make out a sheen of sweat along his upper lip and across his brow. And there were deep shadows underneath his eyes.

Eyes that were a deep brown.

Which was impossible.

Because her father's eyes were blue.

"*You!*"

Edie's voice emerged like a growl, and a deep male laugh filled the space in response, her father's face—no, *not* her father—twisting into a sneer.

And then the sneer was wiped away by what seemed like an involuntary jerk of his head. His eyes flashed, and for just a moment—no more than a second—they were no longer brown, but a deep inky black.

Before Edie could understand what she'd seen, her view was blocked by a pair of male orderlies wheeling a hospital bed past her cage. Lying in the bed was a middle-aged man with greasy, unkempt hair. His body was covered with a dirty white sheet and his eyes were closed.

"Leave him there. By the table."

Mary Sutton's voice. Rising above the squeaking wheels.

A clang of metal on her right brought Edie's attention to Violet's caged-in bed. The man who was not their father was opening the door to Violet's cage.

Edie surged forward. "Don't touch her! Whoever the hell you are, get your hands off my—"

"But Edith, dear." Mary walked calmly toward Edie's cage. "Don't you recognize your dear papa?"

"That man," spat Edie, "is not our father."

Her mind flew back to that day a year ago. The flickering spirit advancing on her as she ran for life. Their father, already in the sitting room when she crossed back, the Veil wide open behind her.

But no. It wasn't possible. Her mother had taken the flickering spirit with her.

"The belladonna." Edie's voice came out like a croak as she turned to the man in the minister's garb. "She forced you beyond. She took you with her."

The man wearing her father's body turned to face her, a cold unfamiliar smile curving onto his lips. "Your dear mother did her best to kill me, girl. She might have succeeded. Had you not come to my aid."

All of the air left Edie's body. Her lungs fought to breathe, but it was no use. A tight band had formed around her chest. Viselike in its grip.

It had been her.

She'd been searching for the medium who'd brought a spirit into life and allowed it to possess a living body.

It had been her.

The flickering spirit had outrun the belladonna, just as Edie had. She had opened the Veil and it had followed her into life, possessing the first living body it found.

If the spirit had tried to take over Violet's body, her twin would have known to resist, as she had with the shadow at the theater.

But her father . . . her father wouldn't have understood what was happening. He would have made the perfect vessel to possess.

Distantly, she was aware that the man possessing her father's body was still speaking.

". . . the man—your *father*, I suppose I should call him—put up a fight. It was some time before I could wrest control of his mind. When I did, I was forced to subdue him. It's why I had no memory of you for so long, Edith. But now I've found you, and I can thank you at last."

Her mother's death. Her final sacrifice. It had been for nothing. Because of her.

"No, Edie! Don't listen to him. This isn't your fault. *They* did this. You can't let him—"

"Silence!" cut in Mary, her voice cold and hard. "Keep up this racket, and I'll sedate you again. Your presence is required, but I don't need you conscious. I suggest you remember that."

The lash of those words forced Edie's mind back to the present. She sucked in a gulp of air, forcing her lungs to fill, and then focused on Mary. "What do you want?"

"I should think that's fairly obvious. I want you to save my husband."

309

Edie blinked in surprise. "But you aren't married."

Had Mr. Huddle's research been wrong?

"Not legally, no." Mary's eyes shot to the possessed form of their father, affection softening her face. "But my soul is wedded to Henry's, and his to mine." Looking back at Edie, she said, "You won't find a record with the county clerk, however. I'm sure you understand why, Edith. It's one of the reasons I so enjoyed the speech you made the other night."

The sincerity of the compliment made her insides twist. A few hours ago, praise from Dr. Mary Sutton about Edie's views on marriage laws would have filled her with pride. Now it only served to reinforce how blind and naive she'd been.

"Henry, do prepare the girl. I'd like to be ready should our friend here need . . . inducement."

The man possessing her father—*Henry*—reached into Violet's cage and grabbed her arm, yanking it forward. Violet yelped in pain.

"Wait," cried Edie. "You don't have to . . . just tell me what you want. *Please*. You don't have to hurt her."

But Henry didn't stop. He held Violet's arm in one hand, and with the other he rolled up the sleeve of her white smock, exposing the skin above her wrist.

"You shouldn't worry, Edith," said Mary as she strode toward a wooden table filled with medical supplies. "Henry is a doctor as well. And he has quite a lot of experience controlling hysterical females while keeping them alive."

Something about Mary's words struck a familiar chord in Edie's mind; but before she could identify it, the woman paused and muttered something under her breath to the two orderlies who'd wheeled in the unconscious man on the hospital bed. Nodding once, both men turned on their heels and left without a word.

"You know," said Mary, as she picked up a silver, glass-barreled syringe and filled its chamber from a vial marked THALLIUM, "you look like her. It's the hair, I think."

In the cage next to her, Violet was struggling against Henry's grip. But Edie could see that her efforts were useless. He was too strong. They weren't getting out of here through physical force.

Think.

Mary wanted something from her. And whatever it was, it was connected to their mother. Maybe if she could finally understand what had happened that day, she could find a way out of this.

"You met with my mother before she died," Edie said to Mary's back. "What did you want from her?"

Mary finished filling the glass chamber and returned the now-empty thallium bottle to the table. Then she turned around, the needle in her hand.

"I went to your mother for help. My Henry was dying and so, woman to woman, I asked her to help me save the man I loved. I'd already found a way to separate his spirit from his wasting body." She tapped the thallium-filled needle for emphasis. "But I ran into a problem with the patients I used in my initial experiments. I could separate their spirit, yes. But when I tried to bring that same spirit back into another form—into a new, healthy body—I failed. I could send them *into* death, but I couldn't get them *out*."

Edie heard Violet's sharp intake of breath behind her, but she kept her eyes focused on Mary. "How did you find my mother? Why did you go to her?"

Mary raised an eyebrow. "A good scientist knows their weakness, Edith. I certainly know mine. And so I did my research. You'd be surprised what a good amount of money, paired with a sob story of grief, can accomplish. Once I ingratiated myself with the right circle, your mother's name came up again and again. She was, apparently, the best at finding a loved one beyond the grave. And I wanted the best."

The final words of Nell Doyle's letter rose into Edie's mind.

. . . grief seems genuine. And yet I find myself compelled to advise caution, my dear.

Edie's eyes flicked again to the unconscious man on the hospital bed. "My mother would never have helped you with a forced possession."

"Not willingly, no."

Edie shook her head. She was missing something. If her mother had known Mary's true intention, why would she have gone into death that day at all?

"You tricked her."

Edie and Mary both turned toward Violet. Henry still had hold of her arm—the angle looked painful—but her sister stared past him toward Mary as she spoke again. "She did offer to help you. Just not the way you wanted."

Mary glared at Violet, and, for the first time all evening, Edie detected a crack in the woman's coolly detached facade. When Mary finally spoke, her voice was low and deadly. "The only *help* your hypocrite of a mother offered was more death. Even after I let her believe my Henry was already dead. That his soul cried out in agony for me. Even after I assured her that the body I had prepared for him had no mind of its own to care. Even then, all she offered him was *peace* beyond. As if he could ever have peace without me."

Mary's eyes flashed to Henry, tears springing to her eyes. But Edie was riveted not by Mary's display of emotion, but by the look Henry gave her as he stared back. Pure, unfiltered adoration. An expression she hadn't seen cross her father's face in years.

Edie closed her eyes. "You agreed," she said softly. Almost to herself, although she knew her voice carried. "She went into death that day to send your husband's spirit beyond the Veil, at your request. She thought you were both in agony, but she didn't know his body was still alive. It's why he was able to resist the binding herbs."

His tie to life wouldn't have helped him against the belladonna, of course. Just as it hadn't helped their mother. But Edie had taken care of that. She'd allowed him to escape.

"But if he was still alive," said Violet, "then how was his spirit able to—"

"He wasn't alive the whole time," interrupted Edie.

The sudden thinning of the Veil. The one part Edie still hadn't understood.

She looked back at Mary. "You killed him, didn't you? While my mother was in the Veil. That's why it thinned so suddenly. How did you know when to do it?"

Mary's eyes still glittered with unshed tears, but her voice was steady as she answered. "Thallium doesn't sever a spirit from its body entirely. I watched him until I saw signs of a struggle. Until I knew Lena had found him in death. And then I . . ." Her breath hitched, but she didn't stop. "I told him to do whatever he had to do. I told him to find his way back to me. And then yes, I freed him from a diseased body that no longer deserved him."

Edie stared at Mary. She and Henry had both taken a terrible risk. It was only luck—and Edie's stupidity—that had allowed their plan to work.

Mary had been desperate. Willing to sacrifice everything for a slim chance of giving her husband a second, stolen life.

"And he did find me," continued Mary. "But then he sickened again."

Edie glanced at Henry. And as she did, she caught another flash of black in his eyes. Another involuntary jerk of his head. She ran her eyes over her father's wasting body. The hollow of his cheeks. The sickly pallor of his skin.

Understanding dawned, and she realized why Mary was equally desperate now.

"The shadow," said Edie. "They're still bound, and the pull from death is draining him."

"A complication," hissed Mary, "that I was ignorant of because your *dear mother* refused to help us. But you aren't going to make the same mistake she did, Edith. You are going to open your precious Veil. You are going to cross into death as you did this evening, and you are going to force Henry's shadow into life. You will free him from this last tether to death. You will make him *whole* again. And then you are going to give him a new life."

Mary jerked her chin toward the unconscious man in the hospital bed. "His mind is corrupted. Believe me when I tell you it will be a mercy when Henry takes him."

Edie met Mary's eyes. "And if I refuse?"

"Then I'll continue with my experiments." Mary glanced meaningfully at the thallium-filled syringe in her hand. "Your friend Ruby was the most promising of the mediums so far, and there have been *quite* a few, Edith. But you stole her away before I could find out if pretty little Ruby Miller could hold the Veil open long enough for my purposes. Perhaps we will have better luck with your sister. Or perhaps she will die too quickly, like poor Nell Doyle, the woman who thought she could hide from me. I cannot say. Thallium is . . . *unpredictable*." Mary raised her shoulders in a delicate shrug. "The choice is yours."

Edie turned toward her twin, despair welling inside her. She'd stalled as long as she could. Learned as much as Mary would willingly tell her. And she still didn't know how to get them out of this basement alive.

She expected Violet to share in her hopelessness; but instead, her sister met her eyes with grim determination. Keeping Edie's gaze locked with her own, Violet slowly lowered her chin.

Trust me.

Then Violet turned to Mary, her voice echoing in the basement as she said, "I'll do it. I'll open the Veil."

30

Edie stared at her sister in silent horror. A scream of denial was lodged in her throat, held back only by the look Violet had given her.

Trust me.

Mary turned toward Violet, her head tilting slowly to the side. "Unless I misjudged your abilities on stage the other night, you are the twin who can channel spirits but lacks the ability to cross into death."

Violet raised her brows. She was wearing a stained white smock, and her arm was still clasped at an awkward angle in Henry's grasp; and yet somehow she managed to look like a queen as she said, "I don't need to cross into death to reunite your husband with his shadow."

Mary stared at Violet, quietly assessing. Then she shot Henry a look, and he released Violet's arm and took a step back. He'd given Violet enough room so that she could have jumped out of her open cage and made a run for it. But Violet, perhaps aware that she was unlikely to get far, didn't seize the opportunity. Instead, she straightened up on her bed and held Mary's gaze.

"You can bring his shadow into life?" Mary asked. "Cut off the drain on his spirit and then assist him in possessing a new form?"

"I can."

Mary pursed her lips. "Dare I ask why you would offer your help so willingly? When it's clear your sister will not?"

"That's easy," said Violet. "Edie thinks it's her fault that our mother died. She doesn't want to help the person who killed her. But I don't think about it that way."

"You don't?"

Violet shook her head. "I want to live, Dr. Sutton. I want my sister to live. Do you know that directly before coming to your house this evening, I was at an audition in San Francisco? I got the part. I'm going to be an actress. They say I'm good enough to go all the way to Broadway."

Mary raised a brow. "Do they."

"Yes. They do. But I can't go to Broadway if I die in this basement as one of your test subjects. I hate you for what you did to our mother. But as I said, I want to live the life that's ahead of me. So I'll help you, and then you'll let us go. That's what I'm offering."

"You'll do this if I promise afterward to release you?"

Violet nodded.

Edie's eyes bounced back and forth between her sister and Mary. She didn't believe for a second that Violet trusted the woman to release them after they'd helped her, but it was clear

318

from the smug expression on Mary's face that *she* thought Violet naive enough.

Mary was underestimating Violet. Just as Edie had done.

"I will require a demonstration," said Mary. "Both to prove your competence and to ensure this is not some kind of trick. If you succeed, I will allow you to help my husband. Your sister's life will of course be forfeit should anything go wrong. And if you succeed in all that, then I will release you both. You will have your life on the stage. Do you agree to those terms?"

"Tell me what you want me to do," said Violet, "and I'll do it."

Mary smiled. A real smile that reached her eyes. "It just so happens that I have a suitable candidate at hand."

Without another word, she turned on her heel and left the pool of lamplight. Mary called out, but the words echoed in the cavernous basement and Edie couldn't make them out.

Less than a minute later came the now-familiar creak of a door opening at the end of the basement. Then the sound of something being dragged across the floor as the two large orderlies who'd wheeled the hospital bed in earlier stepped into the lamplight.

Only this time there was a third figure suspended between them. A man, by the look of his clothes. His hatless, brown-haired head was bowed, and his feet dragged on the floor as if his legs were too weak to stand. As the three figures drew closer, the sharp iron tang of blood assaulted Edie's nose.

And then the drooping third figure raised his head.

A pair of brown eyes flew straight to Edie's face.

Laws Everett was here.

Edie threw herself forward, her palms banging against her metal cage.

"Edie." His voice came out thick and slurred. "Edie, it's *him*. Dr. Ly—"

But whatever he was going to say was cut off by the fist of one of the large orderlies. It collided with his jaw, emitting a dull thud. Blood spewed from Laws's mouth. His head dropped, and his body went limp.

The two men dropped Laws's unconscious body in a heap at Mary's feet before turning to leave the way they'd come, their footsteps quickly fading away.

"We caught this young man"—Mary's eyes swept over Laws's crumpled body at her feet—"attempting to break into the asylum shortly after you arrived. We might as well make use of him."

Edie tried to catch her sister's eye. What was her plan?

But Violet's eyes were fixed on Mary, her face perfectly calm. "What is it you want to see?"

"Open the Veil." Mary's grey eyes glittered with anticipation. "Call a spirit—any will do—and assist it in possessing this young man's body. Shadow and all." She cocked her head at Violet. "Is that within your ability?"

Violet lifted her chin. "Of course it is. As long as I have access to herbs to guide the spirit and shadow." She held out a hand, palm up. "I believe you are in possession of my sister's pouch."

Mary's gaze slid down to Violet's hand. Then she glanced up at Henry and nodded. Henry hesitated for a moment, but then—

320

at another look from Mary—he dutifully crossed the room and retrieved the herb pouch from the same table Edie had stolen the bottle of thallium from, the night before.

"I'm afraid," said Mary, "that during this . . . *demonstration*, we will need to keep you contained."

Violet shrugged. "It makes no difference to me."

Mary gave a satisfied nod. Henry handed Violet the herb pouch and then closed the door to the cage around her bed, continuing to hover nearby.

Violet opened the pouch at once and began digging around inside. First she pulled out a stick of lavender. But instead of preparing to set it on fire, she undid the string binding it together and laid the dried lavender next to her on the bed. Then she pulled a bundle of hellebore from the pouch and proceeded to dismantle it in the same way. She did this again for a bundle of dandelion and then one of fennel, until she had sticks from all four herbs laid out haphazardly on the dirty white sheets of the bed.

From this she assembled a new herb bundle—only this time she bound a mix of all four herbs together, tying them quickly but efficiently with string.

Edie watched her sister closely, trying to track what she was doing. She'd combined lavender, which could open the Veil and calm surrounding spirits; hellebore, the same herb Edie had used to bind Ruby's spirit to her will; fennel, which strengthened fellow herbs; and dandelion, which increased psychic protection from a spirit's influence. It was a combination of herbs that could be used in all manner of ways.

Her old familiar instincts tugged at her, every nerve begging her to step in and intervene, but she forced herself to hold her tongue. Violet had asked Edie to trust her. Something she'd failed to do for the past year. A failure that had weakened and exposed the twins in ways she was only just beginning to understand. She couldn't make that same mistake again. Even if trusting Violet right now meant doing nothing. Even if it meant letting Violet take the lead. Even if it meant standing silently by.

Violet finished the last knot in the string and then reached into the pouch for the matchbook. Edie's mouth went dry at the movement. This was it.

Violet lit the match. And then, just before she brought the flame to the tip of her mixed bundle of herbs, her eyes rose at last to meet her sister's. They had another message to impart.

Violet blinked once. *I love you.*

And then she lit the herbs on fire.

༼ ༽

Violet closed her eyes as soon as the smoke from the herbs rose into the air. For her own part, Edie had to clamp a hand over her mouth to stop herself from calling out. The look in Violet's eyes, the silent message she'd given her before lighting the flame . . . Edie had a terrible feeling about it all.

There was a groan a couple of feet to her right. She glanced toward it. Laws's body was beginning to move. Henry turned away from Violet's cage and started toward Laws, but Mary raised a hand to stop him.

"Leave him. It will be easier to see the possession take hold if he's awake."

A moment later, Edie felt the Veil open. The basement was already cool, but the drop in temperature was sudden and extreme. Violet hadn't just opened a small tear in the Veil as she usually did. No, she'd opened a gap nearly two times the size of her cage.

Edie closed her eyes and tried to feel for whatever spirit Violet had summoned. Surely she wouldn't actually allow one to possess Laws?

But although she could feel *something*... she couldn't glean any of its characteristics. Whether it was young or old. Strong or weak.

Across from her, Violet took in a rattling breath. Edie's eyes flew open at the sound. A split second later, Violet's eyes also opened.

Edie screamed at what she saw. Because Violet's green eyes were gone, replaced by pools of inky black.

Too late, Edie understood.

Too late, she recognized the heavy presence, the faint whiff of belladonna still lingering from her mother's failed attempt.

Too late, Edie realized the purpose of those herbs.

Violet had channeled the shadow.

Edie cried out, horrified, as herbsmoke from her sister's improvised bundle wrapped around Violet in thin, spiraling ribbons, winking in the low lamplight.

Violet had bound the shadow to her in the same way Edie had tied Ruby's spirit to her in the Veil. It gave her sister control over it, but at what cost? How long could Violet stay bound to a shadow and remain in life?

Edie banged her fist against the cage. She screamed her sister's name. But without her herbs, she was powerless.

A strangled sound rang out next to Violet's cage, and Henry collapsed to his knees. His mouth stretched wide in a wordless scream as his head arched back, the lamplight illuminating his eyes.

Eyes that were rapidly flashing between brown and black.

Black and brown.

And then black, black, black.

The shadow had found its escaped spirit at last.

Edie was distantly aware of a woman's scream. Followed by a dull thud.

And then—just as her father's possessed body went suddenly rigid, all movement forcibly stopped—Edie felt it. A sharp pain. As if someone had reached into her chest and taken out half of her heart.

And she could do nothing to stop it.

Nothing but cry out in agony as she felt her sister's spirit cross out of life.

31

Edie's scream tore her apart. It sucked all the air from her lungs, ripped her limbs apart, and turned her blood into ice.

But even as she fell apart, one thought remained clear in her mind.

Violet. She had to get to Violet.

She tore at the metal cage with her fingers until they bled. A sharp poke against her knee reminded her of the warped hairpin, and she quickly swiveled toward the square door in her cage. Her fingers trembled violently as she tried to fit the pin in the lock, but the angle was impossible.

She screamed again in frustration. She howled her sister's name.

She had to get to Violet before it was too late.

And then cool hands covered her own. Large hands with ink stains under their nails. Edie looked up into Laws Everett's bruised and battered face. He was bleeding from the nose and his left eye was swollen shut. She whipped her head around and saw Mary Sutton lying unconscious on the floor; broken shards from the unused glass vial of the thallium syringe were scattered next to her open hand.

"Please." Laws's voice was ragged and hoarse. "Please, Edie. Let me help."

Edie said nothing as Laws gently removed the hairpin from her grasp. She stayed still as a stone while he knelt and picked the lock on her cage.

Less than a minute later, Laws got the lock unlatched, and the metal door to her cage creaked open. Edie threw herself out. She stepped over her father's body. He was still breathing, which meant Violet had taken only Henry's spirit with her into death, leaving whatever was left of her father's spirit behind. But Edie didn't have time for him now. She stumbled toward Violet's bed, her arms already reaching out. Laws was right beside her. He fell again to his knees and, without a word, picked the lock of Violet's cage.

Edie scrambled inside as soon as the door swung open. Violet was lying on her back. Her unseeing eyes were open wide. When Edie's spirit crossed into the Veil, her body stayed alive. Her lungs continued to breathe.

Violet's body was still as stone.

Gently, Edie reached out and closed her sister's eyes.

From outside the cage, Laws cleared his throat. "I'm so sorry, Edie. I can't tell you how sorry I am."

But Edie wasn't listening to him. Scattered around Violet's body were the herbs she hadn't used. And to her left, lying sideways on the dirty white sheets, was Edie's silk pouch.

A hand reached into the cage and rested itself gently on her shoulder. "Edie. I'm so sorry. But we have to go."

Edie shrugged Laws's arm away. She settled into a cross-legged position, facing her sister's body, and began gathering up the dried stems of lavender.

"Edie, we have to—"

"I'm not going anywhere."

Laws made a sort of choking sound in the back of his throat. He moved closer to the cage; and this time when he spoke, it was urgent and fast. "You don't understand. That man, he is— or *was*—Dr. Henry Lyon. The mediomania expert. He and that Mary Sutton woman have been bringing women here, mediums, under fraudulent insanity claims. For the past year, he's conducted all business via post. It's why I couldn't get an interview—"

"I don't care."

"You don't understand, Edie! They have *support*. A whole host of powerful men in the legislature—and beyond—who've been promised a *cure for death*. We have to get you out of here before—"

"I told you. None of that matters right now."

"Please. Your sister is already . . ." His voice broke. "She's gone, Edie. Please, she'd want me to get you out."

Finished gathering the lavender, Edie picked up the herb pouch and reached her hand inside. "She's not gone."

The connection between Violet's body and spirit was still intact. She could feel it. This wasn't like what had happened to their mother or Ruby. Edie still had time.

Laws's face drained of all remaining color. "Please, Edie. It's not safe here. Someone could come at any—"

"I need you to stay and watch her."

"You . . . what?"

Edie finished binding the lavender, stuffed the rest of the herbs into her pouch, and took out a match, ready to strike.

Then she looked Laws Everett dead in the eye. "I'm going into the Veil to save my sister. I need you to watch her. Keep her safe until I bring her spirit back. Will you do it?"

"Edie. . . ."

"You said I could trust you, Laws Everett. I need you to prove it. Right now."

His eyes flashed with an emotion she couldn't name. Then he lifted his chin. "I'll watch her," he said, his voice solemn and low. "I'll watch you both."

Edie nodded her assent. Then she struck the match, held the tip to the hastily tied lavender bundle, and closed her eyes.

CR 20

Edie opened her eyes to nothing but mist. Seconds later, she closed the Veil and was on her feet following the scent of the herbs. She tried not to think about how similar this was to her journey into death a year ago, when she'd been looking for her mother. Tried and failed.

She had minutes, at most, to return Violet to life. Minutes before the connection between her body and spirit would be irrevocably lost. Even now, it could already be too late.

No. She wouldn't think that way. She would find Violet and get her back to life. And then she would deal with Henry Lyon's spirit. Finish what her mother had begun. He no longer had a connection to his original body in life. Once he and his shadow were reunited, the herbs should be enough to force him beyond.

A scream echoed through the mist. Violet's scream.

Edie picked up her pace, sprinting until she found her sister's spirit at last. Bright with the light of the newly dead. Violet's back was to her, and Edie was about to call out when she caught sight of what her sister was facing—and froze.

This couldn't be right.

There was Henry's spirit. She recognized his tall, wiry features from that day in the Veil with her mother, although that unnatural flickering was gone now. Replaced with a weak but steady light.

Towering above him was his shadow. At least three times his height.

Now that Henry's spirit was back in the Veil, this should have been the moment he reunited with it. The moment he became whole once more.

But that wasn't what was happening.

The shadow—so long on its own; so long without the tempering influence of a spirit's light—was absorbing him instead. Just as it had little William Brown.

Edie watched in shock as ropelike tendrils snaked out from the shadow's form, encircling Henry's weakening spirit. His eyes were wide with fear, and his mouth opened as if to scream, but no sound came out.

In the second before the shadow broke him in two, his frantic eyes met Edie's. She saw his plea for help. Silently begging the daughter of the woman he'd killed and the man he'd possessed to save him. And even though she hated the man, even though he'd torn apart her family and altered the course of her and Violet's life, she might have tried to help. If she'd had time.

But she didn't.

The shadow split him open and inhaled the pathetic amount of light his spirit had maintained after a year of borrowed life. Until there was nothing left of Dr. Henry Lyon but a few measly wisps of mist.

Its feeding done, the shadow turned toward the twins. And it was then that Edie noticed the crisscrossing binds of silver herbsmoke wrapped around its form. Binds of smoke that were entwined around her sister as well.

The bind Violet had cast in life still held.

The shadow's oozing form pulsed. It lurched toward them, only to be stopped short by the silver smoke. Held in place, for now.

Edie rushed forward. "Vi! We need to get you back."

But Violet didn't turn around. Instead, she began to walk. Pitching herself forward at the waist as if preparing to carry a heavy weight.

Edie called her name again and ran after her, but Violet looked over her shoulder and held out a hand to stop her. "No, Edie. Please." Her voice was tight and strained. "It's all I can do to—"

A *crack* cut off Violet's words. A split second later, one of the thin silver binds of smoke connecting Violet to the shadow broke off, disappearing into the mist. The shadow undulated again. Straining to break free.

"Vi, what are you—"

"Just *go*, Edie. Please. I can take it on my own. But I don't have the strength to fight you, too."

"Take it on . . ."

Edie trailed off, finally pausing to properly take in the scene around her. The Veil had assumed the form of a windswept desert tonight. A pale blue moon hovered above them, its beams falling on the silver binds connecting Violet to the shadow.

Edie stared at those binds. Stared at Violet struggling to walk. And then she understood what her sister planned to do. She understood why Violet had only needed a small amount of hellebore in the herb bundle she'd made. Just enough to bind the shadow—not to her will—but to her form. Because her twin had no intention of attempting to *send* the shadow beyond the Veil. No. She was going to *take* it there herself.

Edie planted herself in front of Violet. "Vi. You can't do this. If anyone should take this *thing* beyond, it should be me. I'm the one who—"

Another *crack* interrupted her. The shadow pulsed outward as another tendril of the silver smoke-bind broke off, fading into the mist. Violet may have successfully bound the shadow to her form, but it was fighting against it.

Violet shook her head. "You're the one who carried us for the past year, Edie. I know you felt alone during most of it. And I'm sorry. Truly. Because you're not alone. You never were. And now it's my turn. And you have to let me go."

Violet made to start walking again, but Edie jumped in front of her, forcing her to stop. An idea had just formed in her mind. "You're right, Vi. The shadow *is* too strong to send beyond alone, but you just said it. I'm *not* alone."

Violet's met Edie's eyes, quietly assessing. Her gaze flicked to the dark shape behind her. And then Violet was jerked backward, pulled by one of the silver binds. Another *crack* echoed through the mist.

Edie caught Violet just before she fell to the ground. The light emanating from her spirit was growing dim. The strain of the bind was taking its toll.

"Please," said Edie again. "Let me try."

Violet used Edie's arms to pull herself back to a standing position. "We can try. But we have to be quick. I can't risk—"

"Thank you." Edie squeezed Violet once before letting her go. "This will work, I promise."

She didn't waste another moment, quickly digging her fingers into the silk herb pouch and pulling out the unbound herbs, creating a mixed bundle that would bind the spirit not to her own form, as Violet had done, but to the twins' combined will.

As she worked, another *crack* echoed in the Veil. Another bind snapped. Edie and Violet looked as one toward the shadow.

It was spilling out and over the remaining binds, a storm of clouds ready to break.

Violet's voice was strained as she whispered, "Hurry."

Edie decided on wormwood, fennel, and hellebore. A drawing herb, a binding herb, and an amplifier. The same combination her mother had used on Henry's spirit a year ago. She made quick work of knotting the stems together and then she took out her box of matches and prepared to light the herbs.

To Violet, she said, "As soon as this takes hold, release your own binds."

"*If* it takes," Violet said, "I will."

Edie nodded. That was all she could ask. She struck the match alight and lit the herbs. Seconds later, a deep gold smoke rose up in elegant spirals. With one hand, Edie held the herb bundle aloft. With the other, she reached out and grabbed her sister's hand. Violet squeezed hers back. A moment later, Edie felt a jolt of strength flowing down her arms. A tingling sensation snaking along her skin and melting into her core that was exactly like Violet. Wild and joyful and strong.

Edie directed the golden smoke toward the shadow, long, winding ribbons of gold falling in a net around its pulsing shape. With Violet's help, it was almost easy to bind it to her will. For all its size and power, the shadow was no match for their combined strength.

Once she was sure the bind had taken, Edie nodded at Violet. But from the shine in her sister's eyes, she could tell she'd felt it, too. Violet nodded back to Edie, closed her eyes, and released her own binds.

The silver ribbons of smoke fell silently away from Violet's spirit, the smoke disappearing into the surrounding mist. At the same time, a matching puff of silver smoke fell off the shadow's form.

Violet was free.

Edie released her sister's hand and dipped her fingers back into her herb pouch. "Now you have to go back."

A hand caught her wrist before she could extract anything from the pouch. Edie looked up into the fading light of her sister's face. Already, she had been too long in death. Already, a strip of her auburn hair had turned white, leached of its color. Already, it might be too late to save her.

"No, Edie. We send it beyond together."

Edie shook her head. "What I need is a life to go back to, Vi. And there's no life for me without you in it. I can send it beyond on my own. But you need to go back now while you still can."

"Edie." Violet's face twisted in anguish. "I can't just leave you here."

"You aren't leaving me. We both have our parts. Mine is here. Yours is going back to life and saving us both." Edie squeezed her sister's hand and met her eyes. She needed her to understand. Needed her to see that she meant this. That she knew what it was now to shut her out, and that she'd never do it again. "Please, Vi. Go. Go now so that I can follow."

Violet stared at her for a long moment. Her mouth tight. Her eyes unreadable. And then, very slowly, she released her hold on Edie's hand.

Edie kept her eyes on her twin as she reached deeper into the pouch. All the way to the bottom. Until her fingers curled around something twisted and thick.

A belladonna root.

But it wasn't only the gnarled root she took out of her pouch. Edie also extracted a packet of dried bay leaves. Helpful little leaves capable of reversing an herb's intent. When added to belladonna, for example, it had the effect of forcing a spirit back to life, instead of beyond to a final death. The only catch was, when reversed, the belladonna wasn't powerful enough to affect every spirit within its range. But it could take one.

Edie took two of the largest bay leaves out of the packet and carefully wrapped them around the gnarled root, binding them with a spare length of string. Then she took out a match.

Violet made a little sound at the back of her throat, her eyes fixed on the leaf-wrapped belladonna.

"No matter what you do," said Edie, glancing up at her sister, "don't fight it. You'll want to push back against the hold, but you have to let the smoke carry you. Any resistance might weaken the bay leaves and allow the belladonna to force you beyond the Veil."

Violet lifted her eyes up from the leaf-wrapped root. "I won't fight it, Edie. I trust you. Always."

A lump formed in Edie's throat, but she swallowed it down. Violet's light was far too dim. They'd already wasted precious time. She focused instead on the match, lighting it and touching its flame to the gnarled root.

The bay leaves caught fire first, crackling with a pleasant, fireside sound. Then the flame moved upward, licking at the twisted belladonna. The smoke of the two herbs combined to make a soft green color. The exact shade of the twins' identical eyes.

Edie sent the smoke whirling toward her sister until it enveloped her like the thickest of shawls. The herbs reacted to her spirit quickly. So quickly, Edie barely had time to shout out the words *I love you!* before the soft green smoke started to move, pulling her sister back toward life.

True to her word, Violet didn't fight the herb's pull. But she did keep her eyes on Edie as long as she could, until the mist closed around her and Edie could see her no more.

But she could still feel her. A bit of the wild joyfulness her sister had shared when they bound the shadow together. A thread of connection that was stronger now than it had ever been. Strong enough for her to feel the moment her twin crossed back into life. Safe, once more.

Edie allowed herself one single sigh of relief. Then she turned around and faced the shadow in her hold.

It was time to make this thing walk.

32

Edie tried every combination of herbs possible, given her supplies.

She tried the obvious ones, like hazel and hyssop and sage.

She tried strange mixes, like orange peel and fennel and rowan wood.

She tried wild combinations that could easily backfire if she got them wrong.

Nothing worked.

Each time she lit the herbs, each time she directed the smoke toward the shadow, it stayed still.

It refused to walk. Refused to be sent beyond.

The only good news was that the bind she and Violet created had so far held fast. The shadow couldn't move or make a sound. It was frozen in place. Stuck there, in its cage of golden smoke. But even the strongest bind couldn't hold forever. Soon, Edie would have to make a choice. The same choice her mother had made.

She hadn't lied to Violet. She'd thought she *could* force the shadow beyond the Veil with the herbs, now that it was bound. But nothing had worked, and she couldn't afford to wait any longer. The bind was quickly draining her strength.

It wouldn't be a long walk. She could see the thick, shimmering wall of mist from where she stood now. A barrier between the Veil and a final death that was never too far out of reach. But she had to go now. While she still had the strength to cross it.

She could only hope that one day Violet would forgive her.

She tucked the herbs back into her silk pouch. And then, just as she was about to cinch the opening closed, the mist rippled around her. A moment later, a spirit approached.

It had all the hallmarks of the newly dead. And yet its light was muted and shaky. As it drew closer, Edie understood why.

It was the spirit of her father.

His body must have finally died in life, weakened by the possession.

His face wasn't as she'd seen it a few minutes ago in the basement of the asylum. His cheeks were full again, the deep shadows gone, and his eyes . . . they were no longer pools of black, but a clear bright blue.

He paused several feet from her. When he spoke, it was only to say one word.

"Edith."

Her name hung in the air between them. Shimmering in the mist.

Not knowing what else to say to the man who'd ruined her life, to the man whose life she'd ruined in turn, Edie merely nodded and said, "Hello."

He offered her a tentative smile. "So," he said, "this is death."

Edie nodded. "We call it the Veil. It's a place for spirits to . . . prepare."

"Prepare?"

"For a second, final death. Beyond the Veil."

Her father nodded thoughtfully. "And . . . you've been here before?"

Edie nodded again.

"Your mother came here, too?"

"Yes."

"She taught you how?"

"She did."

"And Violet?"

Edie shook her head. It was strange. The matter-of-fact way they were speaking now after years of hiding the truth from this very man. But now that they were here, at the end of death, it seemed the most natural thing in the world.

"Violet can call the spirits to her in life. Only Mother and I could . . . cross back and forth." Edie paused, then she added, "Violet was here, though. Until a little while ago. I . . . I sent her back."

Her father nodded, as if he understood what that meant. Then his eyes looked past Edie, to the writhing shadow bound in golden smoke. Edie followed his gaze.

"I'm sorry," she said, her voice low. "It's my fault his spirit . . . possessed you like it did. I want you to know that I didn't realize—"

"You don't need to apologize to me, Edie."

She turned back toward him. Her father kept his eyes on the bound shadow as he spoke. "There's a lot I didn't understand about you girls. About your mother. A lot I didn't know."

Edie opened her mouth to apologize again; but, as if sensing what she was going to say, her father shook his head and said, "No, Edie. Your mother was right not to tell me. You were right to keep it a secret. Look at how I reacted when . . . when she died."

Edie stared at her father's spirit—dim, but clear—as a question formed in her mind. A question that had taken root back in the basement of the asylum as soon as she'd learned the truth about her father's possession. A small but persistent sliver of hope.

"That day," Edie began, as afraid of the answer as she was of not asking the question at all. "When you saw us . . . when you . . ." She trailed off. Even here, even now, it was difficult to repeat the words he'd hurled at them. To recall the fear and fury in his eyes. But this was something she had to know. Here, at the end of it all, it was an answer she deserved. "Was that you? Or was it the spirit who threatened to lock us away?"

Her father shifted his gaze away from the shadow and looked at her for a long moment. Then, slowly, he shook his head. "I wish I could tell you what you want to hear, Edith. But I was still myself when I said those things to you. When I threatened you both like I did." His eyes darted away. "You see, there may have been a lot I didn't understand, but I believe . . . to some extent, I always suspected that you girls and your mother . . . that there was *something*." He looked back at Edie and smiled sadly. "And so when I saw you that night, cold and still as a corpse—and then just as suddenly alive. When I heard you beg her to come back . . . not as a grieving child would, but as someone who *knew* it was possible . . ."

He spread his hands, splaying his fingers. He didn't finish the thought. He didn't need to. They both knew what had happened next.

"So," said her father, changing his tone. He nodded his chin toward the looming mass behind her. "What are you going to do with it?"

"With the shadow?"

"Is that what you call it? Interesting. I could feel it, you know. Pulling at me. And I always thought of it as the devil. But seeing it now . . . yes. A shadow makes sense."

"I really am so sorry that—"

Her father cut her off with a wave of his hand. "It's not your fault, Edith. None of this is."

"But it is," insisted Edie. "If it weren't for me, Mother would have—"

"Do you remember when you were a little girl?" said her father, a soft smile inching onto his face. "And you would sit on my knee and listen to me tell you stories from the Bible? You always liked it, I think. Although Violet never did. You asked me something once. I wonder if you remember. You said *Father, will God always keep me safe?* Do you remember what I said to you?"

Edie nodded. "You said he would. No matter what."

Her father nodded sadly. "I did. It was the only thing I could think to say at the time to my little girl. I remember thinking, what could ever happen to her? Of course she will always be safe."

Neither of them spoke for several moments after that.

"I take it," her father finally said, "that this shadow, must go to . . . what did you call it?"

"Beyond the Veil. To a final death."

She looked toward the thick wall of mist that signaled the end of the Veil. Was it her imagination, or had it come closer in the minutes since her father arrived?

He followed her gaze, and for a long moment both of them stared silently into the mist.

Then her father turned back to her. "How will you do it?"

Edie pursed her lips. She didn't know how to answer that. Didn't know what to say to a father who had once told her she would always be safe.

And so she said nothing.

"I think," said her father slowly, "that I would like to go, too."

Edie's brow creased. "Go where?"

He waved his hands vaguely, stirring up wisps of mist. "Beyond," he said. "I think I would like to see it."

"But you don't have to go yet. You have plenty of time. You could, um—"

Her father smiled. "I could . . . what? Haunt my loved ones?"

Edie had no response to that. Her father shook his head mildly. "No. I think it's a good time for me to go. You, on the other hand . . . perhaps it's time for you to go back."

He looked pointedly at her head. Guessing at what he saw, Edie unhooked a strand of hair from her bun and inspected it. It was no longer blonde, but bone-white. Her time in death—the drain of the bind—was taking its toll.

She shoved the hair away and shook her head. "I can't go back."

"Ah," said her father. "I believe I see your dilemma."

Again, Edie said nothing. And for a moment, father and daughter stood there in silence. Then her father spoke again. "What if I took it?"

She started. "What?"

"What if I took this shadow with me? Could you arrange that? I've gathered that you have some control over spirits here. After all, that . . . *thing* and I have been, in a way, bound together for quite some time now. It seems only fitting that we make this last journey as one."

Edie stared at her father's spirit. She'd spent the past year learning to despise this man. And then the last handful of minutes trying to decide how much of that had been deserved. And now he was offering to take this burden from her. He was offering her another chance at life.

Could she take it?

"I . . . I don't know," she said. "I was planning to . . . I'd already—"

"Sometimes," said her father mildly, "plans change."

Edie had no idea what to say to that.

Her father took a step toward her. "I understand if you have doubts, Edie. We haven't exactly always been on the same side, have we?"

343

Mutely, Edie shook her head.

"I'm sorry about that. Truly, I am. There are . . . many things I'd like to say to you, Edie. And to your sister if she were here. But as our time is short, I will choose only one. And it is this: sometimes it is all right to let go."

Edie continued to stare at him, unspeaking. He took another step closer, reached out, and gently took the herb pouch from her hands.

"This is what you use to influence the spirits?" he asked. "You burn these herbs in here?"

Edie nodded.

"Very clever. And which herbs do you think might work? To . . . *reconnect* my old friend and me?"

"I think," said Edie, her voice seeming to come from somewhere very far away, "that you would only need hyssop. The bind is already strong. It would only be a matter of transferring it to you."

Her father smiled. "Ingenious. Truly. Your mother must have taught you well."

A lump formed in Edie's throat as she watched her father root through the pouch until he pulled out a paper packet labeled hyssop in the neat cursive hand of the druggist Edie had purchased the herb from. Her father held up the packet to Edie and raised an eyebrow questioningly.

She nodded.

"And how much," asked her father, opening the pouch, "would one use?"

He began to pull out sprigs of the purple-and-green herb.

"That would be enough," said Edie, once he'd taken out six uneven sprigs. Her father nodded, returned the remaining hyssop to the pouch, and then took out a loose length of string and a box of matches. These he held out to Edie.

"Go on," he said, offering her the cluster of hyssop as well. "I'd love to see you do it. Just this once."

Edie took the items he was offering. Her father smiled and took a few steps back, closer to the shadow that loomed in the mist.

Edie bound the hyssop sticks together, wrapping them up with string. Then she lit the match her father had given her. But she didn't touch it to the herb. She waited until the flame was almost at her glowing fingers. Until her father nodded at her one last time.

Only then did she dip the match and set the hyssop aflame.

The smoke curled up quickly, a dusty purple haze that surrounded the dull, fading light of her father's spirit. Half of the hyssop smoke stayed with him, and the rest of it flew toward the pulsating shadow, joining the golden web of smoke.

In an instant, Edie's bind was gone. A heavy weight lifted from her shoulders.

Across from her, her father's shoulders slumped. As if someone had taken a mallet and pounded him into the ground.

For one terrifying moment, Edie thought he would crack under the pressure, that he would falter and fail. But then her father tilted his head and looked up. His lips moved silently in what Edie was sure—even here, even at the edge of death—was prayer. And then, though she could see it took an incredible amount of effort, he straightened up, turned away from Edie, and began to walk, the dark mass of shadow jerking behind him, forced to silently follow the bind.

He looked only once over his shoulder, a fleeting glance. It was likely all the energy he could afford to waste. Edie held up a hand in farewell. He blinked once. And then the mist closed around him.

Edie wanted to wait. She wanted to stay in the Veil until she was sure the shadow was truly gone. She wanted to stay in case her father turned back. In case he changed his mind.

But then she felt it.

The slightest of tugs.

A vibration along a thread that still connected her to life.

To Violet.

Telling her it was time to come back.

Edie turned away from the place where her father had disappeared and pulled out the last of her lavender. But before she lit it, she paused. And then, in a voice barely above a whisper, she sent a single word into the Veil.

"Goodbye."

And maybe it was nothing more than a cloud passing in front of the cold blue light of death's imitation of a moon. Maybe it was simply the ever-present mist, rising up as it always did, cold fingers caressing her face. But somehow Edie knew that even though her mother was gone, even though her spirit had passed beyond, the subtle shift she felt now was her way of saying goodbye.

Slowly, Edie smiled. And then she lit the lavender aflame.

Three Months Later

Edie soared down Market Street, the wind whipping her hair as she pedaled her bicycle as fast as she dared down the city hill. The sparkling San Francisco Bay shimmered before her through a light layer of fog.

A couple of minutes later, she glided up to a two-story red-brick building with Corinthian-style arches on Bush Street between Kearny and Dupont. She dismounted, found a place to leave her bicycle, and then pushed past a pair of double swinging doors, accepting a little paper booklet from a liveried young man who hovered inside the lobby.

She waited to look at the booklet until she'd taken her seat in one of the plush, red-cushioned chairs. The cover featured an illustration of fairies galloping amongst trees. Inside, the pages were filled mostly with advertisements for local San Francisco merchants. But there, crammed at the bottom of the second page, was the cast list for tonight's performance of *A Midsummer Night's Dream*. It was perhaps the most priceless piece of paper Edie had ever held.

"Excuse me, miss," said a male voice from the aisle on her left. "But is this seat taken?"

"That depends," said Edie, not looking up from the program in her lap.

"And may I ask what your answer depends on?"

"It depends on whether I forgive the original owner of this seat. He was meant to ride over here with me this evening, but he never arrived."

"Ah," said the voice. "And would it make a difference if your companion had, say, a very good excuse? If, for example, he had been delayed due to the need to pick up a rather important piece of mail?"

Edie's head snapped up. "No! It came?"

Laws Everett's honey-brown eyes sparkled. "It came." He held out a plain white envelope. Edie's name was written on the front. But it was the return address that held her attention.

Hastings College of Law, San Francisco.

Laura de Force herself had written Edie a letter of recommendation, as well as help secure a partial scholarship from the local women's rights chapter, should Edie be accepted. The two women had met after Laura called on Laws to congratulate him on his article, which he'd written independently and then sold to the *San Francisco Chronicle*, detailing the abuses taking place in the basement of the Sacramento Asylum.

Although he'd left out the finer details of the experiments—no one would have believed that part, anyway—he'd proven Dr. Mary Sutton's culpability in the death of Ruby Miller, clearing Lillian, Ada, Violet, and Edie's names. He'd also linked Mary to the deaths of a dozen more young women from Belden Place and beyond, all of whom had been fraudulently diagnosed and unlawfully committed to the asylum. Their imprisonment had been made possible thanks to the support of several prominent politicians and police chiefs, some of whom had been bribed handsomely, and some—although Laws didn't include this fact in the article—who had been motivated by the promise of a cheat for death.

Public sympathy for the murdered mediums had the bizarre effect of boosting ticket sales for their show, prompting Mr. Huddle to add another week of Sacramento performances. Laura de Force had attended one as Laws's guest, witnessing Edie's politically charged trance lectures first-hand. After coming backstage to apologize to everyone for the lack of response from the local chapter on the matter of the Belden Place women (*too little too late*, Lillian had privately said to Edie later), Laura had all but cornered Edie. Before she knew it, Edie was filling out an application to study law.

But even with Laura de Force's letter of recommendation, Edie knew her chances of acceptance into Hastings were low. The school admitted women now—had been forced to ever since Laura had sued them to gain her own acceptance—but Edie's previous schooling had been . . . erratic, to say the least. She was largely self-taught. She had nowhere near the level of preparation that most of the boys would have—and even some of the girls.

And now the answer was here at last. She'd used Laws's new office at the *Chronicle* as her mailing address since she and Violet had spent the past month bouncing around, staying with her sister's seemingly endless supply of new theater friends ever since Lillian, Ada, and the rest of the tour had moved on to their next stop.

Laws waggled the envelope. "Are you going to open it? Or is this a new form of torture you've devised to drive me mad?"

Edie took a deep breath and then swiped the envelope from Laws's hands. Slowly, carefully, she slid her finger under the envelope's flap.

Laws groaned. "Oh, for Pete's sake. Rip it open already!"

Edie smiled up at Laws. Then she ripped the envelope open in one fell swoop.

A single piece of paper fluttered out. Edie caught it in her hands.

"Dear Miss Bond,

"It is our pleasure to welcome you—"

Edie jumped up out of her seat and threw her arms around Laws. He laughed when she slammed into him, his arms encircling her waist.

"I knew you could do it," he whispered into her ear. "There was never a doubt in my mind."

Edie laughed again and pulled back far enough to see his face. "You're lying, Laws Everett! You were just as nervous as I was."

Laws smiled crookedly. "You should know by now, Miss Bond. I never lie."

He bent his head low and dropped a kiss on the tip of her nose.

Behind them a woman gasped, and a man cleared his throat. Edie blushed, and so did Laws.

At that same moment, the gaslit chandelier hanging over the theater dimmed, and the curtain began to rise. Edie and Laws scrambled into their seats as the actors took the stage.

The play began with the promise of fairies, but then quickly transitioned into an angry tirade by a father who was livid because his daughter refused to live the life he had planned for her. Laws squeezed Edie's hand softly in his. She'd told him everything about her own father's last act in death.

And then the scene shifted, and Violet burst onto the stage. The new streak of white in her hair—a remnant of her time in the Veil—shone proudly in the light. She was playing the scorned lover, Helena, and her piteous, self-effacing pleas immediately drew peals of laughter from the crowd.

"She really is quite good," Laws whispered into Edie's ear.

The other actors left the stage, leaving Violet alone. After a long, drawn-out sigh—one that sent the audience roaring with laughter again—Violet launched into her first soliloquy.

Edie had seen her sister put on a show before, of course. She'd spent hours watching Violet from the wings or sitting across from her at the séance table. She'd seen her sister play every kind of character under the sun. But she'd never seen her like this. She'd never seen her perform with her whole heart on display. It was as if she, by some miracle, had found a place in the world that fit her just right.

Edie shook her head and leaned toward Laws. "No," she murmured into his ear. "She's better than good. She's a star."

Laws squeezed her hand in agreement, and Edie turned back to the stage. Violet finished her speech on a high note, tossing out her last line and receiving another torrent of applause.

And then, just before she turned to exit the stage, Violet's eyes flicked to where Edie was sitting in the crowd.

A thread of meaning passed between the sisters. A thread that had connected them since birth and had grown even stronger in the months since it had been tested.

It was a thread that would no doubt be tested again. A thread that would need to stretch and grow and adapt as they set off on their own individual paths. At times it would be almost too thin to grasp; at others it would be the only thing holding them up.

But as Edie and Violet held each other's eyes for that brief second in the theater—too quick for anyone but them to notice— they both understood one thing would always be true.

This was a thread that would never break.

AUTHOR'S NOTE

This story was inspired by my great-grandmother Edie Bond and her twin sister, Violet.

My fascination with these sisters began with a photograph—a posed studio portrait of them as teenagers—that lived on a bookshelf in my childhood home. I found it strangely haunting. Every time I passed the photo, I paused to make eye contact with the sisters, convinced there was something they wanted me to know.

When I discovered later that both Edie and Violet were avid Spiritualists who regularly conducted séances, my interest in them only grew. But it wasn't until a couple of years ago as I was researching the Spiritualist movement of the nineteenth century that lightning struck, and the final puzzle piece of this story slid into place.

There is a plethora of rich history when it comes to Spiritualism, but it was the work of writer and scholar Ann Braude that truly opened up Edie and Violet's story to me. In her excellent book *Radical Spirits: Spiritualism and Women's Rights in Nineteenth-Century America* (which I enthusiastically recommend for deeper reading), Braude sheds light on the intersection between early Spiritualism, one of the few religions at the time that gave women equal parity with men, and the women's rights movement of the nineteenth century. I was intrigued to discover that during a time when women were rarely encouraged to speak publicly, many influential women's rights advocates developed their oratorial skills by traveling the country as trance lecturers and spirit mediums.

The popularity of Spiritualism created a kind of a loophole through which women were able to publicly make their voices heard. This was during an era when women were strongly encouraged to cultivate a nature that was pure, pious, passive, and domestic— qualities that effectively barred them from leadership roles. But the invention of the spirit medium neatly got around all of that. It allowed women to simply *accept* messages from the spirit world as *passive* vehicles. Suddenly, teenage farm girls were traveling the country as trance mediums, seemingly unconscious on stage as spirits spoke through them about everything from women's and children's rights to marriage reform, ideological individualism, dress reform, socialism, labor reform, and religious freedom. And the public ate it up, as is evidenced by this truly telling quote Braude includes in her book, that appeared in an 1858 edition of the *Christian Spiritualist* after a trance lecture given by the young medium Emma Jay:

"'That a young lady not over 18 years of age should speak for an hour and a quarter, in such an eloquent manner, with such logical and philosophical clearness,' proved to one observer the presence of a 'power not natural to the education or mentality of the speaker.'"

In this book, Edie does consciously use her trance lectures as a clever way to publicly share her own ideas and opinions, but it's important to remember this was a time when most women were erroneously taught that they were inherently *incapable* of public speech. Yet somehow, when they were given the opportunity to open their minds to the spirits, the ideas simply flowed. I'll leave you to draw your own conclusions about the true source of these lecture topics and spirit communications; my own two cents is that many of the mediums who practiced Spiritualism were likely genuine in their belief that the inspiration bestowed upon them was indeed a gift from the spirit world.

While this book was inspired by the real Spiritualist movement, as well as real historical figures, events, and settings, it is also fiction, and as such, I have taken certain liberties while always striving to stay true to the spirit of this time and place.

Laura de Force, or as she was known after she married, Laura de Force Gordon, was a real historical figure. She got her start on the trance lecture circuit at a young age before suing Hasting College of Law for admittance and becoming one of California's first female lawyers. She did not speak publicly in defense of Dorothy Dryer, who is a fictional character inspired by the very real suppression of access to birth control and contraceptives that came into practice after the passage of the Comstock Act in 1873. However, Laura was living in Northern California during this time period and advocating strongly for woman's rights and suffrage, so I like to think that if Dorothy's case had been real, Laura would've had something to say about it. It is also important to note, as Ada and Lillian imply in the book, that Laura de Force Gordon, like many of the prominent women's rights leaders at the time, fell unacceptably short when it came to fighting for the rights of women of color and other oppressed minority groups. And yet despite the racism and prejudice present in the national suffrage movement, Black women and other women of color continued to fight tirelessly for suffrage and women's rights.

Spiritualism's popularity increased rapidly in the wake of the Civil War's massive death toll, and while the character of the somewhat pompous medium Cora Bradley is fictional, her story about being invited to the White House by First Lady Mary Todd Lincoln is based on the real séances Mrs. Lincoln held in the Red Room while her husband, Abraham Lincoln, was president. She turned to the practice of Spiritualism after the death of her eleven-year-old son to typhoid fever and continued to practice it after her husband was assassinated.

The sidewalks of Sacramento really were raised several feet off the ground because of the frequent flooding of the Sacramento River. You can still see evidence of this today if you visit Old Town Sacramento and take one of the Sacramento History Museum's fascinating Underground Tours. Sacramento did not, however, have a gothic asylum with a basement dedicated to supernatural experiments. That is my own invention. The other harrowing asylum practices that Lillian describes to Laws, however, were very much real in many parts of the country. A few years after the events of this story, the intrepid reporter Nellie Bly famously exposed the horrifying inner-workings of asylums in her groundbreaking work, *Ten Days in a Mad-House*, which I highly recommend to any curious readers.

When the real-life Edie and Violet were grown and had families of their own, they built a passageway connecting their homes. To me, that passageway says everything about the enduring love they shared. I think they would have enjoyed the adventure I wrote for them about two sisters who share a bond that is tested, and who must fight to find their place in the world. Thank you for allowing me to share their story with you.

Edie Bond (*left*) and Violet Bond (*right*) at sixteen years old.

ACKNOWLEDGMENTS

I have a habit of making gratitude lists whenever I am stressed, anxious, or overwhelmed. Since writing a book—especially a *first* book—is as thrilling as it is overwhelming and as exciting as it is anxiety-inducing, the wonderful people I'd like to thank for their help, guidance, and support in the making of this book have all appeared countless times in the pages of my journals, the margins of sticky notes, and on the backs of more than a few receipts. It fills me with great joy to officially thank them now.

To my wonderful agent, Sara Crowe, thank you for the phone call that changed my life and for being a champion for Edie, Violet, and myself. We are so lucky to have you and the magic-making Pippin team in our corner.

From our very first conversation, I knew I'd found a kindred spirit in my brilliant editor, Laura Schreiber. Laura, working with you on this book has been one of the greatest pleasures of my life. Thank you for sharing my vision for Edie and Violet's story and for masterfully helping me shape it into its best possible version.

Writing words on a page and believing yourself to be a writer can sometimes feel like two very different things. I keep an always-burning light of gratitude in my heart for the friends, teachers, and mentors who have helped me find the confidence to bridge that gap. Thank you to Elana K. Arnold, Brandy Colbert, Anne Ursu, Jennifer Jacobson, and Gretchen McNeil for not only inspiring me with your own writing, but for helping me find and deepen my own. A very special thanks to Nina LaCour, whose unwavering belief in Edie and Violet's story from the beginning sustained and bolstered me more times than I can count. My heartfelt thanks to everyone in the Hamline MFAC program for creating an inspiring and supportive community I feel so lucky to be a part of.

Thank you to the incredible team at Union Square & Co. for embracing this book with such enthusiasm. Emily Meehan, Tracey Keevan, Melissa Farris, Hannah Reich, Jenny Lu, Daniel Denning, and Chris Vaccari: I could not imagine a better home for this book, and I am so honored to have your talents behind it. My whole heart to the incredibly talented artist Marcela Bolívar and designer Whitney Manger for creating the gorgeous, spooky cover of my dreams. Thank you to Phil Gaskill and Haley Jozwiak for the kind, thoughtful, eagle-eyed, guidance (and for making it look like I know how semi-colons work). And thank you to my sensitivity reader, Amber Williams, for her generous insight and feedback.

No librarians were harmed during the making of this book, but many were consulted. I am eternally grateful for the hard work of the many research librarians who not only helped me dig up obscure essays and facts but who work tirelessly to maintain detailed online databases that make writing historical fiction a true joy of discovery. Thank you to everyone at the Sacramento History Museum and, most especially, to Shawn Turner for answering my countless questions and arranging a special Underground Tour of Old Town

Sacramento during the pandemic with Thomas Legget, the most incredible and informative guide a writer could ask for. Thank you, too, to Jared Jones for his insight into nineteenth century newspapers. Any and all mistakes are, of course, my own.

If you are going to write a book, I highly recommend surrounding yourself with other brilliant writers who will be in the trenches with you. Olivia Swomley, thank you for being my first writer friend and for continually inspiring me with your own work. I am forever grateful for the countless brainstorming sessions and, most especially, for that time you dropped everything to read an early draft of this book so you could pull me out of the depths of despair. I would be lost without my friend and fellow-writer Veronica Derrick, who magically knows when to cheer me on and when to hold my feet to the fire! I am forever in awe of your magnificent writer-mind and am so grateful for your invaluable insights and suggestions. To Lindsey Olsson, an incredible writer and fellow lover of all things fantasy and cute boys with great hair, your support and insight sustains me. I could talk story and magic systems with you until the end of time. Thank you, too, to Alex Fallgren, K.X. Song, Ari Tison, Tina Kim, and all of the 22Debuts for your friendship and support on this journey we call publishing!

To my dear friends Meredith Wieck and Avalon Hernandez, who both quite literally forced me to send them early drafts of this book, thank you for bolstering me during times of doubt. I am so lucky to have friends like you. To Kit Steinkellner, thank you for being my first collaborator and a continual source of inspiration and encouragement. Thank you to Preeti Hehmeyer for befriending me in high school and never letting me go. You have been my lifeline through everything, and I am so grateful.

I am lucky to have grown up in a home filled with art, music, books, and stories. Thank you to my mom, Nancy, for instilling in me a deep appreciation for art in all its forms, and for passing on to me your love of reading, which I am grateful for every day. To my dad, Rick, thank you for "publishing" my first book with a home office printer, spare letterhead, and a stapler, and for telling me I was a writer decades before I believed it of myself.

To Susie Glaze and Steve Rankin, thank you for all those wonderful dinners and for the never-ending encouragement. To Lynne and Kevin Clifton, and to Embry, Ty, and Toren Maynard, thank you for welcoming me into your family and for not minding my habit of scribbling each morning, even during holidays. Most Valuable Cat awards to my writing familiars Dash and Jenova, who took turns sitting next to me each morning while I wrote this book.

My sister, Georgia, is and always will be my favorite person in the entire world. I'm so honored to share this life with you, G. Without you, I'd be lost.

And lastly, to my partner, Blake. Who read every single word many, many, *many* times. I was terrified to show anyone those first few tentative pages, but you insisted on reading them and told me they were wonderful (even though they probably weren't). And then you asked when you could read some more. I love you so much. This book is for you.

TURN THE PAGE
FOR EXCLUSIVE BONUS MATERIAL!

A LILLIAN CHAPTER

AN EDIE AND LAWS SCENE
ANNOTATED BY AMANDA GLAZE

LILLIAN

June 3, 1886

They didn't come at night.

They didn't break down the door.

And they didn't come armed.

They came instead with a single sheet of paper, which was, Lillian thought grimly as two uniformed officers led her to the police wagon waiting on the corner of Market Street, ironic, considering it was a sheet of paper that had landed her here in the first place.

Well, technically, it had been several sheets of papers. But she decided the irony could still stand.

A sneering officer banged the wagon door shut, blocking her view of Ada's tear-stained face, and as he did, another thought occurred to Lillian. One that sent a strangled sort of laugh bubbling up her throat. The officer who was in the back of the wagon with her looked over in confusion, and Lillian tried to regain the regal composure she'd maintained since hearing the knock on her and Ada's front door. But she couldn't stop the gasps of hysterical laughter tearing through her any more than she could stop her mind from playing the same strangely horrible thought over and over and over again.

Because in that moment, she'd realized something. She'd realized that, despite everything, she and the vile Anthony Comstock did have one thing in common.

They both understood, that in the right hands, a piece of paper was the most powerful thing of all.

⊙⯈⯇⊙

Lillian woke with a start.

Her neck was sore, her throat was dry, and her clammy skin was in desperate need of a bath. The light coming in through the bars on the window told her it was morning, which meant she'd somehow managed to drift off for a few hours of sleep.

Her temporary cellmate, Rosaline, a thin waif of a girl who'd been brought in a few hours after she was and couldn't be older than sixteen, was still sound asleep on the wooden bench across from her, but at that moment, the commotion down the hall that must have woken Lillian intensified, and the slight girl stirred in her sleep, blinking open a pair of bleary eyes.

"You will take me to see my client at once. I won't ask again."

The young waif's eyes widened, likely surprised to hear a female voice speaking with such authority in a place like this. But Lillian only smiled and shook her head fondly. Edie had gotten here much sooner than she'd expected, but Lillian had never doubted that her friend would come.

"Your *client*? Miss, I don't think you understand—"

"It is *you* who do not understand, officer. By denying me access to my client, you are in danger of violating both federal *and* California state law. Are you prepared to stand for that charge?"

"Now look here, missy—"

"I am not your *missy*. And if you so much as—"

"Well, if it isn't Officer Sullivan," said a new voice, deeper than the first two, with the barest hint of a Southern twang. "I must say, I'm surprised to see you up on your feet this morning."

"Everett? What are you—"

"I don't need help," hissed Edie, cutting off the officer. "I have this perfectly well in—"

"Of course you don't need help," said the voice of Lawrence Everett. "You are here on a legitimate and—might I add, *lawful*—errand. I have no doubt justice will be carried out in due haste by this upstanding member of law enforcement. It just so happens that I am here to see Officer Sullivan on another matter entirely."

"You . . . you are?" asked Officer Sullivan with, Lillian was pleased to note, genuine concern in his voice.

"I am," said Laws brightly. "You know I like to help you lot out from time to time. And it seems that you *are* in need of some help, Sullivan. Or did you forget that in addition to failing to actually *secure* the fellow you attempted to crip from the Barbary last night on the ship, you also failed to ascertain his name?"

There was a pointed silence from down the hall.

"I'm curious, Sullivan, if you've given any thought to what the mayor of this fine city might have to say when he learns about your lot's attempt to coerce his dear, visiting cousin to a life at sea?"

Lillian clapped a hand over her mouth to stifle a laugh at the same time that a choked cough sounded from down the hall.

"Cat got your tongue, Sullivan? Miss Bond, I wonder if *you* might have a thought on the matter?"

"Well, it's an interesting question, Mr. Everett," said Edie, her voice taking on a studious tone. "If I could hazard a guess, I'd have to speculate that our fine mayor might have more than *words* to share. Kidnapping and coercion are, of course, criminal offenses. And if you add to that the dereliction of duty that Officer Sullivan displayed, on top of the chief's recent pledge to crack down on the horrendous practice of using criminal means to conscript innocent tourists onto ships that—"

"It wasn't me," blurted out the officer. "It wasn't me, and you've got no proof that it was."

"Oh, Sullivan," said Laws, his voice displaying a hint of the deadly edge he usually reserved for corrupt politicians, judges, and industrialists. "You know me better than that, don't you?"

A long silence followed that loaded statement, during which Lillian noted that her cellmate, Rosaline, had closed her eyes and fallen back asleep on her bench. She couldn't say for sure what the young woman had been brought in for, but so many girls like her—wearing threadbare, low-cut gowns, and with dark smudges under their hungry, desperate eyes—had come to Lillian for help over the years that she could hazard a guess. And as it did every time she met a young woman the world had so thoroughly failed, her heart ached to look at her.

Officer Sullivan finally broke the silence by swearing loudly. "Fine," he grumbled. "What do you want?"

"To start," said Edie, not skipping a beat. "You could try actually *following* the law you are sworn to uphold and allow me immediate access to my client."

"And while they're having their constitutionally protected conversation," added Laws, "you and I can have little chat of our own, Sullivan. I believe you are privy to some . . . *details* about a few recent payoffs that I would very much like to hear about. Background only, of course."

Lillian couldn't make out the specifics of Officer Sullivan's reply, but it must have been in the affirmative because less than a minute later, the groan and squeak of heavy metal reached her ears, and then Edie Bond was rushing down the dimly lit hall toward her, long strands of her windswept, white-blonde hair falling out of its pins, the worn leather briefcase her sister Violet had given her when she started law school clutched to her chest.

"Oh, *Lillian*," Edie cried. "I'm sorry it took me so long. Ada has been frantic, but I'm so glad you're—"

"Ada?" Lillian pushed herself off the bench and rushed to the barred wall of her cell. "Is she—"

"She's fine," Edie quickly assured her. "They aren't pursuing her as an accomplice, for now. But just in case, Laws and I persuaded her to stay at my place for a few days. I wired Violet, and she's catching a train to—"

"Oh, no. Violet doesn't need to—"

"She wants to," said Edie. "She said it was only fair to give her understudy the spotlight for a couple of weeks anyway. She'll arrive tonight, and she'll stay with Ada while I, well . . ."

Edie trailed off, her gaze falling to the buckles on her full-to-bursting briefcase. Lillian took the opportunity to run her eyes over her friend's face, noting the tightness around Edie's mouth and the puffiness under her eyes. The extra sense Lillian had had since birth tingled against her skin like warning bells.

Edie was hiding it well, but she was terribly upset.

Not an auspicious sign.

"You might as well tell me," said Lillian, bracing herself and straightening her spine. "I'd rather hear it all at once anyway."

Eyes still on her briefcase, Edie nodded. Then she took a deep breath and lifted her gaze to meet Lillian's. "They have letters."

Lillian nodded. "All right."

"I've seen one of them. They'll be able to prove it's your handwriting."

"I'm sure they can. I've corresponded with several women over the years, but they were all—"

"They're saying she's thirteen," said Edie softly. "Twelve the first time she wrote."

Lillian blinked several times, her mind racing back through her most recent correspolndence. Whenever possible, she tried to meet patients seeking her help with contraceptive methods in person, but that wasn't always feasible. And unfortunately, the mail, ever since the passage of the Comstock Act, which made it illegal for any material considered "obscene, lewd, or lascivious" to be passed through the U.S. Post Office, was not always safe either. Particularly since Anthony Comstock, a man who referred to himself as "a weeder in God's garden" but who, in Lillian's opinion, could not have strayed farther from the path of compassion Christ preached, had decided that disseminating any information about the prevention of pregnancy—and even the prevention of venereal disease—was now punishable by law.

It was widely known among the women—and the few men—who provided contraceptive information to patients that a judge would dismiss a case if the woman being given advice was married and acting with her husband's permission. That was why when Lillian did correspond with potential patients via post, she inquired about their marital status *before* mailing along informational pamphlets. And if they were not married, she found a way for the women to visit someone local to them.

"Beverly Wallace," said Lillian, the memory of a particular letter popping into her mind. She'd found it oddly worded and had not responded initially. But when the second letter had come from the same woman two months later, her compassion had won out.

Edie nodded glumly.

"But she confirmed she was married and seeking advice with her husband's approval."

"She lied," said Edie, a hard edge to her voice. "I'm afraid the reality is that she is the daughter of a woman who thinks the sun rises and sets on Anthony Comstock's fat behind. It's obvious that she sent the letters under the direction of the mother, although I'm not sure how we can prove it."

Lillian nodded again, unsure what else to do. She'd known the risks. She'd done it anyway. Breaking a law—no matter how unjust—came with a potential cost. And it appeared Lillian's bill was coming due.

Ada's face flashed into her mind. Not desperate and tearstained as it had been yesterday before the police wagon door had shut between them, but smiling and soft, the early morning sun lighting on the dimple that appeared only on her right cheek. The smile she reserved for Lillian, and Lillian alone.

Ada had known the risks, too.

Had it been worth it?

Had it been worth *them*?

"I'm sure I don't need to tell you what our chances are of winning this in court," said Edie, her voice grim. "But I spent the evening with Miss de Force and her colleague Mrs. Foltz, and there may be another option."

Blinking away the tears that had formed at the thought of Ada, Lillian lifted her head.

"Mrs. Foltz knows the judge assigned to your case," continued Edie. "If you're found guilty, it will be the workhouse. But this judge in particular is known to be especially open to accepting pleas of—"

"No," said Lillian

"—insanity. But before you—"

"Absolutely not."

"—make any decisions, you should know there's a new place in Stockton. It's quite modern, and they're known for—"

"I don't care if they have rooms full of kittens, Edie. I am not going back to an asylum. Not now. Not *ever*."

"Lillian, you have to understand. These workhouses, they—"

"I'm familiar with their conditions, Edie."

"Then you know you won't last a year!" Leaning forward, Edie gripped the metal bars of the cell. "Lillian, please be reasonable. This may be your—"

"Reasonable?"

The word came out as a shout, causing Edie to jump back, her eyes wide. Even young Rosaline stirred on her bench.

It was rare for Lillian to lose her temper these days. It was one of the things her first stint in the asylum had successfully beaten out of her. But she couldn't help it now. The anger and fear and fury roaring inside her were too much to contain.

Turning on her heel, she paced the length of her cell.

"It is *reasonable*," she said, "to give women information about their own bodies. It is *reasonable* to help a starving mother of five make decisions about what's best for her family. It is *reasonable* to help these young girls thrown to the street—barely more than *children*—protect themselves in a world hell-bent on destroying them. I help women take control of their lives in the only way I know how. There is nothing *insane* about that."

Edie reached out again to grip the bars of the cell. "I know that, Lillian." Tears swam in her eyes. "Of course I know that."

Ceasing her pacing, Lillian squared her shoulders. "Then we're agreed. We won't plead insanity."

There was a long moment of silence before Edie nodded and said, "We won't plead insanity."

Lillian nodded back and resumed her pacing.

"But I won't see you in a workhouse either, Lillian."

Shaking her head, Lillian continued her useless march back and forth across the cell. She admired Edie's spirit, always had. But there were limits to what her friend—however determined— could do.

"I'm serious," said Edie, pressing her face against the bars now. "I know I'm not a—" she paused and lowered her voice—"not a real lawyer. *Yet*. But both Miss de Force and Mrs. Foltz have agreed to help. We'll fight this, Lillian. We will fight this, and we will win."

Turning again on her heel, Lillian paused as her gaze caught on young Rosaline. The girl was still lying curled on her side, but she was no longer asleep. Instead, her eyes—wide in such a narrow face—were bouncing between Lillian and Edie, filled to the brim with an expression that could only be described as awe.

Only minutes ago, Lillian had wondered if this had all been worth it. If she could bear, without regret, the consequences of rebelling against an unjust law.

Looking at Rosaline now, she realized that she could.

More than that, she could bear it proudly.

Because Rosaline was worth it.

They all were.

Turning back to Edie, Lillian lifted her head.

"We fight it," she said, her chest lifting at the spark she saw light in Edie's eyes. "We fight it, and we win."

~an excerpt from~

Chapter 24

annotated by the author (that's me!)

EDIE AND LAWS

Frank, the donkey

The air was cool as Laws and Edie stepped out into the night. He paid a boy to return the donkey cart to the shopkeeper he'd hastily borrowed it from, and then he and Edie turned toward her hotel without a word.

oh, don't worry, Edie. The questions are coming

She'd been expecting the barrage of questions to begin right away and was therefore surprised when they walked the first two blocks in silence, only the occasional rattling of a late-night carriage or hack filling the quiet between them.

Omnibuses, or horse-drawn streetcars followed prelaid tracks in the road. A few years after this story takes place, they were replaced with electric streetcars.

She was so distracted by this unusual reticence on Laws's part that when they cut across K Street at the intersection of Third, she wasn't paying attention to the terrain, and the hem of her skirt caught on one of the omnibus tracks, nearly landing her flat on her face. Edie yelped and Laws instinctively reached out and grabbed her arm just in time, steadying her.

Characters mutually deciding not to let go of each other, but saying nothing is one of my favorite things ♡

She untangled her skirt and regained her footing; but when they started walking again, Laws didn't let go of her arm. And somehow she found herself not pulling away. This close, she could easily smell the faint scent of sandalwood clinging to his skin.

Silence continued to stretch between them; each second driving Edie more and more mad. All she'd wanted since meeting this boy a couple of days ago was for him to stop asking questions and leave her alone. And now here she was, desperate to know what was going on inside his head.

Fact: Edie never really wanted him to leave her alone.

She was about to give up and start the dreaded conversation herself when Laws suddenly stopped walking. His hold on her elbow pulled her up short, and she twisted around to face him.

Values above things.

"Why did you let me believe you were a fraud?"

on this s at can him Edie not the L.

Surprised, Edie blinked up at him. "What did you just say?"

He took a step toward her. "If you're truly able to cross into the spirit world, why did you let me—no, why did you *encourage* me—to think you were a fraud?"

Edie stared back at him. She wasn't exactly sure how she'd expected this conversation to go, but Laws quickly and easily accepting the reality of death—and her ability to cross into it— was *not* one of them.

She raised her eyebrows. "What makes you so sure I'm not a fraud now?"

"No. You can't do that with me now, Edie. Not after what I saw happen back there with you and your friend Ruby."

"Maybe it was a trick. You said it yourself. Us mediums are full of them."

His grip tightened on her elbow, letting her know exactly how he felt about having his words thrown back at him. "And what," he asked, his voice lowering, "about what happened in the asylum? Are you going to try and deny that, too? You forget that I was there with you in that wardrobe. That I *felt* your reaction when that minister—"

"Don't!"

"—spoke. And while I'll be the first to admit there's a lot going on here I don't understand, I know more than you—"

"You don't *know* anything, Lawrence Everett." Heart pounding, Edie tried to take a step back, but Laws pulled her closer instead.

"I know," he said, his gaze fixed on hers, "that Bond isn't your real name. I know you and your sister are not, in fact, alone in the world. I know your mother is dead, but that your father is very much alive. A circuit preacher based in Marysville. A well-respected family man who is desperate to find his runaway daughters alive."

Stunned, Edie could do nothing but stare at him.

His eyes swept over her face, assessing her, before continuing. "I know you told me that I knew nothing about you and nothing

In an earlier draft of the book, Laws wrote an article about Edie and Violet's true identities, and his editor published it over his objections.

about your life. I know I wanted to change that, and so I asked my editor about you and your tour. He was in San Francisco for a couple of years before this, and I thought your name might ring a bell. It didn't. But then I told him a little more about your sister and your trances on stage. I happened to mention the difference in the color of your hair." *Laws's fictional newspaper, the Sacramento Sting, was inspired by "The Wasp," a San Francisco satirical magazine known for the "Sting" of it's political cartoons.*

His eyes drifted up past Edie's face, landing on the white-blonde hair piled atop her head. Her face heated under his perusal.

"And that's when my editor told me about some gossip he'd heard while covering a mayoral election up north in Wheatland a year ago. A story about a well-liked circuit preacher who'd lost *also known as a "Saddle-bag preacher."* both his wife and his twin daughters in the same night. The wife had died, and the daughters had run off. It was the description of the twins that stuck with him, though."

With his free hand, Laws reached up and pulled loose a strand of Edie's hair. Holding it between his forefinger and thumb, he turned it over, examining it in the moonlight. "The twins were described as identical. Except for the hair. One auburn. The other pale blonde." *I love this sweet, tender moment—especially meaningful because Edie is self-conscious about her hair.*

Carefully, almost reverently, he tucked the loose strand behind her ear. His fingers, warm and rough with calluses, hovered at the place where her pulse thrummed against her throat.

"I'm fairly positive I know *who* that minister in the basement was tonight, and that I know now why you and your sister ran. I also know I meant what I said outside those asylum gates. About your needing help." *Laws is not referring to his story about the sheep who jump + wiggle when you sneak up on them, but since that's one of my favorite Laws moments, I'm immortalizing it here!*

His fingers trailed along her throat, pausing when he reached the corner of her jaw. Edie fought the urge to lean into his hand. She needed to get away from this boy who'd seen too much. *Knew* too much.

"I know," he said, his lip twitching, "that you want nothing more than to run right now. I know running is what you do when you're scared. And I know you are terrified right now."

Edie jerked at his words. She made to pull her elbow out of his grasp, but Laws reached down and took her hand instead, pressing it flat against his chest, his hand covering hers.

His hold was loose. She could have easily broken away.

She should break away.

But then he was speaking again, his voice low and soft, his eyes boring into hers.

"I know you were incredibly brave tonight. I know I haven't been able to stop thinking about you since you first barreled into me on that sidewalk. I know that as soon as I saw you again in the Metropolitan lobby, a part of me realized I'd never want to let you out of my sight again."

Closing the last of the distance between them, he tilted his head toward hers. "But there's still one thing I *don't* know, Edith Bond."

His breath skipped across the delicate skin at her throat as he spoke. Edie's fingers curled into a fist, the fabric of his shirt twisting in her hands. She could feel the beat of his heart against her palm. Fast and racing. His pulse matching her own.

"I still don't know," he whispered, his lips so close she could almost taste them, "if you're ready to trust me back."

For a long moment, Edie found it impossible to breathe. All she could do was stare into Laws Everett's eyes. Eyes that stared back with an intensity that set her blood on fire. And then she was lifting her chin. Going up on her toes. Pressing her lips to his.

She knew she shouldn't. Knew that this wasn't just a kiss, but a promise. A promise to trust this boy with the truth about her and Violet's past. The truth about their lives.

You've become so good at lying, Edie. Violet's words.

She didn't want to lie anymore.

As soon as her lips touched his, Laws responded in kind. A soft growl rumbled in the back of his throat, and then Edie wasn't thinking about anything except the feel of his hand tightening against her waist. His fingers spreading across the small of her back, pulling her close. His other hand tracing the edge of her jaw before settling at the base of her neck, tilting her head so he could deepen the kiss.

And then her hands were moving, too. Traveling up his arms, his neck, and tangling in the curls of his hair.

When she accidentally knocked his hat off his head, they both pulled back in surprise.

Laws laughed softly. Edie laughed, too, and started to apologize, but Laws only shook his head, pulled her close, and kissed her again.

And even as she kissed him back, reveling in the feel of his lips moving against hers, a small voice inside her insisted that she shouldn't be allowed to feel this way. Warm and safe in this boy's arms. Not with her father's chilling words still ringing in her head. Not with the image of Ruby's tortured face haunting her mind.

But even as she acknowledged that truth, she recognized another one as well.

She wanted this.

This boy.

This is a powerful moment for Edie — taking what she wants without shame.

This moment.

His ink-stained fingers soft and steady as they cradled the back of her neck. The sighs deep in his throat. The answering sighs in hers.

This feeling of being known. Seen. Of not running away, but running *toward.*

And so she threaded her fingers more deeply into his hair, pressed her lips more firmly to his, and let herself have it.

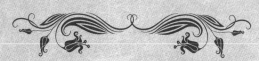

THE
Herbs OF *Death*

A MEDIUM'S GUIDE TO
INTERACTING WITH SPIRITS

LAVENDER

*Opens the Veil of Death
& calms surrounding spirits*

HELLEBORE

*Binds the free will
of a spirit*

BAY LEAF

*Reverses another
herb's intent*